HARD CASE II
The Lure of Hell

by Bernard Lee DeLeo (Author), RJ Parker (Publicist)
Copyright 2013 Bernard Lee DeLeo
Published by RJ Parker Publishing

ISBN-13:978-1490378275

ISBN-10:1490378278

This book is a work of fiction

PAPERBACK EDITION

D0886018

1

Chapter One
Monsters

Stuttering screams of agony reverberated off the dank walls inside the basement of the small elementary school. A naked, red haired woman strapped to a table, writhed in misery, arching upwards with each ministration by the three figures gathered at the table. A battery operated lantern hanging overhead provided the only light, swaying eerily on the pipe as if disturbed at the scene below it. The scream creators, encased in hooded disposable plastic suits with gloves, each held a bloody scalpel. They paused every other moment, savoring the horrific result of their actions.

The two smaller figures on the woman's left moved more industriously than their counterpart on the other side of the table. The smaller of the two giggled with each high pitched shriek, adding another slice to prolong it. Their larger opposite companion held a small HD camcorder, only moving closer to the table in order to add a slice of his own, before moving back a pace to film their macabre collaboration. The giggler lifted free the woman's left breast, dangling it by the nipple over the woman's face. Their victim passed out.

"Wow... that was awesome! She stayed conscious longer than any before," the smaller one of the three exclaimed with another giggle, her Southern accent drawling the last two words. "Did you get it all, Rich?"

The tall man across from her nodded. "I didn't miss anything. God, that was hot! I know Cheryl got off. What about you, Tara?"

Tara smiled at her companions with bright, glazed eyes, and then laughed. "We... are so... sick! Let Cheryl and I hold your stuff. Break her little toe on the right, Rich, before we forget. Otherwise, those FBI morons won't even know it's us doing it."

Cheryl laughed, taking the proffered scalpel from Richard. "I still can't believe we had to leave the shoe off before they got on

2

to the broken toe. We'd probably have to surrender before those idiots ever caught us. This one's naked, so they can all hover around pointing at the toe with arrogant eyes of stupidity. I think we should do one more here before we split up. I don't have to be at the firm until next Monday."

Richard handed the camcorder to Tara and broke the victim's right little toe with exaggerated brutality, leaving it hanging by only loose skin. "There... they won't miss that one. I don't know, Cheryl, it's already Thursday. That doesn't leave enough buffer space between the killings and our flights back."

"He's right Cher," Tara said, handing back the camcorder.

"These cops out here couldn't catch a cold," Cheryl replied. "Even if they get the FBI idiots... that black guy and his skank partner on the case within hours, they'll be spending days doing their 'Criminal Minds' bullshit in the precinct with mockups, profiles, and circle jerks."

"Maybe Cher's right. They don't have that weirdo guy with them anymore we were watching out for. He was only referred to as a consultant, and never modeled for pictures or press conferences. I'm glad we chilled for a time while he was consulting. I still can't figure out how he solved all those cases for those two retards. I wish we could have went up against him just once though."

"Hey... goofy... we can joke around about idiot police and FBI, but let's not start painting a bulls-eye on our chests," Richard warned. "That consultant asshole was good. C'mon... lets wake Red up and play a while longer."

Cheryl followed Tara around the table again. "Are you going to the class reunion?"

Tara spun toward her friend. "Oh hell yeah! This is our ten year reunion, girl. Don't even think about not coming. I'm wondering if we should do one of our classmates. It'll turn Harvard upside down!"

"Damn, Tara, that's not bad," Richard replied, moving into position. "We'll be able to act all frightened and outraged at our poor classmate's horrid death, wringing our hands and weeping while we watch the cops chase their tails. We'll be interviewed for sure."

"I am so in!" Cheryl agreed. "What would be better than to attend a reunion and celebrate our first killing? I love this plan!"

Their victim began to move, and then moan, and then scream.

* * *

The two FBI agents carefully inspected the naked mutilated corpse of a young woman, left in the middle of an elementary school hallway.

"Jesus... Mary... and Joseph..." the woman agent mumbled. "We have to get Clint back with us. We're going over Lundigan's head."

"Shit!" Her companion straightened away from the body, his fists clenched. "I don't want that fucking asshole in with us ever again! We need to get back to basics on this. We'll take a fresh look-"

"We've done the fresh look stuff. We're lost, just like with Montoya. I'm calling Sawyer. If he gives us the go ahead, we're going up to get Clint. I've had enough of this. These monsters are laughing at us! They nearly ripped the woman's right little toe off this time as if to say we're too stupid to breathe. Maybe they're right."

Her partner closed his eyes, picturing Clint Dostiene in his mind's eye with tight lipped fury. He took a deep breath, opened his eyes to glance down at the victim, and then nodded. "I'll call Dostiene's boss, Dennis Strobert. You get on the horn to Justice. We'll need a player to keep Lundigan out of this."

"It's the right decision."

He sighed. "I know."

* * *

Tonto, the huge mixed breed Collie/German Shepherd, let out a low vibrating growl at the door. Clint Dostiene sighed as he slumped back on the pad laid out under his sink, looking up in annoyance to the cosmic forces combining for a work stoppage on his sink plumbing. He stood up a moment later, stretching his six foot two frame out, contemplating whether to pretend he wasn't there or not. His truck was parked in the back of his place, out of sight from the front. Smiling to himself, he wondered how far out in the middle of nowhere he had to go so as not to get any visitors. His sparse neighbors came by out of curiosity or to ask for a favor once in a while. Dostiene endured their visits politely.

That's who he figured was approaching his house now until Dostiene heard Tonto give off an unusual plaintive bark. Dostiene jerked forward, reaching into the cabinet drawer to pull out his hideaway .45 caliber Colt automatic. Instead of going to the front door where Tonto camped out in hackles raised sentry duty, Clint eased out his rear door with the Colt tucked in solidly at his rear waistband. He vaulted his six foot high, locked gate with an acrobat's fluid movement, muscles flowing in sharp relief under his t-shirt. Easing around the side of his house, Dostiene made sure he missed nothing in the near dusk grayness. When he saw the two suits standing on his doorstep, he straightened and walked toward them.

His approach startled the man and woman. They instinctively reached for weapons. When they saw him waving with a confused look on his face, they relaxed. The woman, a five foot four inch brunette, thin to the point of looking sickly, gave Dostiene a tired shrug. Her partner, a tall black man with a goatee gestured at Clint with annoyance.

"Damn it, Clint! Can't you just answer your front door?"

"I live in the middle of nowhere for a reason, Sam - I don't like visitors, but I still get them. Tonto has this weird bark when something ain't right. He just announced you two with it. I have enemies. If I had any family, they'd have been killed already, or in hiding."

"Couldn't you at least leave that very expensive satellite phone on we gave you?"

"I could, Janie, but then I'd be getting calls I don't want. All you have to do is leave an e-mail at the drop we have set up. I get it, and I call you. I bet you two are here about the copycat Zodiac killer or killers in San Francisco. What I don't know is why."

"We need you on this," Sam replied, gesturing at the front door. "Can we please go in and discuss it inside. I'll pay you for the coffee if you have any."

"C'mon in, but I'm really not playing hard to get. I'm out of the game, kiddies," Clint replied, opening the door and pointing at Tonto who immediately sat down next to the entrance. "I have coffee made, so come on in and sit down at my meager kitchen table."

Clint sat down facing the two agents after serving coffee. Tonto curled up next to his chair. "I wish you two would have simply e-mailed me. I could have saved you a trip."

"We know you're still doing jobs for your real master," Sam stated. "Rumor has it you went rogue and took out Carlos Silva near La Jolla when the cartel kingpin came across the border."

Dostiene sipped his coffee, smiling amiably. "Rumor has it, huh?"

"You worked with us in the past on nine different cases with a hundred percent success rate. It wasn't your fault the court let Lynn Montoya go," Janie added. "Your boss at the company told us if we could talk you into doing this, he'd get behind it. He told us the orders on the Silva job weren't specific enough."

Dostiene chuckled. "Denny told you that? For the record, Denny Strobert's a stand up guy. He was happy with our serial killer liaison gig. Forget whatever crapolla you heard on the rumor mill about Silva. Look, I liked working with you two. The Montoya case didn't bother me. Hell, I knew the jury would let her off. That lawyer she had gathered the families of all the rape victims those eight shitheads she killed brutalized. When the prosecutor lost his bid to suppress their testimony, the outcome was a done deal. I only caught her because she had a target rich environment, and I simply shadowed the one I figured she'd get next."

"Yeah, but you lost the bait."

Clint shrugged. "I arrived a little late, Sam. Sue me. You two didn't even know it was a woman doing it. Anyway, that was when Montoya walked and I got my walking papers from helping you two. It was an interesting gig for a while being on loan to the FBI. I'm not ever working for that asshole, Lundigan, in charge of your department again. I'm even having second thoughts about doing anything for Denny. They almost locked me up over that torturing bastard Silva, in spite of Strobert's intercession on my behalf. You both know I ain't ever letting that happen. Now if you'll excuse me, Agents Reeves and Labrie, I have plumbing to fix."

Reeves reached out and grabbed Dostiene's wrist. "This is a bad one, Clint – worst ever. Lundigan has nothing to do with this task force we're forming. We think there's more than one killer. We think the San Francisco thing is only the third locale on their serial killer tour, but we're not even sure of that."

Clint stared at Reeves' hand until he removed it from his wrist. "How do you know that, Sam? Wait a minute… you think those women killed in Los Angeles, and the graveyard of missing women down in New Mexico are tied into the same ones you think are active now in SF?"

"We're sure of it. They imitated the Hillside Stranglers in LA, David Parker Ray in New Mexico, and now they're mimicking the Zodiac Killer in SF, complete with nonsensical coded notes to the police. The bad part is they torture the victims in ways even the original killers never did," Janie Labrie stated. "We missed a tell they gave us on every victim. They were laughing at us I'm sure. They broke the little toe on all the victims' right foot. When we didn't get the clue, they began taking the shoe off the victims' right feet until we got it. It pissed me off!"

"How did you get onto this tell?"

Sam and Janie glanced at each other.

"We didn't," Sam admitted. "Somewhere over state lines with the horrendous killings, coupled with local contamination, we missed it. They included a note on the last victim in San Francisco. They made the locals and us into idiots, and we were."

Janie grabbed Clint by the front of his shirt. "I know you're nearly as psycho as the people we've hunted together. I don't pretend to know what the difference is between you and them.

7

There are at least a dozen people dead that we know of. Put on your Dexter mask and help us get these monsters."

"Unhand me, Copper! You two were never this touchy-feely before."

Labrie chuckled and let Clint go, gesturing at Tonto. "Some protection you have there."

Clint glanced down at the curious face of Tonto, and then back to Janie. "You don't want to ever see what Tonto does if he thinks I'm in real danger. Anyway, what kind of leeway do I get on this. I'll need some bait... hey... where's my old pal Lynn Montoya? She'd be perfect for this gig. I bet the FBI has kept track of that serial killer on legal release."

"Forget it," Sam replied. "Montoya went to Mexico and began plying her trade down there. Word is Mexico's Federal Police caught her, and then sold her to some lieutenant in the Los Zetas Cartel. Hey... what's that look for?"

A grim faced Dostiene stared from one agent to the other. "You should have started out with that news flash. I ain't doin' shit for you two until I get a sit-rep on exactly where she's being held. I also want you to point a bird at the place and get me some surveillance photos. What? You're still here? Get movin'?"

"We don't take orders from you, Clint," Janie replied without conviction.

Clint shrugged. "I'll get it done through another source, but you two turn away here, don't ever come back. Are we clear? Go prattle it to your handlers. I'll wait for the word, but this is non-negotiable. If Montoya is alive, I will get her back up North."

"She's a certified sociopath! We can't just order satellites repositioned to help you get that nut-cake back," Sam reasoned.

"He won't budge, Sam." Janie tugged on her partner's arm as she stood up, while watching Clint sit back with arms folded. "What's the deal with you and Montoya, Clint? You sweet on her or something?"

"When I caught her tuning up that slime-ball, Gradowsky, for the last time with her knife, she looked up at me, smiled, and said 'thanks for letting me finish'. Montoya dropped the knife and turned around with her hands ready for the cuffs. After I cuffed her she guaranteed me she'd walk on all charges. I should have looked her up after the trial, but I figured I'd better put some time between us."

"That's it? Professional courtesy between psychos?"

"You figure to mouth off for a while, Sam, or go try to get me some surveillance photos?"

Reeves motioned for Labrie to stay behind. He walked out the door, his phone in hand. Labrie turned back to Clint with a smile.

"You are sweet on that murdering bitch."

"Hey, I thought we should have let her keep going. If you want to catch these killers of yours, we need her. We can't go baiting traps with some Snow White. If Montoya gets the right opportunity, she'll save on court costs too."

"If that's the way you feel, why the hell did you help us capture the ones we went after together?"

"Think about it, Janie. My boss knows if someone dies around me it won't be by accident. He was experimenting with our collaboration. Strobert makes sure the company pays me very well, and I'm not ready for retirement or prison just yet. Besides, I wouldn't have let any of us minions get hurt just to appease Denny. If we get Montoya up from Mexico, maybe she can snuff these clucks and we'll play it off as self defense."

Janie began shaking her head making noises of disgust. "Didn't you ever watch 'Criminal Minds'? We always bring our un-sub back alive, just like we did when you were helping us."

"I know the tune, but I like having another option."

Janie laughed and pointed an accusing finger at Dostiene. "I see what you're planning. You'll have Montoya there so when the perps die accidentally, Strobert won't think you went rogue. Don't bother answering. What's the use in giggling over the fate of serial killers? We won't ever get that card to play. Here comes Sam."

Reeves rejoined them in the kitchen. He sat down and drank some of his cooling coffee. "There must have been a victim that has a relative high up in Justice. They okayed the surveillance. Proctor told me he'd have something for you in the next couple days. Justice has the Zetas hotspots plotted already. He told me to tell you you're on your own down there when you go. I figured you knew that already."

"Small doubt about that. I'll turn on all my rocket science gizmos. Have the stuff sent as soon as they get it. I'll hook up with you two when I get back from my Mexican vacation."

"I'm writing you off," Reeves stated. "You'll either be dead or rotting in some dungeon, if you're lucky. The cartels have some imaginative people working for them. They catch you alive, and you'll be wishing you were dead."

Dostiene ignored him. "Let me give you some tips on research while I'm away. You know who they're mimicking. Go back where you think they began and throw a dragnet around any recent interest going back at least a year into the serial killers they're imitating. Colleges, authors who've written books on the killers, media reporters that worked the cases – and don't get all funky with your profiles."

"That's actually really good," Janie commented, exchanging glances with Reeves. "We were trying to tie in the methodology and the victims. What do you mean by getting funky with our profiles? It's a proven science."

"Not with a suspected group working together as they mimic other serial killers, it's not," Clint replied. "Sam said this is a bad one. He's right. Don't pigeon hole your investigation to profiles. I have to prepare for extracting my psycho. If there's nothing else, Tonto will see you two out. Thanks for stopping by."

Clint gestured toward the agents as he glanced down at Tonto. In an instant, Tonto streaked attentively next to the agents. When they didn't move immediately, he issued a low toned growl.

"What the hell?" Reeves scooted back from the dog as Tonto bared his teeth. "Call your mongrel off! We need-"

Labrie laughed and pulled on her partner's arm. "C'mon Sam. There's no use bitchin' about going. We've been dismissed."

Reeves stood up reluctantly, glaring at Dostiene. "I won't forget this, you prick."

"One more word, Sam, and I have Tonto drag you weaponless to the door... and he has back up. There's no need for pretense between the three of us. You two know something about me. If you knew everything, both of you would be running toward the door."

"Let's go, Sam!" Labrie pulled the now standing Reeves toward the door. "Call us when you get back, Clint?"

"I'll be in touch." Clint watched Tonto escort the two agents with grim appreciation.

  * * *

Dennis Strobert leaned back in his chair, smiling at the face on his notebook computer screen. "Hey Clint, how's it hangin'? You've been quiet lately. I thought maybe that goofy dog of yours ate you. Still holding a grudge about Silva?"

"We secure?"

"Did I give you a reason to insult me?" Strobert pretended to be hurt.

Dostiene nodded. "I want to know if you got wind of what I'm into now."

"That's two insults in your first two sentences. I've been waiting for your call, pal. I knew you weren't going down there by yourself on some Zeta suicide mission. You need a little firepower, a coordinator, an in and out – all on the down low. What's with you and that goofy broad they have locked up down there, Clint?"

"Look, Denny, you give me a boost for this extraction, and I'll owe you – no strings attached. I'll do a freebie you can claim any way you want."

"Let's talk about that. I think I may have a deal for you. The DOJ wants a piece taken out of the cartels for gunning down our border patrol agent in Texas. They're too chicken shit to make an outright statement, but they're willing to deal a favor if we do it for them. It's a black as coal op, and your shit would be in the wind worse than the Yucatan if you get taken."

"That ain't ever happenin' again, my friend," Clint stated. "Is Laredo still in his hole on the border?"

"Yeah, and he's been whinin' for a month. I'll ask him if he's up for an in and out with fireworks. He still has a fifty mounted in that dinosaur he flies. The favor will have to be done on the ground within hours of when and if you can get your girlfriend out. That going to be a problem?"

"Nope. You thought this all out the moment you got tipped, you pirate. Do you have anyone in mind to give me a hand on this gig."

Denny chuckled. "It just so happens I have my team on the west coast available. They even field a kid to coordinate ops. The kid is what Laredo would have been if we had all the electronics when he was young. If you're through playing mountain man, I could use you on the coast with them. They have as sweet a cover going as we've ever had."

Dostiene's features darkened. "Don't play me, Denny. If they're competent to come on the cartel deal, I'll deliver on the second part. No need making it into a recruitment poster."

"The main three members are Casey Lambert, Lucas Blake, and John Harding." Strobert had never seen surprise on Dostiene's face. He grinned in appreciation and nodded. "Think they're competent enough?"

Clint shook his head in awe. "I admit I've wondered how you skyrocketed up the ladder from handler to chief of ops. Anyone with the balls to cement a crew like that together deserves to be the head of CIA. What kind of cover do they have that's so special you managed to keep murderer's row together."

Strobert laughed. "I am so going to tell them you said that. Here's the deal. John's worked his way up into UFC from his street fighting days. They did a hit during a UFC event last year in Dubai, sweet as you please. They have families, and a bond retrieval/security business run by John's wife. I can freelance them anywhere in a heartbeat, including crossover ops where they need a wet-work option. You can't stay up in the boonies forever, Clint. I have an enclave of the deadliest guys I've ever worked with, raising families, and watching each other's backs. They're like the 'Brady Bunch' from hell."

Dostiene ran a hand over his scalp, clearly stunned. "Damn! You say John's married and his wife's running the op?"

Strobert gestured in a cautioning motion with his hands. "Lora's position is a little strange. She's hella' good making sure

12

everyone is where they ought to be, and she knows Oakland politics. Lora keeps us on the down low, while making those clowns a fortune. I can't explain it all to you. Also, until you get settled as to what you want Montoya for, can you be the only face she sees?"

"Of course," Clint answered. "After they help me open up the cartel can, I'll send them back, and take Lynn out by myself to another LZ. Can you pick them up with a different carrier?"

"That would be my plan. I'll have them plucked out of there to the states at Antelope Wells. If you get back in one piece, they'll be border patrol for a day at the crossing. I don't want you stopped there for any reason. John wants you with him. He needs a top notch investigator to round out their cover gig, and a woman like Montoya who ain't afraid to get her hands dirty. His words – tell Clint I'll get him a house on a hill with acreage and an ocean view if he'll give us a shot."

"That grunt saved my life, and Lucas trained me the same time as Casey. Those guys are family to me. I'll come down off the mountaintop any day to take a shot like you described. I have serial killer business though with the FBI. I heard you directed them my way. Otherwise I would have never heard about Lynn. I owe you one on that, but I see now you had ulterior motives." Clint grinned and shrugged on the screen. "I'm in."

"I'll gather the forces of darkness," Denny replied. "I know you went walkabout on the Montoya case when you caught her. Can you do the same thing when you figure out what's going on with the killers your former FBI partners are begging help on?"

"If you mean let them hack up more women on purpose, that would be no. I've done a little checking, and the perps are taking breaks in between killing sprees. They just did a couple, so I might be able to put off finding them for a short time. What do you have in mind?"

"I have something planned in Las Vegas coming up soon. John and his crew will be there for his undercard fight on the UFC ticket at the Mandalay Bay. It's a rematch with some clown called 'The Syrian Slayer'. John broke his arm in their first match, but the guy has been raging through everyone he's fought since his recovery. He wants Harding in the worst way. A guy who owns a piece of him is a target of interest I'd like to assume room temperature. He'll be there. No one can get close to him. He has a small army around him at all times. He's a player."

"So if I am able to get Montoya away from the cartel in one piece, she might have a couple of options besides the FBI gig, along with a tryout in Las Vegas," Clint replied.

"Without you though the deal goes south," Denny pointed out. "Killers are hard to come by in Montoya's class, especially females. This added consideration is a no strings attached deal. If you want in with Montoya let me know when you get her out safe. If she's too far gone or you want to keep the status quo, then no hard feelings. How's that sound?"

"Too good to be true, but worth taking a look at." Dostiene paused for a moment. "John's the real deal. You aren't blackmailing him into taking me and my psycho on, are you, Den?"

Strobert burst out laughing. It was many moments before he brushed a hand over his face and turned toward Clint again on screen. "Man, I needed that. Yep, if I ever decide I'm sick of living, I'll try blackmailing John Harding… or you. Send me your details on the cartel op. Can I tell John you're interested?"

"Hell yeah. I'll have the plan to you within the hour."

"Until then… until then," Denny replied, disconnecting. He sighed contentedly. *Harding, Lambert, Blake, Dostiene, and a cold blooded female killer, all in one spot, ready for duty with a cover and support cast. Head of CIA… here I come*, he thought with a grin.

Chapter Two
Gronk

I hear Al's super duper i-thingy play its ringtone with Alice's sweetheart, Beater, Beeper, or something. Jafar glances over at me with a grin. I may have growled. Next, the phone bops me on the head, before sliding over my shoulder.

"Mom wants face-time with you, Dark Lord," Alice explains in between giggles.

"The Dark Lord does not do face-time," I snarled in my best Darth Vader voice.

"Get me in front of you, DL, if you know what's good for you," Lora's voice demands in my ear. "You turn yours off one more time and I'm going to staple it to the side of your head."

Jafar and Alice have a laugh fest over that one. I bop Jafar in the back of the head to remind him he's driving. I take the i-thingy in between thumb and forefinger as if it were someone's half eaten hotdog. I smile at my wife's stern features. Lora runs my operations so she figures it's okay to have me on a short leash. I immediately promised myself I'd hear her beg tonight, and not in pain either.

"Hi honey. You couldn't wait another fifteen minutes for us to bring home Beeper's groupie from school?"

"Bieber! His names Bieber!" Alice has deemed it a mortal sin for me to disrespect Beeper. "Mom! Tell DL not to make fun of Justin."

The screen goes blank for a moment with accompanying snorting noises of distress as Lora stifles her laughter over Beeper's disrespect.

"Mom!" Alice notices, and is not happy. "See what you've done now, DL? You've turned my Mom to the dark side."

That was it. Jafar pulled over to the curb, howling in laughter, along with Lora, who gave up all pretense of restraint to join him. I'm leaning back, enjoying the whole thing. I take entertainment where I can get it.

"Mom! The Dark Lord is feeding off of this!" Alice has begun to lose it too, tacking on an admonishment while giggling through it.

"Okay, DL, you've corrupted us all yet again," Lora admits the obvious, coming back on screen as I hastily whip it up so I appear to have been attentive. "Get off at the next block. T's on his way to pick you up. We have a Gronk sighting at the Laurel Lounge, in progress."

Oh shit. "Ten-four, Mistress of the Dark."

"I see in your mottled features you're unhappy with this detour, Dark Lord," Lora zapped me. "Why this sudden squeamishness with working your job for a change?"

Okay, let's dance. "You know I'm fighting tonight, and T is completely mental at me for everything, so yeah, let's throw Gronk into the mix. It's a good payday though, right?"

"Oh baby," Lora replies in her sweetest husky voice. "You and T pick him up at the Laurel, and many in the law enforcement arena will be very happy. Yes, dear, I know you fight tonight and T refuses to even discuss it."

"You sided with Tommy!" I'm enjoying this. I have my life list, and everyone else has theirs. "Maybe you should back a different horse."

Lora smirked... the vixen. "He's right, DL. You're risking our UFC shot in Las Vegas, and for what, so that you can tangle with that goofy Gustavo Dixon? Forget the next block. Get out here and let Jafar bring Al home. I have T in my ear and he says he's thirty seconds from you."

I open the door as I hand the i-thingy back to Alice. That's the problem with all this crap. Everyone has a satellite beam on you wherever you are, and they wonder why I turn everything off. I hear Lora squeaking in protest. "Gronk's at the Laurel, kid. T's picking me up to go get him. Take Al straight home."

Alice launches out of the rear door. She jumps me. "I'm sorry about messin' with you. Be careful, John."

"Hey... what's this all about?" Alice and I have a bond. She's tough, and I couldn't care more for her if she were my own flesh and blood.

Al pulls away for a moment. No tears. Just folds her arms over her chest exactly like her Mom does to me with the same look of aggravated annoyance. "You're doing too much. Your luck's going to run out if you keep going like this. Even Uncle Tommy says you shouldn't be fighting tonight."

"She's right, John," Jafar leans across the seat to ping me.

The look I give him sends Jafar scooting back into place as the driver, hands locked on the wheel, and eyes straight ahead. I put a hand on Alice's shoulder as Tommy pulls up behind us. "I'll see you at home, Al. The fight's not until ten. I thought we had an agreement."

"I'm worried. I know who that Gronk guy is. He looks like Frankenstein."

I laugh. "You mean Frankenstein's monster."

"If he had terminals sticking out of his neck, he'd be a dead ringer for the monster. I read in the papers Mom had on her desk that he killed people, only they can't prove it."

She's a doll. "Gronk's going down, Al. Don't do this. I have to go. I'll be home later to talk about it. Tommy and I don't take chances, kid. What, you think I'm going to get into a fistfight with that clown on a fight night? Get in the car, Al. I love you. Tell-"

Alice grinned and whipped up the i-thingy on me so I could stare into my wife's lovely, but tiny face. Unfortunately, her voice was not tiny.

"Hi hon. Gotta go."

"Don't you move, DL!" The tiny picture amplified a lot of emotion in such a small spot.

Luckily, my partner Tommy showed up, pissed off at the world. He waved at the i-thingy screen. "Hey, Lor, we have to go. Save the lectures for later."

"Oh no... no... no... no... you did not just blow me off, T," the i-thingy voice shouted at him. "I will-"

17

Tommy jerked forward and covered the i-thingy with one very big dark hand. He smiled at Alice. "Take Mommy home. We'll see you there, Al."

"Okay, Uncle Tommy... be careful. Bye, John." Alice retreated into the backseat with the still squeaking i-thingy, and Jafar took off with a wave.

Tommy gives me a shove toward his GMC. "I swear, John! The moment you hear Lora's voice, it's like your balls disappear. Get in the car, and let's get this shit over with."

"You still mad at me?" I'm enjoying all this. Tommy knows it, and it makes him an extra shade of pissed off. He gets in the driver's side and slams his door. I'm already in and buckled up so he takes off.

"If Dev and Jesse weren't on an escort gig tonight, we wouldn't be together, you rock headed, punk ass, white bread, Darth Vader mime! At least have the damn decency to stop grinnin' like a Halloween pumpkin!"

I immediately assume my usual demeanor of an underfed bridge troll, frowning and nodding. "You're right, T! The moment I break Gronk's neck, we'll go back to the house and kill everyone, including Al's goldfish, Gilda!"

Tommy could only hold his grim pose for a moment before losing it. He brayed with enthusiasm, shaking his head, pissed off at himself he couldn't hold the line. "Okay, you got me with that one. John... I thought I was whipped. You, brother, have taken whipped to the undiscovered territory."

"Never presume to know another man's marriage, T. Lora runs our enterprises like she was born to it. You've seen her handle our crew, while threading them into Denny's extracurricular government business. She doesn't ask questions. The business is humming. If it ain't broke, don't fix it. Besides, I love the sound of her voice – good mood, bad mood, happy, pissed off... it's all good."

Tommy shrugged. "Fine, you pussy whipped sap. Now... back to business. Why in the hell do you have to mix it up with Dixon?"

18

I'm serious now. I don't like Dixon. I have two guys working for me, who are just like family: Devon Constantine and Jesse Brown. They claim I ended their careers, but actually although I did beat them, I came up with a way they could make more money than they ever dreamed of. Fightin' them was just business. Dixon was different. "He said something I have to answer in the cage."

My partner did a double take at that answer. "Care to share? I might not be so pissed off if I knew what the hell risking a UFC shot for some pug is all about. Dixon only shoots his mouth off because if he takes you out, he might get a UFC shot in your place. I didn't know you were gettin' so sensitive. Maybe we need to have your hormone levels checked, sissy."

We both ended up laughing our butts off, me at his barb, and him at me laughing over it. Tommy has a right to know, so I explain. "Alexi asked me if I'd meet him for a drink at The Warehouse. He said he had a proposition for me. You know I need to keep him happy, because the old mobster keeps my other masters up to date with any info he gleans from his overseas contacts. Besides, he keeps his word, and he hasn't lied to me. Anyway, I get to the bar, and our good buddy Fiialkov's sitting with that damn polar bear, Dixon."

"Big surprise there," Tommy clucked. "You knew if you refused to fight under his banner, he'd hunt down someone to be his favorite. That albino, Dixon, gives me the creeps. He'd be easier to look at if the sucker didn't have those damn black colored pupils. I still think he has special contacts."

I shook my head. "We've seen him fight. He ain't wearin' contacts. Alexi waves me over, and introduces me. I stick out my paw, and Dixon just grunts. I smile and sit down, nice as you please. Alexi wants me to sign on for a fight with Dixon, using the cage and seating setup the Syrians paid for. He plans on beaming it via Al Jazeera's network for a pay-per-view event in Europe."

Tommy gets to the Laurel Lounge and parks around the corner from the entrance. "I have eyes on Gronk inside. Eric was having a brew when Gronk walked in with a buddy. They went back to play darts, and Eric called me. That was only half an hour ago."

Tommy pulls out his own i-thingy and texts Eric Tamil. Tamil is one of our informants around town. After a few heated keyboard exchanges, Tommy looks at me with a smile.

"Gronk's getting crocked."

"Excellent, Tommy." I'd hoped to avoid a lot of crap with the apprehension. Avery Gronk was not someone anyone in their right mind would mess with. He needed killin', but my cover life would surely suffer unless I handled his demise perfectly. I'm not a perfect guy. "You want the bear spray or the needles?"

Tommy held out his hand. "Give me the spray. I don't want to be anywhere near Gronk."

I handed Tommy the bear spray. Our plan is to blind him, and zap him until he quits moving. We don't fool around with guys like Gronk. The prick's over six and a half feet tall and weighs over three hundred pounds. We've been trying to locate him for a month. We got the ticket from a bond agency in New Jersey. Gronk fled on a drug distribution charge just before they found out he was responsible for two dead bodies with his DNA all over them. We were into the Gronk expense sheet for a couple grand, because Casey and I went down to LA on a tip he'd been seen. If that tip would have panned out, Gronk would be dead, and his body shipped back East. Since he's on our home turf and I have Tommy with me, Gronk has to go down in the traditional manner.

"So tell me what Dixon said."

I wanted to keep my mind on Gronk. Crap! "When I told Alexi I couldn't take the match that close to the UFC fight, he said he understood. I got up to go and Dixon decided to punk me. He said he really loved watching Alice. Fiialkov read the tea leaves and leaped up from the table making surrender gestures, explaining Dixon many times had picked up his granddaughter from school. As you know, Alice and Fiialkov's granddaughter had been in the same class. That didn't cut it with me. Dixon was smiling. I told Alexi to set it up."

Tommy exits the car and I follow. We take up positions at the front of his car, ready to move around the corner to the entrance if Gronk leaves. I stay standing while Tommy sits on his hood. "That stupid son of a bitch wants that UFC shot bad. You do know another killing in the cage after snuffing Rankin in Dubai will end your UFC career once again, don't you dummy? So okay, Dark Lord, what besides bait, which you chomped on, you big guppie, did you think was happening when Dixon mentioned Alice? Even if you got killed did you think your crew would let something happen to Alice or Lora? Hell, your two 'Pulp Fiction' characters, Lucas and Casey would have Dixon out on the yacht with cement shoes in a heartbeat."

Apparently my partner of some years thinks I'm made of stone. "Granted, that wasn't about business, T. Alexi knew Dixon screwed up. Dixon probably thought it was the only maneuver that would get him a shot at me, and he's probably right. Well, okay Dixon, you two bit, albino fuck, you have the Dark Lord's attention. Tonight we play out the Dixon string, T. I know damn well all of you have my back. Come hell or high water, I'm gettin' a piece. If it screws up the UFC shot, too fuckin' bad."

Tommy nodded. "I feel you, John. I'll be there, but it's nice to have an outline."

"You never used to be this touchy feely, brother," I counter. "Maybe you need to put away the evening gown and high heels and get your head back in the game... pussy."

I smile as Tommy is howling his head off, just before he gets a text beep. "Eric says Gronk is coming right at him, and he doesn't look like he... aw hell... he's grabbing him!"

We run around to the entrance to face off with Gronk. I may be a psycho, but I know Tommy isn't, and I like Eric. I'm not letting that ass-hole maim the guy. "Back up out of sight, T. Come out if something happens you can help with."

"Damn it! Sorry, John, I thought we had an easy one, but Eric's been made by someone inside. Got a plan?"

"Yeah, but best we not rake it over the coals. I'll get Eric out alive, but I don't like our chances of him informing for us in the future."

Tommy shrugged. "Eric plays us, but I don't want to see him dead. If you can keep him un-dead, then I'm all for it. Shit happens though. I'll be around the corner."

Gronk exits the Laurel with Eric in a headlock. Gronk's arm's so big, I can barely see Eric's flushed face. His other hand has a knife held under Eric's ribcage on the side. "Get the fuck back, Harding! You ain't taking me in!"

Two things I notice. His partner didn't come out with him, and two, he held the knife too far away from our informer's side. I don't bother starting a dialogue. The Taser needles hit Eric in the middle of his chest. Gronk gets jolted back as I crank up the collapsing Eric. Dropping the Taser, I launch a flying knee right into the still stunned Gronk's solar plexus. It's a money shot. The knife clatters to the sidewalk. Gronk folds heavily after it, trying unsuccessfully for many moments to suck air. Tommy comes around the corner with his bear spray can up and ready.

"You… you Tased me, bro!" Eric's rolling around.

"Watch out for the partner, T, while I handcuff Gronk."

I rolled the barely breathing Gronk over on his stomach. He didn't like it, but there wasn't a hell of a lot he could do about it. I cuffed him. Not wanting him to do anything goofy with his feet, I plastic tied his ankles together. Grabbing up Eric off the sidewalk, I dust him off while he's yapping away.

"How come his partner didn't come out, Eric?"

Eric's still vibrating slightly with his eyelids twitching, but he looks over at the door as if he knew what I was talking about. "I… I don't know, John. When I got grabbed, I didn't see anything else."

I sighed, patting Eric's shoulder. "About how many people are in there?"

"Just a few at the bar. I think the guy next to me tipped off Gronk. He walked back with them, and the next thing I know, Gronk's yanking me the hell off my stool."

I nod as I notice Tommy's already calling inside. Tommy ends the call.

"Red says the guy's sitting at the bar, watching the door."

"Stay here with Tommy," I tell Eric. "I'll bring him out, along with the guy who tipped them off about you."

"John! What the hell? We got Gronk. Let's call it a day."

I try reasoning first. "Look, T, for all we know, his partner's a stone killer. I ain't leavin' until I know both the partner and his snitch. Eric, what does the snitch have on I can ID him with?"

"Ah… oh yeah… ah… he has a red 49er's jersey on."

That'll work. "How about Gronk's buddy?"

Eric's face blanks out momentarily, and his upper lip's still twitching from the Taser charge. He brightens up finally and looks at me like all the gears in his head are working. "He's got a gold ring in his right ear, John."

"Well all right. That's another hundred if you got those two right."

"Really?" Eric brightens noticeably. "Hell, John, I'd have walked back in and ID'd them for you for an extra hundred."

I chuckle. Eric's okay. "Nope. Me and Tommy want you to keep supplying us with info we need. Can you hang around out here for a few moments while I gather up Gronk's associates?"

Eric nods energetically. "Sure, John."

"Let me get the riot gun," Tommy urges, stepping in front of me as I began entering the bar. "What the hell's gotten into you lately?"

"I don't want the lounge lit up over my curiosity, T. I'll be careful."

"You step into that damn bar, and I'm rattin' you out to Lora."

Tommy smiles at my look of complete shock. Shit! I can tell there are going to be adjustments in the future. When Tommy starts second guessing my on scene actions, it means I've been kicked to the curb on procedural matters. That ain't happenin'. I don't bother trading insults with my formerly trustworthy partner. I walk inside the Laurel Lounge and wave at Red behind the bar. 49er's jersey is seated right next to the door, staring down at his beer. I grab him up off his stool and off the floor, holding him in front of me. I spot gold earring at the end of the bar with a distinct look of unhappiness on his face. I point at him while I manhandle Mr. 49er.

"Come along outside, Sir, while we get things sorted out. No one needs to get hurt. Do you have a weapon?"

Gronk's partner shakes his head no. My holding Mr. 49er a few inches off the barroom floor with very little effort has impressed him. "I don't want any trouble."

"That's good. I don't either." I gesture for him to come along. "C'mon outside with me and we'll sort this out. Gronk's already in custody, so it will all be peaceful. Put your hands up and grip the back of your head. Then walk outside in front of me. Are we clear?"

Gold ring nods and clasps his hands behind his head. He walks out in front of me while I stop to quickly plastic tie 49er's hands behind his back under protest. Outside, Gronk's sitting up against the building wall, still looking like he took a knee in the solar plexus. In other words about all he's doing is gasping white-faced while staring at his shoes. I give over Mr. 49er to Tommy. I gesture at gold ring.

"I'm going to frisk you, Sir, so we can all be friends." Gold ring nods and I move behind him. He's not packing so I move over and do the 49er. Our football fan's packing a Glock 9mm in one of those shirt type holster setups. I relieve him of it. Tommy takes it from me while I turn back to gold ring. "Show me some ID, and we'll get you on your way."

He hands me his wallet, and puts his hands back up on his head without my asking. We're not drawing a crowd which is good, but I need to hurry this up. He has a California driver's license, and he matches the picture on it. His name's Charles Stopic, and he lives over on Arkansas Street. Tommy hands me the 49er's wallet. He's local too.

"Call Earl, T. Maybe he'll feel like doing us a solid since we're taking Gronk off the street." Earl's one of our contacts on the Oakland Police Force. Tommy hands me his i-thingy with a grin after making contact with Earl. I barely get out a hello.

"John! What the hell? You're fightin' tonight, and decided to plague Gronk for what... a warm up? You are one sick-"

"Earl!" I need to interrupt him because he's even boring me. "Gronk will be off Oakland streets. As the arguable murder capital of the USA, I figured you'd be more grateful. Can you run two names for me... please?"

Silence for a moment on the other side. "Okay... give 'em to me."

"Charles Stopic and Grant Parsons."

A gasp on the other side of the line did not bode well.

"Parsons?" Earl's voice lowered. "I can be there in ten minutes. Can you stay put?"

"Sure." This is getting good. I might have a few more brownie points to gather for future favors. "How dangerous?"

Earl states it with slow passion. "If you do not have him restrained, do it now or kill him. I don't care which. Do it now!"

I turn away and get out of hearing range. "Whoa there, brother. I plastic tied him, and Tommy has him. What's up?"

"He's wanted for the rape/murder of a fifteen year old girl. He's also killed two cops."

Well, okay then. "Wait one."

I walk over to 49er, and clock him. I'm no stranger to knockouts. Although Grant was restrained, I'm not the police. Yeah, thinking of a fifteen year old girl and two cops dead at his hands possibly made me a little mental. I ain't a psycho when it comes to right and wrong. Tommy steps back. He's seen the look, and he knows this part ain't his gig. I walk back over to a very shaken Stopic.

"Do you know the guy on the sidewalk? Think carefully before you answer, Chuck."

"He... he walked over and told us Gronk was made. Look, I went to school with Gronk. He and I have been friends since 6th grade. When he called me today to meet him for a drink, I said sure. I know it must seem-"

I waved him off. "This will take a little longer than I thought, Chuck. Thanks to Grant's extracurricular activities here, I'm afraid we'll need a little more of a clearance than the local PD for you." I used Tommy's i-thingy to send Denny Strobert a picture of Chuck, and the names, with a text for a rush. It wasn't

25

long before I got a smartass greeting, and a confirmation on Grant, along with an all clear on Chucky.

"Okay, Chuck, you can take off. Stay out of trouble."

Chuck lowered his hands slowly, while glancing down at Gronk, who was still nowhere near his old self. "I...I'll just go then. Will Gronk... ah... never mind. Goodbye, Mr. Harding."

"So long, Chuck." I watched Chucky start out walking, but he was jogging within a few seconds. I walked over to Tommy. "This scumbag at your feet raped and killed a fifteen year old girl, and killed two cops. He's the hat trick, T. Earl will be..." I heard sirens. "Earl will be here shortly."

Tommy gestured at Gronk. "He must have been figuring on partnering up with Parsons. I'll bet he was setting his old buddy Stopic up for a squat."

"Yep. Have a few drinks. Go back to Stopic's place with Stopic in the trunk, and lay low for a few months until they can make their way south of the border. I bet these two have done some time together. Take off, Eric. Give him five, T. He deserves a bonus."

Tommy counted out the money to Eric, who left in a hurry. He didn't need any face time with the PD. It was only a couple minutes before Earl Taylor and his partner, Enrique Rodriguez, arrived with half a dozen squad cars. I figure it was probably orders, because Earl and 'Rique know me well enough if I have a guy, he'll be there waiting. Earl jumps out of his squad car first and rushes over to flip Parsons over. He nods at 'Rique. Earl stands up.

"Thanks John. Too bad you didn't kill him."

This must be personal. I smile and wave Earl back. "Take your peeps somewhere for a few minutes, and I'll guide Grant to the river of no return."

Earl sighed, looking guiltily over at his partner. "We can't do that, Dark Lord."

"You should have told me it was personal on the phone, brother."

"Will you stop with that damn Dark Lord stuff!" Tommy hates my alter ego. "You know he'll be croaking at me now for a week, and humming that stupid Darth Vader theme."

Earl and 'Rique get a laugh out of Tommy's angst, as a few of their PD counterparts walk up to join the group. McArthur Blvd's getting crowded. Since they have Parsons confirmed down, Earl sends the reinforcements on their way. After cuffing Parsons on their own, 'Rique and Earl douse him with some water. He starts groaning after a couple of wet downs. Earl gets in his face. I can see they're recording too.

"Can you hear me, Parsons? Are you coherent?"

Realization is forming on Parsons' features. He sees it would have probably been a better idea to shoot it out in the bar. He looks up at me crossly. "What the fuck you hit me for, Harding?"

I shrug. "It seemed like the thing to do. Hey, Earl, why not take the cuffs off of poor old Grant here and let him have a go? Maybe I can still save the taxpayers some money on his trial."

'Rique plays along. "Damn, John, that's a good idea. Let's get him up and walk him around the corner, partner."

Parsons loses all semblance of rage. He stares open mouthed at 'Rique and Earl as they begin to release him. "Hey… what the hell? You have to take me in. Read me my damn rights and put me in the car!"

'Rique turns his recorder back on with a chuckle. Earl reads Parsons his rights, followed by Parsons enthusiastically acknowledging he understood them. Earl loaded him in the squad car without any trouble at all. By then, I noticed Gronk's beady little eyes taking in the scene around him. He wasn't panting anymore.

"You guys want me and Tommy to take Gronk in? We were going to anyway to get his ticket." It wasn't that I didn't trust my PD buddies, but we had a good deal of money tied up in the Gronkster.

Earl nodded. "Sure, John. We'll write you up for Parsons too. There's a nice piece of change on his head. 'Rique and I will make sure you get it. Thanks for calling this in."

"You two working security tonight?" Tommy wants to know if we'll be able to walk out of our redecorated fight house without eyes in the back of our heads.

"Yeah, T," 'Rique answered. "Should we bet on John or Dixon?"

Tommy grinned, looking over at me. "It's a tossup. I hear it's three to one for John to whup him. You guys can't make any money that way. That's a sucker bet."

My PD buds get a big he-haw out of that line. I shrug because Tommy's right.

"Best to stay away from the action tonight, guys. I have some business with Dixon. Watch our backs tonight after the fight, and I'll settle up at The Warehouse Bar for a five hundred bonus – no gamble."

Earl nodded as he got in behind the wheel. "You got it, brother, thanks."

"Later, John." 'Rique waved from the passenger side of the squad car. "Tommy, you have to come by the Warehouse with John. He'll do the Dark Lord for you, right John?"

'Rique dived into the passenger side, and Earl took off, leaving Tommy steaming. I wanted to enjoy the moment, but I had to keep my attention on the Gronkster.

Chapter Three
Bills Come Due

"C'mon, T. Go get the car and I'll load up Gronk. Let's punch his ticket. We stick to business for the rest of today."

"Fine," Tommy relented with a grin, "but I'm still telling Lora."

Prick. He does that irritating horse laugh of his while he goes around the corner. I turn to Gronk. He's unhappy. "Hey, Gronk, it's time to go."

I get him to his feet in time for Tommy to pull up in front. Gronk holds back.

"Let me go, Harding. You know I'll get free somehow. I'll come back for you and-"

"Shut the fuck up, Gronk!" Tommy leaps out of the driver's side to race around to where I'm holding the Gronkster. He grabs Gronk by his chin. "If you keep talkin', John won't answer, but you'll never make it to the station alive, you moron!"

It was then Gronk felt it as Tommy turned to me carefully. "Put it away, John. Remember what you said – all business today."

My blade had separated the material on his sweatshirt. The tip had probably broken the skin. Tommy was fast. With a flip of my wrist, the butterfly knife closed and disappeared into my back pocket. Tommy takes charge of Gronk, smacks his head into the upper car door frame, and shoves him in the backseat.

"Damn it, John, some folks shoot their mouths off, especially when being taken into custody." Tommy looks away for a moment, and then laughs. "Sorry, John. That was stupid. Now you have to weigh my screw-up into the mix. What'll it be, partner. My bad. I just figured there's a big downside to doing Gronk after our interaction with the PD."

He gets it. We've been around the block together more than a few times. Tommy's just pissed about my Dark Lord stuff. It colored his judgment. I'm not letting it go though just because I

29

love Tommy like a brother. "Do the math and give me a decision, T. Gronk knows you. He knows your family. Forget about me and mine. Granted, he could have kept his mouth shut and came at us later, but he didn't. He wants us to know we're on his to do list. Yeah, I know all the parameters: money, UFC matches, peace of mind... I'll leave it up to you. Make the call, brother."

Me and Tommy are tight. Our connection is way beyond reality. Sure, he recognized talent, and helped me into the back alley fight game at his monetary gain. He also knows if he says the word, I will crawl into the backseat with Gronk and snuff him like an ant on my tuna fish sandwich. I don't take threats well. He knows that, but Tommy can weigh risks, money, and future in a heartbeat. I trust his judgment.

Tommy starts walking around to the driver's seat. "Let's bring him in breathing, John. The PD knows we have him."

I look down into the backseat, staring at Gronk. I whip the butterfly knife out once, twice, three times... before answering. "I'll slice and dice him, and the PD can go fuck themselves. I'll take the rap, and get my playmakers to cover it."

Gronk's head is moving side to side as his mouth jacks out lies about what he will or won't do. I'm thinking Tommy is going to go all in for a moment, but he sighs and gets behind the wheel. "Get in, John. Let's opt for the payday."

The butterfly knife made its practiced disappearance into my back pocket once again. I slap Gronk's cheek affectionately. Then I lean in nose to nose, because I'm getting a hard on for this cheap cocksucker. "I don't normally get to this speech often. You best pray nothing happens to Tommy, or anyone associated with us: family, friends, or even acquaintances. You have no idea what the term flayed alive means. I will teach it to you... slowly... like fifty weight oil flows in wintertime."

I put a period at the end of my speech by making the butterfly knife reappear in a split second, slice through Gronk's right ear, and vanish into my back pocket once again. Gronk yelped in a high pitched tone as the butterfly knife blade reappeared under his nuts, and inadvertently sliced through the outer layer of his pants. Gronk wised up. The sullen wannabe mobster look that had already been replaced by complete compliance, escalated into unabridged fear.

"Want to see it disappear again, Gronk?"

Gronk nodded with passion. "I'm done, Harding!"

I tickled the idiot's scrotum for a moment without losing contact with his eyes. "You're not being convincing enough, my friend. I still detect a lack of passion… you fuck!"

Gronk got passionate. I may have let the razor sharp blade make its cold way to his balls.

"I…I'll kill anyone I hear that… that even speaks your name… anything!"

The butterfly knife returns to its place of residence. I pat Gronk's face once again. "I think we have an understanding. Let me add this: if you escape from custody, I will hunt you down, and flay you alive. I will find you. Is that understood?"

Gronk nodded without speaking. Wise choice.

"Good. I think we're done here, T." Tommy handed me a piece of adhesive tape. I pinched it into place over Gronk's new ear notch. He thanked me. I got out and slammed Gronk's door. Tommy took off the moment I was belted in next to him. "It won't be bad tonight. All business tonight too, T. Fiialkov thinks he finally has a winner. The prick actually bet against Rankin in Dubai… his own white Russian."

"He's a piece of work all right. Alexi knows business. He knows everyone in the area wants you to lose. When you keep winning, it upsets the cosmic balance. Keep doing the damn Dark Lord crap, and I'll be hoping for you to lose."

I heard Gronk grunt in amusement. I glanced back at him and he looked down at his feet. "He obviously figured out a way to get me under his thumb. I might as well be fighting for him. Alexi finds a way to get me to do exactly what he wants me to do anyway."

Tommy laughed, nodding his head in agreement. "You're right, DL. You're his bitch, and you haven't even gotten kissed."

Gronk snickered.

That hurt. "I'm his bitch? What about Ray. Fiialkov can't move without Ray Alexander's nose up his ass. I wonder how much he's into Fiialkov because of betting against me."

"Somewhere in the fifty to a hundred grand range," Tommy replied, getting serious about our subject. "Jim Bonasera got clear of it before that idiot Ray imploded, but they're both still working for Alexi now. I wonder if Ray will be there rootin' you on, Dark Lord."

That's funny - Ray Alexander in the Dark Lord's corner. "I hope not. He's bad luck. I think Alexi keeps him around as a 'Cooler'."

Tommy laughs, nodding his head. "Yeah, every time a big fish starts a winning streak against Fiialkov, he sends Ray to schmooze with them, and deal done, streak ended. You've turned the conversation, but I'm still telling Lora."

Prick. "Fine. I don't care. Lora knows the score."

"She doesn't know the score about you insisting on walking in on a cop killer with nothing but your looks"

I can tell a negotiation when I hear one. "What's it going to cost me?"

"I want to take the family out on The Sea Wolf."

I sat up straight, hearing those words. "You're crazier than a two legged cat, T! That's Lucas's boat. You put a scratch on it, and nothing will save you, brother. Lucas is mental over that boat."

"Make it happen, DL."

"It's your funeral, T. On the bright side you'll have at least thirty burials at sea. That's how many pieces Lucas will cut you into when you accidentally mar the outside of his boat."

"The Sea Wolf belongs to your crew. Stop being such a pansy, and stand up to Captain Ahab."

"I'm trying to save your life here. Let me talk Lucas into taking your family out on an excursion. He might let you steer it or make a couple turns out in open water. How's that?"

Tommy considers it. "Okay... that might be good. Besides, Lucas and I are just like brothers. He'd never hurt me over a couple dings."

Yeah, that's a laugh. "I think I heard Lucas say the same thing about the last guy he eviscerated. Take the example of his partner Casey – a stone killer. Remember the stories about US Cavalry soldiers fighting Apaches. They would put a bullet in their own heads rather than be captured by Apaches. Casey would slit his own throat rather than pilot The Sea Wolf."

Tommy knows Casey. The man's own mother gets chills when Casey's around. "Maybe you're right. Talk to Lucas for me."

I leaned back with a sigh. "You have chosen... wisely."

* * *

We punch Gronk's ticket without incident other than some congrats from the PD. Tommy drops me off at home early enough for me to get a little nap before the fight.

"I'll pick you up at eight, Gomer," Tommy says. "Tell your greeting party I said hi."

I shut the car door while glancing toward my front entrance. Lora and her mini-me, Alice are waiting on the front stoop, arms folded, with complimentary scowls. By the time I look back toward Tommy's car, it's speeding away. He knows trouble when he spots it. At least I know he didn't have anything to do with it, which makes me wonder what the heck my greeting party is all about. I paste a smile on, approaching with shields up.

"I hear you went unarmed into a bar to drag out a cop killer with no backup." Lora fires a volley. "What were you thinking?!"

"Yeah!" Minnie-me puts another exclamation point on.

"Where'd you hear that?"

"That other killer you took down legitimately with Tommy backing you up told the story loud and clear after you dropped him off. He had 'Rique call me, because he said you told him it was important I be contacted."

The Gronkster porked me. I smile. You better pray you never get out of prison, Gronk. Oh, what fun we'll have then. "You and Lora-light go on inside and quit making a spectacle of yourselves."

I get gasps of outrage, but no movement. I walk up, snatch Lora off the stoop, and carry her inside under my arm. Al jumps me from behind with a choke hold. Once inside, I start whistling as

I close the door, with Lora kicking and cursing while Minnie-me chokes me with no effect on the way to the kitchen. I deposit them next to the sink and get a Sprite out of the refrigerator, enjoying the verbal cannon fire from my wife and step-daughter. I sit down with a satisfied sigh. Life is good. The only bad part is Tommy finagled a boat ride without payment.

"Well?" Lora asks, still scowling.

"Well what?" I ask back in full Dark Lord voice. "The Dark Lord does not have to answer to pseudo bosses and mini-mes."

Alice giggles, but Lora is still upset.

"I have a fight tonight. I'm going to bed for a few hours. We can take this case of my insubordination up tomorrow, or have Samira come over and look after Mini-me, and meet me over at the Warehouse Bar. I'll send Jafar after his wife when the fight ends."

Lora's face lightens up. "I can't believe Jafar and Samira are married."

"They're both over eighteen, in love, and her old man gave his consent. The old man's consent was the most important part. They both make great money. They have a house, and an incredible future. I'll bet Jafar's a Dad by this time next year."

"I want to see the fight, John," Alice states.

"Oh, now it's up to me whether you see the fight? Ask the boss. No, don't bother. You already know the answer." I stand up, and chug the rest of my Sprite. "I'll be seeing you two shortly. The Dark Lord needs his rest."

"I'm glad you're okay, John," Lora said.

"I know that, hon. I'm sorry things got scary, but I need to keep the PD happy, and they're very happy with me today. Earl and 'Rique will be watching our backs tonight too after the fight."

"Who will be doing it in the fight?"

I held up my fists, left first, then right. "My old partners here, death and destruction."

"I better call Lucas and Casey."

Smartass.

* * *

The guard at the door waves us into the upgraded warehouse. Thanks to my fight with the Syrian Slayer, we have our own cage and seating around it, not to mention lighting, paint job, and even a concession bar. A big guy blocks our way after we get inside. It's the Big O, a Nigerian fighter who ran his mouth off before I closed it for him. Tommy immediately jumps in front of me. We have money on the line here, and I don't get into extracurricular freebies.

The Big O is playacting for the crowd stopping to see what's going on. That's what got him a special whuppin' the last time. "I want you, Harding!"

"You got him already, O," Tommy reminds him. "If you want a rematch, have your handler call me. He has my number."

"Hidin' behind yo' mamma here ain't goin' to save you!"

I grab hold of Tommy. "Jack's comin', T."

Tommy steps back as Jack Korlos arrives, sap in hand. Nearly as big as me, an ex-boxer wearing all the marks from his time in the fight game, Jack referees matches for Fiialkov. He points the sap at the Big O.

"This is straight from Mr. Fiialkov, get the hell out of the way or you'll never get a fight anywhere again. Stay in the way and I'll move you. Then, the best you'll be doing is blubbering and trying to remember what your name is."

The mention of Alexi's name is enough to put a startled look on the O's face. He steps off, gesturing at me. Jack grins back at me, and motions us to follow him. It was good pre-fight entertainment for the crowd. Alexi moves in next to me with a big smile as Jack runs interference for us to the cage. We never had to worry about this crap until the place got a facelift. I notice the camera crews are already in place.

"Sorry about that, John. The Big O has been steaming for a rematch. I'm not sure why. It took him months to recover from the beating you gave him. He's been wrecking all comers the last few months. I think he's getting pharmaceutical help."

"He had the look," Tommy put in. "You doin' drug testin' yet, Alexi?"

Fiialkov laughs. "We are perhaps a bit too casual for that, Tommy. A few more of these draws, and we may be able to go legit. Maybe whoever wins tonight can give O a match. What do you think, John?"

I see a familiar gleam in Alexi's eyes. "I think you believe I'm going down tonight and it doesn't much matter. You think I'll need a fight after I get whupped tonight, and Dixon takes my spot on the UFC card against the Slayer. Big O would be a perfect consolation match for me after Dixon smacks the crap out of me, huh?"

Alexi smiles, and pats my shoulder. "You can't fault me for hoping, right John."

"With Jack Korlos refereeing I have no problem with the outcome. Are we still fighting UFC rules for this?"

"We have to, John. I wouldn't be able to get a bout on pay-per-view even overseas if we don't have some order in the cage. I have legitimate judges. Jim Bonasera will be doing the master of ceremonies stuff. Ray Alexander will be kept out of the way, although I believe he will be betting a modest sum against you as usual."

"That'll be the least of my problems tonight." We reach the cage, and Alexi veers off with a wave. I nod at Jafar as he walks up next to us. "Hey kid, looks like you get some TV time tonight. That Alexi, he's such a sweetheart, ain't he, T?"

Tommy chuckles as we get set up inside the cage. "Alexi knows his stuff."

"I have been watching Dixon, John," Jafar tells me, getting our equipment bag sorted out. "I am glad it is you who will be fighting him. I wish Dev and Jesse were here to give you tips."

Devon Constantine and Jesse Brown are the other members of my fight night crew, but we have a business to run. "Don't worry about it. You and Tommy keep your eyes open. I'll be okay."

Big O has taken his seat to the right of our position, first row front. He's yelling insults, drawing big laughs from the crowd. I'm not popular here for some unknown reason, except with the cops, and the waitresses around the area. They usually bet on me.

Some of the stuff O is howling in my direction starts to tighten my jaw a little, so I get loose, moving and swinging. Then Dixon makes his way into the cage with his entourage. He's a legitimate UFC candidate, so he stays out of steroid land. Six and a half feet tall, two hundred eighty pounds, with dynamite in both hands, Dixon's the real deal. I would have had to fight him sometime anyway. Dixon stays quiet until the crowd noise lessens. Then he mouths off in a way I did not expect.

"Hey Harding... what, no Lora? What's the matter, you afraid she'll root for me? She is one tight little piece."

I feel Tommy's hands on my arms, but I'm not saying anything. I had a few thoughts about ground and pound, and strategy for stand up. Change of plan.

"While you're recovering in the hospital, I'll go keep Lora warm and safe. That cute little girl of hers is just the sweetest thing. Does she sleep in the same bed with you two?"

"Jesus," Tommy mumbles.

Alice is like Jafar's little sister. I barely have enough time to grab him as he launches. "Easy kid!"

"Maybe you better let the kid take your place, Harding," Dixon jeers. "I bet it would be a better match."

I smile as Tommy gets Jafar back in line. I plan on being everything Dixon ever dreamed of in a match. We were fighting under UFC championship rules – five rounds instead of three. Dixon better start praying I'm dead because I plan on taking him the distance. I see the tight look on Jack Korlos's face. He's been listening to Dixon intently. Jack begins his pre-fight inspection with me. Jack's wearing a grim look.

"Don't make me sap you, kid," Jack says as he checks my gloved hands and body.

I look him dead in the eye, because I respect him. "If I do, don't take it personal."

Jack chuckles. "I won't, but I still won't like it."

Jafar puts my mouthpiece in as Jack walks over to Dixon. It's minty. Neat. "If you are in the hospital after the fight, John, I will put a bullet between his eyes."

Okay. That's not good. It's ruining my buzz. I grab him, getting an inch away from his face. "Concentrate on the fight, kid. Remember Samira, and all the stuff I've taught you about this crap. If there's even a hint of danger with me incapacitated, do you really think Lora and Alice would need protecting?"

That sobers him up. He pats my hand. Jafar knows I have people around me who will make Dixon's last moments on earth legendary. "I'm sorry, John. Dixon zapped me with the Alice dig. I know better than to not think."

I'm right there with you, kid. "No problem. It's all pre-game hype, my friend."

Tommy, who knows me all too well, juts up into my face. "If you kill him we ain't ever fighting in the UFC ever."

I smile at him. I like pain. I like big mouth, no account, cheap ass thugs like Dixon. Apparently, Dixon thought what happened to Van Rankin was a fluke. It's party time, and no amount of reasoning is going to change that. "I'm good to go, T."

Tommy grimaces and backs away, pulling Jafar with him. "C'mon kid. No use reasoning with the Dark Lord. We'll be watching for clues, DL."

I acknowledge with a wave of my hand as Jack strides to cage central. I let the filmy red haze of violence shimmer over my head. See, I don't scare. I don't bleed a lot, and I don't get knocked out. That only leaves one course: to endure. That's where the fun begins. First though, I have to get some quick payment. I know Dixon comes out every match on the attack, a swarming, heavy punching barrage. It usually garners fear when some of those punches hit home. He comes on loud and heavy. Tonight... it will only be for a moment.

Korlos asks us if we're ready. When he gets affirmative nods, Jack starts us. Dixon charges at me ready to counter anything. I'm willing to take the head strike he launches to trade a little peach of a shot I've been working on. I remain motionless as if in fear until he's only feet from me, ready to knock my head clean off my shoulders. At the last second I drop down slightly, and rip death and destruction up under his ribcage while absorbing a couple of his shots. Oh mama, it feels like home. Those shots

38

wake up the big mouth as air intake is reduced to gasps. I leg whip Dixon. Caught unawares, his head bounces. I could have followed it up with some ground and pound, fight ending elbows or fist strikes. Not tonight, brothers and sisters – we're going to the promised land of pain.

Dixon stumbles up to his feet in a feeble guard stance. I can tell in his eyes he's wondering why the hell I didn't follow him down. I give him a clue. While feinting a left hook, I pull back and launch a roundhouse right leg kick to the side of his head that drops him like the sandbag on an old time gallows. I don't follow, although Dixon rattles around on the canvas like a turtle on its back in the desert. An unusual silence has overcome the crowd as if they're sensing this is judgment day for Dixon. They're right in a manner of speaking. He's in purgatory, the place between heaven and hell, but I ain't sending him on his way yet.

Our referee, Jack Korlos, looks over at me with an uneasiness I've never seen on his face before. That's his problem. I have my own problem – how to keep Dixon awake for the rest of the movie. I dance around the ring, hands up in fistic defense as if worried the turtle could shoot up off the canvas and clock me. If Dixon had a brain, he would have stayed motionless and let Jack end the fight. Hey, he's a fighter - an irritating big mouth who doesn't know when to fight and when to spew his verbal hype, but he's a fighter. Dixon works his way back to his feet.

I see in his eyes he knows the game now, and he doesn't like it. His crew shouts out directions, and plans that ain't ever going to work. The one he takes to heart is run, Forest, run. Dixon does laps around the ring, feinting strikes with me in the middle. I decide on a little playacting myself. I drop my hands. I simply stare at him while he's circling like an impotent shark. The crowd starts roaring insults and encouragements, but that's not what this is about. The round ends, heralded by catcalls from the audience.

Tommy and Jafar work over me in silence, toweling me off, and patting the small cut on my eye. They've heard the bells ringing on judgment day too, and they have no idea what to say. I'm certain if they'd seen something special about Dixon, they'd be warning me of it. Tonight, it wouldn't matter. Dixon mentioning Alice to get the fight was low. I chalked it up to hype, especially since Alexi explained about him seeing his granddaughter and Alice together. That last shot Dixon took about my wife and stepdaughter to rattle me sticks; because hey, I kill people. Many times I don't even get to know the reason. Tonight, I have a reason.

Tommy pats my shoulder. "You're good to go, DL."

"I have nothing, John," Jafar adds. "I am liking this fight very much so far though."

I glance back at Jafar. "Buckle up. If you liked the first round, you'll love the second."

I notice something as I stand with the warning horn. Dixon's up on his feet, pounding his gloves together as if he couldn't wait to get at me. I look back at Tommy with a grin. "Dixon got an uplift, T."

"I see it," Tommy mumbles. "You've been here before, John. The only thing I'll add is that the fight would already be over if you had ended it."

"Yep." I clap my gloved hands together. "It should make my carrying this piece of shit easier in the last four rounds."

"Do not play with this man, John," Jafar chimed in. "Anything could happen. Why do you take such chances?"

I turned on Jafar. "Who's playing, kid?"

Jack motions us up, readies us, and indicates the beginning of the round. I smile as Dixon comes at me in deliberate attack mode. He lands jabs, and crosses, speeded up by whatever he got served in the corner. I'm with him, and the round proceeds more in a manner Dixon had hoped for. Only one problem, I don't plan to let this round end without a little extra drama. My left hand jab is like getting hit with a trip hammer. Yeah, I work on it. As round's end approaches and Dixon's confidence builds, I start zapping him with my jabs. It shocks the crap out of him. That's when I leg whip him again. I smile as his head hits and bounces. The problem for my boy Dixon is that I follow him to the canvas, and for ten seconds I blast him with real hurtful shots. I stay away from the obvious head shots, and smash rib shots into him from both sides until the bell sounds. I stand up away from him as he rolls gingerly to the side and stumbles to his corner. Oh yeah, baby, it is so on.

Tommy's grinning when I get to my rest spot. He's shaking his head, but he's liking it. Jafar remains quiet, taking out the mouthpiece, and giving me a quick swig of water. Tommy towels me off, applying coagulant to my numerous bloody spots. What's the use of conversing? I like my crew. If they had anything relevant, they'd be shouting it in my ear. I'm watching Dixon real close when I get a glimpse of him. He ain't happy. Only two rounds in, and I'm afraid that's only the beginning. Pharmaceuticals will help, but after the last round, Dixon's beginning to realize he's been paying for his verbal insights. This round is where I take all confusion out of the mix.

Jack motions us into action. Dixon thinks I'll be satisfied with status quo. I don't think so. He comes out hands high. I smash a beauty side kick into his midsection that sends him into the cage wall. I back off as I watch him writhe in pain. I drop my hands again, with no pretense. If there was any chance someone thought I wasn't carrying this two bit, shithead, I wanted that to end. Dixon scrambled to his feet, looking around as if he didn't have a clue where he was. I smash my hands together. It's the third round. Let's start working for some understanding.

I can tell in moments Dixon got another pharmaceutical uplift. His eyelids are blinking big time. I'm grinning because the four hundred cycle speed hummer he's got going on after his corner visit ain't going to help him. I meet him in the center throwing hands. Difference is I don't care about pain. I embrace it like a long lost friend. Yeah, it's disturbing. So is a lot of reality about me. I pump a left hand jab into his red eye express as he moves forward. It jolts him back to reality with stumbling acknowledgment. With his attention diverted to protecting his head, I smash one of my leg blasters to the side of his knee. It buckles, and Dixon drops. I don't follow. I move to my left slightly and roundhouse his head again. This time I think I've miscalculated at first, but the turtle in the desert stirs, getting to hands and knees while looking around without recognition. I let the time run out in the round without another strike. Jack Korlos's wearing a grim look. Hey, not everyone in the arena can be happy.

Tommy's looking a bit solemn too. He wipes me down quickly as Jafar takes out my mouthpiece and gives me a sip. "I didn't think it was possible, John, but you're making me start feeling sorry for that pug across from us."

I don't answer. Sometimes a bill comes due, and payment can't be deferred. Not wanting to upset Tommy, Jafar merely pats my shoulder as he sticks my cleaned up mouthpiece back in place. I get on my feet for the fourth round. I notice it's still really quiet. Neat. When Jack motions us to get started, I come in all business. I work Dixon's body without pause. I take his flurry of shots in stride. He bloodies me, but nothing will stop my body shots. My right hand lands under his heart, catching him coming in, and I hear the rib crack.

Dixon, white faced, stumbled back against the cage wall, trying to pass enough air to stay on his feet. He can't block the straight on forward kick I follow up with. It shatters his nose. Dixon goes to his knees. I see already I may not have pulled enough off the kick. It's an inexact science. The good part is I don't have to pummel him for another round. The bad part is I don't get to pummel him for another round. I slam into him, getting a rear full naked choke. Two seconds and Dixon will need a séance and a Ouija board to communicate with. Jack pokes me in the forehead with the sap, screaming in my face.

"Don't, John!"

Damn it. "He hasn't tapped out yet, Jack."

Jack snorts, trying not to smile. "That's because he's unconscious. Let him go, kid."

I release Dixon. Jack lets him fall face first while signaling the match was over. He holds up my arm. Dixon's entourage leader makes a run at me, the idiot. I drop him with an overhand right like an afterthought on bowling night. Tommy and Jafar are at my side in a split second, but Jack's already got his security crew in the cage corralling Dixon's hangers-on. The med team is next. A deathly silence hangs over the arena. I turn to Tommy as the medics go to work on Dixon.

"Let's get the hell out of here. I have a sour taste in my mouth only Bud and Beam can cure."

"That was better than sex," Tommy whispers. "Good Lord did you rack him up. You were going to carry the poor bastard for five rounds, weren't you?"

I nod with a sigh as Jafar eases my gloves off. "The whole five rounds if I could. I got excited when he thought that speed ball he took in his corner was going to make a difference."

"Yeah, you did."

"I will go over to your house and send Lora to the Warehouse, John," Jafar says with a smile while stuffing my gloves in the equipment bag. He hands me a towel soaked in peroxide. "Samira and I will stay with Alice. Take your time."

I use the peroxide towel to wipe myself down. "Thanks. Tell her to stay home and call me instead if she doesn't feel like coming to the bar."

"I will." Jafar walks in front of me with the equipment bag after I pull on my sweats, while Tommy takes up a position in the rear. We head for the cage exit.

Chapter Four
Deal With The Devil

Fiialkov's waiting for us with Earl and 'Rique. The PD looks happy, so they must have bet on me anyway.

"I am very sorry about the unfortunate things Dixon said to you, John," Alexi states right away. "I warned him not to provoke you. He is an idiot, and very nearly a dead man."

"I know that wasn't your game plan, Alexi. I see you have my security team ready for the walk out to our cars." I shake hands with Earl and 'Rique.

"They told me you had business with them at the Warehouse Bar. I will call ahead. Your tab is on me. Enjoy."

"Thanks, Alexi. See you next time. May I ask one more favor?"

Fiialkov turns back to me. "Certainly."

"I see the Big O waiting for me down there. If you want him to leave the arena alive, get him out of my path."

"I will take care of it, John. Wait here a moment."

"Great fight, John, if that's what you call that annihilation," Earl exclaims as Fiialkov goes to Big O, points one finger at him, and the O heads for the exit without a word.

"From the looks on your faces, you must not have heeded our warning to lay off the betting." It's clear sailing through the arena. The crowd's too stunned to indicate how they feel about Dixon's judgment day.

"We decided to bet the five hundred you promised us," 'Rique explains. "Odds were only two to one by fight time when we bet. You coming with us, Tommy?"

"Yeah, between saving Gronk's life from the Dark Lord this afternoon, and watching that jackass Dixon nearly yap his way into hell while ending our UFC shot, I definitely need a drink. Do you guys have a driver for tonight?"

44

Earl glanced back at Tommy with a nod. "We have a newbie lined up. You want a ride after we hoist a few?"

"Forget all that," I say, waving a hand. "We're celebrating. We'll have Dev and Jesse ride over when they wrap up for the night. What's the use in having a limo if you don't use it?"

"Oh hell yeah," Earl agrees. "Let a brother ride."

* * *

My Warehouse Bar waitress friend, Marla, greets us when we sit down at the bar.

"I heard all about your night, Champ. Why in the hell do these guys say stuff like that?"

"You have to have an ego to be dopy enough to fight in the cage, Marla," I explain while she sets out all our drinks. We're all regulars. She knows what we want. "Some guys lay waste to a bunch of fighters and lose perspective, and their survival instinct gets blocked. You can bet Dixon heard about what Rankin said to me in Dubai. He decided Rankin's method was right, but he just didn't go far enough."

"Yeah, that worked out real well for him," 'Rique added. "Did you bet anything, Mar?"

Marla laughed. "Oh hell yeah. I got in when it was even odds. Fiialkov already called and told me you gentlemen drink for free. With what I made tonight, I would have kicked in for a free one, but now I don't even have to do that. How much you guys take in, T?"

"I stayed conservative on this one, because we were giving odds. We made about five G's. It would have been much more if I'd known that imbecile Dixon was going to commit suicide by mouth. He shocked the hell out of me. John's probably right about the reason, but damn, that was one righteous beat down. Here's to the Dark Lord."

Everyone laughed and clinked glasses with Tommy.

"He ain't even marked up much for the coming UFC gig, Tommy," Earl added, grabbing my chin with professional posturing."

Tommy sighed. "At least Jack Korlos talked DL out of killing the guy."

"He hadn't tapped out," I protested to much laughter. It was then I saw Lora come through the entrance with Denny Strobert. He's using our Oakland Investigations, Bond Retrieval and Security business to front for Company assets, namely Casey Lambert, Lucas Blake, me, and our IT kid, Jafar Kensington. Lora struck a deal with the devil and threaded Casey and Lucas into our everyday stuff. They're happy with the deal and we can look out for each other. What we needed was a top notch investigator to go legit from the Company. I had my eye on Clint Dostiene. We all chewed sand with him overseas. Clint always had a real talent for sniffing out bad guys. Denny had told me he might be able to get us all together.

Denny's all smiles, escorting Lora. She gives me a big hug, inspecting my face in much the same manner Earl did. "Look who stopped by. Denny watched the fight on the Al Jazeera Channel and called me. I figured even he couldn't mess up your mood here."

"That's hurtful, Lora," Denny complains with pouty lip, while shaking hands with Tommy and the PD. Earl and 'Rique have a lower level clearance Denny instigated with the higher ups in case something got out of hand locally. "I have excellent news to share with John, and here you clip me off like a rabid mongoose."

That statement draws big yucks from my slightly inebriated companions. I've nearly washed away the taste and thought of Dixon. With another quick Marla supplied Beam shot and a chug of Bud, I'm feeling real good about the night. I give Lora a quick kiss. "Save my spot, Hon, while I go find out what possible good news the Spawn of Satan could have for me."

Denny's enjoying this verbal beat down. That means he has something really good, or equal parts good and bad. "Very funny, Dark Lord. Have you chugalugged enough to walk with me for a moment?"

I head for the door with a gesture for him to follow. "Sure, Denny. Let's hear what you got. I hope it's as upbeat as you say or I will be upset, Denny Buzz-killer."

He laughs and nods as we clear the doorway. "I have Clint lined up for a West Coast move. The way we get him is a bit more complicated."

He has my attention now. No more joking around with the master – I need to find out who I have to kill in order to recruit Clint Dostiene. He's the puzzle piece we're missing. If I can get Clint out here, Oakland Investigations will become the most prominent consulting firm in the Western Hemisphere. Best of all, we'll call our own shots. I walk along with him for a moment before saying anything. He waits.

"How do we get it done, Denny? Last I heard, Clint got porked and retreated up to his mountaintop. I didn't know he was even speaking to you."

Denny grinned over at me. "Clint knew I went to bat for him when they tried to railroad him over the unauthorized Silva sanction. When the FBI circle jerk, profiling crew failed miserably with the latest serial killings, they approached me to lure Clint out of his hidey hole. I told them to go ahead. They screwed up not keeping him as a consultant. The FBI went to the mountaintop, but when Clint heard the psycho he'd captured was being held by the Los Zetas down in Mexico, he came undone. First, he made the FBI route satellites pointing at the cartel's compound where she's being held. Then he says he's going in to get this Lynn Montoya out. Then he calls me."

Oh boy. I have a feeling where this is headed. "Clint wants some help for the assault?"

"That sums it up. If he gets it, he's going to handle a little lone wolf op for us. For the team helping, it's an in and out. Then I need a presence at Antelope Wells to make sure if Clint gets the secondary op completed, he and Montoya pass through in country without a stop. Interested?"

I'm a little psycho myself, so envisioning a well armed assault on the Los Zetas with Lucas, Casey, Clint and me stirs the blood, especially if I get to keep Clint. I know there's more to this than that. The Spawn of Satan must be paid in the coin of the realm for something like this to take place. The Antelope Wells crossing is a dead giveaway. Denny wants Montoya, and he doesn't want any local law snagging her.

I'll take a stab at it. "This Montoya has your juices flowing. I thought she was a serial killer who got off on a technicality. If you're sending us to Antelope Wells for safe passage, you've got plans. Care to share?"

"Same old, same old, John. Clint's in love with this Montoya for some unknown reason. In reality, she only killed bad guys. She uses a knife like Edward Scissorhands. I need an anomaly like Montoya with us. I believe Clint can keep her in line, and she'd be invaluable in a lot of situations, one being your Las Vegas gig you almost blew. Montoya can lure our player away from his bodyguards, and we can try her out with you guys backing her play."

"For the record, everything we do on American soil is illegal, Spawn, so what makes the difference if we have a cover story or not? If I'd lost the UFC shot, we could have arrived in Las Vegas the roundabout way by car, set up early, and waited for our chance."

"We don't need to rehash this stuff. You won. They'll be clamoring for you in LV now. By morning, YouTube will have ten versions of the fight, all with subtitles like Harding gets brutal, violent, and murderous with Dixon. What the hell was that all about anyway, John? You carried the poor sap into the fourth round."

I shrug. "Dixon made an error with his mouth. It's over. So, you think Clint's girlfriend can stick this guy with one of your concoctions after getting him into bed, huh?"

"That would be my plan," Denny replied. "The FBI will be watching her and Clint because they'll be there for a legit bust on a serial rapist In LV. I'm getting that set up. It's all wishful thinking if you guys can't get Montoya out of Mexico. Clint sent me a hell of a plan. I put it at our Internet drop for Jafar to get for you. How's the kid doing anyway?"

"His logistics, IT, and hacking skills surpass anyone I've ever seen. We're working on his combat skills so he's not a liability in the field. He's a quick study, and is starting to acquire the adrenaline junky attitude we sometimes need. With his language skills, I have no doubt he will be one of the best you'll ever get a hold of."

"Good. I'm putting him at Antelope Wells to handle logistics. I want to network him with Laredo across the border during the op."

"Laredo Sawyer's still around?"

Denny laughed. "Do we have any other Laredo that you know of?"

"I know Laredo and Clint are tight. Laredo went in and pulled Clint out of the Yucatan. You ever make things right with Dostiene after that fiasco?"

"As a matter of fact I have a pleasant surprise for Clint on the lone wolf gig after he gets Montoya. He will be real pleased with the bonus he's bound to run into on that run. He luckily got free of that traitorous bastard down there just before you, Lucas and Casey went rogue and turned it into an international incident."

Know it all prick. Yeah, the Company can write us off to protect foreign sensibilities. We don't write each other off. What Denny doesn't know is us three musketeers backed Laredo up on the extraction. We did a little population control around the LZ, neat and quiet.

Denny glances over at me. "I bet you think I didn't know Laredo called you three down to protect his old ass when he picked up Clint."

Prick. "It's not that Denny. I just don't care."

Denny chuckles. No one does what he does, or is as good at doing it. That's why I haven't killed him yet. If I ever go to ground though, Denny better be along for the ride. I ain't ever leavin' him behind me to hunt my ass down.

"So, we good?"

"Count on it. You understand if Clint doesn't make it up to Antelope Wells at the appointed time, there will be an incident, right?"

Denny nods as we stand there staring at each other a little ways down from the bar. Denny and I ate sand together. I don't play people I respect. "It's the price of doing business. I have the chance to put together the most dangerous group of individuals I've ever met, John. If all this proceeds as planned, and you absorb Clint and his psycho girlfriend into your West Coast mix, it will be like making the theme of the old 'Shadow' radio series come to life. 'Who knows what evil lurks in the hearts of men? The Shadow knows!'. How's that?"

I busted up laughing. Only Denny could foment a group of cold blooded killers into some nostalgia quote from an old radio show. "Just so you know things could get complicated for you - we'll get it done or possibly ruin relations with Mexico for a hundred years."

"It's good you keep your sense of humor, John. Let's go back inside before Lora comes out and tears me a new one. Let's do this."

"I hope I don't ever want to gut you like a rainbow trout, Den."

Denny patted my shoulder. "Yeah... me too, John."
* * *

A figure ropes down from the old Huey with practiced ease. A big dog is anchored to him. He disengages quickly with the dog staying at his side, but gets low to the ground with weapon at the ready. Only his head moves, sighting in at the surroundings as the Huey flies off toward the horizon. "Dumbbell down."

I snort out my controlled humor. "Hey Clint, how's it hangin'?"

"Five by five, brother." Clint stands up, hands in the air.

We come up toward him like a gentle sand/kaki wave. Lucas gets emotional, going over and hugging his protégé with an endearing embrace that goes beyond protocol. Yeah, that bothers us. It bothers me because I know Casey will torture him with it for the next couple months. Casey and I have MAC-10's in business like directions making sure the reunion doesn't get interrupted.

"Damn! It's good to see you, Clint!" Lucas pulls Clint along with him and we're underway in moments with his dog on our six.
* * *

After scoping out our prep work, we retreat to an area where we've set up a safe camp. Clint goes over the mapping for his retreat points with care on our field laptop. He's always been methodical. Tonight is no exception. Then with the cartel compound structure blueprints up in 3D, he adds his explosive's placement.

"How's that look, Lucas?"

Lucas chuckles. "They'll think they were hit with cruise missiles. We brought enough for those specs. I'm glad you didn't do any last second rethink on them. I'll be close order ground level backup. John and Casey will be at the two vantage points you picked out from the satellite photos you blackmailed the FBI into getting."

"I appreciate this, guys," Clint said. "I'm already on the pad for the Yucatan, and don't think I'll ever forget that one."

I waved him off. "You bring Tonto and your new female experiment out to the coast when we finish, and we're all even up."

"Count on it, John. Give me a little time once I get her North to feel things out, and we'll give that deal in Las Vegas a roll of the dice. You'll be impressed with her. I'm looking forward to seeing you fight. You're nuts. You do know that, right?"

My head dropped with chin on chest, doing my award winning hurt look, while my partners yucked it up. "Not you too, brother. I get raked over the coals now from all sides. I was hoping to get a little understanding from you."

"Hey, it's a sweet deal, and I know Denny loves the cover," Clint replied. "I'm just glad it ain't me getting my head beat in keeping it active. I hear tell you got a yacht too."

"We have to keep it a secret because Lucas claimed it and cut his partners off," Casey remarked. "No one wants to go on board it. One scratch and homeboy here will be at your house drawing a bead on your head. John and I have given up any hope of ever sailing in it unless Denny includes The Sea Wolf in a mission."

"No way Denny's putting the Wolf out on mission." I gang up on Lucas. "Denny's scared shitless he'll wake up one morning with a horse's head in bed with him by way of Popeye the Sailor here."

By this time Lucas is barking out laughter making even Tonto start to look around uneasily.

"Somebody gag him before he brings the whole damn cartel down on us," Casey urges.

Lucas starts waving his hand. "I...I'm done... I'm done. See what I have to put up with, Clint. These clowns get a beautiful sailing ship, and right away they want to turn it into a garbage scow. It has staterooms and everything you can think of for armament."

"Sounds real nice," Clint replied. "I look forward to seeing it."

Lucas grinned. We could see his white teeth even in the darkness. "I'll get you a picture of my baby. I don't allow visitors."

Clint cracked up at that line. "Okay, John, I see where you're coming from on the boat."

I decided to throw chum in the water. "Keep it on the down low, Clint. Once you're with us on the coast, we'll have an intervention for Captain Ahab here."

That busted everyone up, except of course Captain Ahab.

"I'm glad you brought this out in the open, John," Lucas said, his hand stroking his chin like he was musing seriously. "I've decided I'll have to frag you on this op."

"You guys are the best," Clint defused the frag bomb... I hope.

* * *

Casey and I had the high ground with our M107 fifty caliber sniper rifles when the first of the explosives went off in the cartel's armament buildings. Clint's planted C4 packages vaporized them when the munitions went off stored inside. Cartel soldiers streamed out of the other buildings, milling around in confusion, some firing up in the air through the smoky haze. Lucas opened up with the fifty caliber machine gun at ground level while Casey and I killed everything else his fifty couldn't get at. By prior agreement, we allowed women and children housed there to run for the hills. Their male companions didn't make it. Clint worked building to building, clearing each one before blowing it up. He had already disabled their vehicles.

Casey and I then concentrated on the last building where Clint said they kept Montoya. We fired at all targets through the building's windows that were clearly cartel soldiers. I pulped the head of a soldier on an upper floor. Through the window I saw a brief flash of red. I figured it might be Clint's girlfriend, so I broke silence.

"I think you were right about your girl's whereabouts. I just caught a glimpse of her on the third floor."

Clint was out in front of the building by that time with Lucas backing him up. He held up a fist in acknowledgement and went in. After he and Lucas did some mop up work inside Lucas jogged back out.

"We're good, John," Clint said in my ear. "You guys take off. Tonto will see to the grounds. I'll go up and get Montoya once you guys are out of the immediate area. See you for a moment up at Antelope Wells."

"Are you sure you don't want us to stick around and cover your trail to the LZ?"

"Nope. I got this."

"I hope she's all you think she is, meat," Lucas put in.

"Ditto," Casey added.

"She is. See you guys on the flip side."

Tonto busily checked bodies on the ground, only giving us a perfunctory glance as we made our way out of the compound area. We had come down to back up the dog, but he didn't need it. We let Lucas lead at his own pace, him being the oldest, which we never let him forget. I packed his fifty along with my own sniper rifle and MAC-10. Lucas glanced back at me for a moment.

"Think he'll be okay, John?"

I shrugged. "He'll make it. We need to get out of here and regroup at Antelope Wells. If things go bad we can launch back across from there. I'd like Jafar to monitor Clint's favor for Denny with Laredo. They can network and keep us informed."

"I never figured Clint would fall for some dame this hard," Casey said.

"You and me both, partner," Lucas agreed.

"She must be one fine, deadly lady," I concluded.

* * *

Lynn Montoya dove to the floor as a shot shattered the window, and pulped the head of a bodyguard for Louisa Medina. She kicked off her strapped high heels, slithering rapidly to the corner of the room, watching the chaotic scene unfold with detached interest. She knew if it were a rival cartel attacking Medina's holdings, they would kill everyone. Lynn spotted Louisa propped against the bookcase against the far wall with a stunned expression as she cowered fearfully. Lynn crawled in rapid movements toward Medina with a smile of satisfaction. She would either barter Medina for a few seconds of life or choke the life out of her with the last breath she took on earth. Explosions began ringing out in staccato succession as Lynn gained the side of Medina, clasping her right hand in both of hers reassuringly. Medina gasped in shock until she recognized Lynn.

"Oh God, Lynn!" Medina hugged Montoya gratefully. "When they get here, we will both be bought women, brought here for the weekend. We can possibly be spared if they believe us."

Lynn patted Medina's back. "Of course, my lover – we will fool them."

Hope spread over Medina's features. "Yes... we will have to convince them. If we get free, I will make you a princess. You will want for nothing the rest of your life."

Lynn kissed Medina's forehead tenderly. "Cara Mia, we will break free of this. Let me lead. I am very proficient with my sexual skills. The key will be convincing them we are whores of the cartel. As I say, let me lead."

"Of course... my darling. It will be as you say."

The two women remained in each other's arms through the sporadic gunfire and explosions that followed in the next hour. The chaos deteriorated into silence, broken only by an isolated shot at uneven intervals over the next half hour. The door swung open to their room, revealing nothing as the two women watched, one cringing in anticipation, while the other prepared to make calculated decisions. After a brief moment, a kaki clothed

54

apparition lurched in fast to the right of the room, his face obscured by the thin black mask he wore. Lynn stared in disbelief at the blue/grey eyes scanning the room.

Montoya pushed Medina away and stood up. "Oh... my... God! CD, you psychopathic monster! Did you come all the way down here to kill... shit... you came to get me. Well hell, big boy, step up, and tell me it's really you."

Dostiene laughed appreciatively, convinced they were alone. "Hey, Lynn, nice outfit."

Montoya gestured at the red, off the shoulder attire with a slow, tantalizing wave with both hands downward. "You like, sailor? Me give you long time, baby."

Dostiene laughed even harder. "Maybe another time. I'm glad to see you. Who do you have there with you?"

Lynn turned to smile back at Medina. "She bought me from the police. I made myself very seductive for her, Clint."

Medina regained her feet unsteadily, pointing at Dostiene. "You... you know this man?"

Lynn put an arm around the cringing Medina's shoulders. "Yeah, I do, girlfriend – at least in that I'd recognize those weirdo eyeballs of his anywhere. As to what he might have in store for us is anyone's guess."

Clint straightened. He pointed at Medina. "A female cartel leader?"

Lynn looked back at Medina, her hands clasped in a joyous pose for his benefit. "Yeah, Clint... how much can I get for her."

Clint chuckled. "I can't pay you. You know that. I need an intel find to make this rogue mission a sanctioned one. I already have you, so I'm good, baby. I know she must have a lot of money here. She must know where the details of the cartel are. If you were to convince her to fill in all the blanks, I bet you and I would be lookin' pretty good."

"And if I don't?"

Dostiene's eyes darkened imperceptibly to the casual eye as he tightened the grip on his Mac-10 assault weapon. "It's all good, girlfriend."

Lynn laughed appreciatively. "Give me your K-bar, stud. I'll have a chat with Senorita Medina. You have no further use for her, right?"

"Nothing comes to mind, little one."

Montoya's eyes glazed slightly at Dostiene's comment. "No one calls me little one, baby. I like the way you do it."

Dostiene nodded. He handed her the deadly looking knife, turning his back on her to cement their involvement.

Montoya flipped the knife around in professional form while watching Dostiene walk away. "Oh baby. You're the whole package, Clint. Whatever you have in mind, I'm in."

Dostiene glanced back with a grin of acceptance. "I think you'll like your decision. Should I leave?"

"Not unless screams bother you, stud. The only reason I'm not in a burial site somewhere, missing essential body parts, is I noticed Senorita Medina likes women. Apparently one of the adjustments I made down here was to one of her lieutenants. He raped and cut up the women while she watched. She wanted to torture and kill me herself. When the damn Mexican cops sold me to her, I made a very convincing case why I'd make her a hell of a lover."

Dostiene grinned. "It looks like you did all right."

Medina stared back and forth between the two in horror. "I…I'll make you both rich beyond your wildest dreams. Just let me go. You loved me, Lynn. I could tell. Don't-"

Lynn shrugged her shoulders, as she fondled the knife in her hands. "I'll tell you what, Lou. Open up the safe I know about, and give us all the cartel business on your computers. If we had a safe untraceable account to transfer all your offshore stuff, that'd be the bomb, but your buddies would track us down the money trail so we'll take everything you have here. If I like what you give me, I'll let you go out with a painless smile on your face. What do you say, Cara Mia?"

Medina went to her knees, weeping, and holding her hands up to Lynn. "That is no deal! Please… I can give you so much more if you let me live."

"It's a better deal than you gave all those women you let that butcher torture and mutilate. Besides, if we let you live, Clint and I would be watching over our shoulder." Lynn glanced over at Dostiene. "What kind of time do I have for slicin' and dicin' Clint?"

"Couple hours maybe."

Lynn twirled around toward the sobbing Medina. "Hear that, girlfriend? Make a choice or I'll make it for you."

Medina stared into her paramour's eyes with cold recognition. She stood up, a slight smile spreading on her face, coupled with a resigned look of fate. All semblance of fearful weeping angst disappeared. "I should have cut you into little pieces. You fooled me very well. I will tell you nothing... bitch!"

Lynn ran Medina over a split second later, smashing the knife handle into the now screaming woman's face. Montoya didn't stop her attack. She shifted to body-shots with the handle of the K-bar knife, fracturing ribs. Lynn stopped and then struck Medina directly on her nose, mulching it into bloody pulp. She then gripped Medina by the throat, squeezing off her screams, and leaning in closely to her face with a smile.

"You don't know me at all, baby." Lynn looked back at Clint. "If you've become squeamish, Clint, it might be a good time for you to go outside."

Clint smiled. "Naaahhh... I'll stay. I love watching a professional work."

Lynn let out a short acknowledging laugh, and turned to the groaning Medina with the K-bar knife. "You experienced one side of the knife, Cara Mia. Would you like a demo on the other side?"

Lynn put the razor sharp knife up under the squirming Medina. Her first probe provoked a scream of surrender. "That's the girl. I guess you haven't run across the term impalement in your travels. It's a physical blending you don't want, girlfriend. I'm real good with it, right Clint?"

Clint sighed as Medina let out a high pitched ululating squeal in response to Lynn's knife action. "You're the one, baby. No question. She made the rapists who got off jubilant to tell everything. As I recall… it didn't do them much good. Lynn makes that Dexter guy look like a campfire girl."

Montoya wiped the knife off on Medina's clothes before standing up with a sigh. "You're lucky I don't hold a grudge, Lou. She's ready to help. Want to escort her around. I know where most of her stuff is, but we'll need the combinations to the two safes I know about."

She laughed at Medina's widening eyes. "Didn't know I knew about the floor one under your office desk, huh? I'm thinking that's where she keeps all her backups."

Clint lifted the groaning Medina up easily. "That will make things go a little smoother."

Lynn glanced out the shattered window frame at the smoke and fires from the earlier explosions. "Who do you have for backup?"

"Tonto."

Montoya's laughter brought a smile to Dostiene's face as he carted Medina after the gesturing Montoya. "You brought that puppy with you to back up your attack on a Mexican cartel?"

"Don't disrespect Tonto. He's two and a half now. Believe me, he's better at this than anyone I could have gotten on short notice. He liked you. I was training him when I came and got you."

Lynn nodded without turning, continuing down the hallway. "A dog that likes psychos… who knew?"

Chapter Five
Bloody Path To Antelope Wells

A half hour later, Dostiene administered a deadly dosage of pure heroin to Medina. The ghost of whatever last thought she had faded quietly from her features. He patted his pack as he straightened up. "You were sure right about our plunder. I took a look at one of the flash-drives. It has stuff on there guaranteed to get a happy dance back at the DEA. How much did you get?"

Lynn had changed into jeans, hiking boots, pullover shirt and black windbreaker for the trip out. She had stuffed all the money they'd found in a pack from Medina's closet. "I figure it's about two hundred and fifty thousand along with another thirty grand in gold coins. Sure you don't want half?"

Dostiene shook his head. "I'm good. Like I said, you'll need a stash in case anything we do in the near future goes south. Do you have an account set up anywhere or do you want me to get you an alternate drop for your investment?"

"I have a whole identity set up in Mesa, Arizona. I had planned to lay low after I finished with Gradowsky until they sent the damn CIA after me. You do realize it's illegal for you to screw around with us nasty civilians on USA soil, right?"

"I was farmed out for collaboration with those two suits who took you off my hands. C'mon, Tonto will be getting anxious. We have ten miles to cover. I have an LZ there plotted out for a buddy of mine. They won't be looking in on things here for a few hours."

"Did you kill everyone?"

Dostiene led the way out. "I let the women and kids scramble away that were here. I blew up everything that moved on two or four wheels, so they won't be going anywhere."

"Should have wasted them, Clint. You know the cartels. They don't leave anybody alive. You did want this to look like a rival hit, right?"

"Tonto likes kids. He wouldn't let me."

"You big softy!"

Before they left the mansion, Dostiene handed Lynn a mask to put on. She slipped it into place without a word. Tonto appeared instantly at Dostiene's side as he led the way out of the compound. Cartel soldiers' bodies lay in various mangled heaps, some caught in the building explosions, while others were killed at long range.

"What did you use on the buildings, a cannon?"

Dostiene chuckled, glancing back at Montoya. "I snuck into the compound a couple of times over the last few nights. I wired the buildings in the compound to go off by remote, so I could make it seem like they were being bombed. Don't worry about any live ones. Tonto takes care of the survivors. When he glided in next to us it meant we're clear. We have to move fast over the next mile and a half. Then we wait for anything moving on our back trail. We'll continue the pattern until we make it to my LZ. Laredo hates it when I arrive with unexpected company."

"Laredo?"

"Don't ask. He has cowboy delusions. We worked Afghanistan together. You'll like him."

"If he can fly us the hell out of here, I'm in love."

Nearly a hundred yards from the compound, Clint picked up a camouflaged casing, slinging it quickly over his shoulder. Tonto slipped ahead, keeping the pace for his human companions at slightly faster than a jog. The plush vegetation around the compound gave way to a desert panorama with very little cover. They reached a rock strewn rise which Tonto climbed ahead on.

"Your damn dog even knows where you want to stop?"

"What can I say? Tonto's the best. I wanted to make sure our surveillance photos were accurate before making an assault. Plus I wanted to take my time planting the exploding treats I brought," Clint replied over his shoulder, leaving out any mention of the hit squad that assisted.

They reached the top a few minutes later. Dostiene began setting up his sniper rifle, taking the fifty caliber M107 out of its case, and positioning it to fire back along the route they had traveled. He next took out a spotting scope, before giving Lynn a set of binoculars.

"We'll stay here fifteen minutes and then move on. If nothing is on our trail by then we'll make the next spot easy."

Five minutes later, Lynn nudged Dostiene. "We have movement at ten o'clock. I think they're just wandering around looking for a direction."

Dostiene shifted his range finder to the direction indicated. He watched the two all terrain vehicles crisscrossing in a wide trajectory. After a moment, he nodded. "They're trying to cross our trail. I admit I thought this was overkill with the back trail thing. I knew they'd get the word out about an attack. I just didn't think they'd get anyone out here this quickly. Oh well."

Clint eased behind the silenced M107, double checking the readings with his Leupold Mark 4 spotting scope. His first shot took the head off the driver in the lead vehicle just as it closed in on the approaching other vehicle. The driverless all terrain vehicle sideswiped the other one, flipped over and skidded upside down to a dusty halt. The sideswiped vehicle halted, throwing up a cloud of debris. Clint squeezed off his second round, which pulped the second driver's head. He then shifted to the scrambling passenger. As the man leaped from the vehicle, Dostiene blew off his ankle. With the man's screams carrying to their rocky escarpment, Clint turned the rifle on the passenger in the upside down vehicle, slowly trying to work free of the wreckage. The next fifty caliber bullet tore the squirming man's exposed shoulder into bloody tatters.

Lynn smiled at the carnage nearly half a mile away. "I take back the softy remark, you monster. Aren't you going to finish those two off?"

Dostiene hurriedly encased the M107 and his spotting scope. "That would defeat the purpose of wounding them in the first place. What'd you think, I missed my mark? Hopefully, their screams will keep any followers busy. We'll be waiting at the next spot if this wasn't enough to give them second thoughts."

"Maybe the fact they hit out toward our trail is the same reason I ended up getting caught by the Federales."

Dostiene gestured for Tonto to lead the way, falling in next to Montoya on the clamber downward. "I wondered what the hell you were doing foolin' around down in this hellhole. I guess it's a target rich environment, but damn girl, these folks don't play down here."

Lynn shrugged, keeping pace with Clint and Tonto. "I knew I was being watched by the Feds, and I couldn't get near my stash. Mexico seemed like a great place to wait for things to cool down. Unfortunately, I was only down here a week before Medina's henchman spotted me in a local bar. He decided to get romantic. Since everyone was scared shitless of the cartel's soldiers, he figured to tune me up. I should have just given him a quick blow job and been done with him."

She sighed as Dostiene laughed appreciatively. "But no... I had to carve him up like a pumpkin pie. Problem was, someone North had tipped off the Federales. Unknown to me, they were already staking my place out. I had talked Don Juan into driving me somewhere secluded when I realized he wasn't going to take no for an answer. After I finished with him, and disposed of the body, I received my second revelation – Medina had a tracker on Don Juan. She put the Federales on my position. They nailed me before I even got home. The next thing I knew, Medina had me, and I was on my way to the tool shed for recycling. I put on my award winning act with Medina. Since she wanted to play with me, I worked on making myself the best playmate she ever had."

"I should have known not to come down after you," Clint replied. "Here I was thinking you were in a dungeon, awaiting dismemberment, and instead of being an inmate, you're running the damn asylum. Oh well... live and learn. At least I got some good intel for Justice to play with."

Lynn reached out and gripped Dostiene's shoulder for a moment as they jogged behind Tonto. "You came just in time, Hombre. Lou was tiring of me. Naturally, I would have done some damage when I figured it was time, but I'd never have gotten out of there alive. Why did you come for me, and don't give me any of that serial killer crap."

Dostiene exchanged glances with Lynn, before shrugging. "Baby, if I knew that, I'd tell you. I don't. Take the money and run if you think I'm setting you up. I'll cover for you."

Lynn started laughing. "Hey… I never for a moment considered you were setting me up. I'm just curious as to why. What is it that would make a talented agency killer like you come down to this God forsaken dump, and risk everything in an obviously unsanctioned mission to free up a murdering psycho like me?"

"Well hell! When you blurt it all out like that, there's only one reason – I'm mental, and my survival instinct has gone bye-bye."

Montoya gave him a slap to the back of his head. "I thought maybe you might actually like me for some twisted reason. I know. You want to watch, right? You're one of those kind, huh? Wow… it's always the quiet ones."

"Yep, that's me… the watcher."

"You like me. You want me. C'mon, Clint, you little tool, admit it."

Clint smiled over at Lynn. "I sure didn't come down here to cure our illegal alien problem. Yeah… you intrigue me. Speaking of tools, maybe it was my FBI partner team that ratted you out. Can you still work with them if you found out they were responsible?"

"Can I gut them after we solve their serial killer problem?"

"I'd prefer you didn't."

Lynn sighed again. "Okay… I owe you. They get a free pass, but if they work me again, I'm gonna' get me some. Deal?"

"Deal."

At their next two back trail pauses, no one showed up. At the third stop, they could hear the sound of a helicopter approaching. Lynn looked quizzically at Dostiene, a smile spreading on her features. Clint, feeling her attention, glanced over from his spotter scope.

"Something funny here I'm missing?"

"I thought you might have an opinion on the air force the cartel seems to have," Lynn replied, petting Tonto, who waited patiently between them.

Dostiene chuckled and settled behind his M107. "The air force may not be all it's cracked up to be, baby."

Clint squeezed off a rapid fire clip, and the helicopter tail disintegrated. It spun out of control, crashing in a fiery conflagration moments later.

"Well damn, cowboy! You sure know how to show a girl a good time."

Clint began packing up his rifle. "Let's hit the road. They'll know now they're on the right track. We'll go full bore to the LZ, and see if we can bugger on out of this pit before anyone's the wiser."

"Okay, but I owe you a blow job for that little showpiece."

Dostiene laughed, unable for a moment to continue his packing chore. He finally sighed and nodded his head. "No thanks, baby. Payback is the proverbial bitch from you. A simple thanks is sufficient."

Lynn wrapped her arms around Clint, hugging him tightly. "I'm on borrowed time thanks to you. I don't give a shit what you do to me from now to forever. You're golden with me, big boy. I like the way you roll. What, you don't think I could be a sweet thing for you?"

Clint put a rough hand along Lynn's jaw line, while bending down to kiss her forehead. "I think you could be anything you want, baby... until you're not."

Lynn giggled. "We are a pair of eight balls, ain't we? You know me too damn well, or maybe you just think you do. How about I promise you'll never have to sleep with one eye open when you're around me?"

"Let's get the hell out of here. We can kick around sleeping arrangements down the road. Maybe we can get a house with a picket fence, have a couple kids, and join the PTA. We'll even make cupcakes together."

Lynn shoved Dostiene toward the path. "Get moving before you say something that'll warrant me making an adjustment smartass."

Clint and Tonto struck out down the path together, the dog glancing back at Dostiene every few seconds. Montoya watched them for a moment, a tear forming and cutting the dust down her right cheek. She absently batted at it, picturing exactly what Clint had described jokingly. Lynn gritted her teeth, jogging at a faster pace to keep up. *Like it or not, Clint baby... I'm going to get me a taste of that if I'm still alive after this gig.* Montoya giggled. *You little tool.*

They reached the landing zone Dostiene had picked out. Five minutes after they arrived with Clint covering their back trail with the M107 and Lynn spotting, a beat up, Vietnam era Huey helicopter dipped in over the horizon from the opposite direction. It settled in smoothly next to the little group. A gray bearded pilot with a Giants baseball cap and aviator sun glasses waved with a big smile as Tonto bounded aboard to lick his face. Clint helped Lynn up into the helicopter's cargo bay past the fifty caliber machine gun set up in the opening. After he threw their packs on board, Dostiene slid into place behind the fifty, putting on the headset propped on the gun's handle. The Huey began lifting off the moment Clint barked out a hello into the headset's microphone.

"We got company coming, partner. They're faster than me. I hope you still have the magic hand with the fifty."

Clint chuckled, seeing two helicopters dotting the horizon approaching on their back trail. The Huey turned North at full speed. "I'll let you know when to bank, Laredo."

Lynn, who had been scooting into a position near Dostiene with her spotting scope, put a hand on Clint's back. "We doing aerial combat, cowboy?"

"I'm afraid so, baby. What's the ETA, Laredo?"

"Ten minutes, give or take a couple. I bet you can't get them both with one burst, Clint."

Dostiene smiled as he leaned around to check out their fast approaching pursuit. "That's a sucker bet, brother. They're boot camps without more than twenty yards between them, and no elevation difference."

Montoya had been listening intently, leaning out to check on distance. "You two have done this before I take it?"

"In better circumstances," Clint replied. "We're going old school this trip, right brother?"

"Concentrate on not acquiring any new holes in my ride, deadeye. Coming up to pursuit level, Clint – in range two minutes."

Clint glanced down at his watch as the Huey elevated slightly. "Two minutes."

Lynn glanced back at Clint from her sighting position where she could see the two pursuing helicopters growing larger in her scope by the second. She stuck her butt near Dostiene's position, wiggling it. "I'm getting wet, Clint. Want to check?"

Dostiene stifled laughter while gripping the handles on the fifty tightly, resisting the urge to check with all his might. "Damn, baby, this could end up with us tail-spinning in a death arc downwards you know?"

Montoya turned her attention back to the pursuing helicopters. "I ain't riding that horse, cowboy. I see a bad day in the future for those poor playboys in the distance."

Clint took a deep breath after a quick check of his watch, zoning in on what he had to do with practiced concentration. "Ten seconds, brother, from... now!"

The Huey banked perpendicular with the pursuers in exactly ten seconds. The fifty rattled loudly over the wind noise. Lynn sucked air as the cockpits of both helicopters in the distance disintegrated. The pilotless hulks spun downwards to a fiery conflagration below. Montoya turned open mouthed toward where Dostiene worked the fifty into a static flying position, clamping it into place as the Huey resumed course. Montoya began stripping in a no nonsense, hurried rush. She was on him before he could even move clear of the fifty with a moaning, all out, grasping struggle.

"Jesus..." Clint managed to blurt out before chucking the headset.

    * * *

Laredo cleared his throat as they approached their destination. He stroked Tonto's head next to him. "We have touchdown in ten, kids. Flip 'em, and zip 'em."

Montoya stroked Clint's face with a trembling hand. She leaned in close to him from where he held her over his lap. "Damn... that was intense, cowboy."

Dostiene gripped Lynn's face. His answering kiss catapulted them into another writhing climax with only a minute to spare as the Huey spiraled gently down to a perfect landing. Laredo looked down at Tonto with a chuckle.

"You are without doubt the flyingest dog I've ever had the pleasure of knowing, T. I hope the flight was to your liking."

"Arf!" Tonto jumped up with his front paws across Laredo's lap.

Laredo hugged the dog before getting out of his seat. "You're the best, T. You're welcome anytime. Your master is negotiable."

"I heard that," Clint called out as he and Lynn tugged clothes into place. "Don't think I forgot you made me pay in advance, you untrusting prick."

Laredo lumbered into the back, his five foot ten inch frame carrying nearly thirty pounds too much weight. He moved around the helicopter with practiced ease. He gripped Dostiene's shoulder with a brief friendly clasp. "Sorry, partner. I didn't think you were coming back. With gas prices like they are I had to keep my bottom line in mind."

Clint laughed appreciatively, nodding his head at Lynn. "This is Lynn Montoya. The things she can do with a knife would make you wet your pants. Lynn, this aviator is my old buddy, Laredo."

Laredo shook hands with Lynn. "Glad to meet you. It's nice to see Clint with a special lady. I thought he was gay."

They shared a laugh at Laredo's remark. Lynn dug around in her pack, producing a wrapped bundle of cash. She handed it to Laredo.

Laredo smiled down at what looked to him to be a twenty-five thousand dollar wad. "I've been paid, Ms. Montoya."

"Consider it a tip. It's found money anyhow. Will there be any problem for us to get back over the border?"

Laredo jumped down after tucking away his tip. He helped Lynn down with her pack while Clint descended with Tonto and the rest of his gear. "Very generous of you Ma'am. I run this Company safe house and landing field. We're about twenty minutes from the Antelope Wells, New Mexico crossing from here. Clint has a friend that'll pass you through at noon tomorrow. I imagine he collected enough Cartel intel, they'll probably throw him a parade on the other side, so I doubt you'll have any trouble. Follow me. I'll show you where you'll be staying."

Lynn glanced back at Clint, who waved to her as he shouldered his gear. She followed Laredo from the small landing zone to a ramshackle farmhouse with a huge beat-up old barn across from it. Laredo walked by the house, hiking nearly a hundred yards out into the desert. In the midst of some rocks and sage, he brushed away sand with his foot, bent down, and pulled up on a handle. A well oiled, spring assisted trapdoor opened into a gaping portal. Laredo led the way down the stone and steel stairwell, descending to a long open tunnel. Embedded in the walls of the tunnel were spaced alternating, yellow glowing lights on each side.

The tunnel opened into a widening metal encased structure, with a reinforced door, opened by voice and iris recognition. Laredo opened it up. On the other side was an electronics station with banks of video screens, communications equipment, and a computer station only dreamed of by IT specialists. Their next destination was a fully furnished room a few doors down from the entry station. It was designed like a high end hotel room, complete with kitchen, entertainment center, and berthing area.

"Make yourself at home, Ms. Montoya," Laredo told her, gesturing at the inside of the room. "The refrigerator's stocked. The bathroom's across the hall. If you need anything, I'll be out at my desk, getting Clint a secure line to upload his plunder."

"So this is where our tax dollars go," Lynn replied, smiling at Laredo. "Nice. Thank you. This is wonderful."

"You're very welcome. I'll be ready for you in about five minutes, Clint."

"Thanks, brother." Clint waved a hand at the room. "Not bad, huh?"

Lynn clasped him around the waist. "It looks like the bed's big enough for two, cowboy. Maybe you can show me a few more of your moves later."

"I'd love to, baby. That was the greatest helicopter ride I've ever taken. Tonto and I have to stay out on the perimeter. After Laredo and I get my stuff uploaded and the Huey out of sight, I have to make sure we don't get any unexpected visitors. We can't take chances that they didn't follow us on radar. The Cartel could send an army down here. They own some of the Federales stations so we can't get complacent."

"Well damn! I was hopin' you could tuck me in tonight. What the hell do you and Tonto do if an army is moving on us?"

"I light 'em up and they send a Reaper drone across from Holloman Air Force Base for a little surprise party," Clint explained. "It's an act of war, but so is their Federales covering the Cartel drug runs with armored vehicles. They can't track a Reaper, and they can't ID any of its payload. It's just a precaution, baby. Thanks for the offer though. Maybe when we're safe across the border, we'll play house while we hunt for the killers."

Lynn gripped Dostiene's chin, shaking it slightly. "Count on it, big boy. Don't get killed out there."

"Jinx!"

* * *

Lynn went to sleep for a few hours after Dostiene left. When she woke up, a shower, and a fresh change of clothes helped her demeanor considerably. For the first time since her capture by the Cartel, Montoya began thinking about something besides escape. Wandering away from her room toward Laredo's command center, Lynn was surprised to see Tonto bounding toward her. She bent to hug the dog, a sharp shot of desire shooting through her, figuring Clint had already returned.

"I'm happy to see you too, Tonto. Now, lead me to where your master is and you can be my hero of the hour."

69

Tonto licked her face before spinning around to lope in the same direction Lynn had been going. At the electronics display, Laredo had dimmed the surrounding lights as he concentrated on the larger monitors in the center with his headset on. Montoya made no sound to distract him from his work, kneeling next to Tonto and stroking his head, while trying to decipher what was happening on the monitors. Laredo noticed her presence after a few moments.

"Welcome, Ms. Montoya. I have a minute. Is everything to your liking?"

"It's wonderful. Tonto found me, so I figured Clint couldn't be far away. Where's he hangin'? CD told me he and Tonto would be patrolling the perimeter, watching for interested Federales."

"Oh... yeah..." Laredo turned back to the monitors. "He'll explain when he gets back, Ma'am."

Lynn stood up, her eyes narrowing as she tried to make sense of the lights and blips on the screens. "Spit it out, Laredo. I didn't just drop in from a girl scout conference."

Laredo glanced back at her. The look she was gracing him with made the grizzled agent straighten in his seat. Montoya grinned, realizing Laredo knew her past history.

"Clint pays me well for our get-togethers, Lynn. Sometimes when he goes off book, he has to pay the piper to make it happen as smoothly as he wants. DEA had a date when a drug shipment was due to pass by the Antelope Wells crossing. Word was it would have a Federales escort if the border patrol intercepted, meaning overwhelming force against a couple teams of outnumbered and outgunned kids on the border. As payment for you two crossing unmolested at Antelope, Clint agreed to even up the odds."

When Laredo didn't expand on his statement, Lynn did it for him in a questioning manner. "You mean he went somewhere to light up the drug ring for a Reaper strike?"

Laredo chuckled, and then caught himself as he met Lynn's narrowed gaze. "Ah... we don't do Reaper hits inside Mexico, Lynn. The pussies in Washington would shit their pants if they even knew we tracked them on this side of the border. Clint may have been embellishing a bit so as not to worry you."

Montoya spotted a rolling chair she liked on the other side of the room. She retrieved it, and slid in right next to Laredo. "I get the picture. He didn't want to risk Tonto on this one. So… Clint's the 'one riot, one Ranger' on this op?"

Laredo laughed. "Yep. He needed to make it about fifteen miles west of here without a trace and get set up for an ambush. We already have heat signatures confirming a convoy on the way. Clint made it into position after getting the props in place for the surprise party about twenty minutes ago."

"Let me talk to him."

Laredo shook his head. "No can do. We have silence until target is in sight, and only on an emergency basis after that. The Cartels aren't stupid down here. They have some sophisticated gear. It's just not as sophisticated as ours. I'm networked with a new genius near Antelope Wells. He and I are monitoring all communications, so I know where they are, and so does Clint. I beam their signal around and right down to him. He has range, and all logistics."

Adrenaline began pumping through Montoya's frame. Sweat beaded on her upper lip as she focused on the screens, distinguishing the satellite display of oncoming vehicles from the single blip still a distance away. "Is this some kind of message to the Cartel wankers?"

"Yep. They kill one of our border patrol, we kill a whole herd of them, and destroy their drug shipment. If we did this all along the border, we'd fix the drug problem as well as illegal immigration and the slave trade they have going. Not to mention we'd catch some of the OTM's coming out of the sandpit overseas."

"OTM's?"

"Other than Mexican."

"So… if things go haywire, then Clint's the goofy lone gunman?"

"Yep."

Lynn chuckled. "And here I thought Clint was just a whacko killer with a neat dog, and a thing for female psychopath serial killers. Now I find out he thinks he's Lone Wolf McQuade."

"Nope. Clint's more dangerous. He's a believer. When Clint reads about some poor schmuck border guard getting executed by banditos running drugs and work slaves, his first reaction is pack his bag and go down to set things right. That's why he didn't know anything about you getting caught down Mexico way. He hides out with Tonto in some place in the middle of nowhere, turns off his phone and laptop, and goes native. The feds sent two agents up to get him instead of using the e-mail drop he checks on for jobs. That was only a couple weeks ago. He put your gig together in days and just like that I was flying him in."

"Damn. I thought maybe he was sweet on me." Montoya sighed, sitting back in the chair to stroke the attentive Tonto. "Dostiene's a world saver."

Laredo grinned over at her. "He likes you. I didn't say he was suicidal. He wouldn't have done all this for just anybody. Clint mentioned you a couple times after he got you locked up. He lost that sweet gig with those naïve chumps with their profile sheets and behavior analysis books because he let you work that last one over with your knife. They put us back together a couple times in our old Afghanistan hunting grounds last year. Clint told me a little about you. He'd never mentioned anyone ever before, and I've been flying him back and forth since our first excursions in the 'Stans."

Montoya's face darkened. "That cocksucker gutted a twelve year old girl he raped. He got off on some technicality. I was almost done changing his spark plugs when I heard him. Dostiene just stood off to the side with a smile and a Mac-10 aimed at my head. He waves, and says 'finish up, baby, I have to take you in'. He laughed when I thanked him for letting me finish and told him they'd never hold me."

"So you two ain't as different as you let on."

"Maybe... maybe not. Some stuff pisses me off at an elemental level. It haunts me until I do something about it. If you're thinking me and 'Joan of Arc' would be BFF's, forget it."

"He let you do Gradowsky and the one before him. Clint wanted to do some recon, so he pretended to be hot on the trail for a while to study your patterns. Those idiots he was leading around by the hand didn't even know it was a woman they were after."

"Why that no good, rotten..." Montoya laughed. "The prick could have taken me months before. Hell, I did Taylor nearly two months before Gradowsky. He watched me do Taylor, huh? I never felt him at all. Where the hell did he get his training?"

Laredo shrugged. "He was Company when I first flew with him. The killers don't tell you where they come from. I... uh oh... here we go."

"How will he do it?"

"Clint sets up a killing field when he knows where the target will be for certain. You'll see the front target get lit up by Clint's M136. Once the lead vehicle blows, he'll blow the IED's he has planted. There it goes!"

Lynn watched a momentary huge flash with secondary flashes, her hands clenched into fists. A moment later it was as if the column was engulfed in light. Smaller light flashes went off all around the column perimeter.

"That's Clint doing close order combat. He'll use phosphorous grenades on the column until there's no way anyone will know what the hell happened. Then it's a matter of patrolling the perimeter outwards about a hundred yards to make sure there are no survivors. There... see him moving away from the column?"

Montoya watched a smaller signal move away and then go off. "What happened?"

"That's his signal he made it away. We run silent and dark now. Clint covers his back trail in a roundabout path back here, and you two pick up your tickets to wonderland tomorrow at noon... all paid up. He should be strolling in about oh-four-hundred. I'll feed him anything I pick up in chatter or movement anywhere around him until then."

"I'm breaking up with him! Damn it!"

Laredo stared over at her as if she sprouted a horn out of her forehead. "What the hell are you talking about?"

73

"He's killed about a thousand people today and I didn't even get a taste. I'll never catch up with him. We're through!" Montoya started laughing, still juiced from the ambush.

Laredo chuckled and turned his attention to the screens as he widened his satellite reconnaissance area request. "You two are a pair alright. A pair of what… I don't have a clue."

Chapter Six
Collecting Back Wages

The heat from his phosphorous grenade cleanup drove Dostiene outward as he worked the perimeter of his kill zone. The screams of dying men faded with every moment of his unrelenting attack. The secondary blast from his hitting the lead vehicle with the M136 warhead, forced him back for a time while he detonated his shaped charges. He fired his Mac-10 at anything still moving within the inferno, tossing the phosphorous grenades at spaced intervals. When he had completed his perimeter circle, Clint kept his locator on for a few moments while he moved outwards to intercept anyone who had escaped the conflagration. When he was sure Laredo would know he had cleared the blast zone, Dostiene went dark.

Setting off at a dead run with all his gear, Clint covered a hundred yards outwards in seconds, slowing as he reached the intercept perimeter before again moving in a circle around the target. He received a text from Laredo after turning to start his perimeter sweep. It stopped him cold for a moment, before having to clamp both hands over his mouth to keep from howling in laughter: 'GF on my bk. Knife in hand. Breakup asap. Claims U killed a thou tday, she got nuthin. She's mental. Hep me!'

Dostiene texted back quickly before beginning his sweep – 'U big grl!'

Halfway through his sweep, Clint saw movement with his night-vision goggles. Two men nearing his perimeter line stumbled clumsily outward in a zigzag pattern, glancing back at the kill zone every few moments. They had handguns, but nothing else he could see. The short burst from his Mac-10 cut the legs from the two men at the ankles. He then took more careful aim and blasted the shoulders attached to the weapon carrying hands. Both men launched into screaming pain-filled shouts of surrender in Spanish.

"Rendición... rendición!" The two men repeated their anthem every few seconds.

Clint approached them slowly and silently. When he was near enough to see their faces clearly, his hand tensed on the Mac-10. Dostiene willed himself to relax. He smiled, the surprise of recognizing one of the men fading gradually. Clint then fired a burst that pulped the head of one uniformed Federale. The other scrambled away from the twitching corpse, crying out in pain, his one mobile hand clawing in hopeless desperation. Clint flipped him over, ignoring the scream of whining protest.

"Well hell, if it ain't my old buddy, Roberto Perez. Hello, Roberto. Long time, no see, amigo. I never got a chance to thank you for the special treatment you afforded me down here."

The man cried out in hopeless angst, his hand raised in the direction of Dostiene's voice. "Clint? I... I couldn't help you before. I can give you everything... everything you want. I am a Colonel now. I have contacts with... the Cartels. I can-"

"Oh my!" Dostiene cut his plea off. "Roberto... my old friend!"

Roberto began to sob.

Dostiene propped the wounded man up against a nearby rock, comically dusting him off and wiping his face as he made sure the man had no more weapons. He continued in Spanish. "Hey, big R, how's it hangin'? Listen closely. No hard feelings about my captivity under your supervision some years back. You know me, buddy. I have one of those detail oriented memories. I'll make this simple, pal. You tell me everything, including names, dates, places, and Cartel intelligence, and I will put one right between your horns. I'm a business first type guy. You've been a very bad man. It's time to pay up."

"But... but you killed eight men escaping. I...I was under orders to... oh hell... I will tell you nothing! You will kill me anyway!" Knowing his mercy ploy was going nowhere, he clenched his fists, rolling into a fetal position in silence.

Dostiene smiled. "Oh Roberto, you don't know how happy that makes me feel. I was afraid you'd just blurt it out with no pain."

Dostiene patted Roberto's head while injecting him. "Here you go, buddy. This stuff will put you out for a while without damaging you. We'll talk about what I want to know later. I have to go make sure none of your other buddies went walkabout."

Clint plastic tied Perez's wrists behind his back. He duct taped his mouth, wrapped his wounded ankles in duct tape individually before taping them together, and then did Perez's shoulder. His last perimeter search turned up nothing. When Clint returned, Perez had just begun to move around, groaning, and finally barking out thin duct tape covered screams.

"Boy, I sure hope you have something I can use," Clint told the wide eyed Perez, before putting on his pack. He hoisted Perez up in a fireman's carry position. "Damn, Roberto, you've put on a little weight. If we had to go uphill I'd dump you in the fire."

Dostiene headed out on his preplanned route back to Laredo's place, using brush tied to the back of his pack, dragging on the hard packed ground to cover his tracks. It was a tedious and torturous hour to go two miles away from his kill zone. Sweating profusely, Clint put Perez on the ground when he reached a small boulder strewn area. He ripped off Perez's gag tape and squirted water in his mouth from a water bottle on his pack. After taking a few long sips himself, Clint squirted some over his head.

"Oh man... that's heaven. The rest of my escape route will be duck soup without hauling your carcass along."

Perez had begun to blubber incoherently, his pained features contorted hideously.

"Here's the deal one more time. Let me record all the stuff I asked you for, and I won't have to hurt you like this." Dostiene slowly lowered his boot onto Perez's wounded ankles, calculating the man's high pitched screams in intensity. Perez passed out. Clint brought him around again with bottled water and light slaps.

"Madre de Dios... Madre de Dios! I'll tell... I'll tell!" Perez screamed out over and over until Clint covered his mouth while making shushing sounds.

Clint took out a low light, hand held HD camcorder. Over the next forty-five minutes, Clint prompted Perez with questions meant to get the most intel while trying to trip him up. He also

77

acquired the bank names, passwords, and account numbers where Perez had hideaway accounts. When Perez began repeating himself, Dostiene patted his cheek.

"You've been a very good boy. We have whole clusters of stars over us. You watch them, and I'll take all your pain away. For a few moments, you'll be pain free before the trapdoor into hell opens up for your twisted soul."

"Clint! Please... don't do it... I'll make you-"

Clint administered an injection into Perez's neck, holding him upright as his sighs of relief subsided into his final death rattle. After covering him with loose dirt, Dostiene built a rock cairn over the corpse. Sipping water while enjoying the rapidly cooling desert air, he watched the star filled sky in comfortable silence. Five minutes later, he trekked toward the CIA safe house, chuckling as he remembered Laredo's text.

* * *

Montoya strode into Laredo's command center with restrained anger. Laredo glanced her way, noticing Tonto perked up and went to stand at her side. He waited for the verbal retribution with a shrug.

"Still in transit."

Lynn sauntered over to Laredo's shoulder. She stroked his shoulder in friendly fashion. "I don't mean to pry, but it's past 4AM. You wouldn't be withholding info on me, would you, Sparky?"

"Not in this lifetime, Princess. Is there something about going dark electronically you don't understand?"

Montoya nodded and stepped away. "At least he paid my way back. When will you know he bit the big one?"

Laredo launched out of his seat, turning on Montoya while assuming a combat ready stance. "I don't know how far you can push this serial killer bullshit, and I don't really care, Princess. I'd have put a bullet through your head while you were napping if I was playing you. Dostiene's not someone you underestimate. You fuck with him... he gets back to you. I've already explained all the shit I know. Take it or leave it... bitch!"

Lynn smiled, relaxing for the first time in hours. "Thanks, Laredo. I'll be in my room."

Laredo relaxed as Montoya walked toward her room, wondering if he'd need to kill her if Clint's enterprise didn't end well. He shrugged and sat down. Clint was Clint. It would be good or it would be very bad. He resumed his monitoring position, noting Tonto had followed Montoya toward her room. He grinned at Tonto's decision to follow Montoya. Laredo wondered if the dog knew something he didn't.

* * *

At nearly 5AM, Dostiene breached the perimeter of the CIA safe-house. Laredo opened the way in from his control panel. He popped up out of his seat as Clint passed into the Command Center.

"Damn, partner! Did you stop by the zombie apocalypse on your way back?"

Dostiene laughed appreciatively, as he set his equipment down near Laredo's seat. "I had to carry a bleeder for a ways until-"

Tonto ran up to nudge Clint's leg with Montoya following.

"I hope that ain't all your blood, Clint, or I got bad news for you... you're dead."

"You two need to take this comedy act on the road, baby," Clint replied, stripping off his outerwear in a bloody pile. "I was telling Laredo I had a messy bundle to carry a ways before I could give him his last rites. You'll never guess who got clear of the Cartel Roast, brother – Roberto Perez. He had made it all the way up to Colonel."

Laredo's face drained of color as his mouth sagged open. "You... you mean the guy who was supposed to be our gatekeeper down on the Guatemalan border when I dropped you into El Salvador to get Salas in oh nine? I never thought you'd work for the Company again after they threw you under the bus on that one."

Clint shrugged as he kicked free of all his clothing except his underwear. Laredo handed him a plastic bag from one of the desk drawers. Dostiene rammed all his bloody clothing inside of it, including his boots. "State decided since I got Salas, Perez would get tired of screwing around with me, but he was so sure I had the keys to the kingdom he didn't want to let me go. Man, we paid him a bunch of money to make sure I passed through his checkpoint."

Montoya tried to keep silent, but when Clint didn't continue, and began taking items out of his pack, she couldn't hold back. "Don't leave me hangin', cowboy."

Dostiene grinned up at her while he handed Laredo his camcorder. "Be patient, baby. I have some stuff on my cam that just might make us three feel real good."

Laredo hooked up the camcorder to his computer mainframe, and began playing the video. He saw the slightly blurry image of a sobbing Perez clear up before the man began stuttering out names, places, and accounts. Laredo chuckled, shaking his head while he jotted down the account numbers. "Sucked to be him, partner. Are these numbers what I think they are?"

"Yep. I'm hoping we've just regained all that Company money they paid my old buddy Roberto, plus all his ill gotten Cartel bribe money."

"Oh… my… God…" Laredo whispered as his hands flew over the keyboard, launching a myriad of windows on the monitor directly in front of him. "He has over two mil in Belize."

"See?" Clint closed his eyes and took a deep breath. "The circle is completed. Looks like I finally get my back pay bonus from that nasty time I spent with Roberto. I figure you'll have about thirty-six hours before his accounts become untouchable. Is that going to be enough time to clean it up?"

Laredo let out a couple fake sobs as he worked. "You can be real hurtful, Clint."

Dostiene laughed and patted his friend's shoulder. "Sorry… didn't mean to insult you. We hit the jackpot tonight. Half's yours of course. I'll give Lynn a taste out of mine."

"You will?"

"I'd never have run into Roberto if not for you, baby. I figure that's worth a twenty percent finders' fee. Right, brother?"

"Whatever you say, my friend," Laredo replied without looking up. "I'll have this all spic and span in all the right places before you have to head out. You haven't changed anything from those accounts I set up for you, right?"

"Haven't touched a thing. I'm getting cleaned up and then pass out for the next five hours. Wake me up at ten, baby."

"Sure Clint." Montoya watched Clint walk toward the bathroom with Tonto trailing him. She sighed and hunched down over Laredo's shoulder. "How much you figure?"

"Looks like three and a half all told," Laredo replied in awe. "Man... you two ought to just blow off the feds and head someplace cabana boys bring you Mai Tai's all day. As soon as I make certain I put adequate time between me and this bonanza, that's where I'm heading."

"He sure is generous, but I have a hunch Clint would be unhappy sitting around on a beach all day. Like you said, he's a believer. What the hell did Perez do to him?"

"Don't know, Princess, but when I dropped into a spot on the Yucatan Peninsula and picked him up, he looked like he had walked out of a death camp. He had to go to ground after contacting me for nearly half a day before making it to the LZ we set up, and guarded by some black ops friends of Clint's you only read about in comic books. We had to do it dark and under the radar, because of Perez. I have no clue how he made it to the Yucatan."

"How the hell did he get away?"

"Don't know that either. When I asked him, he just grinned and told me one of the guards got too close."

"Damn! He gives me an inferiority complex."

Laredo laughed.

* * *

Dostiene's eyes opened to slits in the dim light cast by a small lamp in the corner of his room. He catalogued where he was, the aches coursing through his body, and the fact he was not alone. Seeing Tonto lying on the covers at his feet, he turned his head slightly to his left. She breathed evenly on her side, facing him. A glance at the digital clock on Lynn's side of the bed read nearly 9:45AM.

"Nice outfit, baby."

Montoya stirred next to him with a giggle and a yawn. She was naked. "I thought maybe I'd work a little for that finder's fee."

"Work?" Dostiene gripped Lynn's hips as she slid smoothly over top of him.

She covered his mouth with her own in a gasping moan. Tonto jumped down with a grunt.

* * *

They passed through the checkpoint at Antelope Wells in the rented Chevrolet Impala without incident. Lynn saw a smile of recognition on the big guard's face. He waved Clint through with a quick gesture. Clint saw Lucas and Casey leaning to the side with big smiles on their faces.

"I guess the payoff was to their liking," Lynn said, looking back at the border.

"That's John. He's one of ours. He would have let me through whether they did or not. My boss doesn't leave anything up to deals with other government agencies. He wanted you to make it North unmolested."

"You know that John guy?"

Dostiene glanced over at Lynn as he accelerated into the USA. "We did a little time together in exotic places. John's a friend."

"You do understand that breaks the psycho code of behavior, right? We don't have friends. We have enablers."

Clint laughed with unexpected zeal at Lynn's remark. It took a few moments before he responded. "You're alright, baby. Okay… John's an enabler. I got his back, and he has mine. He's no psycho. He can use a knife like a master uses a violin. John is a man not to be fucked with."

Montoya saw the grim set to Dostiene's mouth. "Got it. When do we meet up with your retard FBI enablers?"

Dostiene laughed. "Very soon, because I've heard on the news the jackals did another killing. They'll probably be… well hell… there they are now, Lynn. On the side of the road… see 'em?"

"Oh yeah," Lynn replied, spotting the two they would have to work with right away.

* * *

Cheryl began screaming in high pitched harmony with their victim, a blonde haired, blue eyed coed from San Francisco State who looked noticeably like Cheryl.

"Oh God... Rich... this is almost like butchering Cheryl," Tara gasped delightedly. "We need to find one like me somewhere. This is the best West Coast adventure yet!"

Richard looked at his two cohorts with glee. "You two are the fucking best! Yes... we'll find a doppelganger of you Tara. She followed you around like a puppy in that bar. She thought you were the coolest thing on earth. We'll have to hurry though. Doing this one in the same place is fucking awesome, but the risks are high."

"Oh my Lord... I want you bad right now..." Cheryl said, hugging Tara to her, while stroking their screaming victim. "When we get back to the house I am going to scream!"

"The FBI dolts are going to shit when they get called into the same body drop," Tara murmured before kissing Cheryl in a passionate embrace.

* * *

Sam Reeves jumped out of the driver's seat to meet the ambling Dostiene and Montoya. "Christ... I never thought I'd be saying how glad I am to see you. We're fucked! Those damn psychos killed another one in the same fucking place as the last one! They tortured and mutilated her exactly like the first one. I want these bastards so bad I can taste it! I can't stand the sight of either one of you, but as God is my witness I'm your man if you can help us get these fucking monsters!"

Clint's smile disappeared. He gripped Lynn's arm, giving her an imperceptible shake of his head when their eyes locked momentarily. He nodded at Reeves. "I only wanted the cards on the table, Sam. We're in until the end. You two didn't even follow the advice I gave you up at my place, did you?"

Reeves shook his head no, staring down at his feet. Clint held out his hand.

Reeves gripped Clint's hand as Labrie caught up. "Thank you. Anything you need or want, I'll get you. Just help us catch these things!"

Lynn put her hand on Reeve's arm. "I like your passion, homeboy. Can I ask you something just for the record? Did-"

"I made the calls to the Federales," Sam stated, meeting Lynn's inquisitive gaze, releasing Clint's hand and letting his fall to his side. "I don't care if you eviscerate me after this ends. If you can help Clint set these fucks up for us to get, I don't care what you do to me."

A smile spread slowly on Montoya's mouth, continuing slowly to her eyes as she glanced over at Clint and then back to Reeves. "Well hell... me and CD will out monster the monsters for you, and no charge on the ledger. Like I said... I like your passion. Want a blow job to seal the deal, cowboy?"

Labrie gasped, Reeves took a step back while Dostiene laughed, shaking his head.

Lynn clapped her hands together. "You two are adorable. I'm hungry. Take us to lunch and fill us in on what's happened since Zorro came down to rescue me."

     * * *

They ordered their meals and ate in relative quiet, having driven up to Lordsburg, NM to the closest restaurant, called Kranberry's Family Restaurant, which was over a two hour drive from the Antelope Wells crossing. Montoya had driven while Dostiene slept, enjoying everything about the barren landscape, the car, and being free for the first time in over six months. Now, she ate hungrily, noting how wrung out the two FBI Agents across the table from them looked. After the meal dishes had been cleared away, Reeves sipped his coffee as if contemplating how to begin. Montoya did it for him.

"Okay, they've killed again. Let's start with how you two see these killers," Montoya asked. "Tell us what kind of profile you envision fits them."

"We believe them to be two or three men in their late thirties to late forties," Labrie replied. "They're blue collar or unemployed with feral cunning, but very little formal education.

We believe they were abused by a female authority figure – a single mother, aunt, grandmother, or even in a shared foster care home. There would be incidents of petty crime and animal abuse in their backgrounds. Although they have mimicked letters and positions used by other serial killers in the area where the original crimes were committed, they also threaded in elements of the satanic cult murderers called 'The Ripper Crew' from Chicago. They severed the breasts of their victims."

Dostiene sipped his iced tea, his face a mask of concentration until Labrie mentioned 'The Ripper Crew' and severed breasts. He smiled. "Okay, now I know where you two went around the bend and forgot everything we discussed when we worked together."

Reeves leaned forward, his palms on the table. "Fine. We're listening now. What the hell are we missing?"

"The breasts," Montoya piped in, getting a nod from Dostiene. "You two fixated on the one element those fucks threw in there as bait, and built your whole goofball profile around it. You fit your present day killers' round peg into those satanic barf-bags' MO square hole."

"No way!" Labrie argued. "I'm telling you we-"

"Oh for God's sake, Janie… she's right!" Reeves shook his head angrily and stood up. "I have to get some air."

They waited in silence, finishing their beverages, until Reeves returned ten minutes later. Dostiene reached over to pat Montoya's knee. Reeves sat down and folded his arms.

"Lay it on me, Clint."

"They're just killers to me at this point, Sam. They're the total opposites of what you and Janie are thinking. I'm thinking different backgrounds, brilliant, and some shared experiences that drew them together. I bet Lynn here can guess the shared experience."

"College," Lynn answered right away. "Long term relationship, so I'm figuring some degree taking years of postgraduate work. These yuppies have money, high earning jobs, recreational time, and have formed their own sadistic circle jerk."

"But Clint-"

"Forget the numbers, Janie," Clint waved her off. "I explained to you and Sam over and over on the cases we worked, that you have to stop focusing so heavily on the crimes and profiles. You have three completely different areas where these serial killings have been supposedly mimicked... that you know of. Let's look at what you and Sam worked on – profiles. When these loonies started, I'll give you a pass. When they took their act on the road, you and Sam should have caught them, or at least identified them."

"They're the traveling monster corps, girlfriend," Montoya added. "I bet you're right about 'The Ripper Crew' mimic job, but you let it infect your whole investigation. I'm being serious. Did you check flight lists out of the areas and cross them with supposed strangers sharing the same hotel or possibly the same room at the hotel?"

"Once they started baiting you, the startup time was established," Dostiene continued for Lynn. "When the mimicked serial killings stopped-"

"We would have had departure times," Janie whispered. "Sweet Christ in heaven... it's been there right in front of us the whole time. They weren't traveling, setting up new identities, and taking their time before starting another serial killing spree."

"They were on vacation," Reeves mumbled, elbows on the table, and head in hands. "The cold blooded bastards take their vacations together."

Reeves leaped to his feet, fists clenched. "C'mon, Janie. We're dumping the car and flying back to San Francisco. We'll take San Francisco and reach out to our office in LA to work the 'Hillside Stranglers' cases. Can you two take the first area we were aware of here in New Mexico?"

"That sounds good, Sam," Clint replied. "Send the New Mexico files to my Internet Drop. They started in Albuquerque, right?"

"That's right," Janie answered. "They killed five young coeds over the space of two weeks, which we will include all details about, especially the dates. I'll send word to our

Albuquerque field office letting them know to give you anything you want – same with the local PD. Thanks, Clint."

"I'll make sure you and Sam get to look these youngsters right in the eye. If you want, we'll take them somewhere and let Lynn mimic her serial killings on them."

"Oh hell yeah!" Lynn laughed. "That's good... Clint. We'll find them and tuck them away for a long winter's nap."

Sam smiled for the first time. "Don't tempt me. Let's go, Janie."

Janie followed Sam, but glanced back at Montoya for a moment. "Would you do that?"

Montoya let the happy face drop. The sheer menace she projected stopped Labrie in her tracks. "In a heartbeat, girlfriend."

"Uh... okay..." Labrie turned away and hurried to catch up with Sam.

Lynn turned, smiling brightly at Dostiene, who had been suppressing laughter with some difficulty. "Did you like my killer face?"

"Yeah, baby, that was very entertaining, not that you wouldn't do it. Those killers really screwed those two up. If we catch them, the only way they'll be looking them in the eye is on a slab at the morgue. Before I was sent packing after your case, I had them thinking about logistics instead of people."

Lynn covered Clint's hand excitedly. "We have to hurry up to Albuquerque. I want to get a lead before they do. I bet we can crack this sucker wide open in no time. What do you think, CD, three or four killers?"

"Four's too many. I'm figuring three, and at least one's a woman."

"Why don't you like to think of gender?"

"I do eventually," Clint replied. "On your case, Reeves and Labrie tore the rape victims' family's lives apart, looking for a vigilante. Even after I'd helped them nail a bunch of other cases, they wouldn't let loose of the 'Death Wish' type profile. You hit guys all across the country. Granted, you left a bloody calling card, but you robbed them blind. The vigilante types don't steal. Robbing their target would be impure. Not for you. No guy, even a serial killer would have done what you did. The act wasn't angry. It was methodical. I knew you weren't flying into town. You were too smart for that."

"Damn you! Rattling all that off makes me look stupid. You knew I was a woman, a psycho instead of anger driven, a stranger to the marks because I robbed them, and you knew I wasn't flying because you suspected I was on a budget." Montoya patted Clint's cheek. "You love this stuff. You just shuffle in like Andy from Mayberry, and then start gluing the pieces together, you prick! There must have been one last piece that let you find me so you could watch Taylor get it."

Clint sat up. "Hey… oh… Laredo told you."

Montoya giggled while wagging her finger at Dostiene. "You watched the whole thing but didn't take me in. How come?"

Clint lifted a hand in a dismissive gesture. "No one was on my neck yet. When I picked out Gradowsky as your next target, I knew I'd have to take you in. My FBI partners were getting ready to blow. If there's anything they hate worse than innocent victims getting murdered, it's scum sucking rapists and murderers getting offed before the taxpayers spend millions on convicting them to keep the bloated Justice Department on the public teat."

Montoya laughed. "Okay… okay, how'd you figure out Taylor and Gradowsky?"

"I didn't. You were throwing a dart at a select group of large cities, not the marks. Your MO was young victims brutally raped and murdered with their killers getting off on a technicality. That reduced the available target list. Then I factored in wealth, and one last tell – size. You liked the big ones."

Lynn frowned, sitting back with her arms folded. "Now you're pissing me off. What the hell do you need me for? You're like a criminal Brainiac."

Dostiene put his arm around Lynn. "Don't be like that. I did pour over a lot of street level video, looking for a like vehicle in different cities, at different crime scenes."

"Shit!"

"I got a license plate, I got your name, and then I found you with Taylor. I put a GPS tracker on your Accord. I didn't have to figure out Gradowsky. I just waited for you to pick him out."

Montoya whipped up her right hand with the index finger and thumb a millimeter apart. "You're this close to getting cut, CD! This... close!"

Instead of moving away, Clint grabbed her hand before she could pull it away. He kissed her fingers. "I need you on this, baby. I know they have old money, parents with legal teams, and a thousand people who would swear they'd never do anything so heinous. You're the bait for the trap so I can execute all three of these turds."

Montoya grinned. "Oh baby, you know what I like. You need me to get all the way strapped down waiting to get my tits cut off."

"It's dangerous."

"Yeah, and if you're late, I get mutilated." Montoya pouted her lower lip out. "Would you leave me if I get a tit cut off?"

"Never, baby."

"Don't I get to play at all?"

"I'd have to wound one, and that would be even more dangerous," Clint reminded her. "I'll do it if you want."

"I want."

"Male or female?"

"Female. The one who looks to be enjoying it the most," Lynn answered. "Maybe I can set them up to be drugged before I end up strapped to the table. Then I can play with all three. We need to get moving to Albuquerque."

"We're not in a competition."

"Says you." Lynn stood up. "On your feet, soldier! Hey... those two deadbeats stuck us with the tab."

Dostiene chuckled. "Just noticed that, huh?"

Clint gestured to the waitress who came over smiling. He stood up and gave her a hundred dollar bill when she handed him the check. "Keep the change."

The waitress's eyes widened. "Thank you, Sir."

On the way out of the restaurant Lynn hip checked Dostiene, but only ended up bouncing off and almost running into an oncoming restaurant customer.

"Damn it, Clint," Lynn whispered, rubbing her hip while limping to keep up. "What the hell? Are you made of cement? You know you just ruined that girl for serving with that tip. It's a terrible precedent."

"She deserved the tip. We got our meal on time, just as we asked for it. She didn't interrupt our conversation, and she filled our drinks when we needed them filled. What more was she supposed to do?"

Lynn grabbed his arm with a gasp of happy surprise. "I knew it. You were a busboy, waiter, or something like that way back when. Oh, I so got you, CD."

Dostiene kept walking, grinning at being set up so easily. "I let my guard down for five seconds and you nail me. I waited tables once long ago. There... you happy?"

Montoya practically skip stepped at his side. "Oh, I so am! I want to know everything about you. If we're getting married, having kids, and making cupcakes together, I need to know every detail."

Clint held the door for her with a smile. "I don't think so."

Lynn pointed at him as she walked by. "You owe me for deducing you were a server."

Dostiene followed her out, laughing as he walked. "I have to admit, I haven't had this much fun with anyone. You are special."

Montoya turned back into his arms. "I know you're joking around but we were meant for each other."

Clint cupped her chin with his right hand. "I don't know, baby. Think about it. Picture our first fight as a couple. The next morning I'm looking to sing soprano in the Vienna Boys Choir and Tonto rips your throat out."

Dostiene pats her cheek and walks on.

"I...I could change," Lynn called out after him, smiling when she sees his shoulders shaking in amusement. "I know. You could chain me up after a fight!"

Clint is now laughing uproariously as he unhitches Tonto's leash from the post in the shade, and picks up the portable dog bed. After giving Tonto the leftovers from his meal, Clint dumps Tonto's water dish. "See, it wasn't so bad out here in the shade, huh?"

"So, where do we go first?"

"The nicest hotel in Albuquerque, baby." Clint gestured for Tonto to follow and led the way to their vehicle. We stay in style from now on."

"CD! Don't you go soft on me. I want to nail the killers before those FBI profiling nitwits. We need to get there and hit the local PD's database for-"

"Hold on." Dostiene gripped Lynn's shoulders, smiling down at her. "We have a state of the art notebook satellite computer, permission from Langley to join forces with this task force, and a password to anything Langley can hack into. Why the hell should we interact with the local forces of justice? Oh... I get it... you want to screw around with the locals with authority."

Lynn slapped the side of Dostiene's face lightly. "Yeah... kinda. You got a problem with that, CD?"

"I guess not. You want to stroll in there all dressed up like the TV show criminal groups do and demand a task force room and the whole nine yards, huh?"

Montoya's lips tightened into straight lipped angst. "Yeah, I do! Let's have some fun. You know the rumor mill will have me outed as a serial killer. Think about the looks we'll get when I stroll in with you at your side."

"On one condition – you stay calm and professional through all their rantings. Not one snide remark or faceoff. Deal?"

Lynn sighed, turning toward their car. "Deal. I need to go shopping if I'm to look the part though."

Dostiene grinned. "Of course."

Chapter Seven
Killer Trail

The desk sergeant stared back at Dostiene with undisguised hostility. Clint had his FBI ID held up after revealing the initial revelation as to why he and Montoya were there. Montoya, dressed in her new black skirt to the knee, low black heels and white blouse, hair tied tightly back into a bun, was the picture of a professional in law enforcement or business. Dostiene wore his own conservative men in black ensemble.

The florid faced, thinning haired desk sergeant, looked over Dostiene's credentials carefully, although it was obvious he had been expecting them. He handed the ID back. "You like working with serial killers as partners, huh?"

Dostiene glanced over at a smiling Montoya, and then nodded. "Yeah, she's a hell of a lot better than some I've had."

The desk sergeant leaned forward over the counter, his fists clenched. "You think this is some kinda' joke, Agent Dostiene?"

"Nope. I think it's the best chance to catch a host of murderous swine who think it's a joke to torture and maim women. If you have a better idea, please state it. If not, please show us to an area where we can work. We have some ideas to research I believe may bring this murderous chaos to an end."

Dostiene's demeanor impressed the older sergeant. He stepped back for a moment, gathering the folders he had been assigned to give them when they arrived. He looked up finally and stuck out his hand. "I'm Dominic Pantera, Sir. If you two can catch these monsters, I don't care what you have to do."

Clint smiled as he gripped Pantera's hand. "We will catch them, Dom. Guaranteed."

Pantera looked into Dostiene's eyes for a moment and then nodded. "Yeah... I believe you will. Follow me."

Pantera led them to a small office through a gaggle of frowning police personnel. The room was equipped with a computer and desk with chairs. "The password has been encoded already into this station. Anything not in the files I gave you can be accessed on the search line in the computer. Good luck."

"Thanks, Dom," Clint replied. "We'll keep you updated as to our progress."

"Thank you. I'm supposed to be your liaison. My card's in the first index file I gave you with my personal cell-phone number in case you need me. I'm rooting for you two. Thanks to that asshole, David Parker Ray, all of New Mexico is looked at as a serial killer burial ground."

Montoya patted Pantera's arm solemnly. "Look. I did what I did because the freaks I targeted got off on technicalities. They raped, tortured, and murdered, including girls as young as twelve. I never touched an innocent."

Pantera nodded. "Thanks for that. Things have gotten so twisted the criminals have nearly become untouchable. They look for any means to put cops behind bars, thinking we can all function as PC robots in a combat situation. I'm going to look closer at the list you sanctioned, lady. Maybe afterwards... I'll be a fan."

"I think you will be once Clint and I nail these suckers." Lynn watched Pantera walk away without further discussion. She glanced over at Dostiene, noting he had opened up his briefcase, and extracted his satellite link up.

"I get the distinct feeling you're on your way to solving this case before I even get to sit down. You know, of course... there will be blood."

Clint glanced up with a short laugh. "Solving these things is always the last thing to be considered. "We have to be able to present a prosecution case that is flawless, even if we plan on an unforeseeable accident for our misguided perpetrators. Once we have an unmistakable trail leading to them, we'll have all the backing to put them down like the rabid dogs they are. Grab a chair, now that we've pissed off everyone in the station with your presence. We have all the key ingredients already."

Lynn dragged another chair over near Dostiene. "Are you going to use their databases?"

"We'll go through Langley instead. This won't be rocket science anyway. We have the parameters of the murders with the all important dates." Clint's fingers flew over the keys, producing a rapid flow of open windows. "See, we start with separate strangers flying into Albuquerque on separate flights, but near the same time, weeks before the murders began. There's a bunch of them."

"Now you key in the same names flying out to the same place they came from, near the same time up to weeks after the murders." Lynn's hands tightened into fists, her way of channeling the adrenaline rush as she pictured the hunt Dostiene was on. "Damn. There's only around fifty names now."

"Watch how that number drops when I key in three of them booked into the same hotel during their stay." Clint's hands typed in the parameter and he hit enter. Only three names were left: Cheryl Kosygin, Tara Holt, and Richard Jacoby. Clint queried his database again. "That's them, baby. They all went to Harvard law."

"Shit, Clint, that was easy."

"Now comes the interesting part," Clint replied. "We have to start putting together a case. We start a database with their misdeeds coordinated with the facts of when they all arrived from different states here in this city."

"Then you check for their names in the other cities, with the parameters of the other murders," Lynn whispered, hunching over Clint.

"Yep." Clint sat back, pointing at the screen. "And there they are. They always have a few months break before they start up again. Our FBI agent buddies would have enough now to start harassing them and ruin our little plan, so we have to come up with a way to draw them out. I bet you can figure out where we're going to get the next clue."

Montoya stared at the screen for a moment. Then she smiled. "We get into their companies' files and keep track of when they all take vacations next."

"You definitely have the instincts for this, baby. Once we have that, then we'll find out the destination, and a probable target."

"Where's the hard part come in?"

"Deciding whether to go with full disclosure to the FBI, and hoping we can get them to stay low key until we nail the three in the act, or lie our asses off. I'd rather let them in on it."

"I agree," Lynn replied. "They're probably coming up with the same answers we're getting now that you clued them in."

Dostiene chuckled. "Wanna' bet? I'd have to spell it out for them even with the prompts I've already given them."

"Maybe they'll surprise you."

"Maybe. We'll have to meet with them soon if you're on board with telling them."

Lynn gripped Dostiene's wrist. "I don't want you in prison, so I vote on the truth. They'll be grateful, and they'll definitely be more receptive to me being the bait to catch our killers."

"I've already started a query to find out when our trio wants to party next, and… hey… look here. Jacoby's already put in for a couple months away. That breaks their protocol a bit. Something must have caught their eye. Let's see if he's… yep… he's already made reservations for the flight to Cambridge, Ma. The other two have the flights booked, both going to Cambridge. No hotels picked out."

"Maybe it's a social event. That's where their old Alma Mater is," Lynn said.

"On it," Clint replied. "Oh baby… a reunion for their class. I bet you didn't know you graduated law from Harvard. You will when I get all your credentials. I'll find a law office somewhere the Company has relations with so we can make you up an impressive resume with them."

"What if they ask me questions, Clint? I don't know shit about law except breaking it."

Dostiene chuckled. "If someone asks you anything like that, you give them the over the shoulder sneer and say, 'do I look like I want to talk shop'."

"Oh yeah, I can pull that off, especially if I have some impressive credentials. I'll need a complete wardrobe."

"Of course. I'll get on in the security detail or something. They always have them for those wing dings. I'll get to watch you in action. We'll have to make your arrival and entrance legendary."

"Don't they all know each other at these things?"

"Your packet will be waiting for you, and you'll be carrying your invitation. They may have five hundred show up for this, since they're including a couple of Harvard and Radcliff classes. It will be show-time when you get loose inside the Harvard Faculty Club. You'll have to pique the interest of the three killers. Jacoby will probably be your best bet, but with two women in the killer crew, there may be some room for a Lesbos love triangle."

Montoya cracked up, patting Dostiene's back. "I'll think of something. What are we going to do in the time until the reunion? I know even our favorite profiling partners can keep track of those three. As long as they're apart, they're too chicken shit to do anything on their own, right?"

Clint shrugged. "They're only predictable when they're together. They may each have some private horror show going, but you're probably right. So, you think you'd like to play cops and robbers until your reunion?"

Lynn straightened, walking around with her chin in hand as if in deep contemplation for a few moments. She suddenly spun back toward Dostiene, cradling his face in both hands. "Of course I do! It would be such a kick, CD! You and me trapping bad guys together. I'll be the bait. The rougher, the better. C'mon, don't you want to put these Company suicide missions you've been going on behind you?"

"You mean like the one I just pulled off, plucking your shapely butt away from a Mexican Cartel?"

Montoya dead panned her response, hands on hips. "Yeah, like that one."

Dostiene grinned up at her, deciding to play around a little with how Montoya would react to a Las Vegas setup. "Baby... what makes you think we'd be invited in to do something like that by our FBI pals? Desperation is the only reason we're in on this serial killer stuff now. I see prison time in our future if we dabble around on mundane crime business."

Lynn straightened, counting off on her hand. "One, we use extortion to get Reeves and Skanky on board. Two-"

"Skanky?"

"You've nailed her and I don't like it. Let's move on. Two-"

"I did not nail her," Dostiene stated, standing up to face Lynn. He stared at Lynn until she looked away. "Labrie is a good agent. She's just caught up in the 'profile mode' even when there's nothing standard in the case. Her and Reeves have a great conviction record on regular cases. What's this about, Lynn?"

Montoya shrugged. "Sorry, CD. I assumed facts not in evidence. I thought the way she looked at you... you know... maybe you were tapping that. Hell, maybe you should have rocked her world and she wouldn't be all profiled into a corner now."

Dostiene tried not to laugh, failed, and went into full blown laughter for a few moments. "So... let me get this straight... I didn't nail Labrie, which led to the deaths of all these innocent people?"

"Exactly."

Clint bowed his head in deference. "Okay. You may be right. I will forego sexual liaisons with all contacts in my working environments from now on to prevent this heinous outcome."

Lynn giggled, hugging Dostiene. "Like hell. How about if I say I'm sorry for alluding to something that never happened in reality?"

Clint framed Montoya's face with his hands in a firm grip. "This stuff between me and you only works with trust, baby. I have no idea where this is going, but I can tell you it will go nowhere if you back me into a corner. It might be a good idea if we assumed the best of each other instead of the worst."

Lynn moved provocatively against Dostiene while wrapping her arms around him. "Sorry, CD. It won't happen again. How come you're not jealous of me? You must care about me. Otherwise, launching a suicide mission to rescue my shapely butt would have been beyond stupid. What's up with that?"

Dostiene met her pointed gaze with a serious one of his own. "I've never had a relationship with anyone, especially someone who knew what I am. I'm not over thinking our serial killer merger. I know you and I want these monsters. Yeah... you and I are monsters. The fact I don't care should be enough for you.

What the hell am I going to do with some vestal virgin, who hasn't a clue about what we have to do?"

Dostiene grabbed Montoya's hands, grinning at her. "Ever hear that old Bob Seger song 'Night Moves'?"

A startled look enveloped Lynn's facial expression, and then she laughed. "Working on mysteries without any clue?"

Clint's smile spread slowly as he nodded. "That's why I love you, baby. You know my lyrics. What else can I say?"

* * *

Dostiene ended the call by switching off speaker. He smiled at Lynn, who had just walked in from the bedroom. "You heard the last part?"

"Yep. Your buddy Reeves is a happy guy. I thought you calmed him down pretty well. For a moment there, I thought he was going to fly into each of the perp's cities and execute them himself. Maybe he's not as flat as I thought he was. The bad part is you were right. They didn't have anything, did they?"

Clint shook his head. "Nope. They got lost somewhere, and had it narrowed down to a cast of thousands. He was popping the names I gave him into the computer and coming up aces on every front. He's convinced, and he loves our idea to get them. Of course Sammy doesn't know yet what our getting them means. All the details for the cover will be handled. We won't have to do a thing."

When Clint didn't go on, Montoya growled. "Well... what did he say about some practice cases? I heard you mention it."

Clint grinned, having inside info on Denny Strobert's behind the scenes setup. "Sam said to meet him in Las Vegas. They have a serial rapist there that's hit a dozen young women. When he's done, he cuts them from the corner of their mouth to their eye socket. He's been extremely careful. No DNA left anywhere. Las Vegas is a perfect place for him. He's patient – only waits for the dark and a target alone, which happens quite often in Sin City. Hell, he doesn't even have to move around. Sam thinks the sucker waits until he has a lone target away from all cameras or lights."

"But he doesn't kill them?"

"Nope. Scarring only right now. They tried to hush it up to prevent the tourist business taking a dive. It's pretty tough to do that with live victims, and they're talking. Their families are talking too… and demanding action. Most are tourists from other states so the feds have been asked in. It's a hot one, and it'll be breaking all over the news in the next couple days. You can imagine how happy Sam was to have something positive to tell his bosses about our yuppie serial killers, because they're dumping the rapist on them too."

Montoya began stripping. "This will be perfect for me."

Clint watched appreciatively, glancing around their room. "I thought you were ready to leave."

Lynn looked up from where she left her jeans and panties on the floor. "Road trip, right? We're taking Tonto, right?

"Ah… yeah."

Montoya moved up against Dostiene. "I need to loosen up for the road trip. How about you?"

"I do now."

* * *

Lynn looked over at the dozing Dostiene next to her in their rental Chevrolet Suburban. Tonto lay in the spacious rear seat. "Hey Sherlock, we have maybe forty-five minutes until we reach the Sin City limits."

Clint yawned and sat up, glancing out at the bleak scenery on US 93. "Man, this thing is comfortable. What's up?"

"Well you missed the Petrified Forest, and-"

"Hey… I drove the first few hours. You said you wanted to drive, so stop whining about it. Now, what's with the Sherlock?"

"I figured you'd want to go over our action plan before we get there. Why'd you choose the Stratosphere, for example? I wanted to stay at the Wynn's or the Bellagio," Lynn replied.

"We have Tonto. Plus, we want to stay in an out of the way place. It will cost me some extra for Tonto, but all the rape action has taken place between the Stratosphere and the Wynn's. There are a lot of dark spots between the two. The tourists that have been targeted were all staying at the casinos down at that end:

Circus/Circus, the Riviera, and the Stratosphere, or they were walking to the Riviera from the Wynn's direction."

"I see those wheels turning, CD. You've thought of something. Spit it out. I figured I'd just be strutting around in a nice outfit."

"This weasel's smarter than that, baby. The cops have been baiting that hook non-stop since the first couple incidents. We'll be strolling around in the dark getting nowhere just like them. Our guy's chatting up his hits in the casinos, knowing they're staying in Las Vegas, and not just materializing out of thin air. That's why I told Sam we're not going anywhere near them or their field office there. We're checking in for a week. Unfortunately, I'll be the dim sighted guy staying with my service dog, Tonto, by himself. That's the only way the Stratosphere allows a dog in. You'll be the cheap tart staying by herself, having a grand old time on a tight budget, while playing big at the seedier casino stretch."

Lynn giggled. "How will this go over with Sam and Skank?"

"Will you please stop calling her that? Sam will sell it. He'll keep the Vegas PD playing around with undercover cops while we play the long hand. In the meantime, I'll put our FBI partners to work going over every single person on casino video that spoke more than two words with our victims. With the facial recognition stuff they have now, they may even be able to zero right in on the perp, unless he's playing around with hats and hair."

"Okay, CD, I'll bite, why didn't you go into detail with him on the phone?"

Dostiene shook his head. "You should know better than that. They'd put some Barbie trying our ploy and tip our hand to the perp. No way that guy makes you. I'll be shadowing you with different looks. We're not even checking in at the same time. I'll have you let me out at a crowded spot on the Strip with Tonto and my bag. I'll hail a cab from there. You drive on with the Chevy and check in. I didn't make you reservations in case the perp works for the hotel. Get a real nice place with spa and everything there. You don't have a gambling problem I don't know about, do you?"

"Kind of. I very seldom lose, so I'll have to stick to the slots. You'll still sneak up to see me after we're done with our patrol, right?"

"Of course. We'll get settled in and then I'd like you to play down in the Stratosphere tonight, strutting around, and maybe chatting up the bartenders about what places have the best payouts or something."

"Should I be getting loaded too?"

Clint nodded. "Sip a few? Yeah, I think you need to put imbibing on your bait resume in the casino. You won't go getting careless and end up in some landfill somewhere if I lose sight of you for a few seconds will you?"

Lynn laughed but did a double take at Dostiene's serious frown. "Hey... I'm not taking this lightly, CD. You're giving me looks like I'm some easy mark. What happened to trust? If you think I'm lettin' some cowboy rope me into a face disfiguring sex romp, you don't know shit about me!"

Clint nodded over at her, leaning back. "Oh yeah, that's what I'm talkin' about. Just remember to glance around before you exit someplace. Make sure me and Tonto are in the area. Otherwise, fake a quick bathroom break and give us some time."

Montoya reached over to grip Dostiene's thigh. "You wouldn't be admitting to some affection for me, would you?"

Clint patted her hand. "I'm already in love with you. What the hell else do you want from a fellow monster?"

Lynn swerved the Chevy over across lanes to a screeching halt on the side, causing Dostiene to jolt upward, reaching for the 9mm Glock at his waist. "What the hell?"

Montoya grabbed Dostiene's face in her hands, the grim look pasted across her features giving Clint pause. "Don't joke with me! I'm not some tulip you plucked off the road side."

Clint smiled. "What in the world makes you think I'm joking? Sure, we're probably both rated as psychopaths by people who don't even know the first thing about gathering a clue. Just because they don't trust us, want us, or wish they didn't need us, doesn't mean we need to define ourselves by their parameters."

Clint stroked Lynn's side with his right hand with slow deliberation. "I'm only a psychopath in one admitted parameter. I would have killed the entire population of Mexico to free you. I had logically erased your existence from my memory banks after I'd turned you over to my FBI partners. Do I have any idea why the hell you can fill every thought in my head... hell no! When our FBI groupies mentioned you in Mexico, it was me suggesting you be the bait for finding the three slugs that attended Harvard. Yes... I love you."

Montoya released Dostiene, her mouth open in surprise. It turned to tears. She whipped back around, gripping the steering wheel in a death grip. "God, Clint! Could you screw my head up anymore than it already is?"

Dostiene frowned, his usual response to real life situations fleeing him like unwanted serial killers. "I get the distinct impression you think I'm still joking. Lynn, what the hell do you think this is all about? We're fuckin' evil. If we choose to do good deeds, so what? That I care for you? Whoopie do."

Lynn wiped away the tears streaming down her cheeks. "Fuck!"

Moments paused as Montoya struggled with belief and action. Dostiene clasped Lynn's right hand in both of his. "Hey... don't over think this stuff. You already figured I didn't just materialize out of nowhere to 'White Knight' you back to the 'Stars and Stripes'. If me loving you makes you feel uncomfortable then just blow it off. We are psychos after all."

Montoya moaned and kissed Dostiene, pretense, parameters, and any concept of dignity fleeing in an intense moment of utter surrender. The salty taste of Lynn's tears and her moaning intensity of feeling drove a hunger within Clint he could not conceal.

Lynn broke away first, her hand reaching toward her lips. "This... this isn't going to work. Is it?"

"Do you mean whether we're capable of loving each other? Who knows? If you mean my feelings for you will punt our partnership for finding criminals – you don't know me very well. I shoot first and let God sort 'em out later. I've put so many people in the ground, it's a good thing my kills can't follow me around like in that werewolf movie I saw one time."

Lynn laughed, hugging Clint. "Okay... maybe it'll work. I saw that movie. It was... American Werewolf in London."

"That's the one." Clint kissed Lynn again with passion, drinking in her scent, her taste, and her tears. Dostiene pulled back only when the heat and intensity of their embrace threatened a squirming copulation right over the center console. "I should never have let you go after the trial. You could have come back up into the mountains with me and Tonto. They fired my ass anyway off the task force because they suspected I let you carve up that poor old baby killer."

Lynn gripped Dostiene's face once again. "Jesus, Clint... all you needed to do was ask. Hell, didn't you see it in my eyes at his house. I would have screwed you right on top of him. No one had ever come up on me like you did. I was impressed. Now I'm old and used up."

Clint burst into laughter with Lynn only able to keep a straight face a few seconds longer. She sighed after a few more moments and pulled back onto the road to Las Vegas.

"You better get up to my room tonight, cowboy. Do you think our perp will go full bore tonight if he does chat me up, or play it cool?"

"He'll play you. If he hits on you in the Stratosphere you can bet he works there in some capacity. I'll have to be careful making conjugal visits to your room if I see him laying the groundwork with you tonight. Have you given any thought to an extra play on this piece of shit?"

Lynn glanced over with a smile. "Laredo was right. You are a believer. Yeah, I don't like what he's done anymore than you. I'm thinking bringing my knife along will satisfy us both."

Dostiene leaned back in his seat, hands behind his head. "Oh baby, you know what I like. Yeah, I'm thinking during capture you may have to defend yourself, possibly involving a rather sharp groin shot."

Clint sat up straight with a grim look. "He's marked every one of those girls for life. I think it's only fair we return the favor."

Lynn reached over and patted his shoulder. "Calm down, CD. I'm with you. I'll do a little insert and twist he won't ever forget."

Dostiene nodded. "It's nice working with you, Officer Montoya."

Montoya chuckled. "Right back at you, CD. If that prick gets the drop on me, I hope you'll fix him up real good."

"Not happening, my love," Clint stated. "That happens and payback gets biblical, and fuck the G-men. He marks you in any way shape or form and I take him into the desert for a real bonding get together. Did you ever read 'The Carpetbaggers', with the Nevada Smith character?"

"No."

"Some guys skin his Mom and Dad in the old west. He takes one of them into the desert, stakes them out over a red ant hill, slits off their eyelids so they can't close their eyes, puts honey on their stomach and groin, and kicks back to watch them die. It takes days."

"Are you trying to impress me?"

Dostiene laughs appreciatively. "I'm just lettin' you know if anything happens to you, I get biblical, and not in a good way."

"Noted. Hey… here we are on the outskirts of the weirdest city on the face of the earth," Lynn announced, gesturing out at the 'Welcome to Las Vegas' sign' they were passing. Ever wonder what it would be like livin' in a place like this?"

"Hell on earth?"

Montoya giggles. "Figures you'd say that. You could have a place up in the middle of nowhere around here, and drift on down for the nightlife any time you felt the urge, including a little Batman action."

"No thanks. There are so many faces of depravity here, it chills even my blood. I'm a live and let live guy, but this place overwhelms me if I'm here for more than a week. Does something here really sing an aria in your heart?"

"Nope, but I do get a charge out of it messing with your head."

"Hey, this operation gets my blood flowing," Clint admitted, "but it's like operating in a different dimension. I adapt well. I choose to adapt only for short stints though. What do you think about spending Christmas up at my place in the mountains with me and Tonto?"

"I'd like that more than anything. Do you have a house, or is it just a lean-to in the woods?"

"I have indoor plumbing and all the conveniences."

"Well then… I am so there." Lynn pointed at a crowded sidewalk area on the middle of the Las Vegas Strip. "Want out around here?"

"This looks perfect. Remember, everything's in your kit. We test out everything for sound and picture before you go out."

Lynn pretended to nod off and start snoring. "Yes, I remember. Don't get mugged on the way."

Clint opened the door, extending his cane, before opening the rear door to pull out his bag. Tonto, already in harness, waited patiently. "C'mon Tonto, let's go catch a taxi away from this know-it-all ingrate."

Montoya laughed. "I'll only get a shower and nap before heading out, CD. I'll go have a drink at the bar around seven."

"Ten-four, tulip," Clint acknowledged to more laughter.

Clint stood on the curb with Tonto and his bag. Not more than five minutes later a taxi pulled up.

"Taxi, Sir?" The driver called out.

"Just in time. Will twenty extra be enough for my partner here."

"You bet!" The driver hurried around to grab up Clint's bag and store it in the trunk. He then opened his passenger rear door for Clint and Tonto. "Where to, Sir?"

"The Stratosphere, please."

"I don't think they allow dogs, Sir," the driver informed him, hesitating at the curb before closing the rear door.

"I called ahead. They allow service dogs."

"Oh… very good then. Next stop, the Stratosphere." The driver closed the door and ran around to his driver's door.

Chapter Eight
Sin City

Fifteen minutes later, the cab pulled up at the front entrance for the Stratosphere. Clint quickly paid the driver, and accepted help with his bag, and a business card from the driver. One of the greeters immediately assisted Clint and Tonto into the casino to the hotel check-in. The front desk helped him get checked in with a minimum of hassle, after Tonto proved beyond any shadow of a doubt how trained he was. Dostiene put him through his paces, even though the front desk manager did not appear concerned. The demonstration made an impression on the nearby staff as Tonto turned back and forth by command, sat, stood, walked on his hind legs, and even danced in a circle at Clint's twirling finger command. There was even a smattering of applause.

"You have a wonderful dog there, Mr. Dostiene," the manager said with a smile. She had red hair in a bun, and a nametag Clint avoided looking at, while staring at nothing in particular with a nod. "I'm Lois Christianson, Sir. I'll have someone take you to your room. When you're ready to come down for gaming or to dine, just call the front desk, and tell them your room number."

"Thank you, Lois. I will take my meals in, but when I'm ready to try my luck, I'll give you a call."

"It will be my pleasure, Sir."

A young man took Clint's elbow. "This way, Sir."

Clint and Tonto were escorted up to their room in minutes with their guide running interference. Clint tipped him well but noticed the man in his middle twenties eyed him with a predator's bearing. Noting Tonto picked up on the same vibes, Dostiene knelt and stroked the dog's head reassuringly before his canine partner did anything to indicate distrust.

"Do you have a card, my friend, in case I find myself lost down in the casino area or at a loss somewhere else? You have been very efficient in settling us in."

Dostiene looked off casually while waiting for an answer as he straightened up away from Tonto. He chuckled in an offhand way. "Sorry... if you're not available for that type of intercession, I understand completely."

Clint saw the smile of evil intent spread across the man's features, reinforcing at once his initial feeling.

"No... no, Sir, here is my card. Show it anywhere and I will be available if I am near your position. If not, I will be able to get you help very quickly." He grasped Dostiene's hand with both of his. "I am Edgar Constanza."

Clint smiled widely while shaking his hand, and taking the business card Constanza offered into his left hand. "Thank you, Edgar. It's good to have someone at the hotel to contact directly if I have a problem. I know your managers are eager to help, but limited as to what they can do."

Clint turned and took another twenty out of his cash fold, pressing it onto Constanza. "If I need assistance Edgar, you will be my first call, and there will be of course a suitable compensation. I know when I take on an adventure like this, I need contacts locally if something doesn't turn out the way I hope."

Dostiene liked the man's reaction of putting a hand to his mouth in order to suppress an outright laugh. Constanza toned down his reaction immediately as Tonto crouched into a defensive stance.

"I don't think your dog likes me, Sir."

"Tonto is very protective yet gentle to a fault, Edgar. He doesn't know you that well. Think nothing of it. In any case, if I get into a jam, I'll give you a call if you don't mind."

"I am at your service, Sir. Have a great day and don't hesitate to call on me."

"Thank you, Edgar." Dostiene watched the man exit the room with his peripheral vision. "Well, Tonto, I think Lynn and I have our first candidate. Something about that young gentleman has my spidy sense tingling. I should have done a preemptive strike on his ass, and buried him amongst the many in the desert."

Tonto offered a paw, which Dostiene shook. "Good one, buddy. Silence it is for now."

Dostiene's throw away cell-phone rang. "Hey, Lynn. I figured you'd be asleep."

"I think I have a candidate already. He's on the staff. His name's Edgar. He's creepy. He asks too many questions, and he insisted on accompanying me to my room with the bags. The prick set everything up and refused the tip I tried to lay on him. I've already uploaded a picture of him to you. I need to do surgery on him even if he's not the guy... please?"

"See, this is why I love you in our alternate psycho reality."

Montoya laughed. "Oh my God! We aced on the same guy. Tell me... c'mon, what did he do?"

"We blind guys tend to evoke self expressions by suspects they would not normally reveal on their features. I don't know if Edgar's our guy, but he might be someone we should stick around for after we do find our perp."

"Agreed. I kind of miss you already. I'm thinking a hot tub reunion tonight after hours is in order. This luxury spa suite is pretty nice. Do you think I should have gotten the grand suite or something?"

"No. You picked just right. If you'd have gotten too flashy, that might have given Edgar the wrong idea. Depending on how things go, I might be able to swing a visit after hours."

"Good. I'll hit the bar for a drink as we agreed around 7. Then I'll play the dollar slots big time for a while. If I get lucky, I might draw out some extra attention. The outfit I'll be wearing is going to attract attention anyway, win or lose."

"I'll bet it will. We'll do a communications check at 6:55 then, okay?"

"Ten-four, CD. Talk to you then."

Having napped the last couple hours of the trip, Clint put away his things, took a shower, and dressed in jeans, pullover black shirt, and black windbreaker. He gathered up a couple waste bags, hitched the attentive Tonto up, and headed out of his room.

Tonto played his guide dog role perfectly, waiting at the Casino entrance for a Good Samaritan to open the door for the partners. Dostiene thanked the couple who preceded him and held the door open, looking away from them as he spoke. Tonto took over, instinctively heading around the hotel perimeter toward the area less developed in the direction opposite the main Las Vegas Strip. The two didn't return to the hotel for an hour. By then, players in the casino were just beginning to spread around the gaming area in numbers. Tonto endured the attention of animal lovers they were stuck with in the elevator, shaking hands with the teen-aged girl and her parents.

In the hotel room, Dostiene fed and watered the happy Tonto, giving him extra treats. "You were your usual amazing self, T."

Clint removed his electrical gear from the hotel room safe, going over the micro-circuitry device before sitting at the room desk with his satellite uplinked notebook. In moments, he used CIA access to break through the casino security firewalls, hacking into their camera feed archives. Dostiene found Edgar. In the hours until he needed to dress for his shadowing of Montoya, Clint poured over Constanza's patterns and work schedule, crosschecking the victims' recollected times at the Stratosphere casino. The tedious work led to a solid discovery – Constanza interacted with every victim, even the ones not staying at the Stratosphere. Delving into work times more closely, Clint found Constanza on casino video during three of the rapes.

Widening his parameters, Clint traced Constanza's movements in conjunction with the rape dates, and conversations with other men not in the employ of the casino. An hour later, minutes before he would have to get ready, a suspect materialized who matched all dates, times, and parameters. Constanza met the victim in nondescript places near each one of the victims. The man, dressed exquisitely in suit and tie, with hair coiffed perfectly, would watch the women marks, and eventually strike up a conversation with them. They let him buy them a drink, enjoying a lengthy conversation, after which he would excuse himself with class, leaving them looking after him as he exited. Dostiene closed up his laptop with a shake of his head as he eyed Tonto.

"We have a live one, T. He has issues, and he has a playmate who helps him in his twisted endeavors. Little does he know, I'm going to put a real monster on his trail. She doesn't care about his mommy issues, his rough childhood, or whatever perverse shit he's warped his mind into thinking he deserves." Dostiene bent down and stroked Tonto's head affectionately. "We may eventually find out why these two butchers have done all this, but the way they communicate with us may be painful. If you'll excuse me, partner, I have to call the real monster and make sure she gets her electronics hooked up right."

* * *

Montoya swayed through the casino, enjoying the noise, crowds, and banter of passing people. Dressed in a thigh high, off the shoulder black cocktail dress, Lynn smiled at everyone on her way to the main casino bar, C bar. She attracted followers, both innocent and not so innocent. Lynn ordered a bloody Mary, which elicited approval from her small audience. When the drink arrived, Lynn turned to face her groupies, sipping at her drink.

"Hey guys, would this be the appropriate time to let you all know I'm a lesbian?" Montoya watched everyone walk off with varying declarations of response. One hung around, matching Clint's description.

"That's him, Lynn," Clint's voice confirmed.

Lynn leaned forward on her elbows over the bar, drink in hand. She watched the perfectly coiffed, three piece suit edge toward her with an ingratiating smile Lynn figured he worked on in front of the mirror. Six feet of carefully scripted movement slid in next to her.

"Hi, I heard what you said, but you intrigue me. Could we simply have a drink together? My name's Aaron."

"I don't mind, Aaron. I'm Lynn." Montoya sipped her drink, meeting Aaron's smiling gaze without looking away. "You look like you should be hanging out at the Wynn's or the Bellagio."

"I like the people here at the Stratosphere. I win more here too."

Lynn acted surprised. "I get it. You're a local."

Aaron smiled. "That obvious, huh? How about you?"

"I live in LA. My Vegas trips are usually only biannually. I've never met a local other than the casino workers. What do you do around here for work?"

"I'm in real estate," Aaron answered, signaling to the bartender, who came over with a smile and nod.

"Your usual?"

"Yeah, Ben, thanks, and could you get my friend here another of what she's having?"

"Sure thing." The bartender made their drinks in moments, setting them down, and thanking Aaron for the generous tip.

"Do you play the casinos often?"

Aaron shook his head. "I hit them on the weekends, mostly the card tables. What do you like to play?"

"I love the slots. I don't care much for the card games." Lynn smiled, listening to Clint snorting his assessment of her small talk. "I win often at slots. How about you with the cards?"

"I do pretty well. How long will you be staying?"

"I spread my time over the weekend, so I have four nights." Lynn looked over the guy next to her with a knowing eye. She wondered why picturing him doing the rape and face slice was so hard. Maybe they had the wrong guy in spite of Dostiene's track record. "So, how often do you take a girl home from one of your casino visits?"

Aaron laughed. He took a long sip of his drink. "I never take them home. When and if we jointly agree on more than just a drink, I accompany the lady to her room, where she feels more comfortable. Do you play any of the other casinos?"

"I take a walk down the strip to the other casinos to stretch my legs. It's fun walking up toward the main strip and playing the Riviera on the way to the Wynn's. If I stay late at the main spots, I take a taxi back."

"That's a long walk down to the Wynn's," Aaron pointed out. "There's a lot of empty space in between here and the Riviera."

Lynn shrugged, and pointed at her medium heels. "It clears my head. I have my walkin' shoes on. Like I said though, I usually take a cab back. How about you?"

"I play here and Circus Circus on a night like tonight, depending on my luck. If I'm on a hot streak, I may go up to the casinos on the main strip. I'd better let you see how your luck at the slots will be tonight." Aaron held out his hand, and Lynn shook it. "Very nice meeting you. Perhaps we can have a drink together tomorrow night."

"You never know. It's good to meet a nice guy once in a while."

Aaron patted her hand. "Thank you, Lynn. Goodnight."

"Goodnight." Lynn watched Aaron walk toward the exit. A rough looking guy with a dilapidated baseball cap and a worn brown leather bomber jacket sat down two stools over. He ordered a beer. Lynn sipped the second drink Aaron had bought her.

"What'd you think about Aaron?" Dostiene's voice whispered from next to her without looking over.

Montoya chuckled, resisting the urge to glance over in surprise. "Damn, cowboy, you're good at this."

Clint paid for his beer. He took a sip and kept his eyes on it. "You'd have made me in a moment more."

"I like Aaron. He seems like a nice guy. I trust you implicitly, but if Aaron's a bad guy, he's one of the best actors of all time. Am I missing something or have I been contaminated by your FBI playmates?"

Clint nodded. "Maybe a little, baby. Remember the facts I explained. We don't ignore all those coincidences, and let our suave and sophisticated Aaron tempt us into putting our rose colored glasses on. Where this investigation stuff runs off the rails is when we try to reason the whys when we don't have a clue why. You hitting the slots now?"

Lynn stood up, polishing off her drink. "Yep. You'll be around in case I make the casino cry uncle, right?"

"Indeed. Be sure I'm around if you leave for another casino. I know you have the tools to handle any run of the mill mugger, but I don't want to leave anything to chance."

"Understood." Lynn shook her head, mentally admonishing herself for not picking up on Clint's disguise immediately. She didn't want to mention anything about second guessing him on her instincts about Aaron. *I've been around the block a few times, CD,* she thought with a grin. *If Aaron's a serial rapist, I'm Minnie Mouse.*

Walking with a deliberately paced sultriness very few women could pull off, Lynn made her way into a dollar slot cove, where she hesitated for a moment while studying the bank of slot machines. She felt eyes on her, as both male and female gamblers glanced at Montoya. Lynn reached her hand out as she glided up on the second machine from her right.

"There's my bitch!" Her exclamation elicited tittering laughter from other players within earshot. A waitress walking by stopped with suppressed laughter, and asked Lynn if she wanted a drink. "Sure. I'll take a Long Island Iced Tea. If it tastes like one when it gets here, I'll give you a twenty dollar tip."

"That's very generous of you, but not necessary. I will make sure I give you one to your liking." The casino server walked off and Lynn returned her attention to the slot machine.

Lynn stroked the sides of the slot machine, her motions drawing the attention of everyone playing in the room. She swayed from side to side in a slow, provocative manner, as if it were a near religious convergence. Montoya then straightened and poked a finger at the slot machine surface window.

"You will obey me!"

Her modulated outburst elicited another round of appreciative laughter. After putting in a twenty dollar bill for machine credit, Lynn hit the max number of coins, which was three on the machine, and pulled the handle. She won five thousand dollars. Except for the oscillating winner machine whoops of glory, there was stunned silence in the dollar cove. Lynn could hear Dostiene laughing on their com unit.

"Well… what do you know about that?"

"You'll need your photo ID, and social security number, Lynn. Lucky for you we took care of that before you decided to gamble. Hang tight, the attendant is approaching. This is great. If I have made an error in judgment, I should get a look at some other possible candidates."

Lynn looked around after hearing from Clint. A woman attendant approached and shook her hand.

"Congratulations!" The woman with Mandy on her nametag said. "You may not be aware of this, but anything over an $1199 jackpot will require reporting. We make this as painless as possible. May I see a photo ID please, and I'll need your social security number."

"Wonderful."

Twenty minutes later after producing the necessary documentation along with waiting for the machine to be inspected, Lynn had surveyed the people curious about her big win. She had her casino supplied tax form, winnings check, and the Long Island Iced Tea she'd ordered. After tasting it during the machine inspection and delays, Lynn tipped the waitress a hundred dollars, which made her very popular with the local staff. The attendant asked her to clear the machine, so Lynn pushed the max coin button, and pulled the lever rather than push the button. She won a $250 dollar jackpot, which surprised even the attendant.

"I think this machine likes you," Mandy told her as she paid Lynn in cash. "One more time before I walk away please."

Lynn repeated her winning formula, but this time came up empty. The small crowd watching the proceedings gave her a smattering of applause before drifting away. Sitting on her stool, Lynn sipped away at her drink, and fed money into the machine. After nearly an hour, she had only fed back fifty dollars, while sipping her way through a second Long Island Iced Tea. The second drink hit Lynn right down to her toes. Montoya stood up and walked a little unsteadily away from her machine, becoming more balanced with each step.

"You need to get some food, baby. That 'Long Tea' high is distracting you."

"I'm feeling good, CD.

Dostiene chuckled. "I'll bet you do. Want to try a walk on the wild side right away?"

Lynn walked toward the exit. "Sure. What did you have in mind?"

"There's an excellent Denny's restaurant up the road toward the Wynn's. You can get some fresh air on the hike, get a good meal, and then break the bank at the Wynn's."

"I like it! Want to eat with me, or is it too obvious?"

"If only I could. The fish are bitin'. We don't want to jiggle the line and let them off now. After you eat and make Wynn's cry, pick out a bar to have a drink at. I'll sidle up next to you while we imbibe together."

"That'll work too."

"Good. Stick around throwing in a little money while I take Tonto out for a stroll. I'll find you in about half an hour and let you know I'm on your tail."

"Oh baby... I wish you were on my tail now."

Clint snorted. "Damn it Lynn, now I have to walk around with my hat in front of my crotch."

Montoya laughed while detouring to the quarter slot machines near the exit. She fed a twenty in before hitting a two hundred and fifty dollar pay off. She smiled at what happens in casinos when you don't need money. Clint, in his rough persona, played a quarter slot machine near her before walking out the exit. Montoya played another couple of dollars without winning and left, walking out the main front entrance. She walked with a graceful glide toward the stoplight crossing that cannot be taught.

The temperature in early September had cooled considerably with a slight breeze. Lynn walked in the direction of Wynn's casino, breathing the cooling air with appreciation. Soon, she reached the section where a long high fence protected the construction project going on. It was very dark with little area to walk. When she reached a spot near the middle of the construction fence, even the faint light on the other side of the street cast very little illumination her way. More darkness than light continued on along the fence for quite a distance before the next active casino, The Riviera. She smiled, hearing Clint's voice in her ear.

"Man, you have one righteous walk. You have three nomads approaching. They just angled out of a spot one block up on your right. I don't think they're part of our problem, but they do seem interested in you. I can't hold that against them."

"I see them, CD – not impressed. If they come on to me I'll dissuade them on the down low. We can't tell if my earlier date is following me, trying to get the lay of the road, so I won't make a fuss."

"Define fuss," Clint requested, his lips tightening.

"Easy, buckaroo. I'll be okay."

"I know you will. I'm coming up on them from behind. See me?"

"Gee... you ruin everything," Lynn pouted as she came abreast of the three men with hoodies and pants at thigh level. The one nearest her as she passed grabbed her wrist, twisting to come up in front of her.

"Hi, baby doll. Where you headed?"

"Up the road for a little food and more gambling," Lynn answered as Clint came up quick and sudden behind the young men.

"Hey lady, these young chumps bothering you?" Clint asked. "I can tell you sweethearts ain't ever been in prison. When you wear your damn pants low like that in prison it means you want a soul train up the ass."

Montoya tried desperately not to laugh, but the snorting attempts turned into full blown laughter. When the one nearest Dostiene tried sucker punching him, he ducked back and smashed a side kick to the man's knee. It gave out with a sickening crunch followed by a scream from its owner.

"Best pick your boy up and move along, meat," Clint advised, meeting the stunned looks of his victim's cohorts with a steady gaze. "If you don't, you'll be joinin' him. You feel me?"

The two picked up their comrade, who had begun to sob. They retreated toward the block they came from with their friend hobbling between them. Lynn backed away from Dostiene in horror. He acted the part of a concerned citizen, but Lynn's hand gestures and body language made it plain she did not want anything to do with him.

"You hurt that poor kid!"

"Sorry… I… never mind." Clint walked in the direction of the Wynn's, playing for any observer a real attempt to just get away.

Only after a few moments of glancing in the three men's direction and forward toward the Wynn's did Lynn move. "Well damn! Now that was entertainment. You got somethin' against the drop drawer look, Clint?"

"I hate that shit," Dostiene admitted. "Back on point, those jerks weren't our target anyway. I think we played the innocent bystanders' roles very well. Let's proceed as planned. I didn't want you marked up for our real target. We'll compare notes in your room later."

For the first time Montoya took note. "Well then… you must like my choice of outfits."

"I sure as hell like the way you fill them."

"I'm getting into your mind, Ace. I have my butterfly knife. I could have showed them a few tricks and been on my way. You may have hurt that poor young pants dangling nitwit for nothing. Aren't you ashamed of yourself?"

Clint chuckled. "Not hardly. How are you feeling?"

"Hungry. This walk killed my buzz, and put food up into my head."

"Good. I'll grab a bite at the Denny's with you – not at the same table of course, but close. We can still talk to each other. I like being with you… a lot."

Montoya slowed, her mind racing around that admission. "Shit, Clint, why don't we take the money we have and run? We could get a little place by the beach somewhere and go native."

"A couple of reasons, sweetie – we have needs. Those needs may not be what normal people have, but they're just as distracting. We kill people, and it doesn't bother us at all. We both have a sense of what's right and wrong. We get off wasting bad guys. We're an anomaly, Lynn. Money, beaches in the sun, not working – not interested. How about you?"

Montoya snorted amusement before heaving a big sigh. "You're right, CD. If we retired now together, we'd probably either kill a lot of people or each other."

"I wasn't quite as pessimistic as that, but I did figure we might end up in prison."

Montoya began to reply, but slapped at her neck. She felt the dart. "Oh shi… it."

Dostiene spun around, running full out back toward Montoya's last position, cursing himself with each step. He shed his feelings with every movement, steeling himself to think of nothing other than reaching her.

　　　* * *

"Well… hell… Aaron," Montoya whispered, looking up at the man who had grabbed her before she could fall. She fought the debilitating drug with all her will, pinching her leg hard, while moving her head rapidly, trying to fight off unconsciousness. Her attacker held her up against him as if trying to steady her.

"Damn, Lynn," the man said through clenched teeth. He grabbed her chin tightly, giving it a shake "That should have put you out cold already. I'm afraid you're going to have an accident. Recognizing me is not in our plan. My friend's not going to like this."

Lynn grabbed backward with her right hand, encasing the man's crotch and squeezing with all the might she could muster. She giggled at his scream of agony. He pitched back away from her with both hitting the pavement hard. A black van screeched to a halt next to them, Edgar Constanza leaped from the driver's seat, gun in hand, racing around the back of the van. Lynn struggled to stay conscious, reaching for her purse with numb, tingling fingers, smiling at the grainy blackness descending all too quickly.

"Shoot that bitch!" Constanza's partner yelled out while writhing on the ground, his hands at his groin.

"I can't shoot her out here, you stupid asshole!" Constanza reached down to the pawing Montoya a moment before his head exploded. The hollow point .45 caliber slug entered one side of his head, burst apart like a cannon ball, spraying skull and brain matter over his partner, followed by Constanza's brainless corpse.

Vehicles slowed as Dostiene ran up, glancing at the sparse but ever present strip traffic. He watched the man momentarily trapped under Constanza's body, scramble away, coated in blood and brain matter while issuing a keening whine of a sound. Clint made sure the man could see the .45 automatic in his hand. With one hand still cradling his groin, the man used his free hand to make surrendering motions.

"Don't shoot! I give up!"

Crouched between his target and Montoya, Dostiene didn't see Lynn free the butterfly knife from her purse. She flipped it open with deliberate care, staring at the gesturing man across from her. With superhuman will, Montoya lurched past Clint onto her attacker, plunging the blade into his crotch to the hilt. The high pitched scream he emitted with helpless flailing arms ended as Lynn pulled the knife free, and buried it up into the man's heart. Clint, at first reacted instinctively, reaching for Lynn, but had then stepped back, turning to watch for pedestrian traffic, grinning. He turned back as Montoya rolled weakly off the twitching body.

Clint pulled out his iPhone, contacting Sam Reeves while holstering his weapon, and sitting down next to Lynn. He hugged her up against him, waiting for Reeves to answer. When he heard Reeves' voice, Dostiene cut him off. "Sam! We have an officer down and two perps dead. Key into my GPS, and get the meat wagon and an ambulance here now."

"How… shit… okay, fifteen minutes."

Clint set the phone down, still connected to Reeves next to him. He cradled Montoya's chin, watching her battle savagely against passing out. "It's okay, baby. We got our scene airtight now with all the trimmings. Let it go. I'll be with you every minute. That, my lady, was one very sweet wrap-up," Clint whispered.

Lynn sighed, her body relaxing against Dostiene as she lost consciousness. Clint spent the minutes until Reeves and Labrie arrived threading his story together. To their credit, the FBI agents beat the ambulance to them. Reeves reached Dostiene's side first - weapon drawn with Labrie backing him up.

"Are you hit?" Reeves asked, glancing around at the bloody scene.

"No, but while Lynn played the bait, she got hit with a drugged dart. That's how they've been doing this. She struggled long enough for the getaway van to get here. I came up on the scene as Lynn got her knife free with the guy's partner running up on them from the van. He had a gun which he aimed at Lynn. I shot him, and Lynn managed to do his partner before passing out."

Labrie had been inspecting the bodies. She nodded over at Reeves. "They're gone, Sam. I don't suppose you have any way of tying the dead into the actual crimes, do you, Clint?"

"As a matter of fact, I do. We were simply setting up a pattern. I figured they'd move on her in a day or two. They surprised us, me in particular." Clint pulled the dart from Montoya's neck, holding it up for the two FBI agents to see. "The dart explains a lot about how they've managed to pull these rapes off. God only knows how Lynn managed to remain conscious."

Labrie held up a bag for Clint to drop the dart in. An ambulance arrived on scene. Two EMT's rushed over to Montoya. Dostiene backed away, letting them check her vital signs before loading her on a stretcher. Dostiene took out his .45 automatic out, popped the clip, and cleared the chamber, placing all parts in the bag Reeves held out for him.

"Can you two take over here? I promised Lynn I'd stay with her until she woke again."

Reeves nodded. "Go on. I'll need a statement when you can put one together."

"You bet." Dostiene started to follow the EMT's, but Reeves grabbed his arm.

"This looks real good, Clint. Is that Montoya's knife still in the guy?"

"That's the one."

"Okay... go on ahead. We'll talk to you tomorrow."

Chapter Nine
Aftermath and an Airport Incursion

Reeves waited until the ambulance with Montoya and Dostiene left the scene before trading knowing looks with his partner. "I sure hope you find the dart gun on that poor dimwit growing the handle of a knife out of his chest."

Labrie went over with gloved hands and carefully felt through clothing. She found the oversized dart gun inside the corpse's jacket. "It's here, but we better wait for our buddies with the LVPD to get here with their famous CSI unit."

Reeves grinned. "Yeah, that would be interesting. I have no doubt these are the two responsible, although as usual we were a couple steps behind Dostiene. He'll have to clue us in on how he knew there were two. The cops will love this. The rapes and mutilations end. There won't be any expensive trials, and the tourist business goes back to normal."

The approaching sirens caused Labrie to pat the clothing back into place and retreat over next to her partner. "You thinking what I'm thinking?"

Reeves stared at Labrie for a moment. "You mean that these two never had a prayer?"

"Nope," Labrie replied. "I'm thinking I'd like those Harvard serial killers to end up the same way."

"I have no problem with that. There are some people who just need killing. I'll tell you something else I'm thinking - Dostiene has met his match."

Labrie glanced over at the body with a pool of blood under his groin, and the handle of a deadly Balisong knife sticking out of his chest. "Yeah, I think you're right. Did you really suspect Clint shot her with the dart himself to set this all up?"

"Let's leave it at I'm glad you found the dart gun on the perp. With the amount of blood and brain matter all over the guy,

I'm sure some of it got on the gun, and there won't be any doubt Montoya was hit by the dart before the shooting."

"Well, like you said, the PD is going to love us, and the mayor will want to give us a key to the city."

"I can't wait to read Clint's report."

"That makes two of us, partner," Labrie replied as they met with the arriving police officers.

* * *

When Lynn woke up, Dostiene patted her hand he held in both of his. "Hey, baby, how do you feel?"

Montoya smiled at him, a tired upswing of her lips. "I'm fine... just a little out of it. It wasn't a dream. We got the bastards, Clint. Didn't we?"

"Oh yeah. They screwed me up hitting you that quick. It's just like I thought though. No Snow White could have held them up long enough for me to get there. You were incredible."

"Thank you. It's nice to be appreciated. When can I get the hell out of here?"

"The doctor said I could take you back to the hotel whenever you felt up to it. I bought you a robe. Your dress was a mess."

"Help me up, and get that robe on me. How long has Tonto been alone?"

"He'll be fine." Clint helped Lynn into her new robe after he called for the nurse and a taxi. She arrived with a wheel chair. Fifteen minutes later, Dostiene helped Lynn into the back of a Lincoln Town Car taxi.

At the Stratosphere, Clint walked her up to the Oasis Suite. It being Las Vegas, they hardly drew a second look. Once Clint had Montoya in bed, he went to get Tonto for a walk. He jogged with him for a couple of miles, the cooling desert air therapeutic for both man and dog. Clint didn't bother playing blind man's bluff anymore. He stopped in at the desk with Tonto to show his FBI credentials to the night manager with Royal Kershner on his nametag, explaining about the investigation and ending to the rapists' case.

"We'll be staying a while until Agent Montoya and I clear things up." Clint put ten one hundred dollar bills on his desk. "Something on account in case you get worried about Tonto, Mr. Kershner."

"Thank you. That's very generous. Enjoy your stay." He handed Dostiene one of his cards. "If you need anything, call me."

"I will, but we'll be mostly vacationing now that the case is closed. Thank you."

After walking Tonto up to his room, Dostiene made sure he had treats and water before joining Lynn. She was breathing easy, so Clint stripped to his boxers and simply slid in next to her. He fell asleep easily. After getting five hours sleep, Clint made coffee in the little hotel coffee maker, and left a note for Lynn he was going to run Tonto around. She was sitting up when he returned. The Jacuzzi tub was full.

"Good morning, partner," Lynn greeted him. "I have to get one of those dart guns. That's the best sleep I've had in ages."

Clint sat on the bed next to her. "No headache or anything?"

"Nope. Just this weird craving to jump your bones and then jump into the Jacuzzi."

"Sounds good to me. Are you sure you feel well enough to fool around?"

Montoya moved over Dostiene with a moan of pleasure. "I feel a hell of a lot better than our two recently deceased rapists. That was a joke about me not being ready for action, right?"

"Yeah, but not a very funny one, baby. You are definitely ready."

* * *

My entourage and I are waiting at baggage claim when my new i-thingy goes off. It's face-time with Denny. See, this is what happens when some new gimmick hits. Even crusty old government clowns like Strobert start panting over it like a dog in heat. I answer it with my hand in front of the screen.

"What the hell?" Denny starts chuckling.

"Talk to the hand."

123

"Get that catcher's mitt out of the way, John. You'll never believe what went down last night. Clint hit town with psycho-girl, and the two of them cancelled out the rapists their first night in. When I say cancelled, I mean with attitude."

I removed my hand and stepped over to a less crowded spot. "Damn. Those two are like a Reaper Drone. Gee, no long investigations, no read them their rights, court trials, or sob stories, huh?"

"One took a .45 hollow point dead center head, and the other wasn't so lucky. Psycho-girl overcame a drug dart to make a large incision into the other one's dick, followed by a plunge into his black heart. They're over at the Stratosphere. I think she's going to work out real fine."

"That's an understatement. Maybe it would be wise for you to stop calling her names, before she decides to adjust your attitude. Since they fixed up their cover job, has our preferred opportunity arrived yet?"

"Not until tomorrow. Take a day to get settled in, while my new recruits handle fallout and paperwork. I'll call the moment I have confirmation on touchdown. What do you have to take care of for the fight?"

"Check-in, weigh-in, media crapolla," I blurted out for him. In other words, I'll be in the public eye, which means Dostiene and Montoya will be staying far away from me. I'm the distraction over the next few days, even if I see our main target. "At least Clint will have extra time to concentrate on a plan. I'll do my best to be a pain for the Slayer and his crew to deal with."

"Don't do anything to bust this deal up. I hear Dixon got out of the hospital finally."

"Who cares?"

Denny gets a chuckle at that. "Just so they have plenty of security at those weigh-ins. I don't want the 'Slayer' to get too excited and start something that messes with our time frame. I need this fight to go on schedule. If you lost the fight, our boy would probably go on a three day bender to celebrate. What's chances of that?"

Denny living dangerously. Who knew? "I hope you meant if he actually wins, right?"

Denny smiles. "Of course, John. What did you think I meant. I was just asking for your professional opinion about the 'Slayer's' chances. I take it you don't think much of his winning, so I'll have to make sure Clint has his girlfriend apprised of the time limits. She'll have up until fight night to work her magic. I'm glad you came in a full week early. I bet you're going to like the Mandalay Bay. Did you really bring everyone and their immediate families?"

"We made a bundle on the Dixon fight. I decided to keep the troops happy, so I closed up shop for a week. Samira came to Sin City with Jafar. It will be a kick seeing those two wander around this place. Jafar's a little jaded, having already been in Dubai, but Samira has never been in a Las Vegas. We all know it's a working holiday. I'll have enough guys tracking, with Jafar coordinating from hack central at the Mandalay, that we will know everything going on to the minute. The kid worked the last two weeks installing worms throughout every casino on the strip. With the street and light cams, your friend won't be able to sneeze without us knowing about it."

"You're keeping Samira's rather dangerous status in mind, right? There will be a lot of old country, Middle Eastern goons in town for the fight. I don't want anything to happen to our star speaker."

I looked at Denny with the disdain he deserved, hoping the i-thingy conveyed my feelings. Jafar was like my younger brother, and I'd been looking out for Samira since she was a kid. Lucas and Casey adopted Jafar. He sets up their sound systems, repairs and maintains all their computers, and has learned to maintain everything on The Sea Wolf. In fact, he's the only one allowed on The Sea Wolf. We aren't the girl scouts. We have a very good threat matrix. It won't be a haphazard attack from some old school Muslim wanker we have to worry about.

"I see in your face I've stepped in it," Denny volunteers without prompting. "I have to mention this stuff. I'm the bad guy. Where's Samira's dog?"

"With Jafar's parents. They love Haji and Samira. Jafar's old man is back to work and long on the wagon. I think they're figuring on grandkids in short order. Do you need a meet up with all the players somewhere out of the city?"

Denny nodded. "Maybe. Do you think a place like Sam's Town would be far enough off the beaten path? I like their bar area."

"Yeah, I like that place. I'll be training every day, but it would be better to do a meeting late at night somewhere anyway. Let me know." I spot Al on her way over. "I think it's time to go, Denny. I'm still working on a secondary plan B if A doesn't work out. It will be better knowing for sure where our buddy's staying."

"You'll know when I do. I'm thinking it would be better if Jafar just hacks their final plans after check in. They have his check in plans very well hidden."

Al gives me the come on motion. "I have to go. I'll be training starting at 6AM."

"I'll call you then," Denny acknowledges and disconnects.

I'm getting as excited about all these long range plans as Denny. If some stuffed shirt pussy politician ever gets wind of our West Coast band of brothers, they'll probably call in a drone strike on us. I admit I'm frothing at the mouth to run over and tell Lucas and Casey about what Clint and his girl already did, but it'll have to wait. I see all the wives and girlfriends are directing the baggage claim, led by the instigator, my wife Lora. Al grabs my hand.

"You better get over there, Dark Lord. A guy's been hitting on Mom, and I think Mr. Blake is getting ready to make a scene."

"Looking as good as your Mom does today, she deserves to be hit on. Don't worry about Mr. Blake. He won't mess with anyone unless they get insulting. Did you like the plane ride?"

Alice looks up at me as we walk, and shrugs. "I thought the landing was kind of rough."

"I agree. It felt like the pilot forgot to put the wheels down." I pointed at the suit being very attentive with Lora, who was laughing at something he was saying. "It looks like your Mom's having fun, Al. Is that the guy?"

"Yeah. I don't like him."

I spot my whole crew. They're big, mean looking, and dangerous as an avalanche. Devon Constantine and Jesse Brown are my corner crew along with Jafar and Tommy. They have their wives with them. Lucas and Casey are smiling at me with their significant others hanging on their arms. Tommy and his wife have corralled two baggage people with carts, and were having them brought over. Jafar and Samira watched the baggage carrousel anxiously, because I know my young friend is worried about all the electronics gear he's brought along.

"Let's go over by Lucas and Casey, Al. That guy's not bothering your Mom. You can help me pick out the bags to unload so Tommy doesn't start yellin' at me in the airport. They're the ones with big purple ID bows on them."

Al resists my light tug for a moment, watching her Mom still sharing laughs with the suit, and then allows me to pull her along with me. "Aren't you jealous, John?"

That stopped me, as I saw Lucas and Casey edging nearer, having heard what Al said. "Why should I be, Al. Your Mom picked me in spite of all my faults. What? You think she's going to dump me in favor of some silver tongued devil stranger in an airport? Consider this too, young lady. What could I do about it if she did?"

Al met my questioning glance with her 'are you kidding me' look. "You could Gronk him."

That set Lucas, Casey, and the Dark Lord into a laughing binge.

"Yeah, DL," Casey directed. "Go Gronk that sucker."

Lucas is still trying to get his breath. "It…it's the right thing to do, DL. Gronk him."

I immediately switched into Dark Lord voice. "The Dark Lord does not Gronk hapless strangers."

By then Tommy and his wife Rachel arrive to hear the Gronking orders. Rachel's laughing, but Tommy of course is scowling. "I told you to leave the Dark Lord in Oakland this trip! Who are you supposed to Gronk anyway?"

I gestured toward Lora, and her suitor. "Al thinks I'm getting dumped in favor of the suit over there serenading Lora. She wants me to Gronk him."

Tommy smiles and puts a comforting hand on Alice's shoulder. "Don't worry, Al. Your Mom would never give up bossing around all us serfs to be with some new guy. Do you know something we don't? Is your Mom finally getting tired of this Neanderthal?"

Alice giggled, and of course the rest of our audience got a big yuck out of that, including the wives. Al looks up at me though. "I don't want to move, DL."

That silenced everyone, including me. I looked over at Lora and the guy still yakking away, trying to figure out what about the guy would worry Alice. Granted, I am a Neanderthal in a lot of ways, but Lora spent a lot of time training me. It wasn't likely she would want to get a new puppy. I look back around at my friends and everyone's staring at me.

"What did you do, John?" Rachel demands, which gets a smile on Tommy's face.

"What? I didn't do anything." It kind of surprises me when my good looking wife gets some attention, and suddenly I'm chopped liver.

I notice then that Lora is heading our way with the guy keeping pace.

"Damn," Lucas remarks. "I think Al's right. That guy's really hitting on her."

"Told you," Al states, yanking on my wrist. "Gronk him."

"Ah... no."

Lora arrives next to us a moment later. She even seems surprised the guy is still with her. The suit looks around at us all with a curious look. He's a couple inches over six feet, clean shaven, and looks a little like Jafar's older brother. Lora gestures at him politely.

"This is Neal Halabi. He is in the city for the fight too," Lora announces. "Neal, this is my husband, John Harding, my daughter Alice, and our coworkers."

I shake hands with him, noting that at least he doesn't give me a dead flounder handshake. "I'm glad to meet you."

"You are the John Harding fighting 'The Syrian Slayer', are you not?"

I'm not sure if the Dark Lord has a spidey sense, but if I did, it's tingling. Maybe I should have Gronked him. "Yep. That would be me."

"I have a message for you, Mr. Harding." Neal smiled at me like we were friends. "May I give it to you in private, please?"

"Sure, Mr. Halabi. We can talk over here." I gesture at the side of the baggage claim area. I meet eyes with Lucas and Casey. They immediately fan out. Jafar is already face-timing with Denny. Lora directs the baggage handling to my unhappy cohorts without Government Inc credentials.

When we get over next to the wall, I put on my attentive look of curiosity. "Is this okay, Neal?"

The cunning gaze of the predator leaks out slowly across my companion's features. "This is very good. You will lose to 'The Syrian Slayer', Mr. Harding. A large amount of money will be transferred to you after the fight."

I look surprised. "Why in the world would I do that?"

Then it gets deadly. Neal drops all pretense. He's a killer and he thinks I'm impressed. "If you do not lose, you will lose anyway, Mr. Harding. You have a lovely family. Sometimes these sporting events go beyond normal parameters. Let us handle this in a strictly business manner."

I Gronked him. It was a short right hand to the temple, and baby, it was all business. I caught up Neal as if we were old buddies, embracing an old friendship. Casey and Lucas were at my side immediately as we laughed and escorted our inebriated friend along. Tommy's scowl turned serious. He hustled bags, family, and appreciative attendants to handle everything. I motioned Jafar to stay with Tommy. The fun went out for Devon and Jesse as they astutely recognized trouble and acted accordingly. I did catch a small all knowing smile from my good as blood kin Alice. She aced me and knew it. My God, that's embarrassing.

Lucas quickly rented a full sized Chevy Tahoe from Hertz while Casey and I sat with our friend Neal. The SUV was brought around and parked out front. We loaded Neal up and went on a scenic route of Las Vegas as I texted Denny we were in a safe spot to talk. We waited in comfortable silence until Denny got on line.

Denny didn't waste time. "His name is Bishara Khalid. He's a Syrian national, and on the no fly list. Since he's here, he's here illegally. I'm gambling. I don't think this is related to our main visitation. Due to necessity, I set up an immediate meet at a safe house we control only five minutes from the airport. Clint and Montoya are going to meet us there in one hour, but feel free to get started without them. I'll be there waiting. I don't want anything to crab our other deal. How'd we look for eyes on this ding-a-ling?"

"Casey and I combed the baggage claim area in spreading circles," Lucas told him. "It was immediate and we turned up nothing after John Gronked him."

"John Gronked him?"

"Yeah, John's daughter, Alice scoped this guy out in the first minute of his approach," Casey explained. "The term is taken from a case prior to this one. We've officially adopted it since John Gronked this clown a few seconds after he let John know he was supposed to lose the fight, or have family safety issues. If he knew what was happening, he would never have approached us with a threat."

Denny pondered that for a moment. "You're right, Case. I'll keep Clint and Montoya out of the soup for now until you guys find out what this clown was really after. Man, you really must have pissed off the Slayer, John."

"It's probably his handlers. They have more money than brains. To get a guy like this Khalid to face me down in an airport must have cost them a small fortune, not to mention what he was threatening me with."

"Let me make a few calls. I know a couple things now about your companion I'm tying up. I put the safe house address in your inbox. Go there, and I'll contact you."

I wanted to get one thing clear with Denny before he went on his merry way. "You understand that this clown has a date with the desert, right?"

Denny grinned at me from the i-thingy. "Let me see what I can do with him, John. You get final say though. Fair enough?"

"Okay, but don't get cute. If I think I'm getting played, I'll snap this sucker's neck."

"Understood."

Khalid began groaning shortly after Denny hung up and we were on our way to the safe house. We had his arms secured behind his back. I also confiscated everything he had on his person. He was only carrying incidentals like fake ID, and money. He began sputtering and blinking his eyes, trying to focus on where he was.

"Where are… you taking me?"

We ignored him. Why have conversations with dead men?

"If you knew me you would not be doing this." Khalid tried the ominous dark threat gambit. "Free me, and you live. Otherwise, you will all die."

Casey laughed and patted his shoulder. "Good one, partner."

My i-thingy went off. It was Alexi Fiialkov. I hesitated to take the call with Khalid there, but there wasn't much Alexi didn't know anyway with the canary he had working in Interpol. It was just a call anyway, so I answered.

"John, Mr. Strobert told me you have Bishara Khalid. Please let me have him. I will find out anything you want, but I have much personal business to attend to with him. He tortured and murdered my brother in France. You have my word he will never surface again."

Well, Denny must have worked a fat quid pro quo for this turn of events. That means Denny knew about the Fiialkov angle before he even talked to me. That works for me anyhow. "Tell me where and when, Alexi."

"I own the safe house your Mr. Strobert directed you to. Please proceed there as you originally planned. I will meet you in a short time. Thank you, John."

"No problem at all, Alexi." Neal is now staring at me in horror. I don't blame him.

"I will tell you anything you want to know… anything!"

Lucas has pulled over and parked. He doesn't like guessing about this new paradigm. Casey's grinning from ear to ear. He's been watching the transformation from threatening asshole to begging for mercy dead man with interest. Casey, Lucas, Clint, and I have been where this Khalid is now. It's one of the main reasons if we know one of us is in trouble, no government sock puppet is going to tell us to stay out of it. I don't think Khalid will be expecting any help. In fact, my guess is he got complacent, and the airport faceoff was his idea. He thought he could scare some Joe Citizen nobody. Whoops.

"What's up, John," Lucas asked.

"Denny made a trade for a player to be named later. Alexi Fiialkov owns the safe house where Denny's sending us. Apparently, Satan's Spawn saw our Neal, found out who he was, and who wanted him. We're to continue on to Fiialkov's safe house. We drop our buddy off, and then we get back to the Mandalay Bay.

"You must turn me over to the authorities!"

Lucas smiled, started the motor again, and headed for the safe house. Casey and I leaned back in our seats on either side of Khalid.

"Sucks to be you, partner," Casey observed.

* * *

Lora and her Minnie-me greet me together at the door to our suite.

"I saw you Gronk that guy, John," Minnie-me performs a reasonable imitation of her Mom with hands on hips splendor. "Tell Mom who put you onto him."

I looked at Lora, and launched the Dark Lord. "Your Minnie-me is out of control. She walks over in a public airport, points to a stranger, and orders the Dark Lord to Gronk him. I think she needs an intervention."

Alice giggles, but Lora keeps her serious face. "Yeah. Apparently, my daughter has more sense than I do. I'm sorry about that, John."

"Forget it. Alice was the only one of my crew that knew something was up with that guy. It's all on our radar now. I had Jafar text everyone as to this new wrinkle in our stay. Besides, Alice didn't think he was dangerous. She was afraid he'd sweep you off your feet and take you away from me. Alice didn't want to move."

"What?" Lora stares down at her daughter who meets her gaze with her own unblinking attention, which cracks me up. "Why in the world would you think that?"

"You were all over him, Mom. It was embarrassing. I needed to get John before you-"

Alice ran for it with a scream. She saw Mount Vesuvius begin to erupt over Lora's facial features. She streaked into the bathroom and locked it a nanosecond before Lora's fist pounding arrival. "Oh, it is so on, young lady! I'm making the rounds right now of every electronic gadget you've brought along. By the time you emerge from your hidey hole you will be tech free. I hope you brought something to read."

"Dark Lord! You owe me!"

"The Dark Lord is here, little one. Wicked lady, how dare you confiscate the great Beeper from your daughter! The Beeper must be free!"

Alice corrects me with an instant scream through the door, much to Lora's muffled amusement. "It's Bieber!"

"Come out of that bathroom or the only sound you'll be hearing will be beepers on the street outside."

"Okay… but no hitting. I can't help it if you were lining up replacements for the Dark Lord in a public airport. I call 'em like I see 'em."

"Why you little…" Lora looks ready to smash down the door. I'm no use because I'm howling in laughter. "Oh girl, you and I are going to have a long talk about appropriate conversation from a nine year old."

"I hope some of the talk has to do with how to keep a Mom from flirting inappropriately with strangers."

Lora is steaming, and I'm helpless. She of course turns on me. "Alice has never spoken to me like this before you started egging her on, DL."

"Hey... at least her vocabulary is improving. I may laugh, but inside I'm a hundred percent behind you." I make inappropriate motions as if I were behind her. Lora starts laughing, and Alice takes that as a sign she can exit the bathroom.

She smiles up at me. "So, where did you take the mysterious stranger, DL?"

"We don't ask that, Al," Lora said.

"She needs to know, Hon. It turned out, the man was there to prove how close he could get to you and your Mom, Al. He wanted me to lose the fight against Abdul Bacca. If I didn't lose, he threatened that something bad would happen to you and your Mom."

"But something bad happened to him instead," Alice concluded.

"Exactly. I want you to keep your eyes and ears open all the time. You did real good today, Al. I promise you, I won't ever ignore something you tell me. I may not Gronk on command, but I will investigate. All the guys like your new word."

Alice nodded, but turned on her Mom, finger wagging. "You, young lady, will not talk to strangers unless you talk to me first about it."

I saw defeat in Lora's eyes as she accepted the zap in good spirits. She hung her head. "Yes, Dark Lord Junior."

"This has been wonderful ladies. I have to meet my crew at the training facility they set up for us. I should be back in a few hours. I have to go get my bag. Truce?"

Lora and her Minnie-me exchanged looks and shrugs.

"We're okay, John," Lora said with a grin. "She got me good. I know you have to train. We'll see you later after you get back. Should we stay in until you return? I was going to take Alice over to Circus/Circus for their show. Is that okay?"

"Just as planned. Lucas, Casey, Jafar and their wives are going with you and Al. Tommy, Devon, and Jesse will be working out with me. Their girls want to gamble, so Rachel will be leading that excursion."

"Are we going to meet your new friends joining the crew on the coast?"

"Yes. Just as soon as I can arrange it." Lora stored my single sentence item about Clint and Lynn, which means she's already figuring slots to put them in. "With those two in the crew, we are going big time. You're going to like them."

"If Clint's as good at investigations as you claimed, I already like him," Lora replied. "He can do missing persons, runaways, and help out on all the crap Denny keeps trying to push our way too, right?"

Yep. She's on it. "That's the plan, Hon. He's tracked down serial killers the FBI couldn't find, and is in the middle of a serial rapist consulting job for them right now here in Las Vegas. He and his partner Lynn have already wrapped it up."

"Can I meet them too, John?"

"Sure, Al." From the look on Minnie-me's face, I'm thinking she has it in mind to give them the third degree. "I better grab my gym bag and get out of here before Tommy comes up and starts slapping me around."

Chapter Ten
Training Day, Killing Day

Nearly three hours later, Tommy still had Dev and Jesse working me over. We were doing all ground and pound, because that's where I planned to take 'The Slayer'. I had a feeling after the last time when I busted him up with the leg kicks, and eventually broke his arm on the mat, he'd be really humping to get me on the mat under his terms. The good thing was he could not be in steroid land this trip around, because they'd nail him in the pre-fight drug test. I know the lab coats are working on some undetectable Testosterone mix to juice up the fighters, but that didn't work out for a few of the major league baseball players. I was hoping to do the 'Slayer' without him bringing on the extras. I didn't want a disqualification for him either.

I did a sweet roll over, pinning Dev in an arm bar he tapped out immediately from. Tommy was frowning, because he had been tag teaming my two trainers, letting them work me over during the switch together. He also kept them at it for three five minute rounds with no rest. Devon Constantine and Jesse Brown were pros. As part of my team they watched my opponents hour after hour when there is any video of them at all. Since most of my fights are brawls in the warehouse cage, many times they have to go see my prospective opponents fight in person. When we hear of a contender beatin' the crap out of everyone, Dev and Jesse go and take their own videos. Driver and escort work for tourists, along with an occasional bond apprehension rounded out their duties.

"Let's knock off on that lucky move," Tommy announced.

I helped Dev up. Jesse was already chuckling. "Did that seem lucky to you, Dev?"

Dev grinned. "Maybe somewhere in Tommy land, DL. Let's get cleaned up and get this vacation underway. Between punks screwin' with us on arrival, and T the slave driver, I need some downtime."

Jesse clapped me on the back. "That was one righteous move, brother. If the 'Slayer' moves a little slow pulling in his wings, you'll end him. Dev's right, we need to get this party started."

"No party for Lucky here yet," Tommy said. "You two take off. Lucky has a five mile run to cool down with."

Dev put an arm around my shoulders. "Gronk him, DL. Jesse and I will say Tommy tripped."

We all got a hee-haw out of that one, even Tommy. "I'll be okay with the run. You guys go ahead. I'm betting my Circus/Circus crew's not back yet from the shows anyway. You runnin' with me, T?"

"I'm the manager, not some two bit pug due for some road work. Get movin' Lucky before I make it ten miles."

Another hee-haw with Jesse coming to my defense. "That's just mean, T."

"While John was dealing with our airport greeter, I had eyes on the 'Slayer' work out earlier, where he does his business off site, through a contact I have. They must have some kind of secret formula the lab can't detect. He doesn't look any different than the last time, except bigger. I'm doing Lucky here a favor. You can bet old Abdul ain't forgot that broken arm from their last meet up."

I nod. "Tommy's right. If he's that impressive, I'll have to wear him down. See you guys later. We're all on our own tonight, so have fun."

Tommy starts rubbing his chin. "Make sure it's a hill climb on the machine. I'm thinking forty-five degrees."

"I'm thinking maybe I will Gronk you," I reply to laughter from Dev and Jesse.

      * * *

I notice a presence behind and to the left of me. When you've been in the business as long as I have even four and half miles into the hill climber doesn't shut off that sense of self preservation. I speed it up for the last half mile. I'm in the Mandalay Bay Gym so I don't expect a lot of attention. It's quiet this time of day, but there are still people around. I finish off the five miles, and slow down to cool off.

"It's just me, partner," Clint states quietly before walking up next to me. "This gym's a bit nicer than the one down at the Stratosphere, but the machines look pretty close to the same. I watched your workout earlier off site without being seen. You guys ain't foolin' around. I haven't got a look at your opponent yet, but he better be in shape or have a sledgehammer in both hands. Denny told me a little about your last hookup with him."

I smile over at him while toweling off. "Hey, Clint. Yeah, Tommy busts my butt. He likes the UFC stuff, and so does my crew. I like the Oakland warehouse. My present opponent, The Syrian Slayer, refurbished it so he could pound me into oblivion on Al Jazeera pay per view. We have a nice cage and everything."

"How'd that work out for him?"

"Well, he bought the judges, referee, and one of the promoters. I broke his arm."

Clint laughed. "Then it was just like Denny told me. What the hell does he want with a rematch?"

"Tommy says he looks bigger than he did before when he was already mainlining steroids. T thinks the lab boys may have come up with an undetectable booster. We didn't part on good terms, so Abdul will be wanting blood. I plan on giving him some... and of course taking. Lora wants to meet you. Would you and Lynn like to go for dinner with us tonight? We can meet over at Sam's Town. It's out of the way, and they have good food."

"I'd like that, John. How about eight?"

"That works for me. I know our buddy from out of town will be arriving tomorrow, and Lynn will have to go into character. We're still backing you up right?"

Clint nodded. "Yep. Denny has it all planned out according to him. He knows all the places Darzi loves in Vegas already. It will be up to Lynn from there. If we have to go to Plan B, things could get messy, so I'm hoping she can charm him into the last roundup. Do you have any preferences as to when in regard to your fight?"

"Nope. We get 'er done. Denny would like me to throw the fight, so Lynn will have an easier time while Darzi is celebrating a Slayer win. What do you think of that plan?"

Clint smiles and says nothing.

"Yep. That's what I thought of it too. I'd like to make it easy on Lynn, but that is not going to happen unless it's for real, and I admit it's a possibility. One of these days I'll get my clock cleaned."

"Hell, with your damn pain threshold, you'll probably like it better."

Yeah, me and pain are mates. Clint knows it. "I'll let you know when it happens. Maybe, this'll be the time, but-"

"Harding!"

Out by the gym entrance, the opening is filled with 'Slayer' and a four pack of Middle Eastern goons. They're all decked out in suits, looking very impressive. I didn't think the Slayer and his crew were going to hit the party circuit for a while, meaning going out in public, but it won't matter. I know Abdul won't want any rough stuff before payday arrives. We never really traded much talk at our last get together, so other than him being a cheat, I really didn't have an opinion about him. I wave as Clint moves slightly away from me. It's already too late for pretending we don't know each other.

"That's your opponent, John?" Clint whispers over at me. "Damn."

"Yep, that's my pal Abdul," I whisper back at him, as the entourage approaches.

"I am glad to find you, Harding," Abdul tells me, the smile flickering away from his face. "Death is the only way to end our bond, John Harding."

I grin at the goofball. We don't have a bond. We don't even have a connection. I'm going to kick the crap out of him or he'll kick the crap out of me. There is no bond. "So, how can I help you today, Abdul?"

"I have lived only to see fear in your eyes."

Clint starts laughing. One of the thugs in Abdul's entourage moves over and grabs hold of Clint. In seconds, Clint reverses the man's hold, arching his arm up high behind his back. "Don't know what you think you're doin', but I don't like being handled."

Clint pushes and releases the man back amongst his brethren. "I'm sure you gentlemen have business with John I can't help you with, so I'll be going. See you later, John."

"You bet, brother."

"Wait!" Abdul commands, irritated at Clint's tone. "Why do you think Harding will even leave here alive?"

Clint and I both chuckle at that question. He glances around at Abdul and his retinue with professional courtesy. "John will be okay. You don't have enough men here to make me think I need to stay. My advice is to not beard the bear here in his natural habitat. Try your luck in the cage 'Slayer'. If you mess with him now, you not only lose your money, but you may very well lose your life. He won't obey any rules."

Clint glances over at me. "Is this something more than I think it is, John?"

"Nope. Abdul is just marking his territory. I'll see you later, brother."

"Indeed," Clint replied, walking toward the exit.

"Okay," I engaged Abdul. "What's this all about? You won't make any money messing with me outside the cage. Like my friend told you, if I get faced away from the cage, this won't end well. What is it you want?"

I could see 'The Slayer' was getting second thoughts about what he had planned for this ill advised jaunt. "Why don't you back your boys on out of here, and we'll address your issues with me in the cage like my friend suggested. He's right. If you start something here, everybody loses."

Abdul gets testy. He starts jabbing his finger in my direction. "You will pay for what you did, Harding!"

I shrug. I'm already bored with this. My workout's done. Seeing Clint was great. This bunch... not so much. "Look, either take your shot or walk the hell away. I'm going up to my room to get cleaned up. Anyone touches me walking away, and I open up."

I picked up my gym bag and headed for the exit. The 'Slayer' and his crew watched me without interference. I hope he has some good lab enhancements, because I'm starting to get the hots for him. I figured he didn't have enough knowledge or common sense to stay the hell away from me until he could take a shot at me with people watching. He's like a lot of people who take far too much for granted. The 'Slayer' proves he's not entirely stupid by staying put. I wave. It's time for a little recreation.

　　　* * *

Clint found Montoya lurking outside his apartment. She grinned at him while pointing at the door. "Tonto missed me."

Clint nodded while gathering her into his arms. "Yeah, well he's not the only one, babe. You're growing on me in leaps and bounds. My friend, John Harding, wants to meet us for dinner with his little family. Want to go?"

Lynn hugged him tightly. "You mean the guy who runs the West Coast Murderers' Row with daycare?"

Dostiene nodded. "That's the one, and you ain't kidding with what I told you about the Murderers' Row tag. I've been around the block a few times. These guys make up a group you'd have to nuke from orbit. My boss walks carefully when he directs these guys. He put them together, and he instinctively knows if he ever screws them over, he better have a sanctuary at the center of the earth. Hell, one of them trained me. My point is, they've accepted you. We're all part psychopath and predator. What we hold in common is a belief without this nation or a moral foundation, we'd be exterminated. I don't wave the flag with you, but I damn sure believe in it. It's all too easy to spit on everything that has meaning. It means something to me that you don't. I consider the everyday dipshits that whine about not getting enough handouts, and look for any opportunity to spit on their own country in a way I don't even like to talk about."

Lynn moved against him with fervor. "I don't care about anything but you. Lying to you isn't an option. I recognize I'd probably have been dumped into a wood chipper anywhere else on earth. I love you."

Dostiene's face lit up. "I love you too. I've never met another woman who can accept what I am and what I do. I'll do anything to make the other aspects of our lives work."

With a gasp and sob of pure emotion Montoya gripped Dostiene with a physical acknowledgement. "I guess... I'm not as much of a psycho as I thought. I...I don't think I can be Betty Crocker... but I probably can boil hotdogs at a second's notice."

Clint brushed the hair aside from her face with a gentle movement of his right hand. "I like the personal touch, but we have so much money that you can decline any of the domestic duties that repulse you."

"With you... those domestic duties don't seem so bad at all. Want to take your little doggie for a walk together? We can discuss my domestic duties along with my other duties."

"I'd like that." Clint let out an overly excited Tonto into Montoya's arms. She laughed and gagged as the jubilant Tonto launched into a licking attack.

"Damn, dog," Clint protested. "I just took you for a run. I figured you'd be all calmed down. Okay... go get your leash, and don't forget your deposit bag."

After an excited yelp, Tonto ran inside to emerge with his leash and his waste disposal bag. Montoya watched her two companions with hilarity. "You two... need to take... your act on the road."

Dostiene waited until Montoya's laughter subsided. "We are on the road, Lynn."

That set Montoya off again with the very interested Tonto showing his eagerness to get out of the room. She bent down to hug the dog. "Okay, let's go. I don't want to anger a canine capable of ripping my throat out in a heartbeat."

"I love that sundress, Lynn. Did you just get it?"

Montoya brushed her hands over the thigh high, dark blue toned off the shoulder dress with a self conscious gesture. "It's not really a sundress, but thanks. I bought it to wear for you today. It works, huh?"

Dostiene ran his hands over her hips with an approving nod. Tonto nipped comically at his heels. Clint roughed Tonto up playfully. "Apparently I'm not allowed to pause for anything including compliments, babe. Let's get Tonto walked so I can peel you out of that very enticing garment."

"That's what I wanted to hear," Lynn replied. "I'm glad I only wore my medium heels. I didn't know wonder dog would be panting for road time."

As if sensing Lynn's lighthearted protest, Tonto sat down in front of her, offering his paw to her. Montoya laughed and shook his paw. "Okay, you got me. I'm a sucker for a dog that shakes. Let's do this. I'm a little stiff anyway. This will loosen me up."

They walked together toward the elevator when one of the men who had been with Abdul Bacca walked around the corner, hesitating for a moment when he saw Clint. Tonto, sensing his master's feelings toward the man, moved quickly to cut off his progress, growling impressively. Clint smiled, reaching over to squeeze Lynn's hand.

"Whatever you have in mind, partner, keep your hands in sight. My dog Tonto is a domesticated guard dog. He'll rip your hand off at the wrist before you can blink. Then he'll rip your throat out."

Startled, the man who had been moving his right hand toward the inside of his suit coat, kept it out in front of him instead. He glared at the snarling dog. "My employer wishes to know your connection to John Harding."

Clint notes the heavy Middle Eastern accent and Lynn's narrowing look of appraisal toward this new arrival. "Tell your employer John and I are friends. I don't take offense to your boss's curiosity. Take the answer and leave now. A word of advice though – don't start stalking me or I see bad things in your future, what will be left of it."

The man grimaced as Lynn laughed at Dostiene's warning. He pointed at Dostiene as if unaware of anything he had seen or heard. "If I am told to watch you, I will do so. Make no mistake I will-"

Dostiene waved a hand. "You're beginning to bore me. We're going for a walk, and Tonto hates it when his walk is interrupted. Take a hint and let us proceed to the elevator without you following, and everyone has a nice day. Keep blocking our way and I have Tonto escort you to the elevator in front of us. Believe me, you don't want that."

"I kind of want that," Lynn said, giggling at how incensed the man became every time she said anything. "This guy's used to his women in burkas, Clint. I hate these suckers. They run around hiring prostitutes and then go home and beat the shit out of their wives."

The man's hands clenched into fists at his sides as he resisted the impulse to reach for his weapon. It was then the manager, Royal Kershner, who had helped Clint before, walked up on their gathering. He smiled at first until seeing the tense standoff in the hallway. The manager immediately extended his hand to Dostiene who shook it.

"Hello, Mr. Dostiene," Mr. Kershner said, looking uneasily at Bacca's hired thug. "I'm glad to see nothing of note has inconvenienced you during your stay."

The hired thug turned away, walking toward the elevator and entering it. Kershner watched the man's retreat to the elevator with a look of tired experience. "I assume that gentleman was not here to enhance your stay."

Clint chuckled while nodding in agreement to the manager's statement. "He's not staying at the hotel, Sir, but anything other than that, I'm not really sure of."

Kershner's features transformed into a knowing look of professional duty. He pointed at the hallway camera. "I'll review the camera feed, and make him persona-non-grata if seen on the premises other than for gambling."

"That's very nice of you, Sir," Dostiene replied. "Were you coming to see me by any chance?"

"Uh, yes… I was. Although I'm aware of the extenuating circumstances involving your dog, I was wondering how long your stay here with us will be. I've been apprised of your phenomenal success at catching the serial rapist haunting the thoroughfare on our end of the strip, and we would like to extend every courtesy for your stay here. I advised your rooms should be comped, but that small token of esteem was declined."

Clint took out his wallet and put five one hundred dollar bills in Kershner's hand, locking his hand around the stunned manager's hand. "Just between friends, separate of any actual room fees, can we stay indefinitely until I find out how long we need to be here?"

"I didn't mean this to be a money endeavor, Sir."

Clint nodded amiably, reaching out to squeeze Kershner's shoulder. "I know that. Just your timely arrival here just now was worth the five hundred. Thank you. If you could do what you can to make sure our participation in that serial rapist case gets squashed as much as possible, we'd appreciate it."

Kershner smiled. "In that case... thank you, Sir. I will make your stay here an open ended stay on both rooms for you and Ms. Montoya. If asked I'll say neither of you are aware of what happened."

Lynn walked over to put her hand on Kershner's chin. "You know me by name and everything after that rape gig we did, huh?"

A smiling Kershner nodded. "The local PD leaked rumors they overheard from the FBI agents on the case, including your identity. Nothing stays secret around this town. It was also leaked amongst the locals how our rapist met his end at your hand, Ms. Montoya. My compliments, Ms. Montoya."

Lynn laughed, and shook Kershner's extended hand. "Thank you, Royal. I appreciate your noticing the evil end of a bad man."

"My friends call me Butch, and I would deem it an honor if you and Mr. Dostiene would also. I did indeed appreciate that monster's ending. If I can help in any way with your stay, you have my card. Since this interlude didn't last very long, I have another problem to address on this floor so if you'll excuse me, I'll get to that."

"Of course, Butch," Clint nodded with a smile. "We will probably hold you to that offer of further assistance."

Kershner waved on his way by. "I expect nothing less."

On the elevator with Tonto, Dostiene lightly stroked Montoya's arm.

"We'll have to kill that bozo sent to stalk me if he keeps showing up in our business. Even moving you over to the Mandalay Bay in preparation for our foreign friend's arrival may still be a problem if he's staying there with that UFC guy John's fighting."

"Maybe the bigwig's retinue doesn't mix with the fighter's entourage," Lynn replied.

"I'll remain here with Tonto when we do your move. We don't quite have this undercover stuff working as smoothly as we should. My boss would be pulling his hair out over that meet-up in the hallway. It's great practice for going to Harvard to get those scumbags, but Denny only has eyes for his plans."

"Not to worry, Clint. I'll make myself over so that clown won't even recognize me. Do you like blondes?"

Clint smiled. "Oh yeah, but I love you with any color hair."

Lynn patted his face. "That was the right answer."

At the lobby, they made a quick exit, heading in the opposite direction from the busy Las Vegas Strip with Tonto taking the lead. Clint waited until they were well away from the Stratosphere before speaking again.

"If I know Denny, he'll have you booked in on the same floor as our player, Sargon Darzi, and crossing paths as often as possible. We know he's a lady's man… or at least he thinks he is. He's amassed a fortune dealing in drugs, weapons, and the slave trade. We probably still wouldn't touch him except he's working on a gig to broker a deal between the Russians and the Taliban operating on the Afghan/Pakistani border. The deal will fall apart without him."

Dostiene took out his iPhone. He showed Lynn a picture of Darzi. "This was taken in Dubai a few weeks ago."

Lynn examined the picture with care. "He looks young."

"Late thirties by all information we have."

"How do you know he doesn't want someone much younger than me?" Lynn passed the phone back to Dostiene.

"He wants anything he can't have. Darzi's obsessive about women who won't give him the time of day. The last one he wanted was a French diplomat's wife. When you have all the money in the world, the details of reality become meaningless. He pursued. He ruined her husband. He drew her into his game slowly. When he made the conquest, he abandoned her. I guess you see where I'm going with this."

Lynn glanced over at him with a nod of acknowledgement. "Yeah... I get it. I have to attract him, repel him, succumb to him, and kill him."

Dostiene laughed. "You're the best. I believe you have Denny's outline down pat."

Clint heard the tire squeal behind and to the right of them. Three things happened immediately. He released Tonto's leash, threw Montoya to the sidewalk, and drew his Colt .45 caliber automatic. "Tonto! Evade!"

Tonto streaked in a zigzag pattern toward the houses without a split second's hesitation. The black, four door Ford Taurus slowed near them. The barrel of what looked like an AK47 poked out the window of the passenger rear compartment. Clint fired a tightly grouped set of shots, and saw the weapon drop out of sight. He was up an instant later, firing another tightly grouped set of shots into the driver's space. The Taurus powered down, drifting into a parked car on the right. Dostiene knew he had six more shots left in his clip. He ran up on the Ford, seeing the undead inhabitants reaching startled for their own weapons. Clint fired two hollow points into each of their heads before they could clear their weapons.

Dostiene pulled out his phone to call Denny as he raced back toward Lynn, only now regaining her feet. She smiled at him while brushing off dirt. "Damn, these dog walks are sure more exciting than I remember."

Clint snorted a quick acknowledgment, holding up his finger in a wait one gesture. Strobert answered on the third ring.

"I'm here, Clint."

"I got four down, and no regress other than running."

"I've got your location. Keep the GPS on. Stay in place. I'll be there with backup. I'll bring Casey and Lucas. I don't want John in on any interaction. Hold the line."

Clint gave a sharp, two tone whistle, and a moment later Tonto was sitting between Dostiene and Montoya. Sirens were drawing nearer. Clint handed Lynn Tonto's leash. "Take off Lynn. You've already been exposed enough. The jackass from the hallway is one of the DOA's in the car so maybe we'll get a clean start."

"Sounds good. I'll give Tonto a real long walk. I'll see you back at the hotel in an hour if you get clear of this."

Dostiene reached under his right pants-leg, withdrawing a snub-nosed .38 caliber Smith and Wesson revolver. "Take this with you, babe. Keep your eyes open."

Lynn took the revolver, nodded with a smile, and walked briskly away with Tonto. When the police arrived in force, Clint had his hands clasped behind his head, standing in plain sight. Two of the police officers recognized him from the rapist shooting, immediately holstering their weapons and approaching Dostiene.

"Agent Dostiene!" The shorter of the two officers with Seitz on his nametag ran up to Clint while waving at his fellow officers to relax. "What the hell happened?"

"It was a drive-by, Officer Seitz," Clint answered without expanding on why he was walking in the area. He nodded at the other officer with Hanson on his nametag. "My superiors will be here shortly."

Seitz grinned. "Might as well call me Glenn since we're going to be sharing coroner scenes nearly every day."

Dostiene grinned back. "Let's hope that doesn't prove to be the case, Glenn."

Hanson didn't need more than a glance inside the vehicle to see there was nothing anyone would be able to do for the men inside. He reached in with a gloved hand and shut off the engine, as the rest of the officers spread around the car with weapons trained on the interior. "I see an AK-47 and various brands of automatics, Glenn. What there is left of these guys' heads leads me to believe they were Middle Eastern."

Dostiene pointed at the one with the AK-47 still in his lap. "That one looked familiar to me, but I can't place where I've seen him. It was around one of the casinos though."

Denny arrived with Casey and Lucas in men-in-black wardrobe, complete with sunglasses. Each man had a Homeland Security ID held out for the police in attendance. "Who is in charge of the scene?"

Seitz gestured at Denny. "That would be me. I'm Sergeant Seitz. I was on hand at the scene where the serial rapist and his accomplice died. I recognized Agent Dostiene."

Denny nodded, moving nearer to Seitz. "Agent Dostiene is still undercover on another case. Would it be possible for one of my men to get him away from here? He will be available to answer anything and everything you have for questions, but I'd like him to stay out of the limelight on this."

"Of course, Sir," Seitz agreed. "Do you have any clue as to what this is about?"

Denny moved even nearer. "I believe these men are in the employ of Abdul Bacca, the UFC fighter in town for the match at the Mandalay Bay arena. We will have to determine why, but for now, I'd like to keep this on the down low as much as possible."

"I know that name," Seitz replied. "He's the one fighting under the name of The Syrian Slayer. If you'd like, we can process the scene without you or your men, and keep you in the loop."

Denny shook hands gratefully with Seitz before handing him a card. "That would be the best. Thank you. We'll get out of the way then. That's my personal number on the card. Contact me with anything your department can determine about this."

"Will do, Sir."

* * *

Seitz and Hanson watched the four men get into Strobert's car and speed off.

"Damn, Glenn," Hanson exclaimed. "Did you see those guys in there? Man, if you're going to send a guy undercover, that Dostiene character is the one to send."

Seitz nodded. "Yep. There's not much chance in surviving an encounter with him, even when you're in a moving car with three other armed men. We better make sure this scene is done like they do it on CSI, Bill, or we may be walking a beat."

"I heard that."

Chapter Eleven
Take Down at Sam's Town

"What the hell was that all about, Clint?"

"The guy with the AK-47 in his dead lap fronted Lynn and I at the Stratosphere outside my room, Denny. Bacca sent him to find out what my connection with John was. I sent him on his way, wondering if maybe we'd have to deal with him since he saw Lynn walking at my side. I guess not."

Clint's deadpan ending to his explanation elicited appreciative chuckles from his companions. "I sent Lynn on her way with Tonto before the cops got there. No one poked their heads out once the shooting started either. We'll probably be able to keep her clear of this. Any ideas if Bacca would actually send a team out in broad daylight to get me over a non-incident in the hotel?"

"How non-incident like was your get together with Bacca?"

"I didn't think it would even draw a second look, Case. John had the complete attention of Bacca and his retinue. The 'Slayer' was looking to romance John before the fight, thinking he could get a rise. One of his crew put hands on me. I didn't really do much other than send him back over to his side. Then I got the hell out of there. I probably shouldn't have laughed at something Bacca said, but man it was funny. One thing's for sure, those guys don't have a clue who John is. They actually think he's some pug that got lucky in the cage. Listen to this. Abdul tells John, 'I have lived only to see fear in your eyes'."

All four men started laughing. Denny nodded agreeably. "Yeah, I doubt I could have kept a straight face hearing that one."

Lucas glanced at Dostiene in the rear view mirror. "You should have seen what John did to some guy named Dixon back in Oakland. The clown hinted he was going to bed down John's wife and her little girl."

Clint shook his head. "Good Lord in heaven. That must have been some match after that trash talk."

"John made the guy last four rounds," Strobert said.

"If Dixon ever has a lucid thought in his head after what the Dark Lord did to him, it'll be a miracle," Casey added with a sigh. "I'm more interested in you, pal. I saw all those head shots. You're still packin' that damn cannon of yours, ain't you?"

"Of course. I had to get it back from the FBI. In my defense, one of those suckers had an AK-47. I'm taking Lynn over to meet up with John and his family at Sam's Town tonight. Think it will be okay, Denny?"

Strobert nodded. "Might as well. You and John shook the tree, and look what we got. I'm claiming this four pack of thugs on my resume. I'd wager they were all on our watch list, and now they're on our safe list. How'd Lynn do with a close call drive-by, Clint?"

"Cold as ice. If you really do need a female operative in our merry band on the coast, I doubt you could find anyone better. I've met some tough ladies in the game, but no one like her. When I came through the door over at the cartel compound to get her, she hops up and volunteers to get all the info and goodies I'd need from Medina. Man, she went to work on her with my K-bar and we had everything in about two minutes."

"Damn, Clint," Lucas said. "You sure walk on the wild side with your women. We can use her; but what do we do when you two have your first fight, and we find your parts scattered all over Oakland?"

After sharing another laugh, Dostiene leaned back in his seat with a shrug. "Don't know, don't care."

"That's the spirit," Casey said. "Lucas is right. We do need a woman out there with her qualifications. Denny told us you have some serial killer action back East to take care of later for the FBI. Is that the kind where the FBI thinks they'll be getting live suspects, but they get carved up dead perps?"

Clint nodded. "Pretty close, Case. Those three have done things to innocent people that have the FBI agents I work with looking for a quick carving if I can deliver it air tight. Lynn did that serial rapist the other night while still drugged. She fought the drug haze off, flipped open her butterfly knife, and did major surgery. He was trying to give up at the time she opened up the street side operating room for a house call."

"Oh yeah," Strobert whispered. "She's going to be the find of the century."

Lucas pulled over in front of the Stratosphere. They had been doing circles while talking. "Okay, Clint. We've elected Lynn as the woman we most want on the coast. Now… get out. We'll let you know the moment Darzi arrives so Lynn can make an entrance which will attract his attention. Denny has her set up as practically his roommate. I hope she can wrap him up early so we can enjoy the fight."

"She'll play the part. Thanks for coming over to get me so quick. I'm looking forward to coming out to the coast after this Las Vegas gig. We'll be able to get settled in before Lynn and I have to go East to get my serial killers."

"We'll have a real get together after we land Darzi," Casey said. "I know John will be open to staying a couple extra days if the fight goes down like we hope it will."

Clint opened his door and got out. "May not be able to, Case, depending on how the whole gig goes down. Lynn and I may have to head for the Bay immediately. Are you going to have any trouble with the PD, Denny?"

"I'll make some calls," Strobert promised. "I want those bodies ID'd by our people, including anything in that car. I'll get to work on it the moment I get in my room. Let me know if you need anything for the setup at the Mandalay."

"Will do. Tell John fooling around with him nearly got me killed, and I'm really hurt and disappointed."

The three men in the car were still laughing as Lucas drove off.

* * *

I spot Clint with a dark haired beauty near the multi-colored light trees. Alice gawks at the lights and waterfall with undisguised delight. Sam's Town is way off the beaten path, but they have a little of everything: bowling alley, country western bar, pool tables, and a number of restaurants. They also have this light show bar with waterfall and all kinds of tropical accouterments. Clint sees us and walks his lady over. We're all dressed casual as agreed. I didn't bother telling Lora that Clint had killed four men earlier in the day. Although she can take it, I figured it might ruin the mood. I'm hoping we can get the ladies something to drink while they get a look at the surroundings, and Clint and I exchange a few words. I shake hands with Clint as he walks up.

"I like this place better even than I remembered, John. This is my lady, Lynn Montoya."

"Glad to meet you Lynn." I note she gives me a strong handed grip.

"I've heard a lot about you, Dark Lord, very little of it good," Lynn nails me, eliciting laughter from Lora and her Mini-me.

What the hell, I do the Dark Lord for a few moments, complete with outraged voice, and a few new one liners I figured to drop on Tommy to make his head explode. It cracks everyone up, including a few innocent bystanders. Lynn gives me a hug.

"You're all right, DL."

I turn her toward Lora and Alice. "This is my wife Lora, and her Mini-me, Alice. Lora runs our operations on the coast, and Alice is a groupie for some singer named Beeper."

"It's Justin Bieber!" Alice is outraged that I've made fun of Beeper as usual, which causes Lynn to throw a hand up to her mouth and turn toward Clint. "Don't laugh at anything the Dark Lord says, Lynn. He feeds off of it like a roach on a sugar cube."

Alice's first class upbraiding of my behavior has everyone laughing. Finally, Lynn dabs at her eyes and shakes hands with first Alice, and then my lovely wife.

"I'm very happy to meet you both. It must be a real trial being around the Dark Lord on a daily basis."

Alice's eyes light up and she clutches Lynn's arm in both her hands. "Oh Lynn… if you only knew. He Gronks people."

Lynn starts laughing again, perceiving immediately what Alice meant. She nods at last and gestures toward the ornate bar. "I could use a Long Island Iced Tea, Dark Lord. Take Clint here with you. Do you feel like having something, Lora?"

"A Mai Tai sounds good, DL," Lora answers, "and a Shirley Temple for Beeper's groupie."

Alice growls impressively up at her Mom.

"C'mon, Clint." He follows me over to the bar where the bartender asks for our order. "Long Island Tea, Mai Tai, Shirley Temple, two doubles of Jim Beam, and two Bud's. That sound right, partner?"

"Oh yeah, John. Serve the doubles and Bud's before you make the fancy stuff, Sir, please."

The bartender grins when I put a hundred dollar bill on the table and tell him to keep the change. He has our double Beams and Bud's on the bar in seconds before going to work on the more elaborate mixtures.

"Here's to you, brother," I toast Clint, and we throw down half our shots. "Oh man, that makes my eyes water it was so good."

Clint chuckles. "Got that right. How do you like Lynn?"

"I like her a lot. Knowing Lynn's skill set makes it impossible not to fall in love with her."

"That's exactly what I've been trying to explain to our comrades. They think I'll end up in multiple body part dumps all over Oakland after our first fight."

That gives me a big hee-haw. I could almost hear Lucas or Casey laying that one on him. "How's Tonto like her?"

"Tonto's in love."

I threw down the rest of my double, nodding in acknowledgement. "There you go, brother. There ain't no surer way to know a woman's okay than if your dog thinks she's the real deal."

"My thoughts exactly, partner," Clint replied.

The bartender finishes his work and we take the drinks over to our female companions. After we distribute them, we have a small toast, and then Lynn surprises me.

"Lora, let's take our drinks with us, and lead Alice on a tour of Sam's. I'll bet the boys need to catch up on a few things before we eat. I'd like to take a look at the different restaurant menus anyway."

The woman has instincts. Lora glances at me and nods in agreement. "That is a great idea. We'll be back in a little bit, DL. Don't throw so many doubles down that you start doing the Robot where people can see you."

I bow slightly. "Yes, Mistress of the Dark."

The three share a giggle at my subservience while drifting away to check out the sights. Clint and I head back to the bar, where Clint plunks down a hundred for the happy bar keep and orders us another couple doubles and Bud's. When the bar tender moves on to a different part of the bar to serve other customers, we sip our drinks while facing out at the colorful area surrounding the bar.

"How's Lynn feel about our arriving guest?"

Clint shrugs, leaning a little closer. "She's pumped. Danger excites her. Put her in a life and death situation, and she gets giddy. Does Denny have something on tap that will give her some time to put space between Darzi and his journey to hell?"

Because I know what Clint's capable of, I need to find out another key element not on the table yet. "Yeah, he does. I notice you're not too upset with what she has to do in order to get into a position to administer it. Any comment?"

"Lynn and I have no illusions as to what either of us have to do. We're not Brad Pitt and Angelina Jolie in 'Mr. and Mrs. Smith'. If stuff like you're hinting at bothered me, I would never have gone down South to get her. The gig back East will require a hell of a lot more understanding than this op. We have three utter degenerates, all with sexual deviances even Lynn and I are unsure of, carving women up coast to coast. I found out who they are, and we have a plan to get them, but it will involve an understanding Lynn will have to attract both the women and the guy."

Interesting. "Brother, I don't know that I could do what you do."

Clint grinned over at me. "I thought that was the main reason you wanted me out on the coast. If what I do or accept was easy, anybody could do it."

"I'm hoping Lynn doesn't have to play a lot of those type parts. Denny's casting a line in the water with the higher ups to get us a gig on The Sea Wolf down Mexico way I think you and Lynn would love. The Sea Wolf has a master cabin built for a king and queen. If we get the gig, we'll go down there like we're pleasure cruisers. The rest of our women folk can't go with us where we need to go, either physically or mentally. We'd be glad to have Lynn on board."

Clint edged forward. "Man that sounds right up our alley, brother. You're thinking of Lynn and I playing the part of rich folks cruising around without a care in the world – easy pickings."

I smiled. "Yep. It's Denny's idea. Mexico and the state department think the people that have disappeared on yachts down there were targeted either by the cartels or political factions in South America. Denny thinks otherwise. One of the couples, along with all of their crew that were never heard from again, was a Senator's brother and sister-in-law."

Clint chuckled. "Yeah, when the peons are getting plucked it's an unfortunate circumstance. When a Senator's family is involved it's an international incident of mammoth proportions that must be investigated at all costs."

I toasted him. "That's exactly it, and Denny senses these political opportunities like a shark with chum in the water. The Senator beat down the CIA director's door, and it was game on from there. I believe that's the op Denny wanted to see Lynn in action for. This Darzi gig is a warm-up. Rumor has it there are some really connected people in this targeted killing stuff on the high seas. There are no notes, indications, threats, debris, nothing. This is purely because of who they were."

"And they're still cruising in the area? Gee, I guess money doesn't equate with intelligence. Unless... oh, I get it. These couples have more going on than a simple random interrupted pleasure cruise. They were drawn into the area because of something in their lives. We need to know what that mysterious connection is. That's where I come into the picture."

Man, I love this guy. "Yep. Denny needs to know the next couple in the batting order and why, so we can go in their place. He wants this mystery solved."

Clint shakes his head, a smile of admiration creeps over his features. "If the mystery gets solved, Denny figures he'll have a chip he can play under any circumstances. Man, life on the coast is exciting, John. Adding in your UFC fights and other business interests, when the hell do you sleep?"

I decide to let him in on the secret. "Lora holds the whole thing together. She's an idiot savant when it comes to organization. Put plans, dates, criteria, and locations in front of her and she transforms into the Hulk. In ten minutes she has the outline and timelines done. In half a day, you could run the op according to her plan. She studies tactical and combat situations like she's General George Patton. Denny wants to bring her into the company with a title directly under him. She's resistant to that, so I don't take sides. She still has Alice, her Minnie-me, and I think she's been hinting at having another child. I have to get my head around it, because if she decides it's a done deal, we will have a child… period."

Dostiene's been snorting laughter at each step of my enlightenment speech. I think he's recognizing similar circumstances if he launches into a partial domestic situation. He nods agreeably after a moment.

"It can't all be written in stone, John," Clint says finally. "The drawback to what we do has always been if we have something nice, it can be taken away in a heartbeat. If we have kids, wives, or even good friends, we're susceptible to blackmail in undetectable form from numerous sources. What you have out on the coast is a chance to make what we do nearly normal in our personal lives, because we would have protection. The only drawback I see is a reputation has to be earned in blood. That's a problem."

He's pinpointed the problem perfectly. "It is exactly like you say, brother. The only way I can see to bypass the lesson is to issue one on our own. It won't be perfect, but a statement can be made in advance rather than retrospect. We just need to be careful of our targets."

"Now that's what I'm talkin' about, John. If we establish an early warning system for threats, it will be one hell of an experiment. I hear you have a first class tech guy."

"I recruited him in a jail cell. He'd just been arrested for stealing his father's car. Jafar's been in combat both on the ground and at sea on the pirate op we did. He's as good as I've ever seen on electronics, and he's just a kid. We're training the hell out of him. Jafar's intuitive. You're going to like working with him. Even Denny compares him to Laredo."

"A jail cell, huh? I bet you deserved to be there too."

I nodded in agreement, and finished off my beer. "Let's go find the girls."

"No need. Here they come now. They look as if they're getting along pretty well. I've never seen Lynn interact with regular people, and especially kids. It seems like she's doing okay. Alice is hanging on to her so that must be a good thing."

"Alice has a soft spot for benevolent psychos. The first time I met her and Lora was when Lora's sister pressured me into a school meeting to look big and dangerous for the purpose of scaring the girl's parents Al was having trouble with. She looked up at me, grabbed my hand, and led me in."

Dostiene chuckled appreciatively. "John, you definitely have more varied experiences than anyone I've ever run across in this business."

Lora walked up in my face, grabbing my chin with her hand. "Are you still coherent?"

"I'm not doing my Dark Lord robot dance am I?"

Lora and Alice giggled, while Clint grinned, and Lynn was measuring me for how big a shot I could take. The smile spread on her face slowly.

"Who is this Dark Lord guy, and when do I get to see the robot dance?"

What the hell. Ever see a guy over six and a half feet tall with a mug like he belongs in troll-land under a bridge do the robot dance? Probably not. Everyone at Sam's Town with eyes near our spot at the bar saw it. I marched. I sang. I issued warnings during my performance. "Do not laugh at the Dark Lord!"

No one listened, and everyone around us was laughing hysterically, including the bartender as I ended my exhibition with a bent at the waist, limp swinging arm finale. I noted tears were streaming down Lynn's face, while laughing so hard she was having trouble breathing. There was applause, and demands for an encore. That straightened the Dark Lord up.

"The Dark Lord does not do encores! Move along! Nothing to see here!

More laughter, with Clint giving Lynn a hanky to wipe off her face. Lora shook her head. Alice was still laughing and hugging me.

Lora kissed me. "You are something, DL. I just haven't figured out what yet."

"That was the best, brother," Clint added. "We'll be spoiled for going to any shows around here now."

Lynn reached up and patted my cheek. "That was insane, DL. Thanks for the performance. I haven't laughed that hard in a decade."

I nodded with a smile before turning to the barkeep for another round. "I'm dry. The Dark Lord is fading from dehydration. Let's get our drinks refilled here and head in for food. Did you pick out a restaurant, dear?"

"Lynn said she liked the looks of Billy Bob's Steak House."

"That sounds great to me."

"Hey," Alice called out, pointing toward the entrance. "There's Samira and Jafar, John."

I turned to see Jafar leading Samira around the outer light show perimeter toward us. He wasn't smiling and neither was his new bride. All business, Jafar kept walking without turning. It was then I spotted his four followers. I could tell they weren't happy Jafar and Samira had made it inside Sam's Town. I smiled as I saw their followers, Lucas and Casey. They weren't smiling either. Jafar and Samira were like their own kids. I slipped Alice behind me. Lora picked up on it and guided her a few steps back.

Jafar moved Samira next to Alice and spun around. He went from neutral to pissed off in two seconds. His fists were clenched as the four men slowed near us. They went into a huddle, talking rapidly in Arabic, complete with hand gestures. Lucas and Casey spread out near them.

"Hey, kid, I see you found some new friends."

"They recognized Samira and began harassing us along the strip, John. I know not to go on without back up so we immediately hailed a cab and came here. When I saw them get into another cab and follow us, I called Lucas and Casey to let them know we were headed here. They had just returned from dinner so they came right over. These men said many unacceptable things to Samira."

Clint had been listening, having also witnessed the entrance, along with where Lucas and Casey were. Lynn watched it all with professional interest. I could tell how Jafar wanted to proceed, but we were on a mission. He had brought them here for my input.

"You don't think these four have anything to do with the 'Slayer' or Darzi," I whispered sideways to Jafar. "You wanted to make sure. That's excellent thinking, kid. I'm sorry you and Samira's first night in Las Vegas is a little rough. It looks like your new buddies are through with their meeting." I held up my i-thingy and got nice shots of all their faces as they were turning to look angrily in our direction. I didn't want any trouble in here, but I figured we had enough people to end it quickly. I sent the pictures to Denny immediately.

The four turned to leave instead of making any more of a scene. I gave the high sign to Lucas. He smiled and nodded. In seconds Lucas and Casey had the four men stopped, using their FBI credentials. They weren't happy. Sam's Town security arrived and assisted with the arrest, which wasn't needed, but it's always best to be grateful for local help. Denny called to do face-time. He didn't waste any breath on fomalities.

"John. Get those guys. Don't let them out of the casino!"

"Wait one."

I nudged Clint and he followed me. "Denny wants all four put on ice. Do you have your FBI/HS credentials? I need you to be agent in charge and move casino security on their way."

"I'll take care of it." Dostiene pulled out his FBI/Homeland Security ID, holding it up as he drew near the casino security guards. "I'm Special Agent Dostiene. Thank you for your help. We must take these men into custody immediately."

The tall man with Horton on his name tag looked over Clint's ID carefully and nodded. "We will let you get on with your business then, Agent Dostiene. C'mon guys."

As security moved away, the four men being detained began ranting in Arabic, which all four of us also speak. The leader made a racial slur in Lucas's face and got Gronked. It was a short right to the chin that lifted big mouth up two inches clear of the floor. That silenced the other three while Lucas simply put an arm around the guy before he could crumple to the floor, and headed for the exit.

"See you guys outside."

Casey plastic tied the remaining men's hands behind their backs. I face-timed Lora on the way out as Clint and I framed the three men with Casey leading. "Get us a table, my dear. Tell Jafar he and Samira will be dining with us."

Lora sighed. "I knew an uncomplicated night out was too much to hope for. You disrupted the cosmic balance with the Dark Lord robot dance."

I grinned at her. "That is a distinct possibility. Be right there in a few, babe."

I disconnected with Lora as we passed through the door, and reconnected with Denny. "Denny wants these guys put on ice." I held up the i-thingy so Denny could see we were on our way to Casey and Lucas's car. "We're on our way to the car, Den."

Denny sighed with relief. "They're a hit squad. Samira was the target. I had hoped with all the media attention her speaking engagements had generated the idiots still issuing Fatwas for her death would have to back off. I hope you patted those suckers down."

"Was that an insult?" Casey spun around, peering into the i-thingy. "We not only patted them down, but one of these dudes decided we didn't speak the lingo. He did a racial purity zinger in Lucas's face and got Gronked right in the casino."

"Sorry, Case," Denny replied. "I was so excited about having these guys in custody, I forgot myself. Can you and Lucas take them to the safe house? I already contacted Fiialkov. It's empty. I have a team in route to take over there. I'm afraid Jafar and Samira will have to be with someone from now on."

"Count on that," Casey said. "Want Lucas and I to hang around there?"

"No. I'll handle this one. You guys go back to whatever you were doing. Nice work. John, tell Jafar that was a head's up play leading those clowns into a trap."

"Will do," I told him. "Clint and I will be going back to our dinner in Sam's Town. I guess you'll let us know how the hell all of this shit's hitting the fan right now. What the hell is this, the Taliban convergence?"

Denny laughed and disconnected.

"You cannot hold us!" One of the clowns decided to inform us as we continued to where Lucas was standing near their rented Chrysler 300. There was no bad guy in sight so I figured he was in the trunk.

Casey starts chortling over the directive. "You four followed the wrong kids tonight. If our boss wants you taken to a safe house it ain't because you'll be safe."

"That whore and her-"

Casey Gronked him. He didn't knock him out though. Case drilled him right in the nuts. Lucas held the rear Chrysler door for him while Casey deposited the tightly wound ball of pain into the back seat.

"Anyone else have anything to say about my kids?" Casey nodded when the other two men remained silent. "Good. Shove on in there next to your friend. The trunk's full I'll bet, so you two will have to do the best you can."

The two remaining outside the car squeezed in to the backseat with their groaning comrade. "You guys want to come back here? We may go bowling or something after dinner."

Lucas shook his head in the negative. "Our ladies were none too pleased with the break in our gambling excursion. Case and I need to get back to the Mandalay to make amends. Have fun. Tomorrow's arrival day so I sure hope Denny finds out what the hell this is all about."

"One good thing," Casey added. "Between Clint gunning them down, and us delivering them into Denny-hell we may be making a significant dent in the bad guy population."

"Yep. This simple fight cover vacation with a quick takeout is getting a little more exciting than Denny figured. He may also have figured all this was a possibility and we're bait again," I replied.

"I'd vote he knew and we're bait," Clint said.

"Ditto," Casey agreed.

"That's my call too, John." Lucas opened the driver's door while Casey slid in on the passenger side, taking out his silenced automatic to cover the three prisoners. "We're sleeping in, so don't count on us watching your torture session in the gym, DL."

I laughed. "See you guys."

"I hope you win," Clint added. "You hit, we split. Right Lucas."

Lucas popped his head back over the Chrysler roof. "You best get that boy looked at, John. I think he hit his head on the way out."

Clint and I waited until Lucas was on his way out of the parking lot. We were looking into every shadow with wary eyes. There are anomalies on any mission, but this one had zipped past freaky into the danger zone. Yeah, we're killers, and maybe we think we're all that, but we also have a healthy respect for when we seem to be four or five steps behind the action.

"I thought I recognized Samira," Clint said. "She's the Afghani woman speaking out about reformation in Islam for women."

"Yeah, and Samira's damn effective. Like Denny was saying, she's drawn so much media attention, with her popularity soaring, we figured she may have reached the status where self proclaimed imams would stop issuing death decrees. I'm glad I didn't leave her back in Oakland with no one around watching out for her."

"You know my feelings on this crap from experience. When these clowns get tired of mouthing off, they start building bombs. We may have to come up with a proactive campaign to chill out this interest in Samira."

Oh yeah. "I like your thinking. Samira's old man and Jafar have tried to tone her down to no avail. It would be interesting if when one of these jerks threaten her in the media, he winds up sleeping with the fishes. I'm sick of hearing the word Fatwa."

"It's possible we could turn that word's meaning into suicide."

I grinned over at him. "You know there will be outrage, right?"

Clint shrugged. "Into each life a little rain must fall… and sometimes a bolt of lightning."

"There have been many times I've watched one of these imam idiots issuing death warrants on the news, while wishing I had his head sighted in for a fifty caliber can opener."

"I'll start working on backgrounds when I get back to the room," Clint said. "That fighter's staff being involved in a hit really set off the alarms. Follow it with this attempted grab using guys already wanted, and I'm getting real curious as to what Darzi will be bringing in with him."

"Good deal. I'd like another set of eyes besides Denny's on these coincidences. Jafar's still too green when it comes to outside the box thinking, and Denny may get tunnel vision. I know you won't. Let's go eat. I'll get to intro you to Jafar and Samira."

We entered the steakhouse and Lora waved to us. She'd snagged a table with enough room for all of us to eat comfortably. Alice sat next to Lynn, listening to a story she was telling with rapt attention. She wasn't the only one. Samira and Jafar didn't even look up as we approached the table. Lynn did glance up and smile though, halting the story.

"I was telling everyone about when that guy took me while I walked home from school. Don't worry, I didn't get into any details."

"She was my age," Alice said. "Finish Lynn. How did you get away?"

I could see Lynn hesitate, while trying to figure out a way to end the story without going into detail. It made me want to hear how she got away including all the details.

"I… that is… the guy who had me turned his back to me… and-"

"You Gronked him," Alice helped her to much laughter.

"If Gronk means what I think it means then that was it exactly," Lynn replied, putting an arm around Alice's shoulders as Clint sat down on the other side of her.

"Al invented the word and meaning," I explained. "It stuck. Jafar, Samira, this is Lynn Montoya who I guess Lora already introduced you to, and this is Clint Dostiene, an old friend of mine."

"Nice to meet you Sir," Jafar shook hands with Clint.

"Just Clint." Dostiene then grasped Samira's hand gently. "It's nice meeting both of you too. Lynn and I hope to be joining you in Oakland after this project and fight are over. I've been told John recruited you out of a jail cell, Jafar."

Samira giggled, and Jafar nodded in agreement. "Yes, it was just so. He also recruited our friend Devon Constantine on the same night. I had no idea where or what I was headed into at the time; but looking back, it was a very good night."

"What were you in for, John," Lynn asked.

"He Gronked someone," Alice answered for me.

Chapter Twelve
Wet-Work

Dostiene watched Lynn's profile with a slight smile spreading as he listened to her ragged breathing slowly return to normal. Blonde now, in preparation for her move to the Mandalay Bay, and the mission ahead with Darzi, Lynn slapped Clint's hand away from the sensual stroking motion he initiated along her inner thigh.

"Get away from me. I'm mad at you."

Clint chuckled. "For what? We've been making love for over two hours. Was I doing it wrong?"

"You like me better as a blonde. I'm not comfortable with you enjoying the fake me more than the natural me."

"Funny," Clint replied, "you didn't seem to mind when-"

"Shut up, you!" Lynn shifted quickly over him, pinning his shoulders down. "I didn't know what a lecher you were. You also enjoyed helping remove all indications of my dark hair everywhere else too, you pervert."

"I thought I soothed your transition to the bare necessities very well."

Lynn giggled and kissed him. "Yeah, you did that alright. Maybe I'll make you dye your hair blonde and defoliate too."

"After the last couple hours, I'm willing to negotiate anything. How did you like my friends? You sure hit it off with little Alice."

Lynn slipped down inside Clint's embrace to his side. "She reminds me of me. If we make it through this audition, the west coast seems like a sanctuary to me. Do you wonder if we can have a sometimes normal life out there?"

"They're already doing it now, babe. Hell, anyone of us can bite the big one on a mission. It would be nice if we had back-up when a mission ends without needing to disappear off the face of the earth until we're needed again."

Lynn grasped Clint's hand and kissed the palm. "Is someone tired of living like a hermit up in the mountains?"

"Nope." Clint thumbed over at the sleeping Tonto. "It's Tonto. I think he's getting soft on me. All he wants to do is lie around all day, eat, and play catch once in a while. His ears perk up every time he hears the words west coast now. It's embarrassing."

Dositene's reply drew laughter from Montoya loud enough to wake Tonto, who looked around a moment before settling back into a prone position. "Do you have any more surprises for me? You were talking to John for a long time."

"There's a mission on the horizon that's right up our alley. It involves cruising in a yacht as a couple of rich one-percenters."

"Oh baby, I like the sound of that one. We'll have had one momentous time of it in our first year together if we pull through all these adventures in one piece."

"Yep. I figure after we deliver the killers carving up women when we go play on the Harvard campus, we could make this cruise mission our honeymoon." Clint wrestled around laughing with the stunned Montoya. "You didn't think I was going to live in sin out there with you, did you? I have a reputation to think of. What? Am I moving too fast for you?"

Lynn brushed away the tears forming at her eyes, gazing up into Clint's face. "You've turned my life around. If you want to take a chance on something permanent, I'd love to gamble with you."

"What gamble? It's a sure thing. This isn't a very romantic proposal though."

Lynn framed his face with her hands. "It's the most wonderful proposal ever. Maybe we're not so psycho after all."

Clint leaned down to brush her lips in a caress. "That's what I've been trying to tell you, baby."

"Will my being with Darzi make you mental?"

"No, but I've thought of a way safest for taking him out, and leaving open a very fast exit. Add to my little plan the fact he won't be discovered in anything other than a natural passing from this sphere, and I think we have a winner."

Montoya began moving out from under Clint only to be forced back down. "C'mon, cowboy, explain what you have... oh... oh... well... later."

* * *

"How's it look, kid?"

Jafar had hacked into all the security feeds inside the Stratosphere. "It is all clear, Clint. Lucas confirmed Darzi down and clearing check out. Casey has everyone in position. The Mandalay Bay has been alerted the heiress Constance Madrid will be arriving shortly. They have the limo license and all the details."

"Acknowledged. C'mon out, babe. Does Butch have your bags?"

"Yeah. Our Stratosphere confidant is a little confused but right here next to me. We're on our way."

When Devon Constantine glanced out past Clint at the rear Stratosphere entrance, Clint grinned at his companion's surprised look. "She does appear alluring enough, wouldn't you say, Dev?"

"If that Sargon dude doesn't take the bait, he's gay."

Clint nodded. Lynn had not chosen anything gaudy. She dressed in skin tight black stretch jeans with a very revealing red silk, plunge neck, halter top, gathered tightly just past her waist, with back open to the hem. Her now long flowing blonde hair swayed with her every step. The effortless grace of Lynn's gliding approach in strappy black stiletto heel sandals would have made a Hollywood starlet on the red carpet jealous.

Dressed in full limousine attire with all black suit and hat, Clint hurried out to open the rear door of the black stretch limo. He winked at the manager carrying Lynn's bags as he relieved him of the burden, and set them aside for Devon to load in the trunk. "We'll be back in a couple days I hope, Butch. Hold our room."

Their manager acquaintance, Royal Kershner, smiled and nodded, recognizing Dostiene. "Of course, Sir. Perhaps you two will have a story for me at some point. I would love to hear it. The drinks will be my treat."

"Wouldn't mind sipping a couple with you, partner," Dostiene replied as he guided Lynn into the limo. "Agent Montoya and I may have to beg off on the story though."

168

Kershner backed away with a wave. "That will be just fine, Sir. Good luck."

Devon and Clint reentered the limo, and Constantine had the vehicle moving slowly toward the main drag in moments. Clint smiled back through the open access from the front. "Good Lord, you look incredible. Doesn't she, Jafar?"

"Oh yes," Jafar answered. He turned red and looked back to his notebook computer screen. "I will immediately buy Samira the same outfit. As Dev said, Darzi is gay if he doesn't make a play for you, Ms. Montoya."

Lynn patted Jafar's hand. "Thanks. You guys don't think I overdid the cheap hooker look, do you? I was shooting for the casual but elegant starlet look."

"Mission accomplished," Clint replied. "How's our timing, Jafar?"

"Perfect so far. We should be pulling into the Mandalay Bay only moments before Darzi. Lucas says he has three of his bodyguards with him in the limo, and three more following. He says it will be imperative to make enough of a fuss that Darzi will be watching our limo. If he hustles past everyone to the entrance, he will not even catch a glimpse of Ms. Montoya."

"Leave it to Lucas - nitpicking every detail we've been over fifty times," Clint said.

Jafar chuckled. "Lucas says it's either that or end up watching you go into locoweed gear when you screw up. Okay... here we go. Slow down just a bit, Dev. You're good. Turn and take us in. Darzi is two cars back."

Constantine drove into the valet drop off that circled back out. He parked and Jesse Brown in valet uniform brought out a luggage cart. He shifted Lynn's bags from the limousine storage area to the luggage cart. Darzi's limousine parked behind them. Jesse moved the luggage cart toward the front of the vehicle to be out of the way. Dostiene exited the limousine, and opened Lynn's door at the same time movement at Darzi's limousine began. Clint offered her his hand, helping Lynn to make a slow sensuous transition from limousine to walk area. Lynn smiled, casually walking forward slightly, while looking around the drop-off area as

Clint took the luggage cart from Jesse, who then waited patiently to lead Lynn and Clint inside.

* * *

"Oh yeah," Jafar whispered, checking his camera feeds on Darzi's limo. Darzi had caught hold of his lead bodyguard's suit-coat sleeve, while watching every movement Lynn made. "He's not gay, and if he stared any harder at Lynn, her clothes would start to smoke."

Devon chuckled, looking back through the darkly tinted windows at his view of the scene. "He's doing everything in his power to slow his entrance so as to end up behind Lynn. Damn, that girl has good timing. Look, she's gliding in with the guppy on the hook outpacing his guards. Player lookin' for a time on the town. You couldn't ask for a better example of lookin' for love in all the wrong places."

"Yes," Jafar agreed. "Denny says she's one of the most dangerous women alive. That is a high compliment coming from him."

"That Clint seems like a nice guy. I hope for his sake, he can stay on her good side."

* * *

"He's coming right up to her from your right, Clint," Jafar told Dostiene in his earpiece.

Clint turned to face Darzi. "Ms. Madrid."

Lynn stopped, looked at Clint quizzically, and then at Darzi striding up next to her. She smiled at him, shifting not into a pose, but a graceful waiting posture.

"I pray to Allah you will be staying here at this hotel," Darzi said in only slightly accented English. "I am Sargon Darzi, your humble servant forever."

Lynn appeared confused. "I beg your pardon. Do you work for the Mandalay Bay?"

"No... no, sweet Miss. I am merely a traveler like you. I've come to see the UFC fight. Please forgive me for being so forward. You are stunning."

"That is nice of you to say. Perhaps we will see each other again. I'm here to see the fight among other things too," Lynn turned away from him, following the now moving Jesse Brown.

Darzi grabbed Clint's arm. Dostiene stopped the cart, looking down at Darzi. "Yes, Sir?"

"Who is that woman?"

"Constance Madrid."

"Is she here alone?" Darzi asked, while not taking his eyes off of Lynn.

"I am her personal valet and bodyguard."

Lynn had paused, looking back at Clint with a slightly perturbed look, but with such presence, she seemed to be casually modeling for a photo shoot. "Dan?"

"I must go, Sir," Clint said, pulling away from Darzi. Dostiene hurried the cart to the entrance, trailing Jesse and Lynn into the Mandalay Bay. "I think the hook went right through his jaw. I'm not sure you could beat him away with a baseball bat, babe."

Lynn tittered musically. "That would be one bloody Sunday, cowboy."

* * *

A concierge rushed over to Darzi, keeping pace with him as he tried to follow Lynn. "Mr. Darzi, on behalf of the Mandalay Bay, welcome, Sir. Your arrival has been handled. I am here to help you in any-"

Darzi gestured him to silence. "I wish to know where that woman in red is going. What floor is she on, and how far away from her am I?"

The concierge looked confused for a moment, trying to determine who Darzi was talking about. He then noticed Lynn. "Ah... oh yes... Ms. Constance Madrid. A very lovely woman, heiress to some software conglomerate."

The man quickly scanned through the iPad he carried. "Yes. She is on your floor, Sir."

Darzi waved his men on. "Then let us hurry. I wish to know Ms. Madrid's complete itinerary."

The concierge looked stunned, hurrying along to the left of Darzi with the rest of his baggage train and men. "I cannot do that, Sir. If there are any publicly posted intentions, I can make them available to you."

"Good... make it so. You will be rewarded. Perhaps I will be able to have a word with her before she gets into her room. Quickly!"

The concierge, an immaculately dressed Casey Lambert, smiled. "I'm sure that can be arranged, Sir."

* * *

"Stall at your door, Ms. Montoya. The fish wishes to squirm on the hook for you once more before you enter your room. May I suggest Jesse having trouble with the key card?"

"You're funny, Jafar. We'll stall while I pretend to be texting on my iPad. Did you get that, Mr. Brown?"

Jesse smiled. "Yes Ma'am. It will be a few moments before I'm able to open your door."

Clint stayed near Jesse as he pretended problems at the door. Lynn leaned provocatively against the opposite wall, showing her bare back. Darzi's entourage arrived only seconds later. He tried to look calm as he approached Lynn once again, motioning for his men to stay where they were at his room door.

"Hello again, Ms. Madrid. I see you are staying quite close to me," Darzi said with an ingratiating smile.

Lynn straightened, putting her iPad down to tap against her leg. She looked over at Dostiene. "Dan? Did you tell this gentleman my name?"

Dostiene nodded after a moment. "I'm sorry, Ms. Madrid."

Jesse opened the door a second later. Dostiene awaited Lynn's conversational lead before going inside.

"I am very sorry, Ms. Madrid," Casey apologized too. "I also mentioned your name to Mr. Darzi. I am certain Mr. Darzi will be discreet concerning your identity."

Darzi laughed. "Of course... of course... it is a small thing. I will have my men watch over your privacy too, Ms. Madrid."

Lynn smiled a disarming, slowly spreading gem as she glanced around at Darzi's bodyguard detail. "You certainly have enough of them. Not necessary though – Dan here has a room in my suite. I'm sure he will be more careful about running off at the mouth. Well… nice seeing you again."

"Would you have dinner with me this evening?"

"I don't think so. I really need to get settled in. Please excuse me." Not waiting for Darzi's response, Lynn swayed beguilingly past everyone into her room. Jesse and Clint followed her. Jesse closed the door with Darzi still trying to come up with a response.

* * *

Darzi turned to Casey, yanking out three one hundred dollar bills. "Find out her plans for this evening and call me immediately. I will be in my room."

"I will do my best, Sir. Thank you. May I assist you in settling into your room?"

"No. My men will handle that. Go now and do my bidding. I expect to hear from you soon."

Casey nodded and backed away, turning to the elevators. "I will call if I find out anything."

"I must know that woman, Kadar," Darzi whispered urgently to his top man. "Do a complete background check of her. Leave no detail unobserved. Do you understand?"

"I will set up inside immediately and get to work on it," Kadar answered, striding to the door and opening it with the key card.

* * *

Jesse handed Lynn the special universal keycard with a big smile. "It was a pleasure watching you work."

"Thanks, Jess. He'll be taking my alias through the meat-grinder now to see if it's safe for him to come on to me like he's a dog in heat."

"You take care, Ma'am. We'll all be around." Jesse clapped Dostiene on the shoulder. "See you two later."

"I like the crew," Lynn said. "I think we'll enjoy our new Oakland gig."

"You were amazing," Clint replied, kissing her right palm. "As an actress, you'd be making eight figures a movie."

Lynn smiled at the naked desire on Clint's face. "Yeah, but would they let me kill people? I see in your eyes you like what you see. Want to fool around?"

Dostiene grabbed her up off the floor into his arms, heading for the bedroom. "I like what I see so much, I want to fool around until you scream for mercy."

"Oooohhhh... I hope the walls are sound proofed."

"I'll help you stay quiet."

An hour later Dostiene's iPhone vibrated on the nightstand. He checked the screen. It was Casey. "You were excellent as the concierge, Case."

"Even better than you think, Clint. El Dumbass tipped me three hundred dollars to let him know all of Lynn's movements."

Clint chuckled as Lynn leaned against him, listening. "Oh, that is sweet. It may be time for our first unexplained casino interlude. We'll be down in about an hour. I'll have Lynn play Baccarat until dipshit gets word from you to come down. She'll play the 10,000 dollar minimum table. Lynn gasped next to him, and Casey laughed."

"I think you've finally managed to surprise your girl. Tell her they have higher minimum Baccarat tables than that. I'll be watching for you."

"You want me to what?" Lynn had mounted Dostiene, leaning incredulously close to Clint's face. "Are you nuts?"

"You're really good at this. I bet you know how to play too."

"Well, sure, it's the simplest game of all," Lynn admitted. "That doesn't mean I want to play 10,000 a hand."

"I want you to do it and act bored while you do it," Clint replied.

Lynn giggled, smacking Clint's shoulder. "This'll be fun, but... hey... no... we have to get ready. Oh shit... damn it, Clint."
* * *

Darzi rushed down alone without his bodyguards, ordering them to stay put. Exiting the elevators, Darzi headed for the high stakes Baccarat tables he had been told Madrid was playing at. When he reached the special high stakes Baccarat area, a crowd had formed outside the ornately columned room, beyond the elaborate entrance. Edging through the crowd of onlookers he noticed Lynn in a spaghetti strapped black, tightly contoured dress that ended mid thigh. With her long blonde hair falling in a seductive haze around her shoulders, accompanied by a nearly bored sneer on her face, Lynn seemed both drawn to the game and yet content at the gaming aspect. Darzi clenched his hands into fists, flexing his fingers. He wanted this woman. Striding through the crowd, Darzi sat one stool away from Lynn. She had been the only player at the table.

Darzi signaled the attendant to the table. "I wish one million dollars of play. It is good to meet with you again. I see you are doing very well here."

Lynn had won in excess of a million dollars, much to the dismay of the Mandalay Bay dealer, who had been changed moments ago, although Lynn had tipped him with a 10,000 dollar chip. She made a dismissive wave of the hand. "It is not the winning that tests us. Losing divides the addicts from the gamers."

Darzi brightened immediately. "Yes! It is exactly so."

Forty-five minutes later, Darzi was not as open minded toward his losses. Lynn had held her own, fluctuating in the nearly 50/50 match up with the House in a slightly positive manner. Darzi lost, so much so, he fingered his cards with suppressed rage. He noticed Lynn looking at him sympathetically which drove him nearly wild. Then, she surprised him with a look of acceptance.

"I've lost my taste for this game." Lynn haphazardly gestured at her chips, and gave one to the dealer. The manager nearby nodded his understanding. Because of the amount of her winnings, an accounting with the IRS would have to be filed. "Goodbye, Mr. Darzi. Good luck."

As he watched Lynn get up and walk away through a smattering of applause from the appreciative onlookers, Darzi could not remember a time when he was so drawn to a woman. He angrily indicated his intent to leave the table, and waited impatiently for the manager to indicate he would tally his credits. Darzi hurried after Lynn, seeing she had opted for a walk in a long path toward where he could see from the signs left multiple destinations. When they rounded a turn, the black elevators in groupings made it clear there was only one social excursion to be drawn as a choice. Breathing a sigh of relief at noticing the sultry pace of her journey to the elevators with every eye turning as she passed, Darzi slowed to a pace which would allow him to arrive at the same time. He frowned as Clint, joined her, walking slightly behind and to the right.

"Ms. Madrid," Darzi said as Dostiene turned to intercept him.

Clint moved out of his way. "Sorry, Sir, I didn't recognize you at first."

Darzi brushed by him without acknowledgement to reach Lynn's side. "Please, may I buy you a drink?"

Lynn smiled. "I'm going up to the The Mix Lounge. Maybe you better let me buy you a drink."

Darzi laughed. "Yes... I did not do well at the table tonight. You were magnificent."

"In spite of the James Bond movies, winning at Baccarat is luck," Lynn replied. They walked along in silence for a time. "It comes and goes in streaks."

"You are right," Darzi admitted. "My luck was anything but magnificent."

"I notice you didn't bring your guard entourage with you." Lynn never hurried her sensuous stride during the long walk to the group of elevators where The Mix Lounge on the 64th floor could be reached. The number of people thinned out considerably on the trek there.

Darzi gestured at Clint who had moved ahead of them and sequestered an elevator. He now held the doors from closing for Lynn. "I see you brought yours. Perhaps you will let me be your bodyguard for a time."

Lynn walked onto the elevator. "Wait for me down here, Dan. I'll be okay up in the lounge."

"But..." Clint began to protest as the doors shut.

"Although very necessary, having security around night and day becomes exceedingly tedious," Darzi said, jubilant at Lynn's leaving Clint on the casino floor.

Leaning in stunningly natural fashion with an elegance that can neither be copied nor learned, Lynn made a dismissive gesture. "Dan's okay. It's his job to keep me safe. I believe we will be fine in the lounge. The view is breathtaking. Have you been up to The Mix Lounge?"

"Yes. It is very nice." Darzi placed a hand caressingly on Lynn's arm. "You are the most enticing woman I have ever seen. I am completely under your spell."

Lynn turned into Darzi, her hand moving to the back of his head, as he embraced her. She kissed him. Her moan after a moment of heated embrace wiped all else from Darzi's mind, including the pin prick like pain at the back of his neck. Lynn writhed against him until the elevator reached the lounge floor. He let her disengage breathlessly from him.

"You are indeed magnificent," Darzi whispered.

"Find us a table near the window, baby. I have to go to the restroom."

"Of course, my love," Darzi replied as Lynn walked away to the restroom.

Darzi found an open table near the window view amongst the crowded patrons. He began to sweat, as he felt his heartbeat rise and thump in his chest. The wondrous view of Las Vegas out the window began to blur as Darzi gasped slightly for breath. The waitress arriving to take his order, put a hand on the panicking Darzi's shoulder.

"Are you all right, Sir?"

Darzi stared open mouthed up at the waitress, her concerned image fading into darkness along with his life.

* * *

Clint met Lynn a little ways away from the elevators. "You are the best."

"It was your idea about the lounge up on the 64th. He came alone, which made it easy once you kept the elevator clear. I gave him a kiss to remember the rest of his life, what there was left of it."

"Lucas said it was perfect. He sat down near the window and died without anyone even seeing you. Denny called right after Lucas. He said you're hired."

Lynn laughed. "We're on a roll, baby. Did you see me at the Baccarat table? I made James Bond look like a pussy."

"You sure did. Denny said he'd handle the IRS forms, and he'll have the money waiting for us on the coast. He thinks we should leave tomorrow."

"Probably a good idea. Let's go back to the Stratosphere, and see if our friend Royal can arrange a nice table up at their Top of the World restaurant."

Dostiene took her arm. "Sounds good to me. I'd like to see John's fight, but we need to hit the road to complete our disappearing act. Tonto will be happy. I don't know if I can wait to get you out of that dress. Lord in heaven you look good."

Lynn reached up to pat his cheek as they walked. "Anticipation, lover, anticipation. Will the guys take care of my stuff or do we go up and pack?"

"Jesse and Devon are cleaning it out right now. We're going out the door and into a taxi."

"I think I'm going to like working with this gang."

"The one to watch out for is Denny," Clint replied. "We all keep an eye on him."

"Duly noted."

The ambulance was arriving as Clint and Lynn left the casino.

"Gee, baby," Lynn said, as the EMT's swept by them. "I think they're too late."

* * *

Jafar was grinning from ear to ear. I gave him a wake up slap to the back of his head. "Hello, Harding here. Care to share?"

Jafar looked startled for a moment. We were in the limousine, with me driving around while Jafar monitored our mission.

"It is done, John. Clint and Lynn are already on their way to the Stratosphere by taxi. Lucas says it was perfect. Darzi died alone at a table. Lucas thinks Lynn pricked him in the elevator, before sending him to the table while going into the restroom."

"I've already heard the gushing tale Denny told about how she hooked Darzi, and that she won over a million dollars at Baccarat like an Egyptian Princess."

"She is most accomplished. Denny says he is two blocks down on the right."

I have to admit when I stopped for Denny, he dived in and went off like the President of the Lynn Montoya fan club. He started doing that barking laugh of his, and waving his hands around near the divider.

"We're done! Shit, she wasted Darzi like he was a fly on the wall. Watching her at the Baccarat table was easily the most entertaining time I've had since watching you guys lay waste to the Somali pirates. Darzi was so lost at the Baccarat table watching Lynn while losing a fortune, I think he forgot where he was. You should have seen the parting shot she took while leaving the table. He followed her like a dog on a leash. Then he ambles onto the elevator with Clint keeping it clear of other passengers, happily riding to his doom. We need to clone her. Get to work on it, kid. I want twenty of her by next year."

We shared a laugh over that one. It was good to be done with that part. "How about those clowns after Samira? Any luck tying them to Darzi or the Slayer's bunch?"

"Langley's working on tracing their past movements. Lucas and Casey already confiscated everything they had in their rooms. We have all their electronics gizmos, but those have to be hacked carefully or we could lose everything on them. Let's enjoy the moment. If I get a name responsible for those guys coming after Samira, we'll be sure to put a bomb in his house first. I'm with you and Clint on this Fatwa stuff. We're going to make sure there are a few less people to issue a Fatwa."

"It is long past time to try the direct approach. If we let something happen to Samira, her old man will kill me and Jafar."

"I would like to be mission activated for dealing with one of these fanatical ghouls," Jafar said. "Thank you for giving us the go ahead to take this approach, Mr. Strobert."

"Hey, I don't want anything happening to Samira either, kid. Her fan base grows every single time she speaks. She is beginning to garner world wide acclaim amongst women trapped by Islamic Law. Her enemies list is about to get shortened. I sing her praises every time I get together with the higher ups in this ridiculous terror war. We may know more soon from our assassin guests. They thought the ACLU would be waiting for them to apologize for their being detained. Instead, they got Lucas and Casey warming them up before I came in with more gentle persuasion. We're letting them ponder that wonderful experience before questioning them again tomorrow."

I knew Lucas and Casey very well as an interrogation team. We worked together often. That warm up would be tough to sleep on. "I have to go back to work before this evening. This is a bonus getting this stuff out of the way."

"Drive over to the Mandalay, John. I'll drop you and Jafar off and take the limo."

"Sounds good to me. Are you sending Clint and Lynn on their way?"

"Road trip tomorrow. I want all traces of our dynamic duo gone from here. I've already intervened about the shooting. Homeland Security has taken over the investigation at my direction, much to the local PD's appreciation, so Clint is clear of that one. Those two already ended all threads on the serial rapist. I'm so psyched about Clint and Lynn, potential cases keep popping into my head every moment."

I didn't like the sound of that. "It's time to back off a bit on them, Den. They have a full plate with the serial killers in the East, and your Gulf mission investigation."

I saw Denny's eyes narrow and his lips tighten slightly in my rear view mirror. He relaxed after a moment. "Okay... okay... maybe I'm getting a little too ambitious."

"Ya think?"

Denny chuckled. "I always have you to remind me when I'm overreaching, John."

Yeah, I guess you do. "Think about it, Denny. We're not an army. You have a great tool for a sharp incision. We can do innumerable good things, but you need to get a bit more discerning about when to use us and what to use us on."

Denny sighed. "Agreed."

Chapter Thirteen
Slayer

Denny took over the limo, leaving Jafar and I at the Mandalay Bay. I knew Tommy was chomping at the bit to get me working out for the 'Slayer'. He was so into it, he was waiting for us at the entrance. Either Devon or Jesse must be keeping him informed on our extracurricular activities. I remembered the days fondly when the only thing Tommy did was show up at some slimy back alley place in Oakland and say 'how you doin' champ'. He'd bet shrewdly, and I'd win. We were sure on the down low back then.

"We're way behind, John!" Tommy fell in next to us with passion. "I snuck a peek at the 'Slayer' today through a guy working where they're training in secret. You're going to get clobbered if you don't get serious on this fight, damn it!"

"All the peripheral problems are done, T. Let's hit it. I'm ready for anything you have to put your mind at ease. You weren't such a pussy about my chances back in the day."

Tommy grunted and then busted out laughing. "Yeah... you're right. Shit, John, it seems like only days ago we'd be walking into a dank, dark, foul smelling back alley hell like a couple of kings. You didn't scare, you didn't smile, and pain was your friend. We mowed them down back then, you physically, and me financially. I've been ridin' the wave. Maybe it's time for me to step up and quit raggin' the shit out of you."

That was a shocker. I stopped. "Hey, T, you did exactly right all those times. We're undefeated because of you. Have you ever heard me complain? Don't worry about my feelings. You and I are brothers. What the hell? If I lose, so what? I've been paying attention to the 'Slayer'. You keep doing what you do. I'll keep following your direction. I figure Slayer will give me a lot of looks. He'll be stand up and ground and pound. Only I can counteract it. We can train my brains out, but it still comes back to one on one under the lights in the cage."

Tommy glared at me. "Good. That's what I wanted to hear. Now go get your stuff on and let's get to it. I have a different lifestyle now, and I ain't letting your lazy ass regimen sink it for me. I don't care what the hell you do in your spare time. You're mine now, meat!"

Jafar had lost it, and was having a real good time at my expense. I smiled at Tommy. He got the kid's mind off his wife's danger quotient for a moment. Tommy nodded. He grabbed Jafar's arm.

"I'm glad this shit is so entertaining to you. Put your toddler's outfit on too. I'm going to throw you in there to help Dev and Jess with the Dark Lord here. They checked in and they're ready for the festivities."

Jafar stopped laughing as if we'd found the on/off switch to his vocal output. Tommy couldn't maintain his glowering posture and broke into his braying he-hah once again. I wrapped an arm around Jafar.

"C'mon, kid. You can shoot in and take cheap shots at me with the gloves like Tommy does. It never bothers him to be a behind the back, punching asshole during training."

* * *

The arena at the Mandalay Bay takes your breath away when walking from the tunnel to the octagon cage. Tommy stayed next to me, with Dev, Jess, and Jafar at my back. The place rocks with sound. Giant video screens beam from all around. For these events, a sellout crowd up to the rafters keeps the place humming with underlying current, anticipation, and many times, fear. If a fighter lets the noise and people get into his head, he will very likely have a short night. Slayer pressured the UFC into a five rounder, because although neither of us has enough sanctioned fights to get anywhere near a title shot, we have drawing crowd history. Two men died in the cage against me, one by a slow referee, and the other on purpose, when I fixed Van Rankin's mouth for the last time in Dubais.

UFC officials avoid the labels of a blood sport by taking care who they match up in the cage. Deadly blows and choke holds cannot be officiated out of the sport. They belong to the sport. The referees maintain iron control in the fight, but accidents happen. Having watched the Slayer's workouts, Tommy believed his team had found a pharmaceutical concoction to keep up Slayer's steroid regimen that was so far undetectable. Guys take chances because they work in the speed and power department. What they can't do is make you a more skilled fighter. Slayer was hopped up before when I broke his arm in Oakland. He had everything going for him there: referee, fixed judges, and steroid power. It didn't help, but having watched the progress he had made, I had no doubt things would be different this time. At least here, I knew he didn't own the referee and judges.

I picked the Marine's Hymn for my entry theme, same as in Dubai. No need getting fancy. The Hymn would always be there for me until the day I stopped breathing. The crowd loved it. My crew wore black. I wore black trunks. Dev wanted me to start going by the handle of The Dark Lord, but changed his mind when Tommy went mental for a few moments with the rest of us laughing. Lora suggested Cement Head, but Jafar suggested Hard Case. That seemed to fit okay. It wasn't mandatory, but the UFC likes the nicknames for the crowd to get into. I threw aside my robe, and loosened up while waiting for Abdul's grand entrance. He did not disappoint.

He had picked some heavy metal, banging theme I kind of liked. The fans rocked with it, pumping fists, and jumping to the beat. Abdul Bacca and his crew dressed in red and green with crossed black scimitars as their logo, all faces dark and grim, marched to the cage in lock step. It was very impressive because there were a dozen guys with him. They must have drilled together to get hands and stomping feet in sync like that. Tommy slapped me in the back of the head.

"You're stomping your foot in time to the music, dodo!"

"Am not!"

"Yeah, you are, brother," Jesse agreed.

Jafar and Devon were already laughing.

"They're aiming the cameras at you, dummy," Tommy hissed. "Get your head in the game! Maybe you could ask him for a dance when he gets in the cage!"

I looked around at my crew. I looked up at the screaming fans, the huge video screens, and my supposed approaching doom dressed in red and green. I closed my eyes for a moment, my hands in tight fists. None of it mattered. In a few moments I'd be in hand to hand combat. The months and monotonous hours of training were over. No more worrying about whether I'd get hurt in a pickup fight, and lose my UFC shot. I opened my eyes, allowing the noise to flow back over me like a tidal wave.

The Slayer stalked into the cage at the last note of his theme. Nice. He started shadow boxing, and warming up. He didn't look at me or mouth off or make hand gestures. Three of his entourage stood at his back, staring across at me. I waved, and Tommy clipped me in the head again, to my other comrades' amusement. I was in the zone. The flakes across the way had no part in this. The only one who mattered meant business. That made two of us. Our dance card was full. The announcer did his thing to the heightened fan noise as each of us was introduced. Moments later, the Slayer and I stood at cage central listening to the referee's admonishments. We had no plans to follow exactly what he said. I smiled when the ref finished, and Slayer nodded at me. His waiting was over too. I could tell on his face he remembered our last match, but it was not a fond memory.

We backed to our corners while our crew got out of the cage. The referee asked if each of us was ready, and then clapped his hands together for us to begin. Slayer moved at me with deadly purpose, but in his usual swarming manner. He shot out left jabs at me, fast and deadly. I took three in the head before I figured he planned to hammer me into the cage if I didn't do something. Ahhh… pain, my old friend. I decided to let him lead. Each time he threw a rocket propelled left jab, I leaned away while shooting a right leg kick that smacked into his inner left thigh. I could feel my right eye beginning to swell, along with the familiar feel of my own blood trickling down.

Slayer flinched the fourth time my kick hit the same exact spot, throwing off his timing on the straight right he'd planned to follow it with. I nailed him with a left hook under the rib cage that popped his eyes open. Then I took him down. Managing a half mount and some control, I worked out a little frustration left over from those left jabs, while looking for a submission hold. Slayer got to it first.

In a bad moment where I anticipated his movements wrongly, I ended up in a triangle choke, with him working feverishly to attain the leverage he needed. My surroundings began to shimmer in grainy mimicry of a bad black and white TV show. Sound faded away, marking the demarcation line to unconsciousness and death. We're supposed to tap out when we get there, but I tap out for no one. Chilling darkness flowed slowly into my numbing hands, but I kept moving forward, twisting slightly as I went. A memory of nights back in Leavittsburg, hiding by the bridge, when my old man was on a bender brought a smile to my face. Under that bridge with sleeting rain slamming down on me was cold.

I rolled him. His elbow jammed on the mat, loosening his grip. Fighting off nausea, I whipped elbow strikes back into him impossible to ignore. With a grunt of frustration, he kicked away from me, scrambling to his feet. I barely blocked a right leg strike while I was still on my knees that would have ended the fight. The kick opened him to a leg sweep. My answering of the invitation slammed him to his back as the round ended. We trudged to our crews within a storm of noise. The crowd was happy.

Tommy sat me down, and took my mouthpiece. My crew went to work in silence. They stopped blood from flowing, iced the eye, toweled me off, and gave me a few sips of water after I rinsed the blood from my mouth. Tommy grabbed my head with both hands, staring into my eyes. He grinned. We'd been here before.

"It's all cake from here, meat," Tommy said finally. "I figured he had you choked out, so anything you do from here on is a bonus."

"Yeah, T, but the asshole screwed up my singing voice," I rasped out while standing. "I'll never get a gig on stage now."

That jibe induced some unintended laughter amongst my crew. I saw the laughter evoked some surprised looks on the Slayer's side. Everything on me was hurting. If you can't embrace the pain in this game, you shouldn't be on this side of the cage. I grinned while keeping my shoulders and stiffening neck loose. I'm glad I talked Lora out of watching this one. I noticed something the split second before the ref signaled us to begin. He had a cautious look. I've never used a spinning back-fist. Guess what Slayer gets to see first.

Hands up high, while he incorporated a side slanting crouch, I could tell Slayer planned to pitter-pat my eye again with left jabs. The split second before I thought he would launch them, I spun with the back-fist strike. He was quick. Slayer partially blocked it, but the fist hit him just above the ear, and drove him into the cage. I didn't care to hit the mat yet, so I moved in with body shots and close order drill knees. Slayer tried for a takedown, but his speed had slowed with the back-fist. I kicked out my legs and foiled the move. I wasn't ready to hit the mat yet. His breath came in rasping gulps after the pounding I gave him against the cage.

A left hook slammed into my temple like a sledge hammer as a counter to the knee I landed under his rib cage. Pretty stars blasted around in front of my face, but Slayer couldn't follow up because of sucking wind from the knee. We did a toe to toe trade off for a moment with the crowd nearing pandemonium. I caught him with a right cross between the eyes when he tried to pull away. Slayer reeled across the cage to the other side, but the round ended before I could catch up.

I could tell from the faces in my corner I didn't look so good. They worked me over again without comment. That was pretty much my take on it too. If Slayer sent out signals of some weak spot I could exploit, neither my crew nor I picked up on them. Tommy gave me another water sip while Jafar held ice packs to my ribcage. Dev and Jess worked the damage from cuts and my swelling eye.

Tommy moved away so I could stand. "I don't know where you pulled that back-fist from, but you did some damage there."

187

"Don't do it again, John," Dev advised. "Fake it and whap him behind the knee like you did in the first round."

"Yeah, brother!" Jess got excited. "He'll turn the spot to you, trying to position against the back-fist!"

I grinned. I must have looked like a Halloween pumpkin too long on the porch after trick or treat, because I saw worry reflected in Jafar's eyes. "That's good stuff guys."

"You better concentrate on blocking a few punches, meat," Tommy knifed me with that barb as the ref signaled us to start. "Your defense sucks!"

I chortled a little over that line. Slayer thought I was laughing at him, and launched a flying knee. I blocked the main power, but he got up high on my head. The little birdies returned in full force with the twinkling stars as I slammed into the cage. I surprised him with a takedown, nearly getting an arm bar, but the flying knee had slowed my speed. He couldn't get out from under my half mount for nearly a third of the round. I blasted body shots and elbows, letting offense clear my head. Slayer stayed out of my full mount attempts. The ref stood us up, even though I thought I was active enough. By the pained look on the Slayer's face, I think he agreed with me.

When he came in to start the left jab destruction, I faked the back-first. Oh mamma did I get him but good with the leg kick when he went for the fake. He nearly buckled, so I took him down for some more ground and pound. I nearly got him in a triangle choke as the leg gave him trouble, but he shifted to full guard. I stayed in half mount, striking the ribcage while controlling his arm movement. He dropped his arms finally in an attempt to shield his ribcage. I nailed him with a head-shot, he could only turn away from. The damn round ended before I could really blast him. Slayer rolled from side to side for a moment before he regained his feet.

My crew looked a little happier, but went to work again without comment. I was bleeding again, and we didn't want the fight stopped. The wet towels felt like heaven. Tommy took my mouthpiece to wash it while Jafar gave me sips of water. Jess worked to stop the blood flow on my head while Dev iced my eye.

Tommy put the mouthpiece back in. I took silent stock of how I felt. The birdies were still chirping in my head so I figured it would be a bad idea to take another knee or left hook to the head.

"We figure the rounds are 2 to 1 in your favor," Tommy said. "Maybe you should run around this round since you haven't blocked a punch all night."

Everyone chuckled over Tommy's nearly accurate assessment. I stood up, embracing the pain. "I'll think of something."

The ref signaled us to get it on. Slayer couldn't hide his favoring the leg I'd mulched. He shifted to southpaw for added protection. I took a few jabs and smashed my right foot into the inside of his right knee he had extended a tad too far. That really pissed him off. He went into a boxing stance, shooting out bombs with both hands. Crowd noise rocked the building at our toe to toe bombing run. I took a right to the head, countering with an uppercut from my feet. It lifted the Slayer off the mat, dropped his hands numbly at his sides, and put a glazed look on his face I fixed for him. My roundhouse right leg kick to his temple banged him into the cage and out cold to the mat. The referee dived across him, taking out his mouthpiece and signaling it was over.

My crew swarmed me with the crowd hitting a new high note of noise. Tommy and Jess worked me over with towels, but blood was streaming from our bomb exchange, and my right eye peered through a slit of swelled tissue. Jafar took my mouthpiece and gave me water. Dev wiped dry my over the eye slice and pressured a bandage with strips into place. The referee and announcer were next. Slayer's crew had him sitting up on a stool, but he wasn't going to be participating in the after fight festivities. The ref held up my hand as the winner. I went over to the Slayer and patted his shoulder, crouching to look into his eyes.

"Good fight, Slayer."

His mouth tightened, but he nodded. Then I had to endure the post fight interviews that have to be done. The guys doing them know what they're talking about, so it's not like you can blow them off easily with the usual clichés. My head cleared to a point where it seemed the birdies were on their way to the next nest.

Tommy stayed near me, with a semicircle of Jafar, Jess, and Dev making sure I didn't get pushed around by the media inside the cage.

"The Slayer looked like he had you out cold in the first round with that triangle choke, Hard Case." The UFC interviewer observed.

"Yeah, he did. I was only seconds away from blackout." My voice confirmed the aftermath of the choke hold. "I was damn lucky to get out of the first round."

"At least no one died in the cage tonight." He nailed me while smiling like a shark.

I had to move between Tommy and the guy. "You're right. That is a blessing."

Failing to get a rise by baiting me, he asked me to describe the uppercut I disabled Slayer with while watching it on the video screens.

"We were bombing. I took a shot to the head in order to catch him with the uppercut. It could have been me laid out instead of him. He was out of it when I nailed him with the roundhouse kick to the head. Slayer seems okay now when I went over to see him."

"Will you give him a rematch?"

"This was a rematch. I broke his arm the first match."

"That wasn't a sanctioned match. The crowd loved the fight," he said, gesturing at the packed house.

I considered saying there wasn't any use, but then I thought of Denny throwing things at his screen. The rematch could conceivably take place in Dubai, the place Denny refers to as a target of opportunity. I shrugged. "I'll fight whoever UFC picks for me."

"There you have it!" My interviewer spun toward the camera.

I answered a few more questions until UFC officials signaled to Tommy it was time to go. He yanked me toward the cage exit and I followed with my crew keeping the media at bay. It was a joyous, uneventful trek to the dressing room. A lot of the crowd liked me, which didn't happen back in Oakland. A doctor examined me in my dressing room. When he was satisfied my head was clear, he told me to see him after I dressed and he'd stitch up my eye. I smiled at Dev. He knows I hate stitches. They always get infected. Dev would be sealing the leak with those strips.

"That was some uppercut, brother," Jess stated. "I saw you nearly got your ass knocked out landing it."

I grinned while holding the ice pack Dev had given me in place over my eye. "You summed it up nicely, Jess. The Slayer was all business tonight. My head's going to be ringin' for a couple days. You didn't look too good during the fight, kid."

Jafar nodded and shrugged. "I thought he was going to beat you, John. When he closed up your eye with all the blood, I figured they'd be stopping it."

"After that damn choke hold, I didn't know what to think," Tommy admitted. "How the hell you broke out of that is a mystery. You're goin' to sound like a croaking bullfrog for a month."

Dev laughed. "You should have tapped out, blockhead. I figured you to be about ten or twenty seconds away from death."

I stood up with outrage on my face, shifting into the bullfrog Dark Lord. "The Dark Lord taps out for no one!"

My one eyed, croaking Dark Lord drew laughter from even Tommy. "Gentlemen, that was a hell of a payday. Am I right?"

"It was indeed, DL," Tommy replied. "Get your shower, and we'll seal you up. Best keep the ice pack with you in the shower. You're startin' to look like a troll."

"At least we don't have to walk around in mourning like the last time you fought in a nice place," Jess said. "Maybe the UFC will forget about Rankin's death in Dubai and give you a couple regular matches. I wonder if you have a shot at the title in the future."

"Don't know, and don't care," I replied, grabbing up a big towel. "Call Lora, T. Tell her it wasn't as bad as it looked, and that I said she better not have let Al see the fight. We'll be up in a couple hours once we tilt a few. I need me some Bud and Beam."

"I ain't lyin' for you, Dark Lord," Tommy retorted. "It was worse than it probably looked on TV. I hope she's partial to the troll look, because she'll be sleeping with one."

I laughed with the rest of the guys. Yep, she sure would be.
* * *

Alexi Fiialkov left word with our dressing room attendant we would be expected up at the Mix Lounge, and anything we wanted would be on his tab. I had a professional interest in taking the same elevator up that Montoya plinked Darzi in. It was surreal, because I could imagine it. Then getting off the elevator, I could almost see her breaking off for the restroom, ordering him to go get a table, knowing he was already dying.

Jafar went to join his bride and entertain Lori and Alice while we celebrated. Also, he was there to call for help if there was even a hint of trouble around my room. Casey and Lucas had been watching the women during the fight. They joined us in the Mix Lounge. It was nearly empty because the UFC matches were still going on. We took a few of the tables near the incredible window view. In minutes we had drinks in hand. I was the target of course.

"To the Chokestir!" Yeah, Tommy did that one.

"To the back-fist," Devon added.

"To the money," Jess put in.

"Marines!" Lucas of course added.

"Semper Fi," Casey agreed.

"To pain," I stated with respect. "Without it, and the ability to ignore it and embrace it, I'd be just another putz."

We clinked shot glasses and drank the first one down. I looked out the window wondering if Darzi's last glimpse of life was there. Oh yeah, I'm not much on sentiment, but the speed at which Montoya took out the main objective of all this hype will not be forgotten, at least by me. Then I saw Denny striding towards us with the grinning evil of a zombie with unlimited brains to feed on. Suddenly the double Beam I'd inhaled was unsatisfactory. I signaled the waitress. Denny brought over a chair.

"Hi all. Great fight, John. I wrote you off in the first with the choke. I knew you'd never tap out, so I was already racking my head for a replacement when the Slayer snuffed you. Thankfully, you're too damn stubborn to die."

The waitress brought over another double Beam for me, and a double for Denny. He held up his double shot. "To John. He has proven to be the cement head I needed to form this exceptional group."

We laughed, toasted, and threw down our shots. The waitress, sensing rightly we were far from done refilled everyone. Denny then did what Denny does best, mix in business with pleasure with a very amiable demeanor.

"Okay... let's get this out of the way. The assassin at the airport, and the four guys Clint did for, along with the shadow he picked up were all Darzi's. The assassin Alexi Fiialkov dealt with was the key. Gentlemen, we're as good as gold on this op."

Having only been in the inner circle a short time, Jesse asked an astute question. "What about the Slayer? A couple of his guys got aced in this."

Denny shrugged. "Too many layers on that one, Jess. I will get back to you on it when I find out. This stuff is definitely ongoing. This gig has been so successful, on so many levels, our funding is a blank check. I know better than to lie to the deadliest group I've ever assembled. I'm shooting for CIA director. That will mean a lot of pluses. It may mean excess scrutiny. We'll deal with that later. If I ever make director, you bunch will be my palace guard, and I don't mean guarding me. I mean guarding this country."

We toasted that with vigor. I don't wave the flag. I live the flag. My companions share my beliefs, including Denny. If Denny can get to the CIA director's position, I know he has enough common sense and logic to realize what he'll have under his control. He's also fluent in political puppets who believe America takes a backseat to their political ambitions. Denny may smile at some politically correct moronic decision regarding America's safety, but he will not hesitate to make it right in ways not anticipated by our leaders driven by their own image in a mirror. He takes his shots carefully. In these times, a guy who can decipher the political malaise on a daily basis is golden.

I leaned back, sipping my Jim Beam double while looking out at the magnificent view out the window with wary optimism. That changed in a split second as Big O and his entourage arrived. My crew sucked in a glance at my face and came instantly on guard. I understand hype, and playing for monetary gain in the future, but I was getting bored with the Big O. Baatar Okoye had made some unfortunate statements while hyping our first fight. His subsequent beat down with attitude had apparently not detoured his mouth, as illustrated by him showing up to mouth off at my last fight.

"Harding!" Okoye walked up on us, his big smiling face pissing me off.

Casey jumped up as it seemed the Big O's entire entourage planned on invading our space. "Don't know what you have planned here, partner, but it ain't happening. We're having a private celebration."

Big O got the look like he wanted Casey. That ain't happening. I jumped up in the O's face with my marked one. "Don't even think about it! One more word or gesture, and I don't give a shit about the hype or anything else. I will destroy this bar with your face! You hear me, you punk ass loser!"

Big O's handlers jumped him. He wanted it, but I could see doubt running across his face too, because I have none. Sure, I had a couple of Beams in me, but I go all in here, and I don't fool around with rules.

Big O made placating gestures, his annoying smile still making my blood boil. "Okay, okay, we don't want to do this now. We have our drinks, and-"

"Like hell you will," I interrupted his bullshit. "Find another bar to drink in, big shit. Back out to the elevator with your crew, and no one gets hurt. Try and stay here, and I end you! I bet Alexi doesn't know you're here, you idiot!"

Oh boy did I have the Big O. He wanted me so bad, the veins in his neck and forehead pulsed. His fists clenched in violent promise, and best of all, his damn smile disappeared. I grinned from a few inches away from his face. I am a killer. I take pride in it. That I have a moral underpinning in what I do, yeah, I adhere to a code. I've never let it become a suicide pact.

The Big O postures, backing away and pointing his finger at me. "I will kill you when we meet in the cage again."

Tommy put a full desperate leap hold over me as reality wavered into rage. I'm a little tired of being threatened by punks.

I point my finger at him while my crew moves to stabilize his. "I have something better for you. At this hour there'll be very few people using the gym facilities. If anyone's there, we'll slip them a hundred to workout at another time. Our guys here will watch the door while you and I go on in and settle our business. You want me so bad, punk? Here's your chance! One on one, no refs, and no one to stop us. The two of us walk in but only one walks out. If I win, I'm going to kill you. I suggest if you win, you do the same. Let's go."

Big O just stood there. He looked around, but there wasn't anybody with answers or advice standing by his side. He started backing toward the elevator, but that ship had sailed. I started for the O to kill him where he stood. Denny jutted out in front of me, both hands held up in a stopping gesture. Only Denny has that card to play, but I didn't like it.

"John? You've made your point. I don't believe Mr. Okoye wants anything to do with a fight right now. Am I right, Mr. Okoye?"

The Big O met Denny's glance back at him, and then looked away, shaking his head no. His entourage was already very quiet, because Casey and Lucas were smiling at them, weapons in hand. O kept his mouth shut. He led the way back to the elevator without a word from anyone. I looked around and shrugged before sitting down.

"You're wound a little tight, Dark Lord," Casey said, patting my shoulder, while Lucas and Denny showed their ID's to the stunned bar people.

"You going to fight him again, John?"

"If he ever shuts his pie hole long enough, I'd consider it, Jess." Yeah, I'm still a little steamed. "I know Fiialkov didn't sign off on him pestering me here after the fight."

"I didn't see Fiialkov in the crowd anywhere for the Slayer fight. He would have been in the front rows," Devon said. "Maybe that's the reason Big O thought he could get away with this stunt."

"I'm no expert on this UFC stuff," Casey remarked, as Lucas and Denny walked back over and sat down, "but damn, it doesn't seem like a great idea to piss off a guy you're getting into a closed cage with."

"Thanks, John. We didn't need that," Denny added.

I was cooling down quickly, as I began imagining all the downsides to what I nearly did. "Yeah, I didn't handle that very well. It's kind of a carryover from O's big mouth after my last fight, but there's no excuse for me nearly losing it in here. Sorry guys."

Lucas handed me another double beam. "Sip this, enjoy the view, and let's keep this celebration going. Can you even see out of that eye?"

I chuckled and sipped my Beam. "A small slit is about all. I'll have to put a bag over my head before the girls see me. Al will think I got Gronked."

That drew some laughter. "Do you still think we should hang around here for a couple days, Den, or head back to the coast?"

"I think it would be a good idea to get the hell out of here if things work out the way I hope they do, John. I'll monitor how many of the rats scurry out of town tomorrow, and make sure we're clear with the local PD and FBI. Clint's takedown of those four drive-by jokers in the car the other day will need my personal touch to close up. I'm meeting with the local authorities tomorrow. It's a formality to make them feel like they haven't been left out of anything. I'll text all of you once I know for sure how many of the guys we've encountered here stay behind. Darzi's bunch left this morning with his body. We'll see who goes home from the Slayer's crowd. Everyone who had Samira in their sights is either dead, on the way to Gitmo, or on the plane back to the Middle East."

"Are you going to have Clint puzzling out the boat gig?" Lucas asked.

Denny nodded. "Yeah, I sent him the files on the Gulf disappearances to get started on. I hope he can figure out the next target. That shit is strange as hell. I've had some very good people in analysis working on it, but they're coming up with nada."

"What I'd like to know is how you're going to get The Sea Wolf out of port past Lucas if Clint does solve the mystery," Casey observed, generating laughter and a snarl from Lucas.

"One impossible task at a time, Case," Denny replied. "We'll have to do an A-Team on him like they do to B.A. Baracus in the movie when they need him on a plane. I'll have Montoya stick him when he least expects it. He'll wake up out at sea. We'll probably have to keep him handcuffed though until we need him."

Lucas jabbed a finger into Denny's chest while the rest of us laughed. "Oh, you're a funny man, Denny. We need better intel so we don't need my boat. We can send one of those new drones after whatever it is Clint finds."

"I'm sorry, Lucas, but this cruise is mandatory for The Sea Wolf," Denny replied. "We'll have drone backup for the Wolf, but this is going to require a personal touch, including prisoners if possible."

"I like the idea of getting out of here anyway," I said, standing up. "I want to help Clint and Lynn get settled in wherever they like. Sorry about this, but I think I'm calling it a night. I'll walk Jafar and Samira back to their room."

"We'll take care of them, John," Lucas told me. "Casey and I need to get back with our girls too anyway."

"Me and Jess will walk with you guys," Devon said. "That's enough excitement for tonight. We'll have a beer with everyone on The Sea Wolf when we get back to the coast."

Even Lucas chortled a little at Devon's dig. "In your dreams, meat!"

Jesse started to speak, but Lucas cut him short with one gesture. "One more 'let a brother cruise' and I cap your ass right here in the bar, Jess!"

Chapter Fourteen
Date Up North

Lora opened our room door with a smile that quickly turned into a gasp of horror. "Oh my God, John!"

Casey and Lucas were snickering behind me. Lora grabbed my hand and pulled me inside. I gestured the guys inside with me. Jafar and Samira walked out from where they had been watching TV with Al. Samira put an arm around Al while cringing at the sight of me. Jafar, who knew what I would look like, patted Al's shoulder.

"It is as I explained, Al," Jafar said. "John won, but he will be a bit bruised."

Al peered up at me from around Samira's arm. "I don't know, Jafar. He looks like Snow White and the Seven Dwarfs stomped him with pickaxes."

After the laughter died down, Casey and Lucas stood by the door ready to escort Jafar and Samira to their room. Before she left, Samira reached up to pat my cheek. "Do not let Grumpy near your eye tonight, John."

"Oh no... you did not just refer to me as a bad tempered dwarf!" Lora went for her. I caught her up in my arms as Samira squealed, running out the door between Casey and Lucas. There was again much laughter.

* * *

"Hey!" Lynn slapped Clint's shoulder as she looked over his shoulder. "You made me a blonde again. I thought I'd go with the redhead look. That Kosygin broad is blonde and blue-eyed. Tara Holt's brown haired. Don't you think I need to be different?"

Dostiene looked up from the lawyer he was in the process of building up from grade school through Harvard, and into a CIA front firm in Los Angeles as a partner. "I want that same woman who spiked Darzi in the elevator and won a fortune with a bored look on her face at Baccarat. Babe, you were so good, those three won't know what hit them. They'll probably want to adopt you into their killing sprees. You pulled that off so well in Las Vegas, I doubt you could do any better. That is exactly the attitude you need to pull this off."

"I did have a very effective dry run for the character. I can't argue with you on that. It fit me perfectly. You, on the other hand, just want a blonde." Lynn turned away, her arms folded. "I'm not sure I can put up with that kind of disrespect."

They were in a La Quinta motel in Bakersfield, having stopped so as to give Tonto a good workout from the long car ride. They weren't in any hurry. Denny left all the files on suspected disappearances in the Gulf, along with the information on the LA law firm Lynn would be pretending to work for. Clint had also put together a complete background dossier covering the last few years, providing Lynn with time spent on the company's legal dealings in Europe, France in particular. Clint ran his hands up the inside of her thin black silk slip.

"Okay, you got me. Your act at the casino not only roped in Darzi, it completely wasted me," Clint admitted in French. "How is your French by the way?"

Montoya groaned, her hands dropping to her sides. She answered in French, "Not as good as yours. I... I just took a shower. We have to take Tonto out again. He's been dropping his Frisbee on my foot every five seconds."

Clint looked down and laughed. Tonto stared up at him with his black Frisbee clamped between his teeth. When he saw Clint looking at him, he dropped it on Lynn's bare foot.

"Oh thanks, now I've been slimed. Does my knowing French have something to do with this op?"

"Yep. I needed a place where you've been working the last few years in case they wonder why they haven't seen you around. You can do a bored Baccarat shrug, and tell them you've been working for your firm's office in France. Do it in French, and they'll bite like big trout. I know you speak Spanish. You'll be so impressive, I doubt a law question will even get asked."

"Erin Reeves, huh? FBI Sam's going to love you giving me his last name. I like it. Stop that, Clint!" Montoya slapped

199

Dostiene's hands away. When he reached for her again, Tonto intervened with a growl.

"Why you traitorous cur," Clint whispered, grabbing Tonto's head. "Don't you dare side with her."

Lynn dropped down to hug Tonto. "Don't you threaten my dog. Tonto loves me. He knows I won't make him do bad things."

Clint smiled, changing screens to show Lynn what he had been doing for the name. "I had to find a Harvard Law Grad somewhat matching your description, who did not make it into the yearbook. Ms. Reeves dropped out of sight after graduation. It turns out she went on an Italian vacation to Rome after graduation. Erin married a pilot she met there after a whirlwind romance. They have three children. She will not be attending the reunion because Denny made sure of it by giving the family an all expense paid vacation to the Riviera during the Harvard reunion. Erin's never practiced law anyway."

"You guys don't miss a beat. With these three, it's probably a good thing. Do you really think they would check the background?"

Clint shook his head, looking up at the ceiling as if in prayer, which earned him a slap in the back of his head. He laughed. "Lynn, think about it. They're planning a torture murder on their home turf just to get away with it. They plan to cower in a corner with the rest of their classmates, pretending they're paralyzed in fear. They'll be whooping it up when out of sight, knowing what they did. Believe me. Those three will give you an anal exam before they make their move."

Lynn shrugged. "At some point they'll see something they've never seen before. I will have my knife with me. If I see something in their features I don't like, I will start carving. Promise me something, Clint."

Dostiene stopped working the keyboard and looked up. "Anything, babe."

"If they drug me without my knowing or letting you know it's happening, I've changed my mind about waking up staked out in some cellar looking up at those three giggling goons. Let's play that by ear. If you don't hear me call you off, come in shootin' partner. I didn't like that dart in the neck back in Vegas."

Clint stood up and embraced Lynn, holding her tightly. "Say the word and we'll slice all three of them up and make it look like the serial killer did it. We don't work for the FBI. Rather than lose you, Denny would walk in on those three at a party and shoot them all in the head. He only extends a courteous 'bring them back alive helping hand' to a certain point."

Lynn sighed contentedly against Clint. "I'm still jazzed about getting them as we planned. I got a little on edge with the dart in the neck, and then Darzi in the elevator. That was a little more action than I've been accustomed to in a short time. Do I lose my psycho badge for this?"

"Nope, and I'm the only one that counts. Anytime you get a bad feeling about something, you let me know like you just did, and we'll do a preemptive strike on whatever it is. I promise to do the same thing. I always go with my gut. The one time I didn't I ended up as a resident down in a place you never want to go on vacation. When we go on that honeymoon cruise on The Sea Wolf, we're going to enjoy ourselves, but that op better go down real smooth, or I start blasting. Only this time, I'll have the deadliest crew ever assembled firing next to me."

Clint held Montoya at arm's length. "I'll think of something once I know where our three Harvard preppies plan on staying. Put your jeans on while I send this file to Sam, and let's get a beer while we play some Frisbee."

"That sounds wonderful."

Clint went to the room refrigerator and retrieved the beers, sticking them into a small cooler bag he had bought, while Tonto danced and hopped all around him. When Lynn walked to the door with Tonto's leash, Dostiene and Tonto followed with beer and Frisbee. They walked across to the landscaped patch bordering the parking lot, staying in the shade at one end of the narrow grassy patch. Clint flung the Frisbee for Tonto, who jetted under the disc, and plucked it out of the air. He pranced around chomping it while Clint and Lynn sipped their beers, laughing at the self congratulatory dog dance.

"I could get used to this," Lynn remarked as Tonto arrived to drop his Frisbee on her feet. I've never just stood around sipping a beer while playing catch with a dog ever. It's pretty neat."

Lynn picked up the Frisbee and threw it admirably in a straight line.

"You're a natural at this too, babe. John knows we want a nice place with a view, and some land for Tonto. No reason why we can't sit on a step sippin' and throwin' real soon. We don't always have to be psychos."

Lynn giggled as Tonto arrived to deposit his disc. She threw it again. "We'll lose our edge, cowboy."

"You don't know Denny very well. No one has time to lose anything around him. We'll be fine. I'm with you. I like this a lot. It's not that I haven't had alone time with Tonto up at my place in the mountains, but even with scenery it can be pretty bleak."

"It's always tough to have anything in this world. Just about the time you start enjoying something you either lose it or someone tries to take it away."

Clint started to disagree, and then chuckled. "Yep. I think you have a handle on it. I-"

A child's scream, followed by crying turned the two around toward the parking lot direction it came from, and brought Tonto at a dead run to Clint's side where he whined plaintively. Three rough looking men were draped around a new looking, silver Honda Accord. The driver looked as if he were in a heated discussion with them. The woman next to him hugged the crying child.

"Someone order thugs to interrupt our beer sippin'?"

Dostiene grinned over at her, and then down at Tonto. "Heel! Let's just walk past, gabbing away, so we can see what's going on."

Clint set their beers on the ground. With Tonto in a position behind and slightly to the right of Clint, they walked over to the parking lot. "I guess this illustrates what you were saying, babe."

"You don't think these idiots are carjacking these people, do you?"

202

"Nope. I think they're hitting them up for money, and they won't take no for an answer." Clint could hear the guy with a dark green bandanna over his head like a skull cap berating the driver. The driver for his part held his hands up in placating form while leaning away from the driver's window.

"Did you bring anything non-lethal," Lynn asked. "I know you tucked your forty-five under your shirt. I have my knife."

"Sort of," Clint replied, smiling and chuckling as they reached the rear of the Honda. "I brought Tonto the wonder dog. Besides, I haven't seen anything you've ever done in a non-lethal manner with that knife, babe."

Lynn giggled as Tonto perked up. The two men to the rear of their companion with his face in the driver's window straightened while turning to face Clint and Lynn. They had Los Angeles Dodger baseball caps stuck on sideways with the cap bills over their ears. One was black, clean shaven with his arms tattooed all the way up inside his black sleeveless t-shirt. The other was white with a goatee, trimmed to a point, also sporting tats up his bare arms inside the dirty slate gray t-shirt he had on. Both men were nearly Clint's height, but stocky, and heavily muscled. Their leader noticed the interruption and looked up while still leaning with both hands clamped over the window opening. Besides the green bandanna and sunglasses, the negotiator was olive skinned, with a drooping mustache and black beard stubble. His tats were showing more under a black strapped t-shirt with a skull on the front.

"Hi there," Clint said, still sporting a big smile. The family inside the car stared up at him with terrified, but hopeful expressions. "We heard the little guy crying. Are you three here to see what's making him cry too?"

The three thugs did their snorting, hand over the mouth gyrations for a moment. Mustache man waved Clint off. "Yeah, man. We got this covered. These folks just needed directions. Now why don't you and Lindsey Lohan get the fuck away before you get hurt!"

Dostiene heard the familiar, but unmistakable swishing click before Lynn was around him and the point of her knife nearly embedded in Mustache man's throat, causing the stunned thug to back up on his tip toes against the Accord. Tonto made his presence known when Mustache man's companions stirred. They stopped dead in their tracks when Tonto let out a low rumbling growl from his belly up through the open mouthed drooling fangs he showed them.

"What did you call me, Skippy?" Lynn moved the tip of her knife in a gentle oscillation without easing the pressure. Blood began to form around the tip.

"Noth...nothing!"

Clint could tell Mustache man was impressed after looking into Lynn's eyes. He had seen that 'no one home' look before in Montoya's features. Knowing how all this would end without the potential victims' help, Clint asked them for their input.

"Would you folks like to press charges? We'll stay with you until the police come. My partner and I are with the FBI." Clint showed them one of his many legitimate ID's. In country, the FBI special agent badge and ID was the only one he carried with him on his person. "It would mean a lot if you did press charges. This is not the first time these three have attacked innocent people before."

There was a heated discussion in the vehicle. Lynn, meanwhile, smiled enticingly at Mustache man, her knife and hand never wavering. The wife overcame her husband's objections. He turned to Clint. "We'll press charges, Sir. Thank God you and your partner came when you did. We only had a little cash, and they were angry about it."

"Good enough. Gentlemen. Let me have your attention. You will all kneel with hands locked behind your heads. Hesitate to follow my orders, and Tonto here will eviscerate you. He's not patient enough for restraining people, so we don't really bark out orders at him. It makes him nervous. Watch him closely while doing what I tell you. If he stops growling, freeze, because that means you're making a movement he doesn't like. Everyone but Skippy nod your heads if you understand."

The two men not being held at knife point nodded their heads while locking their hands behind their head. They knelt down slowly, staring at the growling Tonto. Lynn eased back with her knife. Mustache man immediately locked his hands behind his head and knelt without a word. Clint called 911 with his cell-phone, identified himself with his FBI badge number, and explained the situation. The 911 operator promised backup within minutes. Tonto moved between the car and the men, crouching into an on-guard position. Lynn with a practiced snap of her wrist made the knife disappear back into her pocket. The little boy peered around his Dad at Montoya while drying his eyes.

"Wow... you're pretty good with the knife."

Lynn glanced inside at him with a big smile. "Thank you. I work at it. Are you okay now?"

The little boy nodded. "Those guys scared me."

Montoya glanced back at Mustache man, the feral look of a killer causing the kneeling man to look away. She grinned when Clint hurriedly leaned in front of her and shook his head no. She turned again to the little boy. Sirens sounded in the distance. "The police officers coming will make sure with your folks' help that they won't scare anyone else for a while anyway. My name's Lynn. What's yours?"

"I'm Bobby. I like your dog. He's not afraid."

Lynn chuckled. "Yeah, these guys don't impress Tonto. If they try and move, he'll impress them though."

Two squad cars arrived, parking in an arrow formation facing the Honda Accord trunk. They shut off the sirens. Clint held up his ID in plain sight as the four police officers exited their vehicles. They converged on Dostiene with hands on their weapons. A clipped brown haired woman with sergeant's stripes and Simpson on her nametag led her three male companions over. She looked carefully at Clint's ID.

"Tell me what happened, Agent Dostiene."

"My partner and I were on our way north on another case. We stopped here overnight. We heard a scream and a child crying, observing these three men in the process of robbing the family in the Honda. We intervened. The family wanted to press charges so we held them here and called for backup. We have not done a pat down on them yet, Sergeant."

"We'll do that right now before I talk to the family. Can you and your partner hang around for the time being? I'd also like to talk with one of your supervisors."

Clint saw Lynn straighten and move toward the female officer. He shook his head at her. "We'd be happy to. Tonto, heel!"

Tonto retreated to Clint's side as the police officers carried out a search of their suspects. They found knives, drugs, and two guns. Clint called Sam Reeves. Reeves answered on the first ring.

"Dostiene? I was just getting ready to call you. We have our three suspects flying into San Francisco to attend a patent law conference at the Hilton starting Friday. Where are you and Montoya?"

Clint grinned over at Lynn's questioning look. "Those three are something else to revisit their prior scene as innocent seminar attendants. We're in Bakersfield. Can you provide Lynn with credentials in time for the seminar from the file I sent you?"

"Already taken care of. Great job, by the way, on the Reeves' background. Could you really not find another name for Montoya?"

"Lynn predicted you'd say that. Can I give you over to a police officer for a moment? Lynn and I had to intervene during a family's mugging here. I need to make sure the suspects get put away, and the family is handled with kid gloves."

Reeves sighed. "Tell me there are no dead bodies... please, Clint."

"Not a one."

"Outstanding! Thank you. Put the cop on. Head for SF tomorrow morning. Labrie and I will contact you there."

Dostiene acknowledged. He walked over and handed the phone to Sergeant Simpson. After identifying herself, Simpson questioned Reeves on what business his two agents were traveling on. Clint saw her redden in the face slightly and her lips tighten. She ended the call with a 'yes Sir, I understand'. Simpson handed the phone back to Dostiene.

"Agent Reeves explained you and your partner are to be kept out of this investigation. He said you would leave me with a deposition in the department's e-mail. He also said you would insist on these suspects being prosecuted to the fullest extent of the law, and he would be checking to make sure that happened. We will handle this family with all due respect."

Clint held out his hand and Simpson shook it with only a slight hesitation. "Thank you, Sergeant, they really had a scare, and we could tell those guys were getting ready to follow through on their threats."

"We'll do our best. With the family's cooperation, we should be able to get them to plea out and no one will have to go to court. Here's my card with personal e-mail. If you can do a deposition for me officially, ASAP, it will speed things up."

"I'll get on it right away. Thank you."

Simpson walked away. Montoya leaned in close. "Do you have an FBI card or something with our phone number that looks official?"

Dostiene took out one of his FBI cards from the ID wallet and handed it to Montoya. She took it over to the family. The thugs had been loaded into one of the squad cars. Sergeant Simpson jotted down notes as she talked with the father. Lynn slipped over next to the little boy and crouched down to hand him the card.

"If you or your folks have any trouble, call us, Bobby."

The little boy looked at the card with wide eyes. He hugged Lynn. "Thanks."

"You bet." Montoya shook hands with the wife, but didn't interfere with Simpson's questioning. "We're staying overnight at the La Quinta if you need us. Bye."

Clint and Lynn walked away with Tonto trailing attentively. When they reached their beers, they moved a little further away and Clint tossed the Frisbee again with Tonto doing his amazing fetch act.

Lynn gulped down the rest of her beer with Clint smiling as he watched. She sighed, belched, and picked another beer out of the cooler bag. "I want a little Bobby, cowboy."

"All in good time, babe. I liked your mothering instincts over there, especially when you got called Lindsey Lohan. Very entertaining. Sam was most grateful with our restraint. He immediately assumed there were dead bodies. He helped change that cop's attitude. I thought for a moment we'd get stuck here. That would have been bad. The three monsters we have a date with at the Harvard reunion decided to return to the scene of their last killing spree. They're attending some seminar in San Francisco together which you will also be attending."

Montoya shook her head in disbelief as she tossed Tonto's disc once again. "Those shits really are something. They're going to land, check in, and toddle around like they're just innocent babies in town for valuable instruction. The good part is I'll get to play my role, and maybe get their attention."

"There won't be any doubt you'll get their attention. I wish I could see you do it, but there's too much of a chance they know me from my work with Sam and Janie."

Montoya shook his arm. "Bullshit. You can play the limo driver and valet for me. I'll make another entrance like I did at the Mandalay Bay. Wear one of those uniform caps, and let some stubble grow on your face. You can trim it nicely. They won't recognize you. If there's a hint they do, we'll cut off their vampire heads and throw them in some waste dump in Oakland."

Clint laughed and took his turn with Tonto. "Okay... that might work. We'll stop for you to buy another wardrobe. I'll get a formal uniform somewhere. We'll turn in this clunker and pick up a limo. I'd call John about borrowing one of his, but he'll have enough on his mind with the fight. You're right. I don't want to miss this."

Dostiene got a text from FBI agent Reeves. "At least Sam is thinking about appearances. He's booked us into a very nice suite at the Hilton where the Seminar takes place."

Lynn toasted with Clint, clinking their beer bottles together. "I get to splurge once again on another eye popping set of outfits and shoes, and a Hilton Hotel suite. Do you think I should tone it down a little?"

"No way! These three will need the Full Monty show to get the attention we want. Playing your valet/driver may have an added benefit. Who better for them to interrogate about you than the faithful man servant?"

Montoya laughed while flinging another Frisbee throw. "Faithful man servant? Really? That sounds good. I've never had one before. I am going to put on such a show for you. I'll drive you crazy, along with baiting our three serial shitheads into wanting to adopt me."

"You had me with the knifepoint in that guy's throat. That was hot."

It was a few minutes before Lynn could speak, or throw the Frisbee. She hugged him, and gave Clint a lingering kiss. Lynn met his amused gaze with stark candor. "We are soul mates, punk. Don't ever try and deny it. We may be the disruption in the cosmic balance that devastates the world, but we were meant for each other."

Clint cupped her chin in his hand. "When I heard you were taken in Mexico, my Montoya switch activated. Everything I did from that moment was meant to lead to where I held your dead body in my hands, or in a position to have you for all time... like now. If it was hold your dead body that happened, I would hate to put a number on the dead that followed."

Montoya grinned up at him. "Ooooh... cowboy, I think you just tripped a different Montoya switch. Let's go inside and bring Tonto out later."

Clint nodded. "Oh baby... you know what I like."

* * *

"Holy hell! Look at that," Richard Jacoby whispered in a stressed voice. "Look at her. Damn! I know you two want to keep a low profile because of our extracurricular events in past months... but damn!"

Tara Holt broke into laughter as she met Cheryl Kosygin's amused glance. "She...she's hot, but we have to tread carefully here, Rich. We're enjoying the past moment. Remember?"

"I know that." Jacoby's eyes followed the stunning blonde in a navy blue one sleeve dress that fit like her second skin. She strode through the huge lobby as if she owned it. A uniformed driver followed her with bags on a cart. "That's not a hotel employee with her."

Just then the blonde slowed and turned to the man following her with the bag cart. She gestured for him to wait there and he nodded.

"I'll be right back," Jacoby told his companions. He hurried over to the man waiting with the baggage cart as the blonde talked with a manager at the front desk. "Excuse me. Who is that woman?"

"I'm sorry, Sir. I'm not at liberty to say," the man answered.

Jacoby took out a hundred dollar bill, pressing it into Clint Dostiene's hand. "Please."

Clint acted as if he were wavering, glancing at Montoya talking at the desk, and down at the bill he'd been given. "Erin Reeves. She's here for the patent law seminar."

Jacoby nodded and walked back with his companions, a big smile on his face. Kosygin and Holt waited with arms crossed in reprimanding form. Jacoby shrugged. "I had to know. Her name's Erin Reeves, and she's here for the seminar."

"You're pushing," Holt said. "So what? You have her name, and she's a lawyer. What? You want a date?"

Cheryl Kosygin squinted in Montoya's direction as she walked toward her man. "I think we had a Reeves in our class. Did you ask him if she went to Harvard?"

"First you're mad because I found out her name, and now you're wondering if I asked for her life story." Jacoby busily checked screens on his iPad. "The answer's no, but we can find out without questioning the help. It's something to keep in mind her driver can be bought. Yes! She was in our class. Here it is right here, Erin Reeves. She's done pretty well for herself."

Holt glanced over Jacoby's shoulder. "What do you mean?"

"She's a partner at a prestigious law firm in LA. We haven't seen her at anything before because our little Erin has been overseas. Hey, she's walking this way. I'm going to play a little. Erin? Erin Reeves?"

Montoya hesitated, but looked over at the approaching Jacoby with the same look of annoyed boredom she had perfected in Las Vegas. "Yes?"

"I'm Richard Jacoby. We went to Harvard together. These are my colleagues, Cheryl Kosygin and Tara Holt. They attended Harvard with us."

Montoya shifted from annoyed boredom to bored indifference. "Small world. Anything else?"

Jacoby was caught by surprise. "Uh… well… I thought maybe we could all get together for a drink."

"I don't think so, but nice seeing you all. Excuse me. I need to get settled in." Montoya walked away with Clint trailing her. Every eye in the Hilton lobby watched her progress.

"That bitch just blew us off like we were three street urchins begging for money," Holt said. "I want her. We need her at the reunion."

"We'll have to be very careful." Kosygin's eyes narrowed slightly as she watched Montoya, a small smile spreading on her mouth. "I want to hear her scream."

Jacoby chuckled. "She's perfect, but unless she already plans to attend, how the hell do we get her to come?"

"Reeves is here obviously for the seminar. We'll have to do our campaigning then," Kosygin replied. "It would be better if Tara or I approach her, Rich. Maybe she's into women."

"Yeah, maybe, but in any case, you and Tara would have a better chance than me. I wonder if that driver is constantly around her. If he's a permanent employee who travels everywhere with her, maybe he's been overseas with her too. I'll get started finding out if they have adjoining rooms and where in the hotel they're staying."

* * *

Clint and Lynn rode the elevator up to their floor, smiling in satisfaction at the first run in with their targets. "Did you see Holt's eyes when you blew them off? You got them good. I'm going right back down there to buy a drink for you somewhere before I come back up. I'll ask at the desk about something. They might still be there, and decide to pump me again."

"They're hooked. I hope they're still down there. We don't have anything real exciting so bring me up a Mai Tai."

Clint laughed. "I don't think so. You may have a Martini, or a Manhattan. Besides, they have fully stocked bars in these places, and room service."

"Okay, bring me a Martini, shaken not stirred."

* * *

Kosygin grabbed Jacoby's coat sleeve. "There's Reeves' driver over at the desk. Let's all go say hi. He's attractive."

"Good idea. It will save us doing detective work finding out the room," Jacoby agreed.

"Don't piss him off, Rich," Holt said as they drew near to Clint. He had finished his conversation with the desk attendant and had turned, walking in their direction.

Jacoby stopped Clint. He pressed another hundred into Clint's hand. "Hey, big guy, my friends and I want to know what room your employer's staying in. She was in our Harvard grad class. We want her to come to the big reunion."

"I can't tell you the room number, Sir," Clint replied, holding the card so Jacoby could see the room number.

"Would you know if Erin's coming to the Harvard reunion?"

"I think I heard some mention of a reunion, but I don't know if she plans to attend. I'm sorry she wasn't more polite. She'll be having a cocktail at seven in the bar. Maybe you'd have better luck talking to her then. I have to go."

"Okay, thanks." Jacoby waited until Clint was out of hearing range before speaking. "Let's make sure we're down in the bar already when she comes down."

"If we need to distract the driver, let me handle him. I wouldn't mind giving him a tumble," Holt said. "If he goes with her to Harvard, we'll have a hell of a time getting her strapped in for the scream-a-thon. We'll need a plan better than any we've had to come up with so far."

"Maybe we'll be able to get a better read on this Reeves bitch in the bar if the princess deigns to talk with us," Kosygin replied. "We better have a way to entice her."

"I know exactly how to entice her," Jacoby announced, holding up his iPad. "I have a very good friend that is the son of Harold Cunningham, the senior partner at her firm. Brad took a look at her records. She's been overseas for years. He's working on an intro for me."

"I doubt that tying any of our names in with hers is a good idea," Holt cautioned. "Your friend will remember this hook up idea of yours later on when the princess screams her way onto our table, and into eternity."

"It may work just the opposite though," Kosygin replied. "If we establish at least a cordial relationship here, we can play that card once the deed is done. Think about it. We entertain Reeves. When the cops move in for the big investigation, we're right in the middle of the whole thing, because no one else will even know who she is."

Holt laughed. "That's the price you pay for being a stuck up bitch. The only people who know you, are your killers."

"And we'll know her inside and out," Jacoby added.

Chapter Fifteen
Baiting Monsters and a New Home

Lynn and Clint stood out on the balcony overlooking a beautiful San Francisco view. Dostiene had returned with her martini only moments before, and removed a beer for himself from the refrigerator near the bar.

"I could get used to this. They must have still been down there, huh?"

"Oh yeah, and you have a date to be down having a cocktail at the bar around seven. We have to figure out a way you can allow them to include you in a conversation without giving up your haughty act. You can't just turn from Erin Evil to Suzy Sunshine in a heartbeat, babe."

Lynn sipped her martini. "I'll think of something."

"I'll bet. Maybe you can-"

Clint's iPhone vibrated. He looked at it. "Great... face-time with Denny. Hi, Den, how you doin'? We're fine."

Strobert chuckled. "You're more than fine, or at least your partner is. Lynn made such an impression on the Harvard Unholy Alliance, Jacoby called in a favor at our LA firm storefront. The senior partner is supposed to pressure Lynn into playing nice with the banditos. Harold Cunningham's one of ours. His son knows Jacoby, but his part in all this will not be revealed. I told him Lynn would make a good impression. You two are surpassing anything I had envisioned or hoped for."

"Hey Lynn, I think Denny's sweet on you. Anyway, you've certainly made the next part easier, Denny. We were just wondering how to allow an approach by those dweebs in the bar. Thanks. We'll give you a complete rundown tomorrow."

Strobert smiled. "Until that time, hoss. I texted Sam Reeves and let him know about your progress. Sam texted back his thanks, and let me know that you and Lynn were playing Batman and Robin in Bakersfield."

"Just two concerned citizens standing up for the rights of families everywhere not to be robbed and harassed by goons. Sam was very happy with us because no one died. Believe me. That took a lot of effort on my part. Lynn wanted to stake them through the heart, cut their heads off, and burn the bodies."

Montoya nearly choked up her sip of martini. "Did not!"

Strobert laughed. "I'll talk to you tomorrow."

"You're a lot more entertaining than I remember."

Dostiene toasted her. "I can't hold a candle to you, but I do want to try and be more than a one trick pony. I don't want you taking off on me out of sheer boredom."

"I doubt that will happen." Lynn reached down and began easing the hem of her dress up with the free hand not holding a drink. "Ever make love against a balcony railing, cowboy?"

"Not until now, baby," Clint whispered, as he set their drinks aside, and eased up tightly against her."

* * *

"There's the sentry," Holt whispered to Jacoby and Kosygin as they walked toward the bar. "I'm glad we decided not to wait in the bar like idiots for her to come down. She makes him stay in uniform. That's helpful. I bet he doesn't like being positioned outside the bar at her whim."

"It would still be a disadvantage if he were hanging around at the reunion," Kosygin replied. "We might be able to use him though. He's just a hired dummy with a cap. If Rich keeps slipping him hundred dollar bills, he'll think of us favorably when he sees us."

"Like now," Jacoby added, pressing the aforementioned hundred dollar bill into the hand of a bored looking Dostiene. "Thank you for the solid tip."

Clint smiled. "Yes Sir."

They entered the crowded bar without drawing any more than cursory glances, even though both Kosygin and Holt were dressed in eye catching strapped gowns of black and red. All male eyes continued to flit to the bar, along with many female eyes. Montoya sat or in more accurate terms, reclined in a pose both sultry and provocative. One leg was drawn up, leaving a wide expanse of leg showing in careless comfort. The sleeveless, slit at the thigh, black dress both clung and hung away in all the right spots. She stirred her martini with blonde hair falling loosely around her face in haphazard fashion, deep consideration etched across her features. Classical music spun softly from the excellent speaker system, which at the moment played an aria by Bocelli.

Jacoby indicated a table near Montoya's perch where she seemed to be ruling over the rest of the room. "Man... she owns the place. Every person in here is aware of her, and yet she is aware of nothing other than her moment."

Holt glared at Jacoby, but Kosygin shrugged. "Rich is right. You can't teach that kind of natural poise. It makes her all the more tantalizing, Tara. She's everything we've been hoping for. What are the chances of her falling into our laps like this?"

"Slim and none," Holt replied. "This is beginning to worry me. I know this is a rather popular law seminar, but to have an old classmate from our Harvard graduating class show up here from an overseas work station has the alarm bells going off. You checked her out, right Rich?"

Jacoby nodded. "I get where you're coming from, but she made partner in record time through the clients list she grew in Europe. What is it specifically you're worried about?"

Holt shook her head as if in confusion as the waitress took their order and walked away. "Timing I guess... and she's just so damn perfect. I want to carve her up like a pot roast. The too good to be true theme keeps playing in my head."

"You wouldn't be jealous of Ms. Perfect would you, Tara?"

"No more than I am of that damn Southern Belle act you put on, Cheryl."

Kosygin smiled, batting her eyes, and holding up a hand under her chin. "Why whatever do you mean, Tara?"

Holt growled, waiting until the waitress served them and Jacoby signed for the check. "When you do that I want to strap you to a table."

"Our Erin Reeves seems to be affecting us all in a manner we're not used to," Jacoby said. "I'll tell you what, Tara. Let's just pretend we don't know she exists. If she comes over to make small

216

talk after the way she originally blew us off, then maybe we should consider letting this particular idea pass."

"That makes no sense, Rich," Kosygin objected. "If your phone call worked, why wouldn't she approach us... if of course she ever emerges from that trance of perfection she's in?"

"Because she'd be pissed off about getting nudged in our direction, no matter who does it. Good one, Rich. I like it," Holt agreed. "Let's wait her out and see what happens."

Montoya did not make them wait long. She took the last sip of her martini, and lithely moved away from the bar with a smile for the bartender. Every eye tracked her path from the bar, including the Harvard graduates. She never glanced at them. Her unhurried gait, clutching the small black purse in an easy swinging motion lent poetry of movement to Lynn's exit.

Jacoby sighed. "She's the real deal. I'll be back."

"I'll go with you," Kosygin said. "Save our spots, girlfriend."

"Fuck you, Tinkerbell," Holt retorted.

Jacoby and Kosygin caught up to Lynn as she cleared the entrance.

"Erin!"

Montoya smiled at the approaching Dostiene before turning toward Jacoby's voice with what could only be interpreted in body language as bored annoyance. Jacoby waited for Kosygin before taking the last few steps toward Lynn. He waved with a small smile.

"Hi. We talked earlier. I-"

"Richard Jacoby from my grad class at Harvard," Lynn finished for him with a hand twist. "As I said at our last meeting, small world, only now, annoyingly so."

"I was wondering if you had heard from my friend at your firm?"

Lynn smiled, but said nothing. Her amused silence put Jacoby immediately on the defensive. She made no effort to expand on their conversation, but only waited.

"Look, Erin," Jacoby pleaded his case. "We're only interested in catching up on old times with you. We've heard you've been overseas since almost after we graduated."

Montoya laughed. "Okay… let's get serious here. I barely remember you and your friends, and I know none of you have any reason to recognize me. You've done some detective work and found out some facts. Let me make another fact clear: if you think Harold Cunningham orders me into meet ups with grad groupies, you're mistaken. Cut to the chase. You're boring the hell out of me."

Cheryl Kosygin laughed. She held out her hand. "I'm Cheryl Kosygin. We would just like to invite you to the Harvard reunion event coming up. Have you heard about it?"

Lynn hesitated perfectly before grasping Kosygin's hand in a firm grip. "I've heard. We all get the same notices no matter where we are."

Lynn released Cheryl's hand with a speculative look. "I'm mildly intrigued. Is this some kind of gag? Why the hell would any of you care whether I went to the Harvard reunion or not?"

Her question caught them flatfooted. It was obvious they had no idea the question would come up, and their irritated exchange of glances confirmed it.

"You two are so cute," Lynn said.

"We want to hang with the rich and famous," Kosygin blurted out. She accompanied her goofy answer with a wide unnatural smile, before giggling in much the same way she did with a scalpel in her hand, while standing over a helpless victim.

Montoya laughed, pointing at Cheryl. "That was funny. I admit I'm curious, but not enough so to adopt you. You bunch seem a little clingy to me."

"Come have a drink with us," Jacoby replied. "We're not as clingy as we seem. We're impressed. Hell, everyone in the bar back there is impressed just like we are. My friends and I at least have a shared past with you. Maybe we have more in common than you think."

"I'm going to dine in my room with a little wine. If the three of you would like to join me, I'll give you one more chance to tell me what the hell it is you want. I bet you already know my room number, don't you?"

Jacoby shrugged. "Guilty. We'd love to dine with you."

"Come up in about half an hour," Lynn said, turning away.

"We looked like idiots, Rich." Kosygin watched Montoya walk away with Dostiene trailing, her mouth formed into a grimace. "She doesn't miss much. Most people would be flattered at attention from their peers, especially in a seminar setting like this."

"Reeves could care less," Jacoby agreed. "We better come up with something explaining our interest in stalking her or little Erin will boot us out of her room."

"Come on. Let's get in with Tara. I think I have an idea. It's thin, but I think we can sell it. We don't have anything to lose. Let's loosen up a little. It's not like she's after us for anything. At least we intrigued her enough to get a meal. I can't tell you how much I want that bitch!"

Jacoby took Kosygin's arm. "I'm with you on that. C'mon, let Tara hear your idea."

* * *

Clint leaned against the elevator wall. "You should be outlawed as bait. You're like those electronic gizmos they outlawed for fishing."

"I'm more like throwing a stick of dynamite in the lake."

Dostiene cracked up. "Yeah, you are. We have to try and narrow the area we use you in because of collateral damage. That was an interesting play inviting them to the room, and putting pressure on them to come up with a believable lie."

Lynn sighed happily. "Let the games begin."

* * *

Dostiene answered the door, still in full uniform, including cap. When he saw it was the unholy trio, he opened the door wide. Not for the first time did Clint harbor dark thoughts about simply eliminating the three perverted monsters. Their pursuit of Lynn proved beyond any doubt what they were up to. While the three entered, Holt smiled at him in a speculative manner. He did not return it. Clint glanced at Lynn, sitting at the room bar in much the same manner she did down in the Hilton bar. Watching her in action like this made Clint's blood pound. Not for the first time did he wonder at the incredible good fortune that brought them together. Clint shut the door and strode over behind the bar.

Lynn gestured at Clint, without looking at him. "What can he get you to drink? I'm having Champagne, but I believe the barkeep here can make you whatever you desire." Lynn smiled. "Within reason of course."

"That sounds good to me," Holt said, and her companions indicated Champagne would be fine with them also. "You look fantastic, Erin. Thank you for humoring us. I know you must think we're stalking you or something, but in reality, we have a business investment I believe you'll find interesting."

Dostiene served the Champagne with deference befitting his position, and the smooth expertise of someone familiar with all facets needed at times in his true vocation.

"No need to put the sales pitch on," Lynn told Holt. "I reward persistence if it proves entertaining. I have been considering the Harvard reunion on my own. I did not, however, feel it necessary to share that with anyone. I'm sure you understand."

"Of course," Kosygin replied. "I'm sorry we came on so strong. We should have simply approached you at the seminar, but it will be crowded as hell, and full of lawyers."

Lynn chuckled, and held up her glass. "Very good, Cheryl. Don't bore me with business right now. I'll hear you out at Harvard. Make your proposal there, but make it very, very, intriguing. To the reunion."

The unholy trio joined right in. "To the reunion!"

Clint grinned. The toasting scene brought to mind three kids with cap guns baiting a grizzly bear.

* * *

It was only a short trip home. We spent more time in the airport than we did on the plane, which was just fine with me. I popped a few aspirin before we took off. My head throbbed a bit anyway on the flight back home. Pain is my friend, but I like to be able to hit back when I'm enduring it. Our women folk won a little money gaming with Casey's wife Suzan winning a thousand on a dollar slots payout. Casey didn't bother telling her he had won a lot more than that on the fight. The swelling went down quite a bit on my eye, but Alice claimed I looked like I lost the fight.

The limo dropped us off last. While I helped the driver with our bags, the Sparks Twins, Jim and Kara came rambling toward us. Alice immediately ran back out of the house to greet them. Minnie-me hatched plots with the twins at every opportunity, along with their cohort from down the street, Darin McBride. Mostly it was Minnie-me directing the show. I waved at Mrs. Sparks as she sauntered up after the kids. She grabbed my chin with a look of distaste.

"My Lord, John, you surely did get marked up this time. Do you wear your Dark Lord mask when someone rearranges your face like this?"

Lora arrived in time to yuck it up with Della Sparks while I paid off our limo driver. "He only has half a face mangled this time, Della. I'm thinking of getting him one of those 'Phantom of the Opera' half masks."

I waited until the ridicule on my behalf dwindled. "Yeah, the 'Slayer' got his licks in. Besides, I'm always good for a laugh, right?"

Della's eyes narrowed. "I don't know, John. A scream might be a better word."

The twins drifted over with Minnie-me to join in on the festivities. Jim and Kara checked me out with their eyes wide and mouths open. Alice is already giggling, so I'm certain she's already cooked something up with her peeps.

"Wow, John, Alice is right. You got Gronked," Jim announces.

Kara peered up at me while Della and Lora laughed. Lora gave Della a quick report on what getting Gronked meant. "I'm sorry you got Gronked, John."

"I'm okay, Kara. It's just a little swelling." I didn't crouch down or anything. Kara would have probably run for it the way she was looking at me. I was already like the neighborhood troll, only in a good way. People reported stuff to me like a break-in or drug

221

dealers sniffin' around the neighborhood. If it was something mild, I talked to a few of my friends at the PD. If it was serious, I deposited the problem in an abandoned building or something. Our neighborhood watch had tripled in membership, so we did what we could without getting violent.

One gang-banger put out the word he'd bust a cap up my ass in a drive-by. The PD found him gutted by the side of a building on East 12th Street. No witnesses or evidence could be found. The PD ruled it a homicide, of course, but unsolved. The gang accused me of doing a preemptive hit on their leader to the police. When the laughter died down, they told the gang there wasn't any evidence of my involvement; but if the bangers really thought I did it, maybe they should take the hint and stay the hell away from me. I put out the word quietly I would exterminate their gang if there were any more threats from anybody in the city. It's been quiet since then.

"Will your eye turn back to normal?"

I hesitated, because I never think of things like that. I shrugged. "I think so, Kara."

"You're not fighting any time soon, are you, John?"

"I'm done for a while, Della. I'm going to concentrate on the business."

Della moved closer to Lora and I. "I heard Cinnie Noonan is back in the Bay."

She's on our list. A working girl Madam and drug dealer, Cinnie took the next step and killed one of her girls who got out of line. Born and raised in Oakland, Cinnie went into business up in Seattle, where she started her drug distribution and prostitution business. Noonan's killing of her employee made all the Oakland news outlets, because of the mention she had roots in Oakland. Della had went to school with her, as she had with another notorious and now deceased classmate, Terry Nelson. We have an open ticket on Cinnie. A firm in Seattle took on the parents of the murdered woman's request to find her killer. They in turn sent the file out to our firm in case she touched home base.

"We have a notice on her," Lora told Della. "The parents of the woman she murdered want Noonan found and brought to trial. Do you have any idea about her hangouts?"

Della shook her head no. "I stayed away from Cinnie. She was a cold hearted snake, even in high school. I don't know how she ever made it to graduation. I heard after she got out of school, she made enemies, and that's why she ended up in Seattle. Any arrest on sight warrant ought to be a shoot on sight order for Cinnie."

"Thanks for the tip, Della."

Della waved as she turned toward her house. "You be careful with that one, John."

"I'm always careful, Della." That drew laughter from both Lora and Della. I get no respect, even in my own front yard. As I'm carrying the bags in, I'm wondering if Clint and Lynn were done with their serial killer meet up Denny told me about. The way Lora is stalking me, I figure she has her own take on this. "What's the payday on Cinnie?"

Lora smiled. "Ten thousand is what the reward is. Apprehender keeps eighty percent."

"Not bad if I can interest our new investigative branch in the operation. I won't call them direct, but I think I'll give Denny a call, and see how they're doing. We may be piling on a little heavy. I don't want to work them so they pack Tonto up and go walkabout up in the mountains again."

"Please don't scare them off," Lora said, holding her hands clasped as if in prayer. "I like Lynn, and we need an investigator of the caliber you say Clint is desperately. Jafar doesn't have that instinctive sixth sense for it yet. He's more nuts and bolts like I am."

"And me," I admitted. "I'm decent at making leaps in logic, but compared to Clint, I'm a novice. If Jafar works with Clint like I'm hoping for, the kid will be Clint in a few years, at least in the investigative part. Nobody can be Clint in combat."

Lora moved up against me. "Not even you?"

"I'm a hammer. Clint is a weapon of mass destruction. Denny doesn't mess with him much. He kind of nurses him in the direction he wants him to go. Denny knows if he crosses a line with Clint, he could wake up in the middle of the night with a grenade in his mouth - and Clint holding the pin in one hand while waving goodbye with the other."

"Have you any ideas on places they'd like to live?"

"Yep, I lined up a place already in Lafayette. It's on an acre of land, and the house is set back a ways from the road with tree covered front, all of it fenced in with a security gate. I can't wait to show it to him."

"I love your little place here, and I really like all our neighbors. I know we could have a bigger place, but I'm not sure if I want one."

"Let me know if you change your mind. You already know me well enough to understand I'd stay here forever. We can visit anywhere we want and stay as long as we want. There's always been a good feeling for me when I come home to this place, but if you ever get the urge, all you have to do is say something."

"Alice loves your house too. It's goofy, but she even likes the school here more than the one she went to in San Leandro."

I watched Della negotiating with Alice, who of course wanted to keep the twins. She was tired of us adults. Della gave in and Alice took her peeps inside past Lora and I. The peeps made a wide detour around me as is understandable when passing a full sized troll. I looked over Lora's shoulder. She had suddenly become engrossed in one of her iPad pages. I started laughing. It was a very nice shot of Clint standing in a cap and driver's uniform, glowering with arms folded. In front of him was Montoya posing in the persona she had been busy baiting killers with – a sultry half lidded annoyed look with one hand on her hip. The caption said they were checking out of the hotel and would check in with us when they crossed the bridge.

"Text them our address, and tell them to come over," I told Lora. "That'll save me having to interact with the Spawn of Satan. Every call I make to the Spawn goes on the mental tab he keeps on me. We don't need his permission to go after Cinnie. Clint's developing a sense of humor. He would never have sent out something like that to anyone before Lynn."

224

Lora sighed. "Another killer tamed."

"Actually, we just pick our shots before we reestablish control."

"Very funny. I just sent Clint the file on Cinnie that we have on record with a note we have a tip she's in the area."

"Way to take it easy on him. What happened to the please don't chase him away?" I grinned at Lora's sour expression. "Good job. Crack that whip and get those two in line."

"Maybe I need to crack the whip on you, DL."

I brushed a hand down over her arm in a stroke meant to glaze her eyes over, combined with the 'I want to rip your clothes off and have my way look' I gazed at her from my troll face with. It worked in spite of my appearance, in spite of having kids in the house, and in spite of sending a work file to a known killer. Our lips met in a sensuous exploration which had both of us gasping in a manner unbefitting our station as parents and kid watchers.

Lora pulled away. "God, John... don't. You're driving me nuts."

Yes! The Dark Lord's mission is complete.

* * *

Clint's iPhone went into his personal ringtone of 'Bad to the Bone' in the middle of an intense love making session after doing the funny photo shoot for Harding. Lynn cried out, shuddering and gripping Clint with all her might. They remained locked together, both unable and unwilling to break the moment. Lynn giggled, tears starting from her eyes, beginning to trail down her cheeks. Dostiene could not stop. The utter abandon Lynn provoked in him surfaced and could not be shut off. More time passed before either of them could escape the moment. Lynn rolled away from atop Clint, her body sweating and vibrating with release.

"May...maybe we should just stay here another day."

Clint chuckled, stuffing his hands behind his head. "Let me see what the Dark Lord or his minion, Lora, texted us. You and I are not meant for downtime. We writhe passionately and collect bliss in moments between what we are, and what we do."

Lynn popped up on top of him for a moment to kiss Clint's nose. "Good! I'm glad you said that."

Much to Clint's amusement, Lynn leaped from the bed to retrieve the message. He watched her with grinning appreciation as her expression turned from interest to excitement. By the time she turned toward him, his physical appreciation had become evident. Montoya covered herself provocatively with her hands.

"Don't even think about it. Get your ass up, and let's get to the other side of the Bay. We have a new mission."

"Apparently, enjoy the moment is not part of your make-up either." Clint shifted to the side of the bed, enjoying the disarray Lynn's presence in his life evoked in him. He held out his hand. "Let me see what the Dark Lord has in store for us."

Lynn streaked to his side, one hand holding him, and one hand holding up his iPhone for Clint to see. "It's a murderer. John needs your magic, Obi-wan. I know the Dark Lord has me in mind for the apprehension, so get on it, and don't stop until you have this abomination in our sights."

It was many moments before Clint could speak. "You... you're something else, lady. Okay... okay... give it to me."

Dostiene took the iPhone from Lynn. He sped read through the message and attached file. In moments, he was up pulling his clothes on. "This is right up my alley, babe. It gives me a chance to enlighten you on another facet of our nonviolent resources."

In moments, Clint had tied in his satellite hookup with the information provided in Lora's message. "We know facts, babe. Here is a list of Cinnie's schoolmates, and here is a list of her brushes with the law back to first grade."

Lynn gasped in comedic form. "You are so out of line! Keep going."

"We don't want to focus on Cinnie just yet. Let's see what kind of calls her friends and cohorts have received." Clint entered the data parameters into the query screen he had created. In moments it reduced the number of calls originating from a source shared to three, and then to one. "Our Cinnie is using a burn phone, but that's no problem, because thanks to her calls I can triangulate her whereabouts. See?"

Lynn backed away within sight of Clint gesturing at him in mock horror. "You are scary good. Harding should be revoking your group invitation... you monster!"

Montoya dropped her hands in resignation, huddling up next to Dostiene. "Oh... never mind. I forgot. I'm a monster too. Where's the real monster at?"

"It looks like she's in East Oakland at a friend's place that was on her call list. I hate to say it, but these deadbeats seldom change. If one of them gains notoriety, and reaches out, they can't resist. No matter how many years go by, they flock to the gig like moths to a flame. Cinnie thinks she has a crew already, but what she really has is an arrow pointing right at her head."

Lynn straddled Dostiene, pushing him back on the bed where he had been sitting with his satellite laptop, while carefully shifting the device to the side. "One for the road, cowboy, and then... oh... oh shit!"

* * *

I knew who it was. I peeked. Then, I opened the door in full Dark Lord form. "Hello. You have arrived at the Dark Lord's abode. How may I be of service?"

Alice, the little minx, popped out from behind my leg. "Hi Lynn. Don't mind DL. C'mon in." She reached out and took Lynn's hand to pull her inside while gesturing at Tonto, who didn't hesitate for a moment.

"The Dark Lord gets no respect here!" I let my shoulders droop in defeat while gesturing the laughing Dostiene inside. "Never mind. C'mon in, Clint. Show me how many ways you've already made me look stupid in front of my wife with the Noonan file."

Clint pointed at me with distaste. "You don't look so good, brother. I thought you won the fight."

"Oh... you are so funny." I tilted my face up to the light. "I think it's the lighting that calls attention to the very slight imperfections from my recent struggle."

Clint moved past me, patting my shoulder, while looking at the watch on his other wrist. "Whatever helps you sleep at night, brother. I've been here for over two minutes, and you have not offered me a beer. Is this a new form of polite hosting I'm unaware of?"

"You know of course, this means war."

Clint chuckled. "Yeah, but does it mean a beer, or do I have to go down to the corner store?"

"Follow me." I know when I'm in the company of a better prick, but I can't help myself. "I've never mentioned the time I saved your life, my friend. It was an incredible experience. Perhaps you recall the time?"

Clint waved me off, taking the beer I handed him from the refrigerator. "Yeah… but what have you done for me lately?"

Then I slammed his disrespectful ass. I handed him a set of keys. "I bought you a house. It was perfect for you. Everything's on in there, so get directions and move in. I'd give you directions, but you've hurt my feelings so you can just find it on your own."

Clint held up the keys while laughing his head off. "You… you're the best! I was concerned. I figured you'd make us bed down with you. Did you make sure we have some furnishings? What about dishes, and accoutrements? TV? Fresh soap? Does-"

"Please shut up! Please? I made sure you have furnishings, you ungrateful-"

"Ungrateful?!" Clint cut me off in mid sarcastic diatribe. "You saved my life. In many cultures around the world that means you're responsible for me from then on. In other words, I hope you plan on coming around to garden every other week."

"Did you see the fight? The 'Slayer' was a smartass too."

Clint gripped his chin in thinking mode. "I think so. That was the live action demo on how to block a left jab every two seconds with your right eye. Very informative. Are you thinking of making a workout video?"

"No, I'm thinking about a live action demonstration."

"I'll call Lynn. She loves doing that stuff."

"Don't even think about it. She's as good with a butterfly knife as I am. I have a family now. Show some respect."

Clint shook his head, hand rubbing the back of his neck. "You poor guy. Someone cut out your stones, and you didn't even get to wave goodbye. Is that what all this UFC shit is… trying to grow back a pair?"

Okay, that cracked me up. I held up my hands. "I'm done. Let's go on to my next humiliation. How did you do with the Noonan file?"

"Pretty fair. We can go pick her up tomorrow. Lynn wants a piece."

My mouth may have hung open for a moment, but I quickly covered it, pretending an unexpected cough. "If you've found Cinnie, I'll let Lynn have it anyway she wants. I figured to take Noonan down hard with the full crew. She's up for only one killing, but I have a feeling Cinnie has a few bodies buried in places no one will ever find."

"I saw that part in Noonan's file about being questioned in relation to three women who worked for her in the past disappearing under mysterious circumstances. We'll find out what happened to them. Cinnie's staying with an old classmate she dealt drugs with in high school. She definitely has delusions of getting her old band back together. The classmate's name is Adrian Stenson. The address is on Morgan Street, only about a mile from here. I figure we can hit it around four in the morning, and catch them both in a drug and alcohol stupor. Lynn will tidy up Cinnie while you and I entertain anyone else that might be there."

Damn. I'm starting to feel insecure. "Do you want to stay over tonight since it's close to me?"

"Are you kidding? I'm taking Lynn over to our new house. We'll turn in early and be back over to your place at four. I want to make sure Tonto has adequate space at our new residence. Otherwise, I may have to file a complaint."

I could never get more than two words out of this guy in the past. Now, he's a standup comedian. I figure this has to be Lynn's handiwork. I'm not sure how one psycho turns another into a mouthy smartass, but she's done it. I like him better this way. Who knew? "I believe he will find his space to be completely satisfactory. I like your plan, but I'll bring in one more for the party as a driver and lookout, who can monitor the police band while we go in."

"Jafar?"

"Yep. The kid doesn't panic, and he never screws up the tech stuff."

"Sounds good. Want me to ask Lora if you can come out and play tomorrow morning? I don't want you to get grounded."

"Did I ever show you the knife trick where I make the blade disappear?"

Clint laughed. "No, but Lynn showed it to me the other night in Las Vegas. The guy she was showing it to me on didn't like the trick at all."

"I'll bet."

Chapter Sixteen
Mean Girl and War in Oakland

Cinnie Noonan groaned, her face stinging from the open hand slaps she was enduring. Then she noticed her hands and feet were restrained with plastic ties, and fastened together uncomfortably at her back. Her head throbbed already from the Tequila she had gotten wasted on the night before. She began protesting, trying to twist away from the slaps. They stopped. Cinnie squinted up in the darkness at the face now hovering over her.

"What the fuck… what the hell do you want!?"

"Hi girlfriend. I'm glad you asked. There's a reward for your ass from the girl's parents. You know… the girl you shot through the head in Seattle. We're going to take you back to Seattle for trial, or depending on what you tell us about the other three girls you murdered, torture and kill you here."

"You don't scare me, bitch! You think you're a mean girl, huh? Mean girls piss their panties when they see me!"

The woman talking to her giggled. "You are so cute!"

Cinnie watched the woman turn on the nightstand lamp she was facing. Then she saw a dark colored bottle with an eyedropper held where she could see it. Noonan began to sweat. She felt the t-shirt she was wearing pulled up from her waist. The woman pinched off her nose. When she opened her mouth to breathe, a small rubber ball was stuffed in her mouth, and her nose released. Lastly the woman sealed her mouth with a piece of duct tape.

"There we go," Cinnie's captor announced. "My little demo may be a bit painful. We don't want to wake the neighbors. This bottle has diluted sulfuric acid in it. I'm going to put just a tiny drop inside your ear. You're not going to like that, honey, but it's to get you in a more helpful mood."

Cinnie thrashed around, trying to scream, but the only sound she managed came out as a muffled high pitched whine. She tried to look up at the woman while shaking her head in a violent but silent pantomime rhythm of no. Noonan felt a knee pressing onto her side, and a hand shoving the right side of her face into the bed mattress. Then Cinnie felt a pain so excruciating, she passed out. Open hand slaps brought her around to consciousness again. She went back to the muffled scream as the whole side of her head felt like it was on fire. The woman's hand cupped her chin.

"C'mon now, mean girl. That was just an itsy bitsy drop. Think about what it'll be like when I start on your eyes. Tell you what. I'll give you one chance to be helpful right now. What do you think, mean girl."

Cinnie moaned, moving her head again violently only in an affirmative direction.

"That's my little mean girl. My name's Lynn, by the way. You're going to be my very helpful friend the moment I take out your gag, or I'm going to show you my mean girl. You don't want to see my mean girl, honey."

Noonan felt the duct tape taken off carefully, and the ball plucked gently from her mouth. She gagged for a moment. "My... my head... it-"

"Uh oh!" Lynn grabbed Noonan's chin again. "Misunderstanding here. You think I care. I don't. When I ask you something, you answer yes Ma'am, no Ma'am. I'll have my video recorder on. Best get talkin', sweetie, or we'll have to give you another bite of rubber ball. I want you to start out with your full name real official and serious. Then I want you to say you know all your rights, but you need to confess your crimes, and where you've put the bodies. I'm going to cut the tie holding your feet and hands together. Once I get you sitting up straight on the bed, I'll turn on my camera and give you the signal. You won't need any reminders to behave, will you?"

Noonan looked away from Lynn, because she saw no weakness and no mercy. "No... I mean, no Ma'am."

Lynn pinched her cheek playfully. "That's my good little mean girl."

* * *

232

I watched Clint chuckling as he listened in on the interrogation, shaking his head. I had to take my earpiece out because Lynn was cracking me up too. My job involved being the glowering watchdog for Adrian and her gangbanger boyfriend, Putz or Struts or something like that. We had slipped in with no trouble at all. As Clint suspected, our Cinnie and her friends got wasted. Clint and I took care of the peripherals while Lynn locked herself in with Noonan. We didn't want to secure these two, because although we had the right to go after Cinnie as bond agents, I didn't want to rough up these two. I had already run their names through Jafar. They were clean, except for the usual drug and petty crap.

"What's your bitch doin' in there, man?"

Uh oh. I saw Clint tense, but then he relaxed. He's a pro. We don't let hurtful words throw us off our game. Putz opened his mouth again, and I grabbed his nose. Believe me. When I grab your nose, you don't move. Two things become apparent. One, you ain't movin'. Two, you'll do anything so I won't grab it again, because I make sure it feels like I'm going to rip it off and hand it to you. I leaned down.

"Listen here, Putz, you don't want to say anything else and start annoying me. When I get annoyed, I start tearing things off of you. You don't want that, right?"

Tears were starting at Putz's eyes as he shook his head no as much as I allowed him. I released him and patted his cheek while Adrian looked on in open mouthed fear. "We'll be done soon, so just relax a few moments longer... silently of course."

It was only five more minutes before Lynn guided a very subdued Noonan out fully dressed. Lynn was smiling at us. "Let's go, boys. We're all set, right, Cinnie?"

"Yes, Lynn," Cinnie mumbled with head down.

I gave the two Cinnie peeps a final warning. "Okay, folks, we'll leave you to the rest of your day. Take some advice. Don't follow through on whatever Cinnie had in mind for you. I'm going to be watching you two, so you better watch out, or I'll be coming here for the two of you one early morning."

Lynn guided Noonan out with Clint close behind. I had their backs. My hand was on the butt of my Smith & Wesson 9mm auto as they loaded up in the already running car with Jafar behind the wheel. I backed the rest of the way to the car and got in on the front passenger seat. No sign of anyone charging out the front door with a gun so Jafar started us toward my house.

"Did you find out, Ms. Montoya," Jafar asked.

"Yeah, Cinnie has been guilty of a few more atrocities she's not being accused of."

I was sitting in the front seat, watching the interview replay. "This is great, Lynn."

I uploaded it to Lora, who I had standing by with a text Noonan was in route. She would in turn contact our clients up North, and let them know the details. We now had a complication, and one simplification. The confession makes it plain Cinnie killed her first in Oakland. That complicated our taking her up to Seattle, because she would have to be charged here for the killing in Oakland. The other three were committed in Seattle. This all mattered in that we wouldn't have to transport. We'd get credit for the apprehension, and Oakland would handle incarceration and charging. Seattle would probably send someone down to transport Noonan. By the time we arrived at my house, Lora had news and directions.

Lora met us as we exited the car. "I put in a call to Earl first. He and Enrique are working the morning shift. They're on their way over. I told him we'd make it a joint deal where they were made aware of our plans for apprehension, with them as the official arresting officers. You can imagine the happy feet those two got hearing that."

I nodded. "That was good thinking. How did your idea go over with the firm in Seattle?"

"They loved the confession and apprehension. They promised to handle the details with the parents up North. I knew the delay in Seattle getting Noonan wouldn't bother them. With the confession the way it was done, the chances of her ever getting out will be slim. Do I want to know how Lynn got that confession?"

"Nope." I glanced back at Lynn having a personal conversation with Noonan. She owned Cinnie. Some things go to an elemental level. Whatever happened in the room had changed Cinnie forever. Until today, our murder suspect thought she was a monster. As Denny had envisioned, Noonan met a real monster. No contest. I watched the former monster looking down at her feet, with tears streaming down her cheeks, while enduring a final bit of advice given by the real monster. "No need for management to get involved in details. Thanks for making all that happen in a short car ride back home."

Lora gave me a little hug. She knew the players and the perps. She was still a little foggy about why some on our team were still running around loose, while the perps who in many cases had killed fewer people, or did less horrendous things, were sent to prison – mainly through our efforts. That she could live in our world, organize it, and deal with it on a separate plain of existence was a mystery to our crew and Denny. To our credit, we didn't question her ability, we rolled with it. With me, I loved it. I knew talent. First and foremost, she loved me – not an inconsequential endeavor. Earl and Enrique rolled up as Lynn gave Cinnie a shoulder squeeze that the former monster cringed at.

Earl, Enrique, and I huddled up for the moment of transfer. "John… you look like shit."

"Gee, thanks Earl. Listen, can we get around my mug and go straight to the details of the arrest we're handing you two slackers?"

That got some laughs, accompanied by fist bumps by Earl and his partner. "Sorry, John. 'Rique and I won a couple grand each on your set to in Las Vegas. Your favorite waitress over at The Warehouse went all in on you and came away with ten grand. You, my friend, are a very popular man amongst your friends. Now today, you hand us a gift like Noonan?" Earl stopped, sobbed, and continued my send up, "I love you man."

"I actually had very little to do with the apprehension." I gestured Clint and Lynn over while making eye contact with Jafar. He took charge of Noonan. "This is Clint Dostiene and his partner

Lynn Montoya, both in our employ, and with active FBI credentials."

They all shook hands with the proper respect. This is the way this shit should go down. It seldom does, but once in a while we get a win the way we want it.

"We have it from here, my friend," 'Rique said, helping Noonan into the backseat of their squad car. He pointed at Lora. "Thanks for the gift, Lora. We won't forget it."

Lora went over and patted Enrique's arm. She said exactly what was needed. "We need you guys. You know that, and so do we. I sent all the particulars of the apprehension to our client in Seattle, but I dubbed a copy and put it in your e-mail."

Earl gestured at the very docile Cinnie Noonan. "Why do you figure Noonan confessed and gave up so easily?"

"She seemed ready to bare her soul," Lynn replied with an award winning speculative look. "I think she needed to tell someone, so we helped her out."

Earl smiled. "Okay then. Welcome to the neighborhood."

We watched their squad car pull away with Cinnie. I liked the way that one worked out. "Thanks to you two, we had a very fulfilling morning. Go enjoy your new house, and we'll call when something else pops up on the screen. I guess you'll be tying all the loose ends on the Harvard bunch until you finally get to fix them up with permanent quarters in a gray bar hotel somewhere."

"Clint and I like to keep busy, so give us a call if anything comes up, Lora. I'm not too sure how the Harvard problem will end up, John. We haven't figured out what ending we'd like to have for that story."

I liked that. It's always best to keep all your options open with murdering psychopaths. "If you need special backup at anytime for the gigs you two handle with the FBI, we have the best backup in the world."

"Let me factor that into my thinking, John," Clint replied. "It opens up a couple of options if I had a team."

"Then consider it done, brother," I told him. Hell, I'd go gut them for him. What the hell do I care about three murderous shit-heads? "I guess you already know I'd go with you and fix these three up. Hell, we'll bury them in Canada."

Clint laughed. "If they're dissolved into a liquid form, we wouldn't have to go far at all."

Yeah, I laughed because Clint and I, along with Lynn come from the same deep dish pizza. I noticed Lynn giggling at our exchange. "It's nice to have so many monsters in our employ."

"What about you, Lora?"

"I go where John goes... always. It's nice having you here, Lynn."

Lynn looked around with a big grin. "It's nice being here in monster land."

* * *

For a split second I woke up in the Afghan mountains, wind howling like mad, freezing cold, pitch black, and a single sound out of place. Like then, I moved. I sealed Lora's mouth, taking her scantily clad body up with me. She struggled at first, before realizing who had her. I carried her toward Al's room, put her on the floor outside the bedroom, and whispered shushing sounds while releasing her mouth. We have a safe room inside Minnie-me's bedroom.

"Take Al and get in the safe room. Hit the alarm in there we have to everyone else's place. We're probably not the only ones under attack."

Lora didn't argue or say a word. She ran in to Al's room to gather her up. I went back to our bedroom and retrieved my Heckler Koch Mac-10 machine pistol, night vision goggles, and a flash-bang from my spring open safe. I didn't know how many, but I knew they were pros. They disabled my alarm system, which was state of the art, while barely breaking stride. Not knowing the inside of my house would work in my favor, but only for seconds. Once they acquired a target, this would be a war. I had no doubt they brought enough firepower to turn my house into wood dust.

I didn't give a crap about what they did or didn't do in the lower part of the house. I knew they would have to come upstairs to get at me. Right now, these guys figured we were sleeping like babies or they'd be storming around with a full out attack. This wasn't a social call. Whoever sent them wanted a statement made. My little family was meant to die bloody in our beds. I'm thinking they're hitting at least Jafar's place. He also has a safe room. I made sure Jafar knew never to take even a whimper from Samira's dog Naji for granted. The kid knew to get Samira and Naji into the safe room and hit the alarm - nothing else.

I didn't have a dog like Naji. They're terrific, but no matter how hard we try, having an early warning system like Naji blunts us. We depend so much on the animal, we forget our own senses. My house is sound proofed. I heard the single click made while they entered. They came upstairs silently, inching with precision up each step. When the first guy cleared the stairs, I shot him in both shoulders, and lobbed the flash-bang in amongst them. I whipped off the night vision goggles and hugged the wall as my military grade flash-bang blew out eardrums and blinded them.

In seconds I was at the stairwell, protecting my wounded guy while executing what turned out to be four other black clothed guys behind him. Then I waited out of sight with my buddy. No need to go rushing around getting myself shot. I either got them all or I didn't. I listened for an escape out my door. When I didn't hear anything, I dragged the unconscious survivor toward my bedroom. After getting him trussed up so he couldn't move, I dressed quickly and carried him to the stairs. I threw him down the stairs over his dead comrades' bodies. He hit with a satisfying crunch. When his landing didn't attract gunfire, I followed him down, collecting weapons as I went. I don't leave live killers behind me. I made sure each had journeyed to hell before moving on.

I knew they had a driver. I left my house through the back, circled around to the street, staying near my neighbor's trees. Lora always kids me because I know when there is a different car or truck anywhere on our street. The black SUV parked two houses down with the engine running and a very nervous driver made the discovery pretty easy. My sound proofing the house had limited the noise, but a few lights were going on around my house. I put three grouped shots through the SUV windshield which pulped the driver's head. Did I worry about killing an innocent person as I ran up on the SUV? Sure, but sometimes you have to take the shot.

Luckily for me, the driver was armed and outfitted like his compatriots. I turned off the engine, and retreated into my house.

Dragging my criminal associate into the kitchen, while he screwed up my carpet with blood, I stuffed some towels into his clothing to stop the flow a little. I wet one towel and worked on waking him up while calling into the safe room. The crunch I heard when I threw him down the stairs originated from the way his right ankle was bent.

"John?"

"I'm fine. Don't come out of the room until I come get you. Did anyone get through to you yet?" Our crew is supposed to call in immediately after they make sure everyone is safe at their location.

Lora's voice was cracking, but she held it together. "Everyone has called in. Jafar was the only one who has intruders. Lucas and Casey are on their way over to him now. Lucas just called and said ETA in five minutes. Denny said to call him the moment you can talk."

"I better do that now. I'll call you once I sort things out."

"Okay, John."

Next up, I had to contact Satan's Spawn. Denny answered on the first ring. "Five down here, and one live one, Den."

"Did you get the driver?"

"Starting out with an insult is a bad beginning, Spawn."

Denny chuckled. "Lucas called. Jafar told him the attackers found the safe room and were in the process of finding a way to get in. Lucas and Casey killed the driver on their way in, and threw flash-bangs to disable the very surprised bunch getting ready to blow up the house in order to get at Samira. We have some live ones. I briefed Clint and Lynn just in case we needed them. How's cleanup?"

"Messy. I'll drive their getaway SUV up to the house and load them all. Want me to meet you at the house of pain?"

"That's the plan. Lucas and Casey will be headed that way shortly with their bunch. I made sure Tommy, Dev, and Jesse were okay. We're lucky. They restricted their attacks to old news. You were best man at Jafar's wedding, and the one assigned to guard

Samira at first. Everyone knows now. This is war until we find out who issued the order. Then we clean house. This was a failed statement. We're going to make one they won't ever forget."

"See you in a few." I hung up. It only took fifteen minutes for me to load the bad guy's van. I told Lora to stay put. No way I wanted her and Al running around the house until I had a chance to clean things up a bit. By the time I made it back out to the van, it was still quiet on the street, as the lights had gone back out. Thankfully, no one had called the cops. Clint and Lynn pulled up behind the SUV.

"I'm pissed, John," Lynn said, hands on hips. "You had a party and didn't invite us? What the hell? We've only been here a couple weeks and you're already shunning us?"

Yeah, she's been here cracking us all up for a couple weeks. Her and Lora have bonded, with Minnie-me mimicking them both now. "I didn't want to freak you out. I know how faint you get at the sight of blood."

I got her and Clint with that gem.

When she could speak again, Lynn gestured her acceptance. "O...okay, you got me on that one. We're here to clean up and watch Lora and Minnie-me until you get back."

Clint had been inspecting the leftover carnage with professional interest, peering up the stairs and my spatters in the stairwell landing. "You should get a dog, John. The Rock was a long time ago. Besides, he died with his boots on."

Rock was a dog we had with recon back in the 'Stans. He died saving our butts. "I know, but I have Samira's Naji, and now Tonto. Besides, although I didn't hear them like Tonto, I still sniffed them out in time to welcome them properly."

Clint shrugged. "You're going to need a little reconstruction here. We'll clean things up a bit and let your family out of the safe room." He slapped his forehead comically. "Sorry, Lynn. I'll be cleaning up a little. I nearly forgot about the fact Lynn doesn't clean up anything."

Lynn gasped, but then giggled. "Fine. Maybe I'm not a domestic chore Goddess. I'll give you a hand here, honey-pie. In return, I don't want you whining about my shortcomings for at least a month."

"Whining... whining? I'll have to buy a month's supply of paper plates and plastic silverware in case I have to be gone for a month, so I'll still be able to find the kitchen when I get back."

I was already laughing my ass off as the Bickersons were still trading shots. My wounded buddy was probably getting lonely out there with his dead friends. "Thanks, you two. Keep this up and you'll have your own radio show. I think it took Lora and I at least a month before we were at each other's throats over domestic chores. It wasn't actually a fight though. I've always cleaned my place myself. Lora thought it was her job to clean the house. It was resolved pretty fast when she decided it was okay with her if I cleaned it."

"Only one problem with that solution, John," Clint said. "I can't clean as fast as Lynn trashes the place."

Lynn giggled again. I began to think she was playing Clint. The look in his eyes when he grinned, convinced me he was remembering all the little tells she probably left him.

"Oh, you dirty... no good... rotten..."

Montoya was laughing so hard she nearly collapsed on the floor.

"Take off, John. I believe my partner and I are about to have a breakthrough."

"I'll call with an update, you whacky kids you."

* * *

By the time I reached our homemade house of pain, I only needed to drive right into our unique warehouse. This is where we bring special guests when we're out of options or time. It's not sanctioned, on any of the expense sheets, or acknowledged by people at the Company. Those who arrive here for interrogation will eventually wind up in disposal, because the people who interact here know we only have one purpose – protect the United States of America and each other at all costs. The quick and the dead meet here for the last time.

Casey met the van while closing up the door behind me. "Hi, John. Thanks for the wakeup call. You know of course everyone in the kid's neighborhood will think he and Samira are terrorists, right?"

I shook my head sagely as I left the SUV. "Like Clint says, into each life a little rain must fall. How much of a remake will we have to do on his house?"

Lucas joined his partner. "We hardly scratched it, unlike the last time I allowed Casey to join me on The Sea Wolf."

Casey launched into hands in the air exasperation the moment he recognized the melody from that familiar tune. "Oh for God's sake! I knew it! I knew you'd bring up the knocked over beer. All joking aside, John, we need to have an intervention here. The next time Lucas mentions that spilled beer... there will be blood!"

I played the hand Casey dealt me with relish as I watched the storm clouds form over Lucas's features. "I believe you're right, Case. We need to recapture The Sea Wolf. I'm sick of this tiptoeing around. Let's bag this cheap Captain Ahab mime holding our ship hostage." I pumped a fist in the air. "Free the Wolf... free the Wolf!"

"Yeah! That's what I'm talkin' about!" Casey joined me for another call for action while Lucas stomped around like a real life Ahab.

"Knock it off you nut-cakes," Denny ordered, walking out from the back room. "Let's forego the usual banter. I didn't see this coming and I'm not happy. We almost lost two valuable assets and John."

Lucas and Casey cracked up at that remark.

"And unacceptable collateral damage," Denny added. "The good news is our counter measures and crisis reaction were exceptional. Bad news is our electronic stuff sucked. Bring your wounded one to the interrogation room. We better get to him first while he's still breathing. We'll do the others later."

Thus started a long but information rich day. No, they didn't list names of the people behind the attack. They were two separate cells operating in the San Francisco and the Los Angeles area. They were a motley group with origins in Palestine, Jordan, Saudi Arabia, Iran, and Chechnya. Once we had immediate identities, Denny relayed the information to Clint and Jafar. They would work in tandem to find even a thread involving shared financial or business interests, and any trace where they crossed paths with a common source.

We three musketeers clean up our own interrogation room. Denny also has area contacts who do things on a moment's notice, along with resources for incarceration. He's a full service horror show for enemies of the United States. His own personal rendition squad flies in to collect guys he wants to put on ice for a while until the information we get checks out. They come in by military means and fly out the same way. The clean up was nearly finished when Denny came in to update us.

"Jafar and Samira are at your place, John. I sent a crew in to fine tune your house. They specialize in crime scene cleanups. Clint and Jafar will work together with the stuff we have so far while the trail's hot. We salvaged a lot of their electronics, which I shipped over to Clint and Jafar. We're moving in any direction we need to the moment we get a target. Go on home, tighten up your defenses, and get ready to rock and roll. A statement will be made about Samira these assholes won't ever forget."

Denny didn't get any argument from us. I wanted to know if Strobert had any ideas. "Did you have favorites in the area?"

Denny shrugged. "I have a wish list. There's a Saudi Imam in the Sacramento area, practicing the favored terrorist sect of Islam – he's a Wahhabi practitioner. He issued a Fatwa allowing rape of females fourteen and older found not to be adhering to Islamic law. Samira is a favorite target of his."

I thought I knew who he was talking about. "Muhammad Abdul Azim?"

Denny smiled. "You must have heard Jafar talk about him."

"Both he and Samira have mentioned that guy. Samira thinks too many people laugh him off as a whacko. She says he has a large following. The kid hates his guts."

"Let's go pick that sucker up," Lucas said. "We'll take Jafar with us. He needs some seasoning. Does this Azim have kids and a wife?"

I chuckled. "No. He's a player. Azim pulls the Muslim persecution card at every opportunity, while defending honor killings and female genital mutilation. It drives Samira nuts."

"Sounds like a primo candidate for an adjustment," Casey said. "I'd like to see how Jafar does with something like this. He has a personal interest. We can monitor whether he can keep his feelings in check."

"That would be my angle too," Denny agreed. "I have no doubt about his outlook, but I'd like to see if he can handle something more in a gray area of right and wrong."

"I doubt he'd care about whether Azim goes bye-bye," I replied. "He lives in Davis at a house on Almond Lane, with access."

"Have you been mapping this poor man, John?"

"Yeah, Lucas," I admitted. "I've thought of twisting his stupid head off more times than even I like to admit, because he's been on my radar since Samira married Jafar. The kids live in our neighborhood under our protection. I like the idea of making a few of these religious icons disappear, instead of allowing them to order other peoples' deaths on a whim. I figured if Azim kept shooting his mouth off about Samira I would have no choice but to Gronk him."

That got a few laughs.

"I'm in agreement. I doubt we'll need many lessons if one of these weasels spews that Fatwa bullshit and ends up off planet a few days later. I take it you have a plan already on tap, John?"

"I do, but it involves the overuse of our new assets," I admitted, cringing as I saw the Spawn of Satan grin knowingly. Lucas and Casey immediately disseminated what was passing in front of them. They switched immediately to hosts of the Harding roast.

"Case, I believe the Dark Lord has had the audacity to lecture the Spawn of Satan on the deployment of his assets. Woe on to the Dark Lord for such an affront."

"Oh the shame, DL," Casey piled right on, abandoning his cohort in the retaking of The Sea Wolf. "You have forbidden Spawn from deploying Clint and Lynn according to his perverted

244

schedule? You indeed have ventured into the forbidden zone of discourse with Satan's Spawn!"

I caved like a tulip in a tornado. "Okay... okay... I need Lynn to play dress up with Clint and go over to Azim's place, plant a few camera feeds, and bug the house. He may already be familiar with the rest of us. We do want to know what he knows before we snuff him, right?"

"You know, DL, you're sounding a lot more like Denny every day." Lucas shook his head, regret lancing out with each word.

"Pretty soon he'll be dressing in those butt ugly suits and gaining thirty extra pounds around his waist."

Denny pointed a warning finger at Casey. "You're lucky I have a sense of humor. John's right. If we're going to play with these people for a while, there's no use in cutting off a solid illegal information gathering as long as we're all on board. We want this kept in house at Murderer's Row. Azim is on our shit list whether he's connected with the two cells we've uncovered or not. Any objections?"

"Hell no, Denny," Lucas answered. "If you and your mime have your hearts set on Azim, then Case and I are in all the way, right Case?"

"Hold on, Lucas," Casey countered, waving his hand. "If we do this, do we have to take orders from Denny's dupe here?"

Strobert was already laughing. I just beckoned with my hands. "C'mon... let it all out. This is because you guys ended up on a working vacation in Las Vegas. You two thought all was right with the world in Sin City, and the only thing to do there was sip whiskey, win a fortune, and watch me get my butt kicked. Get over it."

"We've lost our brother, Case," Lucas said, putting an arm around the shoulders of an equally grieving Casey as they walked toward the exit. "We never thought you would pass over to the dark side for real, DL."

"C'mon, Lucas. Denny's Gronked him. His soul is gone, leaving only a vapor trail. God help us all," Casey finished with fervor.

I watched them leave like two mourners at their grandma's funeral. Strobert finished me off with a pat on the shoulder. "Go on to your house. Now that you've joined management I'll need you to go over and check on my other employees. Report back with any new development, DL."

"Good one, Spawn." What's the use of arguing when you've already been Gronked.

Chapter Seventeen
Jafar's Final Word

Clint pointed at the screen on Jafar's laptop. The two of them were sitting in Harding's den where work related business was conducted, their laptops open side by side on a desk. Lynn stayed with Lora and Alice while the work crew fixed the home. "You're getting it now. Stay on that path. Section off links into categories in the database we created. Don't memorize or get drawn away from our template. Let the software handle recognition once we provide all the facts. Getting bogged down in financial records, events attended, or acquaintances will only cloud up the picture. What we're doing is a little like the data mining the feds do when scanning millions of items on the Internet. We don't want targets at this stage. We want keywords, locales, and interests we can base a wide search on through every database in existence. With enough connections, no matter how slight, you'll see what would have been thousands of suspected sources reduced drastically."

Jafar nodded, smiling in appreciation as Clint sat back down to handle his list. "The Company instructors were much less imaginative than this."

"You're real good, Jafar. Don't let the profilers ruin your intuitiveness. Never set out with a fixed template. Build your query database with an expandable template, adding parameters as you go. The FBI likes to highlight their hotshot profilers, but they fudge their stats all the time. They are nearly useless with random acts. If crimes were all committed by people the victims know, then sure, the FBI or local cops can round up the usual suspects. Random burglaries, killings, thefts, identity thieving rings, or nearly anything involving unknown perps who move their base of operations will stymie law enforcement agencies. They have guidelines not to catch perps, but to protect their own asses when they find nothing. Then they point at their guidebooks and profiling sheets claiming they did everything possible."

Jafar chuckled. "You do not have much respect for law enforcement."

"I have respect for their dedication. I just don't think much of their tactics. Working with John and the crew you're part of, will be my first opportunity at going after bad guys without my hands tied behind my back."

"John told me you have already found the serial killers the FBI could not locate at all who have been mutilating and torturing women all over."

"Yep. Lynn and I are going to get them. Then we'll find out how many those monsters have actually killed no one knows about." Clint glanced over the screen networked with Jafar. "I think we have enough to send out our first query into the system. He opened up another window, and typed for a moment with blinding speed before hitting enter. "Now we wait. This is our check of whether we're establishing the right query."

Clint didn't just input the data and relax. He tracked progress on parallel screens. His brows knitted. He focused a laser like glance of admonishment over at Jafar. "Okay... I get it... you think you can dick over the old guy. What's with this Azim character? You've jacked the data real nice so he comes up as a suspect. I'm beginning to think you're disrespecting me, kid."

Jafar's eyes widened. He had no illusions as to Dostiene's abilities at a computer or in mass casualties. He had been interacting with accomplished killers and knew when he was in the presence of a very dangerous man. "I am sorry, Clint. I jacked the input because Azim has said things about Samira to end her life countless times. I want him dead, and I would like the opportunity to do it myself."

Clint grinned. "Hell, kid, you didn't have to fudge me. You have a reason to want someone dead, just tell me. You want Azim to shine as a mastermind with the two cells that John, Casey, and Lucas have decimated. We can make it happen. I can tell in your face you want Azim in a private setting."

Jafar's face lost all semblance of dissemination. "I love Samira with all my heart and soul. Azim has said things about her that can only be answered with death. I wish to beat him to death and piss on his grave."

Clint laughed, clapping Jafar on the back. "That's what I'm talkin' about. All we have to do is figure out who the real sources are, and then we'll fix Azim up for the adjustment too. What we can't do is substitute him for the real perps. Keep the mission foremost in your mind, Jafar. Opportunities always present themselves if you stick with the prime objective. You've already told me enough about this Azim character to make me want to go take care of him right away. How serious are you, kid?"

Jafar met Clint's gaze without looking away. "As serious as you and Lynn are about fixing those Harvard serial killers."

"Definitely serious enough then. Well... well... it looks like we don't have to set your buddy Azim up at all. Look who just popped up as the front runner even without your helper items. I bet you're not the only one looking at Azim. Strobert always has a wish list stashed away for a rainy day. My guess is Azim's name won't surprise him much. Here's a Chechen pretty high up on the list of probables – Ruslan Umarov." They waited in silence for a moment until the database query ended with one other name – Saud Morcos.

Jafar gripped Clint's arm, pointing at the screen. "John picked that guy up on a bond skip two months ago. He should have been deported back to Iran."

"What did he jump bail on?"

"Threatening witnesses in an attempted honor killing. The eighteen year old girl got away with her life, thanks to a neighbor down the street from where they lived. He heard her screaming for help, all bloody and beaten. The neighbor hid her and called the police. The girl's uncle and brother were arrested for attempted murder. When it came to trial, jurors in the case complained to the judge about their families getting threatening e-mail notes. They were traced to Morcos."

"How did John get involved?"

"The bail bond company that agreed to post a bond for Morcos already knew it was a bad risk, so they got a big up front fee and hired John to make sure Morcos didn't skip. I tracked his expenditures. When he bought a ticket to the East Coast, John was waiting for him at Oakland International. Lora informed security around the United entrance. Then, John and Tommy faced him up when he was dropped off. He spit on John and got Gronked. Tommy said John hit him so hard, people nearby fainted from pain in commiseration."

Clint laughed appreciatively. "I think we've hit the trifecta, kid. No one posted bail for that Morcos guy. You're right. He had a limited visa, and should have been thrown out of the country. I see they released him on an unspecified technicality. What a crock! It looks like it's up to us for the judicial correction. There, I uploaded it to Denny. We'll see if he reacts the way we want him to. If he doesn't, we'll do it anyway but tighten up our rules of engagement. I'm sure Denny will want to question the guy, and his two cohorts. We'll try right now to nail the point of origin for these two cells, but it may not be possible without a few tidbits of info from this rung on the ladder."

"You have not seen Mr. Strobert's warehouse they call the 'House of Pain'," Jafar replied. "They have a 100% success rate when questioning known terrorists. I do not know why that Senator keeps claiming torture doesn't work, because it works every time in the 'House of Pain'."

"I bet it does. There's a reason we have ways to take ourselves out under hard interrogation," Clint replied. "No one can withstand the stuff human beings can dream up for torture."

"I heard you were taken, but you did not kill yourself."

Clint shrugged. "The guy who had me interrogated lacked imagination. He wanted me alive as a card to play on people over him later. His guards eventually became complacent. Let's work on this project with the assumption we'll proceed immediately. Call up Morcos's last known address. We'll make sure he's there when we go to collect him. With his building plans, I'll be able to give John a few suggestions on taking him."

"John has not said how he met you. Was it overseas?"

Dostiene stared solemnly at Jafar as a picture kaleidoscope played in his head for a moment. "I was already in the Afghan mountains with a Company team, scouting for an offensive against a developing Taliban force near the Pakistani border. It was a joint operation with the Marines. They sent Marine Recon units ahead of their regimental force to hook up with us. Strobert worked liaison duties between the Marines and us. I laser guided a target for demolition by the Air Force. A mortar round knocked me out before the Air Force arrived to decimate the Taliban encampment."

"Denny knew my last known position. He had his eye on John already from prior actions. He asked for volunteers to go get a man down, but the officers rightly labeled it a suicide mission, promising once they secured the area, my position would be the first checked. Harding spoke up then, claiming he was familiar with the area from the last time Marine Recon had been on scout in the area. John's squad leader backed him on a one man retrieval mission, and the officers reluctantly agreed."

"When I eventually came to, I was bumping along across the Dark Lord's shoulders. He nearly had me all the way back when a Taliban force encountered our back trail. John saw we weren't going to make it. He backtracks to rocky cover and checks me over. John grins and hands me his .45 caliber sidearm with extra clips. 'Do you know how to use one of these,' he asks. I laughed and nodded at the sarcastic prick. He and I took out an entire Taliban team from ambush before some of their main force started catching up. By then Marine Recon teams had moved into a nearer position. The Marine snipers mangled everything within five hundred yards of us. John helped me to our forward positions. I was seeing double which had made our fight in the rocks exciting. Every time I missed, John would have a new remark about my shooting prowess. I only laughed and killed at one time I can remember. That was the time."

Jafar listened to Dostiene's accounting of the meeting with rapt attention, completely forgetting about what they had been working on. When Clint finished, Jafar quickly told him about his overnighter with John in jail, complete with a detailed description of Harding's adjustment of Terry Nelson he had only mentioned before in Las Vegas. He watched with amusement as Clint howled in laughter at John's remark in jail after knocking out Nelson, when he warned everyone down to a sitting position or they would be partying with him. "Everyone sat down... even if it was on the cell floor."

Clint clapped Jafar on the shoulders. "God... good story, kid. Yours is funnier than mine."

"John told me that night we were very much alike, in that his drunken father came home to beat the crap out of him when he was young. Instead, John Gronked him and left the area in his car. I know in taking this position, I am in the company of highly skilled and very deadly men. Please let me know if I am ever out of line. You do not know me very well yet, but please know I do not wish to offend you by accident. I should have been truthful in this business I have with Azim. I apologize."

Clint waved him off. "Forget it. If you're thinking I won't cut you the same slack as the rest of this crew you're wrong. I'm sure Denny is stirring things up, even as we speak, with the new stuff we've provided him with."

"I hope to be an agent all of my friends here can depend on. Samira loves our home and she does not ever wish to move. I will make sure she gets her wish or I will be dead."

Clint fist bumped with Jafar. "Amen, brother."

* * *

I watched our new guest, Muhammad Abdul Azim. He woke up finally, his head probably throbbing. He then realized he could not move his limbs. His eyes darted back and forth, because we had also strapped his head in place. Our buddy Azim was not happy. That touched a happy place in my soul. See... Jafar and Samira were like my kids. I remembered back to when I hid out with Samira and her family in a cave when she was just a little girl. She stepped up. She didn't whine or complain. Jafar knew she was a keeper the moment he laid eyes on her. Jafar wanted Azim like a snake wants a big fat rat.

After our info gathering phase, we hit our targets hard and decisive. The civilian population would never know because these particular people had made the deadly mistake of taking on

Murderer's Row in their natural habitat. I unfastened Azim and gave him some aspirin, massaged his shoulders, head, and neck. He was very tense, mostly because he recognized me the moment he saw my smiling face come into view. Saud Morcos and Ruslan Umarov were next to him, but still unconscious. There were no other survivors of our foray. All but these two had been left with a Denny Strobert cocktail syringe full of afterlife potion. We didn't fool around with niceties. All the bad guys were dead... all of them. Yeah... the newspapers would be full of speculation. We didn't care, because we have a pact. Our West Coast Murderer's Row incorporates one basic tenet – we do not allow foreign entities to allow our Constitution to become a suicide pact. Our select group, when we have incontrovertible proof someone around us has decided to shit on our country or our friends, we take those facts and act on them in ways beyond the law. Boo hoo. Light a candle and move on. Allowing known terrorists coupled with ACLU lawyers to reach our perverted justice system with judges who've negated their positions by either selling out the constitution or their moral integrity, doesn't sit well with us.

"He's fine, John." Jafar hovered in a way only passionate interest explains. "Tell him about the deal."

Azim perked up, as he rubbed his previously fastened parts. I could tell he knew who Jafar was. His brain was humming, trying to make sense of it all without any facts other than he had went to bed the night before and woke up here. "What of my family?"

"They're fine, pal," I reassured him. "Unlike your ilk, we don't make war on wives and children."

"I will tell you nothing." Azim hung his head in a defiant posture with his hands clasped in tight fists.

"That really hurts our feelings. I'm at a loss here, Jafar. How could we have been more obliging? Mr. Azim has taken an immediate dislike to us." I got a kick out of Jafar simply smiling but saying nothing. The kid never disappoints me, except of course when he sides with Minnie-me against the Dark Lord.

"He hasn't even heard our deal yet, John," Jafar picked up where I left off.

Azim wasn't stupid enough to leap up and start engaging us. He had thought about it with serious consideration, but knew instinctively it would end badly for him. "What is this deal you speak of? I want a lawyer. I will speak with you no longer."

I shook my head with the proper amount of sadness. "We don't allow the ACLU in at this level, Mr. Azim. You are far beyond their traitorous clutches. The deal my young friend speaks of is a chance you have right now to actually hook up with your ACLU buddies and their scum sucking lawyers. All you have to do is take on my friend Jafar here. If you win, you get the ACLU promised land of traitorous lawyers. If not, he'll probably beat you to death. I'm hoping he lets us test your theory about 'you will say nothing', but it's his call. See, you decided to go Jihad on his wife Samira. We've decided to retaliate. Sucks to be you."

Azim looked at Jafar and I with his beady little eyes trying to perceive what his chances were. "I am listening."

He seemed a bit too cocky so I walked over, grabbed him by the neck and lifted him free of the floor with his hands batting and pummeling my hand. After a minute's attitude review, I put him on the floor again. "I don't like it when you assume too much, meat! Be careful how you react to us in any way, shape, or form. You feel me?"

Azim sputtered, choked, and made placating gestures to the effect he understood.

"Okay," I proceeded. "My brother, Jafar, wishes to kick the crap out of you for what you have said and intimated about his wife, Samira. I'm in agreement. Here's what you get on my word: ability to call in any ACLU traitorous dogs you want to if you win. If Jafar wins, you get a chance to tell us everything, along with a quick painless death. What do you say?"

Azim grinned. "I know you will not abide by your own rules, but I wish to kill this young pup anyway. I agree to your terms. Let us begin."

Casey came out of the shadowed part of our greeting room. He helped Azim into the gloves and explained how the camera feeds would be focused. Azim shook his head, in obvious disdain for the professed rules. "I am not stupid! Get out of my face. I know you will break your word if I win and kill this young piece of shit!"

Casey grinned over at me. "Well hell, John, let's start slicing on this prick now. He only thinks we won't get everything out of him."

I don't conduct business like that, even with Azim. I could always get him later. "I gave my word, Case. Azim will get what he wishes if he wins. If I short change Jafar, what the hell do I do for respect in what I promise? I promised Jafar a life and death meet up with this sack of shit. I don't like it any more than you, brother."

Clint's chuckle from the shadows made me look up. I figured he had a more direct intent in mind for Azim, but he surprised me.

Clint walked forward, putting a hand on Jafar's shoulders. "You trained him, Dark Lord. Don't go pussy on him now."

He was right of course. "Let's do this."

Casey helped Azim into the MMA gloves as I did with Jafar. In moments they were faced off at each other, and I could tell from the expressions we wouldn't need much to get things going. I gestured at our would be opponents. "Get it on!"

Azim charged across at Jafar, who sidestepped the flying knee he launched, and floored the passing Azim with a lightning quick, back of the head strike. Jafar let Azim regain his feet, gloved hands clenched at his sides. Both of them, as if by prearranged signal moved in on each other. I was about to find out how well I had done as a teacher, because I could see Azim wasn't some unpicked posy. To his credit, Jafar remembered to keep his rage in check. He impressed me over the next few moments. Azim landed shots with purpose, catching Jafar coming in with a couple left hook stunners. The second shot put Jafar on his butt.

Azim launched a side kick to Jafar's head, he narrowly rolled out of the way of. Blood gushed from his nose Azim had flattened with the second left hook. Yeah, I watched my pupil's handling of the first broken part I knew about. He spit blood without taking his eyes off Azim. Jafar was in shape, but besides the blinding pain a busted nose causes, it affects your wind. I noted he acted as I had schooled him – short breaths where he could, and react to the fighter not the nose. Azim threw a straight right hand, Jafar rolled down under while leg whipping his opponent. He caught Azim completely by surprise. The leg whip worked perfectly. Azim landed flat with the back of his head bouncing off the cement floor.

Jafar went into full mount position with elbows and hammer fists. In seconds, the stunned Azim went from in danger to near death. Jafar did as I had coached him. After his first devastating flurry, the kid went to measured strikes, waiting until he had a clean shot before pummeling Azim. I shook my head at Clint and Casey as they moved forward to save our interrogation subject. They grinned and returned to watchful positions. The kid didn't let up when Azim's head no longer showed any signs of moving in between blows. He held up finally, his gloved hands dripping blood, and his breathing ragged. I noted Morcos and Umarov stirring into consciousness during the last takedown.

I walked over next to Jafar. "You done, kid?"

He stood up to face me. A bloody mess, with a flattened nose, Jafar smiled. He looked like a ghoul. Taking a deep, gulping breath through his mouth, Jafar held up a finger. "Almost."

That said, the kid leaped into the air. He came down full bore with a right foot stomp that caved in Azim's face, killing him instantly. Well, this payback stuff is hard to predict. Satan's Spawn would of course be displeased, but I could tell by the chuckling laughter behind me, Clint and Casey thought the ending was pretty entertaining. For me, when you decide to make statements branding a man's wife a whore, prostitute, and mark her for death, sometimes that ill advised talk comes back to haunt you. Jafar played it through. He walked over to the wide eyed Morcos and Umarov, shaking a bloody fist at Morcos.

"You are next, dog! Cut him free, John!"

Yeah, the kid was on a roll. I could tell in his eyes, Morcos didn't want any part of the raging bloody specter dripping Azim's blood on him. "I think we should give our buddies, Saud and Ruslan a chance to talk, kid. You know Denny. He'll be wanting an accounting as to what happened to Azim. A cooperative Morcos and Umarov might make him a bit more receptive as to Azim's sudden departure from planet earth. I believe Saud here for sure wants to be helpful, right pal?"

Our Saud couldn't move much, but what he could move, he moved in a violent show of affirmation. Naturally, that tickled my two comrades. Umarov mimicked him even though he hadn't been asked. Clint and Case knew we had methods far beyond a Jafar beat-down to get Morcos's cooperation, so they weren't really concerned with whether Morcos or Umarov would help us out. They knew both would... eventually. I uncovered Saud's mouth with a rip of duct tape. His face contorted momentarily with Jafar hovering around him dripping blood.

"I...I want to make a deal."

Yeah, Saud, that'll happen. "See, kid. Saud wants to be helpful. Maybe you won't have to grind his head into bloody pulp. You know of course we're going to make you clean up Azim from our floor, right?"

Jafar leaned over with his broken nosed, blood dripping face, to smile into Morcos's eyes. "Yes, I am very good at cleanup, John. No problem."

* * *

We were meeting in Denny's bat-cave. He loves our warehouse House of Pain. I could tell Strobert was less than happy with our results. His mind, of course, amped into the future, which limited his ability to enjoy the moment. He sees scenarios where he keeps these mooks alive somewhere secret so he can return to them like a garden of infamous information. I'm more of a day to day guy. They're not like a set of your mother's good china. You break them, and you go get some more.

Denny stared at me, gauging how his perspective would mesh with mine. He correctly assumed it wouldn't, sighed, and shrugged. "At least you allowed me to keep a couple."

"I aim to please." What the hell's the use of trading barbs with the Spawn of Satan? I can't predict what he sees in the future. I do have an imagination of sorts though.

"You could have stopped the kid from stomping Azim into eternity, John."

"Was there a question for me in there, Denny, or are you just blowing off steam?"

Strobert waved me off. "I get it. The teams from Homeland Security hit the spots Morcos and Umarov gave us. We did well. It's my job to caution you as my company rep to keep the bigger picture in mind."

Denny was already laughing when I couldn't keep the look of angry disdain off my face. Note to self – work on the poker face with Strobert. "You can kiss my big picture ass. The kid killed Azim in cold blood. It's his first, and I have no doubt he could do it again. He's tested goods. Jafar knew what you wanted. He knew what I wanted. He looked me in the eye, jumped up and stomped Azim into hell."

"I get that, and believe me, I'm arranging future missions in my head with that in mind. Staying in the present though, any suggestions for immediate procedure you'd like to share?"

I consider my answer to Denny carefully. "I think we sit tight now with all channels open for threads entwining into what we've done. You have Morcos and Umarov for bad guy input."

Strobert nodded. "That's how I figure it too, John. Okay, let's take a breath and keep the feelers out. You still thinking about backing Clint with a team?"

"Whatever Clint needs to get those wankers is exactly what I'll provide. Clint's already worked out a wish list and I agree with it completely. I know he sent it to you too."

"I have it, but interdivisional camaraderie dictates a different ending. I'd like you to make sure we have live suspects."

I laughed. It was a few moments before I could engage coherently in the conversation. "Fuck you, Denny! Those people have to die. If you're not onboard with that, maybe you better duck into the cellar and stay away from our obvious need to happen scenario."

"I'm getting pressure for an FBI show trial, John. It's one I can't ignore."

Rage would have been the common reaction here, but I knew how things worked with this stuff. The same FBI minions who owed most of their latest successes to Clint, wanted him to put aside his serial killer end game and play ball, but Clint already told me they'd take whatever he gave them. No way I'm forwarding that determination by a guy who should know better. Who knows? Denny may be lighting me up as a test for all I know.

"Fuck you, Denny. Let me lay it on the line for you, partner. It don't matter how many government agencies try to sack our op. We will kill these three, Denny. I don't care where they are, or how many people we embarrass, they die, period. If it hurts your ambitions, I guess you'll have to lay low out of this."

Denny looked me in the eye without turning away. "That's what I figured. Any chance you keep the team on the West Coast, and allow Clint and Lynn to do this on their own?"

"Clint's already requisitioned the West Coast Avengers. Our participation is a done deal. Best to figure out your involvement or non-involvement in this, Denny. We want you as CIA Director, but if you think we'll cave on psychopaths killing on sprees, you're out of your bureaucratic mind!"

"Understood," Denny acknowledged while looking away. He held out his hand after a moment and I shook it. "I don't want to end up so jaded I don't know right from wrong. I'd rather have all of you at my back than the Washington fucks any day... any way."

"Good to know, my friend. I never figured you for a kiss ass serial killer stance... at least I prayed not. We'll make this serial killer trio demise as righteous as we can, but know this: their deaths are a forgone conclusion, and any ripples in the force will be dealt with extreme prejudice. You feel me, brother?"

Denny didn't waver. "I got it, John. Know this, no matter what I face, I ain't ever going to screw my team over... ever. It has nothing to do with fear or political complications. When things get unsavory or too hot to handle, I'll take the heat, and join you all. It took years to have something like we have out here. I'm not pissing on it over a few complications. I hope their deaths look good, because there will be a spotlight on them."

He's got me there. "With the way my newest members work, I'm not real sure that's possible. You saw what happened in Vegas to the serial rapists. I'll do my best to express your desire for a good looking death scene, but in the end, it will be Lynn and Clint who make the final sendoff scenario after they find out where all the bodies are. Best if you work on an ending where the bodies are burnt to a crisp and maybe the info found on a hard drive."

Denny nodded."Not bad, DL. How are Lora and Alice doing?"

"Alice still insists on sleeping in the safe-room. I guess it will take a while to earn her trust back. Lora keeps to herself about it. She knew what she was getting into. Your cleanup crew was the best, Denny. They had the place looking better than before the attack by the end of the day. I think Lora cut me some slack because of it. Let's call it a night so I can go home and take the girls out to dinner or something. They'll probably refuse, thinking they'll get killed in the restaurant parking lot, but hey, I don't make the rules."

Denny laughed, nodding his head in agreement as I spoke. "You ever think of going into management full time, John?"

Yeah, but all the scenarios end up with me forcing unintended consequences. I've been around Strobert long enough to know how management works. I probably couldn't cut it. That's why I have a day-job. "Nope. Not doing that. You're the best I've ever seen at it, Denny. I'm not you. We both know that."

Denny grinned. "I thought the same way as you back in the day. Keep it in mind, John. I could use a second in command I can trust. It's a joke at your expense with the West Coast Avengers, but you have the tools for it."

"I'll keep it in mind. I have so many things working the right way, I'm not going to change what ain't broke."

"Fine. I'm not wanting you anywhere you don't want to be, but it is something to think about, John. I could use the backup if I ever get the directorship."

"I would help for sure. Whether I make it official... I don't know. It doesn't seem to me you need much help, Spawn. How about if the West Coast Avengers help you out as a team? That sets the right tone for me."

"Interesting idea, Dark Lord. Take off and make the attempt at a night out. My advice is to rent a movie Al wants to see and order a pizza."

Probably a good idea. "Thanks, Den. See you later."

Chapter Eighteen
Outside Agitator

While I'm driving home, pondering my predicament as the butt of a Company management joke, I see my young neighbor Darin McBride being stalked by a herd of idiot gang-bangers. I'm upset, because after Darin helped me out with the setup of the now deceased gang-banger, Terry Nelson, I had made a few permanent adjustments to the adult supervision trying to make everyday citizens' lives miserable in Oakland. I couldn't single out Darin because that would be like putting a target on his back. Something about this gang shenanigans bothered me. I smelled trap. Darin was walking while looking back over his shoulder uneasily, but the bangers weren't approaching any closer. I called my nearest West Coast Avengers neighbor, Devon Constantine. He answered on the first ring.

"Dark Lord?"

I heard muffled laughter in the background. "Is that Jess with you, Dev?"

"Yeah, brother, what's up?"

"I have a situation here. You and Jess want to come over and be bait?"

"Give us the 411 and we'll be there. What do you want us to do?"

"I have a herd of gang-bangers stalking a neighbor of mine, a kid you two know who lives up the street from me, named Darin McBride. I have a bad feeling this is an extension of the hit put out on me and Jafar. I don't want my young neighbor to die because he's connected to me. They're following him along 38th Avenue toward our street on Lyon. They're at Penniman now."

"We're on our way. We'll load up."

"Front the bangers. I have your back on what happens after."

"By your command, DL."

I listened to the muffled laughter with the hope I was wrong about this. "Stuff it, Dev. I'm on point, and I am armed. You and Jess make sure you are too. DL out."

I kept back from the event. I had parked for a time after spotting it. No way would I ever allow Darin to get jumped without me interceding. These bangers following him weren't kids from his school. They had the look of hard corps made bangers over the age of what I think of as youth stupidity. If they moved on him, I knew there would be a hot time for John Harding today. Darin was under my protection. This was a bad situation. It meant that either I was being followed, or my car was bugged, and whoever ordered it knew me far too well.

I took out my .45 from under the driver's seat while I waited. Then I spotted him. He trailed the herd by about twenty-five yards. His slacks and thigh length leather coat were black. A thin material black hoodie covered his head and parts of his face. Dev and Jess arrived in front of the herd next to Darin. Jess motioned for Darin to get in the car. He knew my two friends. With a relieved look, Darin jogged across the street, and slipped in the back seat. The bangers stopped, starting to do some catcalls while moving toward Dev's car. Jess and Dev got out of Dev's GMC Terrain. They leaned against the hood with their arms folded.

By that time, I had exited my car and come up on Mr. Hoodie from his blind side. He hesitated, trying to make sense out of the new kink in the scene, because it wasn't Dev and Jess he wanted. I Gronked him. The straight right I threw into that tender bunch of nerves at the base of the skull dropped Mr. Hoodie like he was shot with a cannon ball. He was unconscious before he hit the sidewalk face first. The Uzi he had his hand on under the coat clattered to the walk too. The bangers were stunned.

I plastic tied Mr. Hoodie's hands behind him while watching the herd. After my play on Hoodie, Dev and Jess ran over to bookend the bangers with weapons in hand. Once my hunch about a setup proved true, they knew there were no innocents here. With Mr. Hoodie on my shoulder, I jogged over to my car and stuffed him into the trunk.

* * *

"Stay here with your head down Darin," Jess said. "Bait up, brother."

Dev smiled over at his long time friend. They served together in the same sandpit overseas. "Let's set up out front, Jess. That should attract some attention away from the Dark Lord."

"On it." Jess exited and took up his position next to Dev in front of the car. "Have I tol' you how sick I am of these pants down, pathetic excuses for humanity?"

Dev chuckled. "Many times, my brother." Dev waved at them, a circular motion with rolling finger meant to say 'bring it on' in body language.

"I think you upset them," Jess said, mimicking his partner, as the bangers became more virulent with their gestures. "One or more of them probably has a gun."

"Oh... Jess... I'm so scared. The Dark Lord has his nasty ass .45 Colt in hand even as we speak. You've seen him shoot. What's chances anyone at this distance from where DL is sneakin' up on that dimwit in black, survives raisin' a weapon on us?"

Jess snickered in appreciation of that word picture. He straightened. "Uh oh! DL has seen enough."

Dev cringed. "Oh shit! He Gronked him. Let's move."

Jess rushed to the inner sidewalk side, weapon aimed. "Hands on the top of your heads, my little thugs! Don't make me tell you twice or someone gets knee capped!"

One of them reached, but by that time Devon was five feet away with his 9mm Glock pointed in his face. "Yeah, kid, draw that piece right on out. I'll pump half my clip through your head, but hey, it's your call."

Devon's person of interest slowly eased his hands up to the top of his head. Jess pointed at Mr. Hoodie getting transported to the trunk of Harding's car. "Looks like we're collecting today, Dev."

"Shit! That means he'll be calling Satan's Spawn for the rest of these pixies." Devon waved a warning finger at the group. "Listen up! Drop down on your knees. Keep those hands locked behind your heads."

* * *

I called Strobert after loading my trunk, and taking out a pair of Nitril gloves.

"Hey, John. Miss me already?"

"Check this guy out, Den." I give him a close up face-time with the i-thingy after pulling back the hoodie and positioning my trunk occupant's somewhat sidewalk scratched face. "He had seven bangers following a neighbor kid of mine, while setting up behind them with an Uzi."

I face Denny back with me while shutting the trunk. He considers it all for a few seconds.

"I'll send Casey over to pick up the trunk luggage. His face looks familiar. We'll have to let the PD take the bangers. I'll see if Taylor and Rodriguez are on today, and send them with a meat wagon over to pick them up. We'll have to use a Homeland Security angle to keep them incommunicado until I check out this situation. It looks like Alice had good instincts about not moving out of the safe-room just yet."

Yeah, she did. "Agreed. Can I tell the PD anything about Mr. Hoodie and his Uzi or are you going to make him disappear. They won't know how serious this was without some explanation."

"Tell them everything, John," Strobert replied. "We can tell anyone looking into what happens to Hoodie we did a rendition to Saudi Arabia or something."

I like it. "Good call. Talk to you later. You don't need me over at pain central, do you?"

"Nope. I'm going to see if Lynn wants to do a little lab work."

Denny disconnected, and I went over with Dev and Jess. "I'll do the frisks, guys. I have my gloves. Spawn is gathering the PD for a pickup."

"Do Punky Brewster here next to me first, John," Dev says, pointing at the guy kneeling near him. "He was going to reach for something when we threw down on them."

I laughed when I found a .22 auto in Punky's pants-down back pocket. "Wow, kid, Dev would have made you eat this if you'd pulled on him."

"They use the .22's for execution, John," Jess pointed out. "How bad's the guy in your trunk?"

I continue my rough pat downs. "Bad enough for some special encouragement to tell us what this gig was all about. Spawn will be using Homeland Security to keep these boys incommunicado until he finds out. He plans to let our new daughter of darkness do the honors."

"Sucks to be him," Jess states with solemn surety. "That girl gives me the creeps."

"The grapevine has it her and your buddy are having a 'War of the Roses' at their new home," Dev adds. "Fifty says he ends up in the Bay."

That cracks me up. I have to take a moment before resuming my banger frisk-a-thon. "Best not to presume to know what goes on between those two, brother."

The sirens start wailing toward us from off in the distance. I finish my task, and plastic tie my little prayer group's hands behind their backs. They don't like it, but I can tell in their eyes they recognize me. When I finish, I help them get sat down on the sidewalk where we're beginning to draw a few gawkers. Once I have them in place with Dev and Jess keeping an eye on them, I walk over to Darin. He waits for me to speak attentively. Like I said, he's a good kid.

"Where did you pick up this bunch?"

"I noticed them right after I crossed the freeway overpass, John. I don't recognize any of their faces. Do you know what they want?"

"Me, I'm afraid. When the cops get here, tell them what happened. I'll get this straightened out."

"I haven't had any trouble since Nelson."

"Sit tight, Darin. I'll send the cops over when they get here. I promise to end the trouble."

"I like Alice. She's really cool."

Figures. "Now, you are in trouble, kid."

Darin snickers. I push his head back inside the car, and walk over to meet the arriving squad car. I catch a break when I see it's Earl and 'Rique. They know the score, so the preliminaries

THE LURE OF HELL

should be short. I know Denny warmed them up. Dev and Jess had already put away their weapons after I finished plastic tying the crew on the sidewalk.

"I don't know these guys, John," 'Rique said. "Strobert warned us they might have been shipped in."

Earl gestures at the plunder I had set out in front of their owners. "That looks like a jackpot. They decided to bring a little of everything, including the drugstore. Have you asked them anything yet?"

"I'm leaving that to Strobert. He's calling in HS for a meet at the station once he gets a little background music from the one in my trunk."

"This can't be good, John," Earl states the obvious. "Imported bangers following your neighbor kid down the street as cover for an Uzi packing assassin waiting to spray you – I can imagine what's going through your head. We already got briefed on your house attack. What's next, a bombing?"

Good question. "I'll have to get back to you on that, Earl. I doubt these guys know anything other than they were recruited for a nice payday, but we'll know more when Strobert gets to talk with trunk-man."

"If it's all the same to you, John, Earl and I are going to load these guys up, take your neighbor kid's statement, and then get the hell away from you."

It's hard to argue with logic like that. "I'll be in touch."

"From afar, I hope," Earl zings me.

"Prick."

* * *

Lynn looked around at the plastic coated lab interior and the naked figure strapped onto the table in front of her with an appreciative smile of malice. She saw the eyes of her intended subject darting around in frantic recognition of the setting he was in. Montoya had picked out a skintight black outfit with her hair tied tightly at the back of the head. No mask was needed, because her subject probably would never leave the table alive. If he did, it wouldn't be anywhere he'd be identifying anyone. A tray of frightening utensils lay on a portable stainless steel table next to the strapped down former assassin. His head was free to move. He moved it enough to take in his environment. Lynn took a deep breath as the realization of how turned on she was filtered into her mind.

She whipped out her butterfly knife, click-clacking it in and out of fully closed to fully open position with an expertise Lynn knew her buddy on the table recognized with undisguised fear. "Hi, cupcake. Don't pay attention to that surgical table. I'm old school. Drugs and shiny stuff don't get me off. I need a more subtle appreciation of my talent. Screams soothe my black soul, so don't hold back, honey."

Lynn played her part as Strobert entered the room, striding past Montoya as she clacked her knife back into neutral with obvious reluctance. "C'mon, Spawn. What the hell? I haven't even started... damn it!"

Strobert waved her off. "We allow our captive audience some leeway, Lynn. Mr. Ghassan... nice of you to join us. We're here to ask you a few questions. Let's not quibble about details. Get me on your side with who sent you."

Ghassan didn't answer swiftly, prompting a quick click-clack and slice across his groin area as Lynn darted in without orders. Ghassan screamed as he watched the blood welling up.

Strobert smiled at Lynn while Ghassan's eyes were tightly closed. "Lynn! No cutting unless I say so!"

"Quit babying this prick! Let me flay him for a while. He'll tell us anything you want to know. So what if he speaks in an octave higher?"

Denny walked over to grasp Ghassan's hand. "Sorry about that Kamil. My employee incorporates all the usual traits a cold blooded torturer needs, but she lacks restraint. Was there something you wanted to share with us?"

"Musa El Mofty!" Ghassan gasped out. "I know I am... dead. Leave me intact! He despises Samira Karim and her father. El Mofty blames Harding for why she is not dead. Because of his hatred, we have lost our only..."

"Oh yeah, baby!" Lynn was at the assassin's side in a heartbeat when he hesitated. "Don't tell this bad man anything. We'll work it all out after he leaves."

"Lynn." Strobert shook his head. "Kamil just wanted to catch his breath. I won't let her hurt you. Take your time. If you prove valuable enough, I might even keep you where I have a few other helpful ex-terrorists. When a situation arises here or overseas, I get my consulting group together, and they come up with likely scenarios. That sound like something better than being eviscerated by Lynn here?"

Ghassan's face brightens. "Is there such a thing?"

Strobert shrugged while Lynn glared at Ghassan. "It is if you have some very interesting information. If the info is just mildly amusing, I'll still give you a painless death. Take a shot. Impress me."

"El Mofty is in the country. He will be in San Francisco later today from New York!" Ghassan looked at Strobert expectantly.

Lynn patted Ghassan's cheek. "Aw, that's so sweet. You think after giving up El Mofty's name that we won't know everything about him and every movement he makes."

"So far you're not exactly blowing my skirt up, Kamil," Strobert added.

"He… he knows he has lost assets on the West Coast. El Mofty plans on bringing up recruits through Mexico. One of the cells lost during the attacks on Harding and Karim was his only asset in the Los Angeles area. I had to contract those young hoods from Hayward to run interference for my attempt on Harding. I am the last one alive from our cell in the North Bay Area."

Strobert smiled. "That's more like it. Who was to meet El Mofty today? I assume he is flying in. He wouldn't be stupid enough to be seen with you, but does he usually have a limousine service pick him up at the airport?"

"Yes, I contracted SFO limousine service to meet him at baggage."

Lynn started giggling. She patted Ghassan's hand. "Oh, that is just the best. You have a better limo service than that one, right boss?"

"Indeed I do."

* * *

Denny face-timed me while I was riding in our limo with Jafar next to me. Devon and Jesse were up front. "Forces of Darkness Limousine Service, the Dark Lord speaking."

I elicited laughter from my cohorts in the limo and the ones already networked with me, but Denny had his game face on.

"Are you sure it's a good idea to meet him in person, John? I think Clint or Lynn would have been better."

"You said yourself we don't know how many bodyguards El Mofty has with him. Jafar will be out on the side with his El Mofty sign. Clint and Lynn will be inside the baggage claim area counting bodyguards. Lucas and Casey are outside baggage claim ready to stuff bodyguards. They can't be armed, so we have this covered. I know you don't want to lose your new kingpin of terrorists. Jafar will load El Mofty, and the rest of our posse will coral the bodyguards. Tommy's waiting in an SUV to swoop in for all the rest."

There were assenting grunts of approval from the rest of our players all linked up to us.

"Sorry, John... I want El Mofty so bad I can taste it. Call me after you land the big tuna."

"Will do." I reached over and grabbed Jafar's chin, checking out the makeup job Samira did on him. "Your wife did a very credible job covering up the facial you got from Azim. How's it feel?"

Jafar grinned. "Loose, but I'll tape the nose after we get El Mofty. Samira immediately called her father after I came home. He was very pleased I had beaten Azim to death. He forced me to give him every detail of Azim's killing. Badee called me son."

More laughter in my ear as everyone heard of my young friend's intercourse with his father-in-law. "Good one, kid."

"Moffy's flight's on the ground," Clint informed me. "Case has your spot zoned and airport security informed. You can park it."

Devon nodded his head in the driver's seat. When we came around, he pulled into the spot with Casey's direction. Casey then moved into position again.

"Wait until they see him leaving baggage claim, Jafar. Get out then with your sign. Guide him in and follow the Moff inside."

"Okay, Jafar," Lynn's voice said. "Coming at you. He only has two mooks with him."

"I'm on approach right now," Tommy said.

Jafar jumped out with his sign up. El Mofty, a well dressed, rat faced, fat ass in a gray shark skin suit, around five foot eight inches tall, strode toward us. Jafar opened the limo door for him. The Moff looked in, saw my smiling mug, and then I reached out to drag the tuna inside while Jafar gave him a kick in the ass from the rear. I noticed the bodyguards get handled before Dev had us on the road. Then it was time for an introduction, although I could see the Moff knew me. He couldn't struggle because I had the entire front of his suit jacket, shirt, and tie twisted up in a noose around his neck. With his face turning purple and consciousness fading, Jafar plastic tied his chubby little hands behind his back. Then I released him gagging and gasping against the seat. I face-timed Denny.

"Forces of Darkness Limo Service here with a passenger."

"Nice, John," Denny said, as he was put face to face with the Moff on my i-thingy.

"Let... let me out of here... immediately! I have diplomatic immunity!"

Everyone was still on line hearing the Moff making demands with audible enjoyment.

"Denny, let me have Moffy," Lynn pleaded. "He disrespected me in baggage."

"The minx threw herself at him as his minions gathered the bags, Denny," Clint said to much laughter. "She almost blew the whole mission. Moffy wanted her in a carnal manner right there on top of the bags."

I could hear Lynn giggling, and even Denny chuckled at that word picture.

"This is an insult! You will all pay for this! You-"

"Shut him up for a moment, John," Denny said.

I grabbed hold of the Moff's ear. "Stay quiet for the boss or I'm going to rip this off and feed it to you."

El Mofty, already crying out like a girl because of his ear, shut up instantly upon hearing my threat in Arabic. He nodded his understanding. I released him. I kept Denny in front of him.

"Okay… here's how this works. All life as you know it is over. My guys are taking you to a place where if you're superbly helpful to us, I will give you either a quick death, or a chance to help us even more. While you're riding there, think of all the ways you can impress me with your helpfulness."

The Moff spit on my i-thingy. "I… will tell you nothing!"

"He just slimed my i-thingy, Lynn," I complained.

Lynn sighed in a way most people would think of as contentment. The rest of us who knew her, immediately felt our balls trying to crawl up inside our bellies. "Sucks to be him, DL."

Chapter Nineteen
Final Reckoning

Richard Jacoby stood next to his murderous cohorts, Tara Holt, and Cheryl Kosygin. All were in fashion dress. Jacoby wore a black, pinstriped suit with red tie, while Holt had on a silvery, low cut silk dress with black high heels, and Kosygin's one shoulder black, thigh high dress left her right shoulder and chest bare. They were a stunning trio. The Harvard Faculty Club's outside area sparkled with lights and subtle streamers spotlighting the tenth anniversary Fall gathering. For the moment, only a dozen guests mingled outside.

"This fashionably late shit pisses me off," Tara said.

"She called me," Jacoby replied. "Why would she bother if she planned to stand us up? At least we have a legitimate business venture to discuss with her. Other people will see us together. The proposal will give us perfect deniability once we have our Erin Reeves party."

"I'm nervous," Cheryl confided. "I want that bitch. I'm glad we decided on getting her tonight. Doing her on the first day will throw this reunion into chaos. Because we had a business deal with her, we'll be the stars. Our classmates will be commiserating with us over her loss, and the cops will be respectfully reserved in their questioning."

"It's agreed then? We go tonight?"

"I don't know, Rich," Tara said, shaking her head. "She'll have that big driver guy with her. How the hell do we get her alone without him knowing she's with us? He's like her shadow."

"Sorry," Jacoby replied. "I forgot to tell you the great news in the call. I mentioned trying to get her driver in as an escort to see where she planned to have him in relation to the reunion. Erin and her driver had a falling out. She came without him. In her words, 'what could possibly happen to her at a Harvard reunion'? I should have told you two that right off."

Cheryl grabbed Jacoby's arm, shaking it in her excitement. "Oh my God, Rich! We're doing this! We'll get her over to your place for the business sales pitch. Everything's set up. We are so going to get some tonight."

"Calm the hell down, Cher," Tara urged. "Sure, Rich has all our portfolios on the law office we've been looking at in reality set to make a partnership pitch, but that's a long way from getting her on our table without being seen."

"That's why I spent a small fortune to rent the mansion on Littleton Road," Jacoby said. "There are no neighbors near the place. If it looks like we got her there without anyone seeing or her reporting the location, we can load little arrogant Erin into the trunk after we finish playing. Then we take her some place without cameras. That will be the tricky part. We should wait for the following night. Then we can walk around at the reunion events asking if anyone has seen Erin. It's risky, but it wouldn't be such a turn on if it wasn't."

"I like your idea about putting space between our play date and our dump date," Tara agreed. "It'll give us a day to find a proper dump site. I hope they put the FBI idiots on the trail. We'll have to make sure we set her up so obvious even the yokels around here will call it in for federal help. I say we do a note on her belly."

Both Cheryl and Richard Jacoby laughed at Holt's statement. Cheryl shut up suddenly.

"There she is."

"Holy hell," Jacoby whispered in awe. "People will certainly know she's been with us."

Lynn, aka Erin Reeves, glided onto the patio area with an entourage of classmates trying to stay near her without making it obvious they were stalking her stunning figure. Her mauve, twisted two strap dress, completely open but for where the material extended down over her breasts to a belted middle, ended tightly at mid thigh. Only the strap material at the back provided any coverage of skin at her back. The elegant black stiletto heels seemed as comfortable on her as a pair of worn sandals would on another woman. Her blonde hair hung in waves over her shoulders.

"Fucking bitch!" Tara hissed under her breath. "She makes me look like a boy. Smile kiddies. Here she comes to get her pound of flesh. Look at the idiots following her around like lapdogs."

Lynn approached the three with careless grace, giving them a little wave. "My favorite classmates. I don't see a drink in your hands. Waiting for me, are you?"

"You look wonderful," Tara exclaimed.

Lynn waved her hand. "This is the place to do it, Tara. Richard told me you three have a real opportunity for your own law office here in the Harvard area. That's rather ambitious with the competition I'm sure has alumni roots a mile deep. I hope this collaboration has to do with some foreign interests."

Jacoby did a double take. That would be the only way a new firm could get off the ground there. "Yes. We wish to cultivate any contacts you've developed overseas of course. It will be challenging. You would be our main ingredient for overseas interests. We would want you in lead position at our firm. We bring a vast amount of seed money to the mix."

Montoya allowed a slow appraising smile to turn her lip upwards. "Your proposal intrigues me. I could use a new challenge. Let's get a seat and a little Champagne while we make our presence known inside."

"Would you be interested in an earnest discussion tonight," Cheryl asked. "Rich has a wonderfully scenic mansion rented on Littleton Road near here. We could really kick back in comfort."

"Littleton Road, huh. I remember that country pathway. There are some very scenic places out there. I'd like that."

"I think you'll have to fight off our other classmates," Cheryl said. "They'll want to keep you against your will. You look stunning."

"I think we make a very attractive group," Lynn replied. "Lead the way inside, Richard."

Jacoby grinned happily. "Of course, Erin."
* * *
A shadowy figure in a tuxedo moved toward the door inside. "Did you get all that Clint? Those freaks mean business."

"Every word, Case," Dostiene replied. "You had the place wired perfectly."

"How's Tonto behaving?"

Clint looked over at Tonto, who had his head sticking out the passenger window as he pawed over the protesting Jafar. "He's bonding with Jafar on the way to the place I found out Dick-head rented on Littleton Road. We're headed there now. Jafar will drop Tonto and I off before setting up a tech base down the road."

"John and Lucas are planting the bugs on Lynn's rental and Jacoby's Expedition. They'll follow the players as discussed. Jafar, make sure you check in once you have all of us on screen. We take no chances with the walking dead."

Jafar chuckled while groaning under a misplaced paw. "I will contact everyone the moment I am situated."

      * * *

Lucas and I stayed silent until we hooked up everything. We were all agreed with Lynn. No way, no how would she wake up drugged out on a table with those three Casey had dubbed the walking dead, standing over her.

"Lynn is something else," Lucas remarked as we returned to our vehicle. "It's hard to reconcile that fashion model we saw tonight moving like a princess with the woman who walked out of the Moffy interrogation. Fifteen minutes with her and he begged to tell us his life story."

I gave him the wave off. "The Moff spit on my i-thingy. He had it coming. Once he spit on my i-thingy, karma came to get him."

Lucas laughed. "Yeah… Lynn karma. Denny will be working the stuff she came up with for months. I like it that he knew what the hell was going on with those people behind the boat disappearances in the Gulf. Maybe we won't have to take my baby down there."

"That mission is on tap, Lucas, and The Sea Wolf is going. Clint and Lynn are getting married after this op. Then they're honeymooning on our mission with the Wolf. They get the main cabin too."

I watched Lucas's blood boiling, threatening to shoot out of his ears. I laughed at him. "You best take a step back, my friend. Clint and Lynn are in, and the Wolf is going hunting. You feel me?"

Lucas nodded. "Yeah, Denny-light, I got it. I just don't like to hear it from Denny's Minnie-me."

I hung my head. "That's cold Lucas. I thought we were brothers."

"We were until you became another management suck-up." Gronked again.

* * *

"This is very nice." Lynn relaxed in the spacious barroom on a leather recliner.

"The three of us are thinking of buying it as a kind of personal home base," Cheryl replied. She sat across from Lynn on a matching leather loveseat while Jacoby and Tara opened and served more Champagne.

"I really love this place, Erin," Jacoby said, while pointing out one of the glasses to Tara on the already made up serving tray. He opened the Champagne, before easing it into an iced bucket, and following Tara over to the glass table between the couch, loveseat, and recliner combination. "You'll really like this California Champagne."

Tara put the indicated glass in front of Erin. While Jacoby filled it for her, Holt put out the other three glasses. Jacoby then filled those. The four held up their glasses and toasted.

"To a very profitable and exciting partnership," Jacoby stated.

They sipped the Champagne in a comfortable silence for a few moments. They had conversed amiably at the reunion get together, with Lynn asking more serious questions about what would be expected of her. They were pointed enough to keep her three targets off balance until Jacoby angled for a ride out to his place where he had the business plan.

Jacoby leaned forward animatedly. "I almost forgot. You have got to see the basement in this place. It will be like a home theater and business meeting room with those huge fifty inch screens for networking from anywhere."

"Sure," Lynn answered. "I'm a little buzzed. A tour would be a chance to walk it off a little. Lead the way."

The three Harvard killer cohorts exchanged knowing glances when they stood. Jacoby led the way, with Lynn on his arm. "Hang on to the railing, Erin," he advised as they reached the steps leading down to the basement, and he switched on the lights.

On the basement level, the area appeared huge because of the massive shadows. Only a single medical type table with accompanying rolling cart of instruments stood in the center of a single overhead flood lamp, which cast the area around the table into total darkness. Lynn let go of Jacoby's arm as Cheryl Kosygin giggled, unable to control her anticipation.

"It's really tough to tell about this room's potential when it's decked out like this." Lynn sighed with icy contentedness. "You three sure did step in it this time. It's too bad you don't have three tables, but I see a couple folding chairs over there. I guess two can watch while I entertain the first. Then, one... and then none."

"What the hell are you talkin' about, bitch?" Holt grabbed Lynn's hair. Tonto charged out of the shadows, leaping into the screaming Tara's chest, and catapulting her to the cement floor, his fangs at her throat.

"I... I don't feel so good," Cheryl mumbled as she passed out onto the floor.

A sweating and confused Jacoby stumbled toward the staircase, but lost his balance, ending up in a pile on the floor. Tara was the last to lose consciousness as even the adrenaline from Tonto's attack couldn't keep her awake. Clint came out of the shadows next. He took Lynn into his arms.

"Hello, cowboy. Want a quickie before we get started. I owe you for that wonderfully delicious drug switcheroo you pulled off."

"Oh baby... Jafar?"

"Yeah Clint."

"Main mission done. We have the room for the next half hour. Send John in to get Tonto then."

"Ah... okay, Clint."

* * *

Lucas and I were laughing, but Jafar turned to us in confusion. "What is it Clint means about-"

Sounds of something besides interrogation began in all our ears. Jafar quickly disconnected the network. "Oh. I see. Clint liked the dress Ms. Montoya was wearing."

"I believe you have a firm grip on the situation, kid."

I waited a half hour and then went into the house. At the top of the cellar stairs I called down. "Knock... knock!"

"C'mon down, John," Clint said.

When I reached the bottom of the steps, Tonto leaped over for kisses and hugs. Luckily, his mouth wasn't all bloody. I worked him over the way he liked, before checking out the room. The guy, Richard Jacoby, and his blonde friend, Kosygin were duct taped to two folding chairs at the side of a medical gurney. Tara Holt was strapped to it, naked and screaming. I could tell from the way Clint and Lynn were laughing, that they hadn't even touched her yet. So much for the cold, hard, serial killer. Lynn duct taped her mouth, and waved at me.

"Hi John. Clint's going to stay with me tonight down here. We'll find out where all the bodies are buried, and what's been going on with our three bad people. Of course they only thought they were bad. Isn't that right, my little mean girl?"

Lynn pinched Holt's cheek. Holt passed out. Lynn made a disgusted snort. "It's a good thing you packed the smelling salts, baby. We're going to need them."

"Yep," Clint agreed, patting his partner's butt. "Can you take Tonto, John? The smell of blood drives him nuts."

"You bet, Clint. I'll leave my SUV out front, and the keys on the bar upstairs. Denny told me he made peace with your FBI buddies. They're satisfied with an ending with all the facts, but no killers. He's sending in a team in the morning." I tossed the body bags down on the floor I had carried in with me. "Just put them in these for transport. I think there's going to be a fire where their

279

DNA will be discovered as the cause of many heinous murders, which the FBI and Denny found on a partially burned laptop."

"See." Clint put his arm around Lynn. "I told you Denny would handle it. Now, Sam and Janie will get some peace without pestering the shit out of us."

"I like it," Lynn said, staring into the eyes of Jacoby and Kosygin. "I don't think Rich and Cher like our plan. What do you think, John?"

I walked over where I could see into the faces of Lynn's folding chair audience. The hollow eyed horror in their eyes touched me… but not in the way they hoped. "I think they've found out they're not cut out to be monsters - but I believe they've also found out about karma, and that payback's a bitch."

Lynn giggled. "Clint wants me to play dress up with him at the Harvard reunion some more."

I nodded at my two monsters. "Have fun kids. I'll see you back in Oakland. C'mon, Tonto, our part here is done."

Clint hugged Tonto and framed his face with a hand. "You behave yourself with the Dark Lord. Don't spoil him rotten before we get home, DL."

I patted my leg, while heading for the stairs. "Let's go, Tonto. Steak every night with the Dark Lord."

Tonto bounded past me up the stairs.

"Prick!" Clint called out as I followed.

Yep, I grinned to myself. The Dark Lord's comin' home with a new mission. I had a honeymoon cruise to plan with the Spawn of Satan. There were other fake monsters out there to be dealt with.

The End

Made in United States
Orlando, FL
12 April 2023

32035553R00154